LONDON AND THE SOUTH-EAST

David Szalay was born in 1974. *London and the South-East* is his first novel.

DAVID SZALAY

London and the South-East

VINTAGE BOOKS
London

Published by Vintage 2009

2 4 6 8 10 9 7 5 3 1

Copyright © David Szalay 2008

David Szalay has asserted his right under the Copyright, Designs
and Patents Act 1988 to be identified as the author of this work

First published in Great Britain in 2008 by Jonathan Cape

Vintage
Random House, 20 Vauxhall Bridge Road,
London SW1V 2SA

www.vintage-books.co.uk

Addresses for companies within The Random House Group
Limited can be found at: www.randomhouse.co.uk/offices.htm

The Random House Group Limited Reg. No. 954009

A CIP catalogue record for this book
is available from the British Library

ISBN 9780099515890

The Random House Group Limited supports The Forest
Stewardship Council (FSC), the leading international forest
certification organisation. All our titles that are printed on
Greenpeace approved FSC certified paper carry the FSC logo.
Our paper procurement policy can be found at
www.rbooks.co.uk/environment

Typeset by Palimpsest Book Production Limited,
Grangemouth, Stirlingshire

Printed and bound in Great Britain by
CPI Bookmarque, Croydon CR0 4TD

'London and the south-east of England, which together account for over 30% of GDP, are markedly wealthier than the rest of the UK. According to data from the European statistical agency, Eurostat, the Greater London area is now the wealthiest region in the EU.'

The Economist Intelligence Unit

'If women did not exist, all the money in the world would have no meaning.'

Aristotle Onassis

1

Dieter Flossman has been on Paul's mind a lot these last few days. Managing his software firm in Stuttgart, it is unlikely that he thinks about Paul at all when they are not actually speaking on the phone. Paul, on the other hand, thinks about Dieter all the time. While he waits on the platform of Hove station in the morning; throughout the slow, stopping journey; when he sinks to the Underground at London Bridge, and when he is lifted out of it at Holborn, Dieter is foremost in his thoughts. Exactly a week ago, with very little fuss, after a single short, sharp pitch, he sold him a full-page, full-colour ad in the automation systems software section of *European Procurement Management*. (Dieter did not know, of course, that his ad would *be* the automation systems software section of *European Procurement Management*.) Paul faxed him an agreement form, which Dieter said he would sign in time for the positioning of his ad to be discussed at Paul's 'pagination meeting' at the end of the afternoon. Paul went to the Penderel's Oak. It was his first sale in some time.

On Monday morning, the fax was not there. A quick call to Dieter elicited an apology, and an assurance that he would send it through immediately. A further call, towards the middle of the afternoon, and Dieter's secretary, Frau Koch, said that she thought Herr Doktor Flossman had already signed the fax, and that she would send it as soon as she had a minute. She took down Paul's fax number. The next morning, there was still no fax. And then Dieter seemed to disappear for a few days. Paul was calling him so much he knew his fourteen-digit number without having to look it up. Every day, the first thing he did when he arrived at work was phone Dieter.

Dieter was never there, only the severe Frau Koch. Herr Doktor Flossman, she said, is always busy. If he has something to say to Herr Doktor Flossman, he should put it in an email or a fax. Frantic, Paul got Elvezia to phone pretending to be his secretary. He got Murray to phone pretending to be his boss. He tried to flirt with the impervious Frau Koch, and when that did not work, stabbed the white mute key with his finger and unleashed a stream of obscenities. 'You fucking fucking fucking fucking *bitch* . . . Yeah, not to worry. I'll call back tomorrow. Oh, tomorrow's the weekend, isn't it. I'm playing golf up in Scotland. Yeah, very nice. Looking forward to it. You been to Scotland, Frau Cock . . .'

That was this morning.

And now Dieter is *there*, is saying, 'Ah, Mr Barclay, we speak at last!' His tone, wonderfully, suggesting that the wretched week of silence was simply unfortunate, that there was nothing sinister involved.

'Better late than never, Dieter,' Paul says loudly, still smiling.

'Yes indeed.'

Dieter's English is faultless. It is difficult to tell, from his voice, how old he is. Paul imagines him to be in his mid-fifties; lean, sinewy, probably a mountain-biking enthusiast, a potholer, a weekend naturist. The voice is good-humoured in a boring, irritating, overbearing way.

Starting to doodle, Paul says, 'How you doing?'

'I'm very well. But I think that's just because it's the weekend tomorrow!' And Dieter laughs – he *laughs*, as though he has said something funny. Paul laughs too, more warily, in what probably seems to Dieter a more English way – but what he takes for Englishness is in fact the sarcasm, more or less open, that Paul is unable to prevent himself from putting into his laugh. 'Yeah, I know what you mean. I do know what you mean.'

Suddenly more serious, Dieter says, 'What can I do for you, Mr Barclay?'

'Well, it's about this ad, Dieter.' Paul maintains a weary, we're-both-busy-men-of-world tone of voice. His style, as a salesman, is modernist – that is, he is almost an anti-salesman, scrupulously avoiding any of the formulaic patter, the importunate over-sincerity still taught in the training room. From the start, he had felt his way towards a more subtle style – offhand, low-intensity. It is a style that has served him well; though in truth, less and less so in recent years. Is this because it is becoming more difficult to sell the space? It seems to be, and Paul sometimes wonders why this is, what has changed. Possibly the prospects, through unending exposure to salesmen and sales techniques. Possibly, he sometimes feels, he himself is losing the underlying pressure, the vestigial old-school salesmanship that is always essential, even to a modernist. It seems likely that he brings less energy to the task than he used to. Possibly it is the product itself – the various publications in the Park Lane portfolio are no less useless now than they ever have been, are still simply pretexts, utterly stripped down, for selling advertising space. With the possible exception of the in-flight magazines – very much the firm's prestige publications – it is unquestionably a waste of money for anyone to advertise in them, for the simple reason that they have no readers. Some are sent out as junk mail, but in most cases the only copies printed are those sent to the advertisers themselves. In any normal sense, then – certainly in any sense that the advertisers would recognise – these publications *do not actually exist*. They are like a stage set, an illusion, a fiction sustained from the sales floor. This minimalist approach to publishing had been very successful at first. Now, though, it seems more and more difficult to sell the space. Or maybe it isn't. Paul is never sure. Perhaps his memory is playing tricks on him. He sometimes thinks it would be worth improving the publications, or getting some *proper* publications – becoming, in essence, a *proper* publishing company. But then the whole point, the whole idea of Park Lane Publications is that it is not a proper publishing company.

*

3

He was in the Penderel's Oak with Murray when Andy walked in to tell him that Flossman had phoned. They had been there since twelve, in an awkward, dark, dead space near the toilets and the cigarette machine. Lifting his eyebrows, Andy made a drinking motion. A few minutes later, treading with his eyes on his brogues, he was holding pints. He landed them on the table, shoving them among the many empties. 'All right,' he said plummily, pulling up an upholstered stool. 'All right, lads.' He turned his head to take in the muted ragu tones of the pub. The other people there were mostly tourists putting away late lunches, traditional pub fayre – pies and square-cut chips, the sauce in sachets, the cutlery wrapped in maroon paper napkins. 'Michaela in today?'

Paul shook his head – an emphatic no.

'Will she be in later . . . ?'

'What are you *doing* here, Andy?' Paul said. 'Why aren't you at the office? Why aren't you on the phone?'

'What are *you* doing here?' Andy laughed.

'Don't fucking laugh.'

'Just a quick one –'

'You don't have *time* for quick ones! What's your problem?' Andy's boyish smile wavered, went slightly bewildered. Paul said, 'You're not here to have a laugh. You're not going to make any deals sitting in the pub all day. No wonder you never make any deals.' Andy was not smiling any more. 'Why aren't you on the phone, *now*, calling people?' Flushed – his full face as crimson as the lining of his chalk-striped suit – Andy said nothing. There was nothing for him to say. In his five months at Park Lane Publications he has made only one 'deal' – sold a quarter-page mono ad to a Belgian keyboard manufacturer – and that in his second week, when everything seemed to be going so well.

Slowly, with showy sadness, Paul shook his head. 'You've got to sort yourself out, mate,' he said. 'You're taking the piss. If you don't make any sales it's because you're in here all day. You don't make

4

enough calls. It's a numbers game. You've got the leads. You just need to make the fucking calls.'

Andy nodded. 'Yup,' he said. 'Yah.'

'Go back to the office,' Paul said. 'Go back to the office, and get on the phone.'

Andy gulped down half of his pint. Then the other half. 'I'll see you later then, yeah.'

'Yeah.'

'See you, Murray.'

'Yeah, see you later,' Murray muttered. And then, when Andy had gone, 'He forgot his umbrella. Fucking tosser.'

He was soon back, though. Within minutes.

Paul said, 'What are you doing here? Why aren't you on the fucking phone?'

'There's something I forgot to tell you.'

'What?'

'Flossman called.'

'Flossman?' Hurriedly, Paul stubbed out his cigarette. 'When? What did he say?'

'Um, I don't know. That you can call him this afternoon if you want. And he's going somewhere on Monday.'

'Where?'

'Um. I don't know. China?'

'For fuck's sake. When did he call?'

Andy hesitated. 'About an hour ago?'

'For fuck's *sake* . . .'

'Is there a problem?' Murray enquired.

Paul stood up. 'I've got to go back to the office, mate.'

'You're not serious . . .'

'Yeah I am, unfortunately. I've been trying to speak to this cunt all week.'

'Flossman?'

'Yeah.'

5

'You staying here, Murray?' Andy said. He said it – so it seemed to Murray – with a sly, mocking smile.

'No,' Murray said, without thinking.

'What ...' Andy seemed surprised. 'You're coming back to the office?'

Squinting scornfully, Murray shook his square head. 'Why wouldn't I?'

'Well ... Marlon.'

'*Who?*'

'Marlon.'

Still Murray did not seem to follow. 'Marlon?'

Smiling as though the whole thing were some kind of joke, Andy said, 'He says you nicked one of his leads. He's telling everyone he's going to punch your lights out.'

'What, that little shit?'

'Yeah ...'

'I'll punch *his* fucking lights out.'

For a moment, there was an uneasy silence. Murray was still sitting down. 'Should we go then?' Andy said. Slowly Murray swallowed what was left of his pint, and stood up, a tall man in a shapeless blue suit. Quite pale, he did up his jacket and they followed Paul towards the front of the pub. 'You coming back?' Paul said when he saw Murray. Murray nodded. 'What about Marlon?' Murray shrugged – like the nod, a small, tense movement.

Despite the hurry, and the drizzle, when Andy said, 'Should we have a quick doob?' Paul stopped. 'Get a move on then.' They were in an alley near Lincoln's Inn Fields, grey old office buildings looming on all sides. Murray seemed nervous, making strange munching movements with his mouth and staring at the words CITY OF WESTMINSTER on the side of a dumpster. Paul was also preoccupied, impatient. If Andy's good at anything, he thought, it's making spliffs. In the rain, the wind pouring intermittently down the alley, he made the spliff in the palm of his hand, dipping into his pocket for what he needed.

6

The result was something that looked like it had been manufactured by a machine. They smoked it quickly, in silence, ignoring the inquisitive looks of purposefully striding passers-by.

The entrance to King's House, a nondescript office building on Kingsway, is on a side street, a glass door tinted greyish brown. Wobbling slightly, the small, gloomy lift went up. There is some other company (Winchmore Leasing Ltd) on the first floor; Park Lane Publications has the second and third floors; the fourth floor has been vacant since the spring. Paul looked at his watch, an old Swatch with a red plastic strap. Three twenty – four twenty in Germany.

Tony Peters' team occupies one half of the upper sales floor, Paul's the other. The room is long and low – when salesmen stand on their desks to 'power pitch', their heads are not far from the off-white ceiling panels – and usually loud with overlapping voices. There are windows down both sides – on one side the sad, unleaving plane trees of Kingsway; on the other a grey jumble of roofs and fire escapes. Even with so many windows, at this time of day, and this time of year, the room would be dim were it not for the extensive strip lighting. Paul stopped at the cooler to drink several paper cones of icy water in quick succession. Frustratingly, the dryness of his mouth was almost unaffected. In his intoxicated state, everything seemed unnaturally intense, and at the same time not real – as if he were lying in a hot bath imagining it all. 'Come on!' he shouted – he heard himself shout – as he crossed the grey carpet towards his team at the far end of the room. 'Get on the fucking phone!' He shouted it only out of a sense of obligation, and everyone ignored him, except Elvezia who looked up sceptically from her magazine, then let it fall shut and started to leaf through some old index cards. It was, everyone understood, Friday afternoon. Paul took off his jacket and sat down. There is a large whiteboard on the wall behind his desk, on which the names of the ten members of his team are written, and their total sales, and their sales this week – a column filled with zeros. Different-sized zeros, some blue, some black, some red, some green, but all zeros. Some of the zeros – Andy's for example – have been there so long that it is probably no longer possible to erase them. In the total sales column some of these indelible zeros have been incorporated into later, larger, multi-coloured numbers.

Without preliminaries, Paul picked up the white handset of his phone and punched in Flossman's number. The long pulses of the foreign tone in his ear, he pulled off the plastic lid of his tea, fished out the sodden bag, and burned his mouth with an impatient sip.

'*Koch!*'

'Oh hello,' Paul slurred, smiling, 'it's Charles Barclay.' Not, of course, his real name. His sales name, his *nom de phone*. For various reasons, most of the salespeople use pseudonyms. In some cases because their real names are considered inappropriate – too foreign-sounding, too difficult to spell. Andy for instance, who is of Polish descent (Andy is short for Andrzej, not Andrew) has a surname consisting of a dozen consonants, mostly Zs and Ws, and one isolated vowel, somewhere in the thick of it. His sales name is David Lloyd. (When selecting a sales name, the names of banks are often felt to have the right tone – one young man made a promising start to his career as James Natwest.) In Paul's case, his real name – Paul Rainey – was not particularly problematic. He has had numerous identities over the years, though; switching whenever a dissatisfied advertiser is furious enough to demand his dismissal, and he is 'sacked'. 'Nicholas James' was 'sacked' in February, since when he has been 'Charles Barclay'. 'I think Dieter tried to get hold of me a little while ago, Frau Cock,' he said. 'I was in a meeting. I'm just returning his call.'

'Oh, yes, Mr Barclay.' Frau Koch's tone seemed changed – more congenial. 'Yes, but Herr Doktor Flossman is in a meeting himself at the moment.' *For fuck's sake*, Paul thought. 'In about twenty minutes, I think, he will be finished,' she said. 'You will call back?' Startled by this unexpected transparency, Paul said, 'Right. Fine. I will call back.'

8

'Thank you, Mr Barclay.'

'Thank *you*, Frau Cock.' He dropped the handset into its plastic berth and looked at his watch. Three twenty-seven. Drink the tea, he thought, have a fag, then phone Flossman again. Satisfied, his plan thus in place, he slid his chair back on squeaky wheels, put his feet, his scuffed black lace-ups, on the desk, and waited.

Smirking, walking slowly, it took Andy ten seconds to traverse the sales floor. Paul watched absently as he walked towards him, knowing that he should say something along the lines of 'Where the fuck have you been? Why aren't you on the fucking phone?' He was unable to summon the energy. The office was hot and soporific, the hubbub of voices dull. He felt the warmth of the tea touch his fingers through the cardboard cup. Still smiling, Andy sat down. He seemed to be waiting for something. His face expressionless, Paul stared out over the sales floor. 'Where's Murray?' Andy said.

Paul shrugged. 'Dunno.'

'He was in the smoking room. He said he was coming back here.'

'He hasn't been here. Why aren't you on the fucking phone?'

Suddenly serious-faced, Andy dug through the snafu of papers on his desk, trying to look purposeful. Then he saw something that made him smile again. In a boxy pale grey suit and large-knotted lilac tie, Marlon was strolling, strutting, towards them. His head, in its colour and texture, reminded Andy of Silly Putty – something from his prep-school days. There was a time when every boy in the school, it seemed, had to have a little red plastic egg containing a blob of flesh-coloured putty, and Marlon's broad nose and prominent chin, as well the semi-glossy surface of his pink scalp, all recalled it. He spends so much time in a Covent Garden gym that many of his fellow members are under the impression that he works there – which in an informal, voluntary way he more or less does. Not mopping the changing rooms, of course, or manning the till in the shop, but helping people with the machines, and dispensing detailed advice on warm-downs and stretching. 'Where've you been?' said Paul. Marlon held up a long cup of soya milk latte.

'Marlon!' Andy called respectfully, in a sort of stage whisper, across the desks. 'Marlon!' When Marlon finally looked up, Andy's smile widened. 'Have you seen Murray?' he said. Unfitting the lid of his coffee, Marlon shook his flesh-toned head.

'I think he's hiding from you. He thinks you're going to punch his lights out.'

'Will you get on the fucking phone?' Paul said to Andy. He looked at his watch. Three thirty-eight. Twelve minutes.

The smoking room was cold and, despite the wide-open window, smoky; grey, and loud with the perpetual groan of the traffic where Kingsway and Holborn meet. The cleaners seem to have permission not to clean it, though they all smoke themselves, and big, abandoned newspaper pages stirred in the chilly draught when the door croaked open. Unusually, Paul had the narrow space to himself, and taking advantage of this, he dragged a slick of phlegm up from his mid-throat and spat it into the metal bin. On his way there, he had almost met Lawrence, the director of sales. For the sake of his health, he was going to walk down the two flights of stairs, but he had heard Lawrence's nasal whine speaking to someone in the stairwell, and had tiptoed back up and taken the lift. This had made him feel quite small. 'Fucking Lawrence,' he said, quietly, to the empty room – an act of defiance so minor that it only increased his sense of oppression.

Lawrence, it seems, has become obsessed with the underperformance of Paul's team. And his team *is* underperforming. There are only three more weeks of selling left on *European Procurement Management*, and the sales target looks more implausible every day. Paul knows, in fact, that it will be missed, but he still tells Lawrence not to worry, that there's 'a lot out there'. Which there isn't – so when Lawrence presses him for details of what, exactly, is 'out there' the evasive sketchiness of his answers tends to lead to unpleasant-ness. The publications, in any case, never meet their sales targets – not *European Procurement Management*, not the in-flight maga-zines, not *Asian Procurement Management*, or *International Finance and Financial Policy Review*, or any of the others. The targets are not so much targets as notional figures – aspirations at best, ambi-tions that everyone, even Lawrence, has tacitly accepted will never be achieved (though they are raised a little every year), unattain-able standards condemning the salespeople – all of them, ultimately – to the misery and stress of perpetual, soul-wearying failure. This is the same for Tony's team, and Simon Beaumont's, and Neil's, and the Pig's – so why, Paul wondered self-pityingly, sitting on the low chair, its brown wool torn to reveal yellow foam (which has itself been picked away by nervous fingers), does Lawrence single him out?

Lawrence's obsession with Paul's team and its failings has, over the past few weeks, focused more and more intensely on Andy. On the phone Andy does not even sound desperate any more; he just sounds dead. Paul had had high hopes for Andy. He had nurtured him, bought him little presents (a bong, a Zippo with a marijuana leaf on it), bought him pints in the Penderel's Oak – all of which was, of course, substantially self-interested, Paul being on an over-ride and getting a few per cent whenever a member of his team makes a sale. Andy was posh, plummy – unintimidated by talking to other posh people, or foreigners. On the phone he could sound much older than he was. As the weeks passed, however, it became obvious that, in some subtle way, he had the wrong vibe, the wrong something, the wrong *je ne sais quoi*. And perhaps most impor-tantly, not enough need. Paul thinks that he must be getting money from his parents – or someone – because not having made any sales since then, he has not been paid since June.

Andy starts to stutter as soon as he sees Lawrence walk onto the sales floor. Looming over him, Lawrence presses the earpiece of Andy's phone to his head (he has an odd way of holding the earpiece – in the palm of his long, hairy hand), and stopping his other ear with his index finger, he listens, with his eyes shut, to Andy's pitch. 'Good morning,' Andy says, his voice shaking in a way that it only does when Lawrence is listening in. 'Could I speak to Dr Rüthke, please.'

'Who is it, please?' A German secretary's voice.

'It's David Lloyd.'

'And where are you calling from, please?'

'I'm calling in association with the International Federation of Procurement Management.'

'What is it concerning?'

'Is Dr Rüthke there?'

'What is it concerning, please?'

'I'm calling in association with the International Federation of Procurement Management.'

'Excuse me?'

'I'm calling in association with –'

'Could you send a fax?'

'There wouldn't be any point sending a fax.'

'Please – could you send a fax?'

'I don't have a fax. I'm calling in association with the International Federation of Procurement Management. I need to speak to Dr Rüthke. Is he there?'

'Are you selling something?'

Andy laughs in the way that salesmen usually do when they're about to deny that they're selling something. 'No,' he says, laughing, 'I'm not selling anything. I need to speak to Dr Rüthke. Is he there?'

A towering blue-suited presence at his shoulder, well inside his personal space – Andy can smell him, his BO, his halitosis, his after-shave – Lawrence's eyes squeeze more tightly shut.

'Rüthke.'

'Oh. Good morning, Dr Rüthke,' Andy says, moving uneasily in his chair. 'My name is David Lloyd, and I'm calling in association with the International Federation of Procurement Management. From London. How are you?'

There is a short silence. 'Yes?' Dr Rüthke says, impatiently.

'Um, I'm calling ... I'm calling from the ... I'm calling from Park Lane Publications,' says Andy. 'We publish *European Procurement Management*, in association with the International Federation of Procurement Management.'

'Yes.'

'Do you know the International Federation of Procurement Management?'

'No.'

'Well, it's an international organisation made up of the national institutes. I understand you're involved in the manufacture of industrial thermostats, Dr Rüthke?'

'Yes.'

'Well, I'm putting together *European Procurement Management*, in association with the International Federation of Procurement Management. It's published twice a year, in January and June, and goes out to the purchasing managers of Europe's thousand leading multinational companies, such as Philips, Hoechst and BMW. I'm putting together the January 2005 edition of the publication, in which there will be a major section on industrial thermostats. We have a limited amount of advertising positions available in this section and I'm calling Europe's leading industrial thermostat manufacturers –'

'We are not interested.'

'Not interested in what?'

'Not interested in advertising in this publication.'

'Who are your main clients, Dr Rüthke?'

'We have a very limited number of clients.'

'Can you give me some examples?'

'We are not interested. Thank you.'

At this point, his mouth in close proximity to Andy's enflamed left ear, and in a vicious monotone whisper, Lawrence starts to dictate a pitch of his own, kicking the desk until Andy takes it up. Lawrence's pitch, though, is no more successful than Andy's – is in fact almost identical, except that Andy's delivery, previously flustered and faltering, suddenly has the flat, hesitant and disconnected feel of a simultaneous translation. When Dr Rüthke is still not interested – and increasingly irritated by the inexplicable pauses that have started to appear in the middle of Andy's sentences – Lawrence drops the earpiece onto the desk and, with spittle accumulating in the corners of his mouth, shouts, 'For God's sake! For God's sake – get *angry*!'

The Gents, with their pinkish marble surfaces and warm halogen lights, were put in for the previous tenants of King's House – obviously a posher company than Park Lane Publications Ltd. Finding one of the stalls occupied, Paul tapped the varnished wood of the door. 'Murray?' he said, after a few moments of unforthcoming silence. 'It's me.' Silence still. 'I know you're in there.' Paul looked at his watch. Three forty-nine – time to call Flossman. 'Murray, I know you're in there.'

'What?' Murray's voice, deadened by the door, was irate.

'Are you planning to do any work this afternoon?' Paul said, irate himself.

There was another long pause, then Murray said, 'I'll be along in a minute.'

Paul sighed, and for a moment, thinking vaguely of Michaela – the petite Kiwi barmaid from the Penderel's Oak – he inspected himself in the mirror. Often, he and Murray perch up at the bar, imagining themselves to be flirting with her. They watch her always-smiling small figure as she moves, wearing a tight black skirt, twee blouse and clip-on bow tie; and often, in the dead heart of the afternoon, when even the Penderel's Oak is quiet – the only sounds the automated pippings and whirrings of the fruit machines, and the mumble of the traffic from outside – they lounge there, making innuendo-laden small talk with her, and offering her cigarettes, which she accepts, and drinks, which she doesn't.

Paul shoved a puffy hand through his pepper-and-salt hair. He is not handsome. Shortish, plump, his face unevenly flushed and already showing split mauve capillaries here and there, he looks ten years older than he is, which is thirty-nine.

On the sales floor, he lifted the white handset of his phone and was about to start entering Flossman's number when he saw the note, unobtrusive among the papers that completely cover the surface of his desk. It was written with a purple highlighter pen in Andy's almost retardedly childish handwriting. It said: *Flosman called*. Paul looked at Andy, who was on the phone, and seemed to be trying to avoid his eye. 'Oi, Andy,' he said. 'What did Flossman say?' Andy just shrugged and shook his head. 'When did he call?' Paul said. Andy put his phone on mute for a moment. 'A few minutes ago.'

'And what did he say?'

'Nothing.'

'What do you mean *nothing*?'

Andy shook his head, and unmuted his call. Frowning, Paul entered Flossman's number into his phone. The long tone, once, twice, then . . .

'Flossman.'

Expecting 'Koch', Paul was taken by surprise. He sat up straight and, his face forming itself into a wide, insincere smile, said, 'Dieter. Charles Barclay here.'

'Ah, Mr Barclay, we speak at last!'

'Better late than never, Dieter.'

'Yes indeed.'

'How you doing?'

'I'm very well. But I think that's just because it's the weekend tomorrow!'

'Yeah, I know what you mean. I do know what you mean.'

15

'What can I do for you, Mr Barclay?'

'Well, it's about this ad, Dieter. My secretary said we still haven't got that fax through yet. I think she called, um . . .' Paul pretends to have forgotten Frau Koch's name. 'She called your secretary, who said she'd send it through. She doesn't seem to have done that though. I'm sorry to get you involved in this, Dieter, it's just that I'm going to be away next week . . . There's . . . Well, in the States, and if we could get this wrapped up before I go . . .' His voice is slow and level and unworried. He has done this so many times before, has been in precisely this situation so many times, that his mind is unengaged, and his eyes wander over the mess of his desk, while his mouth gets the well-worn words out. 'So if you could just make sure we get that this afternoon, Dieter . . .'

'Yes, Mr Barclay. But we have decided against this.'

Said as though it were something insignificant.

There are innumerable moments like this, of course, and the humiliation stings because they demonstrate so starkly – after all the standard banter, which sets the salesman and the prospect up as equals – the underlying asymmetry of the situation. Stunned, furious – feeling as though he has been physically struck – Paul says, in a voice which still sounds almost unflustered, 'Right. I thought the decision had already been made though, Dieter. I thought you'd decided to go ahead.' That was undoubtedly the impression that Dieter had given him. He had said, 'This is something we will be doing.' He had said, 'We will confirm this today.' He had said, 'We think this is a good idea.'

Now he says, 'Yes, but I think we have other priorities at the moment.'

Paul is suddenly unaware of the humming sales floor around him, is aware only of Flossman's disembodied presence in the white plastic handset of his phone. In short sickening pulses, during which the sales floor comes back, briefly and intensely real, he feels the appalling, ridiculous tenuousness of this link with Flossman – the link on which everything depends. During these moments, Flossman seems not even to exist. And yet Flossman is everything. 'Dieter, if I could ask you, let me just ask you, what *are* your priorities?' And without waiting for him to answer, 'Remember that *European Procurement Management* is sent to the purchasing managers of Europe's top one thousand manufacturing companies, companies like Philips, Hoechst and BMW.' It is the sort of line Paul usually eschews, the sort of line that his style of selling has eliminated, but in situations like this – with panic setting in – what else is there? The oblique, modernist style is useless here. Faced with traditional salesmanship, however, Flossman immediately sounds weary. 'Yes,' he says, sighs, 'I understand.'

'So, if I could just ask you, Dieter, what *are* your priorities?'

'Well . . .' He seems to be on the point of answering – of telling Paul what his priorities are – when he hesitates, and says, 'But we have decided not to do this. Thank you for thinking of us, Mr Barclay.'

Paul experiences a moment of pure frustration. Frustration that there is no way to *force* Flossman into the publication. There is, in fact, no point prolonging the call any further – contrary to the orthodoxy of the training room, it is more or less impossible to turn a situation like this around. Experience informs Paul of this, and, normally, he would wind up with a bruised, embittered goodbye. His voice is still level, though nothing remains of the laconic tone with which the call began. He says, 'I understand, Dieter. I understand. If I could just ask you though – who are your most important clients?'

The conversation is now an undignified tussle – demeaning to them both – and Flossman is openly impatient. 'I . . . I don't know, Mr Barclay. I must tell you, we are not interested.'

'But you said you were interested last week.'

'Yes, but now we are not interested.'

Despite his enormous sense of injustice, of having been misled – lied to even – Paul knows that it would be useless, worse than useless, to dispute what Flossman said and meant or didn't mean last week. All the power in the situation is, as always, with the prospect, and Paul is terribly aware of his own powerlessness. He says, 'You have clients in the automotive industry?'

'Of course.'

'Such as which companies?'

'Mr Barclay –'

'DaimlerChrysler?'

'Yes. Mr Barclay, I have told you –'

'Could I just –'

'I have told you we are not interested.'

'What I was going to say, Dieter –'

'If you have anything to say, please send me a fax.'

'Let me just say this – is General Motors a client of yours?'

Flossman sighs. 'No,' he says. 'Now, Mr Barclay . . .'

To persist, Paul knows, is totally futile. Flossman now dislikes him. Flossman is irritated, even angry. Nevertheless, he says, 'What I wanted to say, Dieter, what I wanted to say is that I'm constantly speaking with . . . Actually, just today, for example, I've just come from a lunch meeting with a chap in GM – very senior individual on the purchasing side . . .'

'This is bullshit,' Flossman says dismissively.

For a moment Paul is so shocked, so insulted, that he is speechless. In sixteen years of selling, surprisingly perhaps, no prospect has ever openly put it to him that he is lying. Of course, there has been insinuation, there has been euphemistic scepticism, there has been innocent incredulity. Never this.

'What did you say?' He is stunned, his voice quiet.

Flossman laughs edgily, aware of having transgressed something, some etiquette – and also, it seems, elated to have done so. 'You are speaking bullshit,' he says, with a smile in his voice. The outrageousness of this is simply too much. Paul's face blooms an alarmingly deep red. 'I am speaking bullshit?' he says hoarsely. '*I* am?'

'Yes, you –'

'No.'

'You are speaking –'

'*No.*'

'– bullshit. You are –'

'*You* are speaking bullshit, Flossman.'

'– a liar, Mr Barclay.'

'– speaking bullshit, Flossman.'

Flossman is laughing.

'*You* are speaking bullshit, Flossman!' Paul shouts it several times more, his hatred – ardent and humiliated – the hatred of the long-oppressed for the oppressor. Suddenly, though, there is no one there, no one on the end of the line. A small plastic silence. It is finished, and pulling his jacket from his seat, ignoring the looks that are fixed on him from all over the suddenly quiet sales floor, he sets off purposefully, urgently, for the Penderel's Oak.

2

A painful knot of self-hatred, Paul wakes, as usual, in the pre-dawn darkness. Unseen, the seconds tick, trudging over the eventless desert, the depression of the hours of darkness – and the depression is huge, immediate, though he knows that in the morning it will look melting and pale, like the moon will in the sky. The morning, however, seems infinitely distant. Though the pain is located mainly in his head, stirring slightly under the duvet he starts to find mysterious secondary pains everywhere, especially down his left side. If only it were possible to smother himself in sleep again – to sink into insensible fathoms with his eyes stuck shut. If only it were possible ... And now, worse, things are whelming up – surfacing – memories – he is unable to stop them. Yesterday afternoon and Flossman. It is all still there, exactly as it was.

Lying in his tepid bed, wheezing shallowly, eyes shut, ticker fluttering, his head a tightening knot of pain, he is once more sentient of his self, and his situation. His life is exactly where it was at four o'clock yesterday afternoon when he hung up the phone and walked, stony-faced, off the sales floor. The escape was no more than a temporary oblivion. And now, like objects thrown up by the surf on the shifting pebbles less than a mile from where he is lying in the dark, he starts to find odd things littering his memory. The oddest sees him scrambling on a train track among the surprisingly large stones and heavy sleepers of the rail bed. Some people watching him, laughing, from the greenish light of a station platform. Him shouting at them to 'fuck off'. Them pelting him with empty cider tins and half-eaten kebabs wrapped in greasy, sauce-smeared paper, scattering shredded cabbage everywhere – the memory squeezes his eyes more tightly shut, shoves his chin into his chest. And how did that situation end?

How, for that matter, did it begin?

Darkling, mortified, his memory feels its way. He had expected to find Murray in the Penderel's Oak, but Murray was not there. The pub was fuller than it had been when he left it an hour earlier. He wandered up to the bar, hoping to see Michaela, but she had still not started her shift, and he leafed uninterestedly through an *Evening Standard* that someone had left there. He had just read something about house prices, and was searching through the sports section, looking for the snooker, when Murray appeared. 'Where've you been?' Paul asked. Murray answered in profile, staring at his own reflection in the dim mirror behind the bar. 'Where d'you think?' he said. 'At the office.'

'Did you see Marlon?'

'That little shit?' Murray paused. Then, offhand, 'I think so.'

'So it's all sorted out?'

Murray had still not made eye contact. 'Is what all sorted out?'

'What do you think?'

'Oh aye.'

'What did you agree?'

'What did we agree?'

'Yeah.'

'We agreed that he should fuck off and stop whingeing.'

'You agreed that?'

'We did.'

Implausible. Paul, however, did not press him; he would hear on Monday what had happened.

The trail of his memory soon peters out in the sweat and thumping noise of the Penderel's Oak. Then there are only little fragments of time. For instance, Murray – very full of himself once a few drinks had steadied his hands – performing his poems. Leaning towards

Simona – a leathery old-school saleswoman in her fifties – and saying, 'Get yur gums aroon' mae plums!' Simona billowing smoke into Murray's equally leathery face and telling him, in a voice that was the product of more than a million cigarettes, to fuck off. Murray shouting, 'Get yur lips aroon' mae bits!' In Murray's opinion, these poems were simply more upfront than most other literature, with which they shared the same essential message. Later, he was heard saying, 'Get yur larynx aroon' mae phalanx,' unsmilingly, to a young woman he did not know. And later still Paul has a memory of him saying, 'Get yur nozzle aroon' mae pizzle,' to Michaela, whose response – 'You're disgusting. You're really disgusting' – he seemed to take as subtle praise, and smiled.

And suddenly Paul remembers that he himself had been holding – *holding*! – her small hand, which she tugged away when Murray sidled up to them. They had been talking. What had they been talking about? More awake than he was, he stares into the darkness, trying to see.

One thing is distressingly sure – he has nowhere near enough memory to fill the many hours that he must have spent in the pub. He has perhaps one hour of memory proper, and then some fragments, pseudo-memories with a dreamlike lack of edge and integrity. Even to use the word 'fragments' is to exaggerate the solidity of these episodes, to make them sound more substantial than they actually are. How much time, for instance, had he spent locked in a cubicle in the Gents? Or was that a dream? If it happened, it was potentially quite a long time – perhaps as much as an hour. Was that before or after he had spoken to Michaela and held her hand? Who had come into the Gents looking for him, knocking on the door? Had he really shouted at them to fuck off? And had *Eddy Jaw* been there, in the Penderel's Oak? It is not that Paul has any memory, as such, of his being there – just a vague feeling that he was.

Later, he remembers being at London Bridge station – it was probably between nine and ten o'clock, the time that he usually stumbles out of the pub and, without really knowing what he is doing, starts the long journey home. Michaela was prominent in his thoughts, and while he does not remember exactly what he was thinking, it is evident that he had, at the time, an exaggerated sense of the significance of a little hand-holding and slurred speech. And then, the incident on the rail bed. How had that happened? *Where* had it happened? How had he extricated himself from the situation? It occurs to him that the ladder of plum pains down his left side may have something to do with it. On the other side of the bed, Heather moves, asleep. Paul is strangely surprised that she is there. He has, needless to say, no memory whatsoever of arriving home last night, of taking out his lenses, of going to bed, and her presence – though it is her absence that would really have been strange – is somehow unsettling. It, more than anything, seems to emphasise the hole that has appeared in his head. Shutting his eyes, breathing through his nose to preserve what little moisture there is in his mouth, he hunkers painfully down to get through the next four or five hours of nothingness.

Later still, he is sitting up in bed, mortifying himself with a foul cigarette. The curtains are open, and the windows white and untransparent with condensation. Only when the light had struggled up, and the noises from outside become more frequent, until they were more or less continuous, had he surrendered, at last, to the gravity of sleep. It was too late. The children were audible on the landing; and Heather sat up suddenly, sat puffy with sleep on the edge of the bed, squeezing first one small yellow foot, and then the other, with her hands. With a scraping scream, she opened the curtains – and Paul, pissed off at being woken from what seemed like one whole second of untroubled sleep, pulled the duvet over his hurting head. Having opened the curtain, Heather left the room – and she had opened it, of course, to express her anger at what had happened last night. She was not that angry – only so much anger can be expressed by opening a curtain – and nothing that extraordinary had happened; only that Paul had stumbled in unusually drunk and unusually late, at midnight, when she was watching the History Channel and drinking white wine, the kids long since upstairs in bed.

When she comes back, twenty minutes later, to remind him of all the things they have to do this morning, he gives up trying to sink into the bed – fervent dreams and tired solid reality mingling in his mind – and sits up, and instinctively lights a cigarette. Heather stands in the doorway, in a pink dressing gown, which is tightly and neatly tied at her thick waist like a sturdy overcoat. She is quite heavy-featured, but with large blue eyes and curly blonde hair. (Someone once told her that she looked like Sarah Jessica Parker, and sometimes she nearly believes it.) Looking at Paul – his flabby ashen face, his round white shoulders, his downy tits – she worries. She worries that he is becoming less attractive from one week to the next, and the implications of that for a future she imagines in terms of years, but even more she worries about the damage that he must be doing to himself, the devastation he must be wreaking on his own poor frame. She does not like to think about it – still less about *why* he does it – and during the prosaic day, when there is always something else to do, it is usually easy not to – the moments of massive worry, of worry turning to fear, panic, terror, always find her at night. Then his wheezing, whistling breath as he sleeps beside her speaks of a self-destructiveness, a self-negation that she finds terrifying – and underlying it, of course, the fact that it is difficult to imagine that someone who lives the way he does is not unhappy. Has he always lived like this? When she forces herself to look, she can see that things have been getting worse for a long time now, but slow decline is easy to ignore. Nothing dramatic has happened. He has been drinking more and more, but has always drunk too much. He seems depressed a lot of the time. Especially since he tried to stop the Felixstat. Then something dramatic *had* happened, and hurriedly, in a panic, he had snatched for the pills that he had been so determined to quit, saying they stole his energy and made him satisfied to live with mediocrity. Since then – it was six months ago – he has started to remind her, in ways she finds painfully sad, of the Paul she first met, fragile and self-destructive. And without the open-handed, kind, twinkling, funny qualities of that Paul, except in isolated moments, which nowadays she finds herself pathetically treasuring because of the way they make her feel that everything might be all right. Not this morning though. This morning he is ugly and sullen, and last night he was loud and stupid and not funny at all.

The sound of two televisions showing the same thing – Paul can tell from the squeaky voices, and he knows anyway, that it is a cartoon – fills the narrow landing behind her. Oliver and Marie both have TVs in their rooms, though most of the time they watch the same thing. Oliver and Marie are not Paul's children. They don't call him 'Dad', they call him 'Paul'. They haven't seen their father ('Dad') – a Dr John Hall, formerly of Brighton, East Sussex, now of Sydney, New South Wales – for nine years, since Oliver was two and Marie two months, and only know what he looks like from photos. A few photos which Heather keeps hidden in a drawer. The manic, high-pitched voices of the cartoon remind Paul, with some nostalgia, of his university days, of watching *Dangermouse* and *Dogtanian and the Three Muskehounds* with a mug of tea, a spliff and a young woman called Geraldine, Doc Martens under her long, black, Victorian skirts, a pale face with round cheeks, fuzzy black hair, depressed and depressing poems. Dutifully, he had read these poems, and said that he thought that they were good. (Sometimes he wondered whether the 'badger-headed thing' was him – even then he had a tuft of prematurely white hair.) 'Can you please ask the kids to close their doors please,' he says, slowly and quietly. For a moment Heather considers this. She takes a small travel alarm clock from her dressing-gown pocket, looks at it, and says, 'I want to leave in half an hour.' Paul turns his gaze to the white windows. 'What time is it?'

'It's nine thirty. Half an hour, Paul.' And when she goes there is a brisk barrage of door sounds as first Marie's, then Oliver's, then the bathroom door are closed. In the quietness, he queasily stubs out his less-than-half-smoked cigarette. Standing is a mistake. He sits down urgently on the edge of the bed. Then, with a look of intense concentration on his face, like someone walking a tightrope, very slowly, he descends the stairs and slips into the peach enclave of the downstairs loo (even the toilet paper is peach, and quilted, with little rosebuds on it) and throws up.

Throughout the day, without looking for them, he finds little pieces of last night. In Sainsbury's, for instance, being jostled by bad-tempered people and knocked by their trolleys in the non-foods aisle, waiting while Heather compares two oddly shaped bottles of something, one puce, the other aquamarine, he suddenly remembers stepping out of a stationary train into emptiness, and hitting the big stones of the rail bed. Yes. He had stepped out of the wrong side of the train – that *had* happened – a painful pratfall for the laughing young people eating kebabs on the opposite platform, a pratfall only possible because of the old slam-door rolling stock still in use on his commuter route. It didn't even occur to him at the time, kneeling there and trying to work out what the fuck had happened, that he could have been killed by one of the fast expresses that occasionally howl along the line. Then what? He had been pelted with food . . . Heather drops the puce bottle into the trolley and they move a few metres along the aisle. And then some people, yes, some people had helped him onto the platform – the memories materialise. The platform, from the rail bed, had seemed very high, and the two men had taken a hand each and pulled, his scuffed shoes scraping at the wall. He had fallen back, onto the hard rail, with a clang. And lying there on his back, the men shouting at him, he had wondered whether he could be bothered to move. In the end, they had pulled him out like a dead weight, his ankle knocking

26

against the platform edge. And where was that? And why had he tried to get off the train there anyway? The whole thing seems more and more dreamlike, and at the same time more disturbing. Where had he been? Waiting in the enormous queue, mesmerised by the song of dozens of checkout scanners, he remembers that he took the eight eleven train from London Bridge – remembers being astonished even then how early it was. He should have been home at nine thirty, at the latest, not twelve. Had he spent two and a half lost hours blundering around the SouthEast Trains network? Where had he been? Perhaps he got on the wrong train at Haywards Heath. That had happened before.

And in McDonald's, where they take the kids for lunch on Saturday after the shopping, the first bite of his Big Mac in his mouth, he finds with a small jolt of adrenalin something that Michaela said to him – that she was splitting up with what's-his-name ... On the other side of the table Oliver has ritually separated his Big Mac into two separate 'sandwiches', and Heather is munching a Quarter Pounder With Cheese, holding it with as few fingers as possible, her eyes empty, wiping her mouth with a paper napkin every few seconds. Marie has gone to the loo, leaving a small pile of mustardy gherkins. What else had Michaela said? What had *he* said to *her*? He remembers saying something ... And during his driving lesson, moving slowly down Church Road towards an ethereal winter-afternoon moon, while his instructor, Graham – a gentle Christian with a little gold cross dangling from his ear lobe – is telling him something about orphanages in Romania and how he might help, he remembers that Eddy Jaw *was* in the Penderel's Oak last night. He remembers seeing him talking to Murray, and walking up to him and saying, with an unintended edge of genuine belligerence to his voice, 'You still drinking that fucking shit, Jaw, you poof?' (Eddy, as usual, was swigging a Bacardi Breezer.) It was, on reflection, quite an aggressive thing to say to an old friend he had not seen in years – not since the sad demise of Northwood in ninety-seven.

What was his surname? Not Jaw, that was just what everyone called him. Staring at some shabby rainswept Victorian villas, Paul squeezes his facial features together in an effort to remember. The name is not there. And what had Eddy whatever-his-name-is been doing in the Penderel's Oak anyway? Had he said something important, something interesting? Even in the absence of a specific memory, the idea is teasingly persistent. Perhaps Murray would be able to tell him on Monday.

Towards the end of the afternoon, he takes Oliver to the snooker club. It was once a bingo hall. The front entrance, the long row of glass doors through which the old foyer gathers dust, is permanently locked, and they walk down an alley at the side to an unpromising-looking metal door watched over by a security camera. Buzzed in, they climb winding, unheated, concrete stairs with iron banisters, up, up, Paul panting, until they emerge into the semi-darkness of the hall. The bar glows in one corner, and here and there islands of green are illuminated in the huge, indefinite space. Oliver's obsession with snooker is sufficiently intense, sufficiently single-minded, sufficiently almost-worrying, for it to be possible that he will make it as a professional one day. He is not interested in anything else. The walls of his room are covered with pictures of Ronnie O'Sullivan, and in imitation of his idol, he wears an Alice band around the house, though not to school. His cue, a birthday present from Paul, is on permanent display in his room, and from Heather he has pestered permission to stay up late during tournaments. Paul is proud of all this, having introduced Oliver to the sport himself. These days, when they play, he is pleased if he beats him – it happens less and less. They don't talk while they play. Oliver is a silent, serious child, and Paul's attitude to snooker is solemn. 'Set the balls up, will you, Oli?' he says, and heads to the bar for a Foster's and a Coke. He was himself introduced to the sport by his own father, and their relationship, such as it is (and Paul, as much

28

as anyone now, looks at these things with a critical eye), is still heavily dependent on snooker to give it any form or content at all. There are other things sometimes – other things that they talk about – but only in the context of playing snooker, or talking about snooker, and always safe in the knowledge that snooker is never far away. And although Oliver is not his son, Paul had felt it important, as the years went by – though he had never really articulated this, even to himself – that he should have *some* kind of individual relationship with him, and that snooker should be the basis of such a relationship seemed obvious and natural. (At a loss about what to do with Marie, he had included her in their early trips to the club, but she had not taken to it.)

Paul himself had once harboured hopes – probably never realistic – of being a professional player; hopes which foundered in 1980, when at the age of fifteen he was knocked out in the second round of the National Youth Championship in Wolverhampton – not, from a wider perspective, an unrespectable achievement, but certainly not good enough for a would-be pro. Even then, Jimmy White – who had just turned pro himself and was unknown outside the world of snooker – was his hero. They were, in many ways, Paul often thought, so similar. Jimmy was simply a more high-profile, a more heroic, a more epic version of himself – a version of himself who appeared on television. What Paul might have been – who knows? – if he had beaten that flatulent Welsh boy in the second round of the tournament in Wolverhampton. If he had not missed that easy blue in the deciding frame . . . They do perhaps have points of similarity, Paul and Jimmy, though not most prominently the ones that Paul likes to point out (they are both, in his opinion, mavericks, flair players) – more a dingily raddled appearance and a perceived lack of ruthlessness and steel; and if it is hyperbolic to talk about 'tragedy', a sad sense, at least, of something squandered. It is probably these unacknowledged, and perhaps only subliminally noticed similarities, which underpin Paul's long-standing admiration and affection for Jimmy White. An affection not shared by Oliver, incidentally, who when questioned describes Jimmy, with characteristic forthrightness, as 'disgusting'. Paul's other favourite players, Stephen Hendry and John Higgins (and *their* appeal is perhaps that they exemplify, in professionalism and solidity and steel, qualities that he finds lacking in himself), are also dismissed by Oliver as 'annoying' and 'boring' respectively.

Taking the drinks, and tucking two packets of crisps under his arms, Paul returns to the table, where Oliver has finished setting up, and is knocking the cue ball the length of the now illuminated baize, trying to bring it to rest as close as possible to the baulk cushion. It is the sort of thing he would happily do for hours. Paul wins the toss, and taking off his jacket (his suit jacket, worn with a round-necked jumper and jeans and scuffed work shoes) he steps up to break. He overhits it, and leaves a red on for Oliver. Not an easy red, but Oliver has become the sort of intimidating opponent who punishes most lapses, and Paul sits down – partly to put pressure on the eleven-year-old, and partly because he assumes that the pressure will not tell. It doesn't. With a sharp *clock* the ball drops into the pocket. The white scoots into the pack and – quite luckily, Paul thinks – positions itself for a simple black. All day he has had a voracious hunger that seems unsatisfied however much he eats, and he pulls open the pack of prawn cocktail crisps with a sort of urgency. Oliver sinks the black, and having to stand on tiptoe, replaces it on its spot. Paul lifts the pint of Foster's to his lips and its smell sickens him for a moment. He soldiers on, sipping, scowling, stuffing the sweet-and-sour crisps into his narrow mouth. Even now it pains him to think of that easy blue he missed in Wolverhampton. On such small things our lives depend, he thinks. Fate. It may be the case that ever since that miss – and if he had potted it, he has to admit, he might have missed the next shot, or failed in the next round – it may be the case that he had given up on his life even then. Not entirely of course, but as a serious, wholly worthwhile undertaking.

He remembers the way his legs shook as he returned to his seat, after the blue had rattled in the jaws of the pocket and rolled a little way over the table's green plain, and the umpire saying, in a heartless voice, 'Rainey, thirty-four.' He remembers that he had tears somewhere near, though not actually in his eyes. He has no memory of the Welsh boy finishing the frame, only of standing in a light shower of applause to shake his damp hand . . .

Clock!

Oliver seems to be putting a break together. The most extraordinary thing about his game, Paul thinks, is not his precise and assured potting, nor his intimidating nerve and determination; it is his break-building. He has an amazingly mature ability to think several shots ahead, to plan ahead . . . So, after Wolverhampton, life had gone on, but maybe his attitude to it had changed. Nothing seemed worth full engagement. He had drifted – that was for sure. He had been drifting, it sometimes seems, ever since. He pulls the crisp packet taut and pours the last orange-pink crumbs into the palm of his hand. Then he lights a cigarette. With the hangover, he feels emotionally oversensitised, as well as intellectually dull and physically depleted – everything seems moving, seems full of mysterious significance. There is something savage about the way Oliver plays, a savage precision. Killer instinct. He has a winner's attitude. He pots the black, and the white spins back turbulently to align itself with one of the few remaining reds. Paul knocks the rubber butt of his cue (he uses one of the dodgy club cues) twice on the floor in restrained appreciation. Oliver ignores this, his focus intent on the next task. It is sometimes difficult, watching him, to remember that he is still a child, who weeps when he is disappointed or prevented from doing what he wants. Like the time Paul promised to take him to Sheffield, to watch some World Championship matches at the Crucible. Heather vetoed that. While Oliver cried in his room, Paul had tried to reason with her in the kitchen, where she was doing the washing-up. As soon as he started to speak, she said, 'Paul – no.' He sat down at the table, and lit a cigarette. It was summer and outside the windows the garden – the damp rectangle of overgrown grass and old tennis balls and tangled washing lines and slugs – was still half sunny. He started again, but she turned to him, her hands in pink rubber gloves and said, 'No!' He knew there was no point pushing it, that her stomach for a fight over this was far stronger than his own. 'I'm sorry, Oli,' he had said stiffly, ashamed of being unable to deliver on his promise, 'your mother doesn't want us to go.' He did not even ask her why she was so opposed to the idea (she later said it 'wouldn't have been fair on Marie') – if he had it would only have made her angry, only have made her point out the obvious fact that Oli is her son, not his. And he is hers. Paul is not his father. (Though there are naturally times when she wants him to perform the part.) And Paul, it must be said, is pleased to be shielded from any sense of ultimate involvement, is pleased to feel that, theoretically, he is under no obligation, that he is simply filling in for someone else, informally, temporarily. That the whole domestic set-up is merely provisional – he feels safe with that, which is also why he never pushes her on it, why he sometimes seems so passive. He looks up. Oliver is standing there, surveying the table and chalking his cue the way he sees the professionals do on TV. Paul notices that the people at the next table, two old men, have stopped playing and are watching Oliver. It *is* quite a break he is on. He finesses the last red into the side pocket and, his chin still on his cue, watches as the white rolls against the end cushion, setting it up precisely to pot the black, which is stranded there. One of the old men nods, and lights a cigarette. Ned the barman is passing with a clutch of empty glasses. 'Eh, Ned,' says the other old man. Ned stops. 'This boy's got a maximum break on.' And Ned, too, becomes a spectator. Now with four sets of eyes on him, but seemingly oblivious to them, Oliver sinks the black. Ned winces – the cue ball has not travelled far up the table and the shot for the yellow, which is still on its spot, is extremely difficult. Paul, who is resisting the urge to stand lest it put more pressure on Oli, watches in silence. He wishes the spectators – Ned is staring open-mouthed at the table – would all fuck off. And now more of them are emerging from the shadows, as word of what is happening spreads through the hall. In the middle of it, Oliver shows no sign of even noticing them. He seems as focused, as unflustered as if he were on his own. He takes his time. He pots the yellow. There is a short spate of applause and then the watchers, perhaps sharing Paul's worry, stop their hands. What is left should be easy, were it not for the pressure, the immense forces of the pressure, which distort it. (And there is also the fact that everyone there has lost sight of – he is eleven years old.) When he pots the black – and he nearly underhits it – there is a strange, strangled exclamation, and then people are applauding and laughing and talking excitedly to strangers; except Paul, who is still and silent, and Oli himself, who had seemed the oldest of them all a moment ago, when the final ball fell with a quiet rustle into the rigging of the pocket, and is suddenly a child again, small, with an unsteady expression on his face – not a smile, exactly – as though stunned and scared by this moment of success, so often imagined (imagined uninterruptedly, in fact, for several years), so many times unsuccessfully attempted – and wondering, 'What has happened?' Or even, 'Who am I?'

3

It is a perfect Monday morning. Late November. Cold grey gloom outside. And raining. On waking, in the dark, to the alarm's infuriating high-pitched stutter, the first thing Paul does is fumble on the light. For a few moments it stings his eyes. It is not a day on which he expects anything significant to happen. Heather drops him off at the station on her way to the small solicitors' firm, Gumley Rhodes, where she does part-time secretarial work. For an hour, he sits squashed against a wet window, someone else's newspaper in his face, and a morsel of hashish under his tongue. When he arrives at London Bridge, he has a slow subtle floaty feeling in his limbs, a peaceful fug about his whole person. He takes the Northern Line to Bank, and there transfers to the Central Line. From the mighty escalator at Holborn, he watches the adverts slide down through his field of vision, until delivered by it, via the low ticket hall, into daylight and rain, he crosses Kingsway, and enters King's House through the taupe glass door – tentatively, fearing some sort of fallout from the Flossman incident. He knows, however, that this is paranoid – there is no sign of fallout nor will there be.

Paul is always one of the first onto the sales floor in the morning. Murray is usually the last to arrive.

'Murray,' Paul says, when he does, 'is it just me, or was Eddy Jaw in the Penderel's on Friday?'

Murray looks surprised. 'Eddy Jaw?' he says.

'Yeah.'

'Don't think so.'

'I'm sure I saw him.'

A few uninterested heads turn to see what Murray will say.

He shrugs. 'Might have been, yeah,' he says. With an unlit cigarette in his hand, he stands up. The double-breasted front of his suit, especially when unbuttoned, seems too big for him, there seems to be too much blue cloth – masses of it, a dismantled marquee.

'I'm sure he was . . .' Paul says.

And suddenly, on the point of leaving, Murray says, 'Yeah, he was. I saw *you* talking to him.'

'Me? I was? What were we talking about?'

Murray leaves without answering.

It is, Paul thinks, as if he's offended – as if I've offended him somehow. And he sifts his scant memories of Friday night, looking for something that might account for this moodiness. Nothing that he can remember. Perhaps something happened to Murray over the weekend. What Murray does at the weekend is a mystery to Paul – the two of them operate an informal, unspoken don't-ask-don't-tell policy on the subject, and in fact hardly speak of their lives outside the office at all. (They are always hearing about Andy's life, though. Every Monday he has a new story about some Annabel or Alexandra he's lusting after, who's always 'gorgeous' – all the girls in Andy's stories are 'gorgeous', if they're not 'mooses' – and whom he met at Jezza's or Josh's party on Saturday night.) About Murray's life, however, only the occasional slight snippet filters out. Every summer he has a barbecue in his small suburban garden but only people from the office are there, and not many of them – typically the Pig and Neil and Simona and one or two others – a few of the transients who happen to be on the team at the time – as well as Paul. It is a long-standing tradition now, Murray's office barbecue. So Paul knows where Murray lives, and what his house is like – two-up, two-down, not unlike his own minus the extension. He also knows that before he knew him, Murray was married, and divorced, and thinks he may have a brother somewhere – all in all surprisingly little, given that they

35

have worked together, on and off, for over fifteen years. These days, particularly, Paul finds Murray's life quite depressing to think about – in the intensity of its seeming loneliness, no woman, a desperate financial situation – so he seldom does. When he does, it is with pity, and mild horror.

The morning is unexceptional. Paul reads *The Times*, and does what he can of the quick crossword. Tony Peters holds a team meeting – which Paul watches, sneeringly, over the top of his paper. He dislikes everything about Tony Peters' team – the tidy desks, the smart, well-behaved salespeople, the way they laugh at Tony's jokes, the strict timekeeping, the team meetings . . . Later, the slow clock nearing eleven, he listens in to one of Andy's wooden, underpowered pitches. 'Yes, many of our readers are in the chemical industry,' Andy is saying when Paul activates the earpiece and, shaking loose the tangled coils of the cord, puts it to his ear. 'Would they be potential clients?'

'We have clients in the chemical industry.' It's another German. 'And also, of course, in other industries.'

'Like what other industries?'

'For example, the food industry.' The German is civil, but sounds bored.

'That's very interesting,' Andy says. 'We have readers in the food industry as well. Such as Nestlé.'

'Do you have something you could send me? A fax?'

'Of course. But if I could just ask you whether you'd like new business from Europe's leading multinational companies?'

Obligingly, the German says, 'Yes, I would. Of course.'

'That's good, because as I've said, our readership includes the purchasing directors of Europe's thousand leading multinational companies, such as Philips, Hoechst and BMW.'

'But if you could send me something.' The German is more insistent now. 'Let me give you my fax number. It is forty-nine for Germany.'

'Yes.'

'Then . . .' There is no hope for poor Andy, Paul thinks. He replaces the earpiece and returns to his desk. No hope at all. He leafs through some old leads – the dead catalogues of international industry fairs, obscure publications full of advertorial, directories. Listlessly, he taps in a number. A company called Sunny Industries, in Mumbai – though the lead is so old it is still down as Bombay. It is in an ancient directory of Indian companies, and he chooses it because it presents him with the MD's name and direct-line number. He watches Murray while it rings. All morning, Murray has managed to pretend not to have noticed that Marlon is there – which is not easy because Marlon's desk is directly opposite his own, and Marlon is there. Paul notices that Murray's eyes take on a strange, empty, defocused quality whenever they pan across it, as they often must. Yes, he has been very quiet this morning, Murray. Uncharacteristically subdued . . .

Earlier, Paul had heard separately from several people what had happened on Friday. Murray, it seems, had waited in the Gents, sitting bored in the locked stall, until he thought that Marlon, who usually left the office early for the gym, would be gone. For some reason, however, Marlon was not gone. What's more, there was a strange atmosphere of eerie stillness on the sales floor – something must have happened. Sitting at his desk, Marlon had his back to the entrance. Murray had hesitated, and then – after momentarily making eye contact with a smiling Andy – had turned to leave. And it was then that he heard Marlon's voice. 'Oi, Murray!' Involuntarily quickening his stride, he had pretended not to hear. When Marlon shouted again, though, it had been impossible to keep up the pretence with any sort of plausibility. So he had stopped, and turned, and seen Marlon stalking towards him, saying, 'I've got a bone to pick with you, Murray.'

This was the situation, more than any other, that he had wanted to avoid.

'That was my repeat,' Marlon said.

'What? Was it?' A half-hearted show of ignorance that only seemed to infuriate Marlon further. 'You fucking know it was,' he shouted, staring up at Murray, who quickly said, 'If it was, I'm sorry.'

'I don't care if you're sorry.' Not knowing what to say, Murray had looked at the floor – had tucked his strong chin into his neck and looked at the worn grey carpet and the dark blue tassels of his loafers. 'What are you going to do about it, Murray?' He found it hard to believe that this was actually happening, that he was being dressed down by Marlon on the sales floor, in front of everybody. He could not look up from the carpet. He has had dreams like this – nightmares in which he is publicly humiliated by little men like Marlon, and in which his father, a short man, often figures. 'What are you going to do about it?' Murray seemed unable to speak. He had had to force the words out. 'What do you want me to do about it?'

'I want you to give me the commission next time you get a deal in. If you ever get another deal in.' An obviously preposterous demand, and Murray had looked up, finally, just to make sure that Marlon was joking. He did not seem to be. 'You lost me the commission on my repeat by fucking it up,' he said. 'You shouldn't have even been calling them, and you fucked it up.'

In mute protest, Murray shook his head.

'You shouldn't have even been calling them . . .'

'That was never a deal.'

'Yes of course it fucking was.'

The tension, to some extent, had fallen away – some people, bored by the routine spectacle of two salesmen arguing over leads and blowouts and commission, had gone back to what they were doing – and Murray had said, more emphatically, 'That was never a deal.' And for an infinitesimal moment, unnerved by something in Marlon's eyes, he had feared the worst. Marlon, however, had not punched him. He had said, in a voice that everyone was able to hear, 'You're a wanker, Murray.' Then he went back to his desk, and after standing in the doorway for a while, with what was technically a smile on his square-jawed face, Murray had slipped away . . .

'Yes!' shouts a voice in Paul's ear.

'Yes, hello,' Paul says. 'I'd like to speak to Abhijit Bannerjee, please.' There is an offputting echo on the line.

'Yes, that's me. And who is this please?'

'My name's Charles Barclay, Mr Bannerjee. I'm calling from London . . .'

Half an hour later, Paul hangs up. He has been trying to get rid of Mr Bannerjee for most of that time, but Mr Bannerjee's persistence, his intense will to sell, was unstoppable. He agreed – 'Yes, yes, very good, of course' – to take a full-page, full-colour ad within the first few minutes of the call, and then he started to sell. *What* he was selling, Paul was not sure, but he knew the tone. There were references to 'tea gardens' and 'boutique hotels', 'software' and 'airport taxis', 'databases' and 'cheap labour one pound a day'. And he kept explaining how he had people, many people, who would be 'the hands' of some protean enterprise, which would make 'a billion' and involve 'boutique hotels'. He said he had developed machines with true artificial intelligence, and that he had also developed property in London in the seventies. Whenever Paul tried to steer the conversation back to the full-page colour, Mr Bannerjee would say, 'Of course, yes of course, we are going to do that,' and then start talking, with torrential enthusiasm, about something else, some other business he was proposing to start – software or construction or tea or boutique hotels. The boutique hotels seemed to be the only fixed point in this maelstrom of entrepreneurial zest – they featured every few minutes, and always as a spin-off from something else, from the tea gardens, the airport taxis, the thousands of toilers entering data for a pound a day – though how this last would work was not entirely clear. After about ten minutes and several attempts to talk Mr Bannerjee through the agreement form, Paul began to give up on the full-page colour. Mr Bannerjee asked him when he was going to be in Mumbai. Paul said, 'Probably not till next summer.' Mr Bannerjee then said that he would be in London in a few weeks, and suggested they have a meeting. Paul was evasive, spoke of being extremely busy. Mr Bannerjee said he would be staying at the Hotel Henry VIII in Bayswater – did Paul know it? Paul fibbed, and said he did. Mr Bannerjee suggested the bar of the Henry VIII as a possible meeting place – 'or maybe they have conference rooms, I don't know'. The call ends with Paul saying that he *really* has to go, and that he will send the agreement form through, and Mr Bannerjee saying that 'of course' he will send it back straight away.

By this time, it is almost twelve. 'Coming to the Penderel's?' Paul says to Murray, standing and pulling on his jacket. Surprisingly, Murray responds as if this suggestion were something unexpected. After a moment of strange puzzlement, he says, 'Aye.' But with a distinct lack of enthusiasm.

The pub is deserted when they arrive. Paul's phone had started to ring as he was leaving the sales floor, and though he had hesitated, and half turned, he had not answered it. He is still wondering who it might have been. He wonders if it might have been Mr Bannerjee, whose long, supercharged spiel has left him exhausted and muddled, and oddly inspired. He is even starting to wonder whether perhaps he *should* have agreed to meet him at the Hotel Henry VIII, whether perhaps something might have come of such a meeting. 'Like what?' he asks himself, derisively, as he stands at the bar. And in answer summons the examples of Angus MacMilne, who so impressed one of his prospects that they offered him a job in the City, and of Pax 'the Fax' Murdoch, another former fellow salesman, who went out to Bangkok to set up a telesales business there – which turned out, extraordinarily, to be an international scam run by the North Korean intelligence service, though Pax did not realise who he was working for, or why, until it was too late.

'Morning, Paul,' Michaela says.

'Morning? I think you mean afternoon. Never in the morning, Michaela.' It is two past twelve. She laughs, and without waiting, starts to pour three pints. She likes Paul. He is 'nice'. 'Nice' in a way that Murray – who makes her uneasy – is not. Setting his cigarette in the glass ashtray on the bar, Paul reaches into his pocket and fishes out the exact amount of money for the pints – he knows it well. He finds he is irritatingly shy with Michaela today, after what happened on Friday – the more so when, standing there, he suddenly remembers telling her that he and Heather were on the point of separation, which just isn't true. 'Good weekend?' he says, smiling softly. Michaela shrugs her small shoulders. Andy is at the fruit machine, and they hear the metal of his winnings yocker into the trough. Scooping out the coins, he looks at Michaela, a cigarette stuck sexily – so he thinks – to his lower lip. And from the table, Murray stares, his face set in a virile scowl that he hopes she will see. All three of them find the unspoken hopes of the other two – of which they are all more aware than any of them think – contemptibly ridiculous, evidence of a comical degree of self-delusion. Paul puts the pints on the table, and he and Murray watch suspiciously as Andy wanders to the bar and says something to Michaela which makes her laugh. Murray mutters a few poisonous-sounding words, and Paul wonders if his unusually taciturn and preoccupied mood has something to do with his car, his Mercedes S-Class. It seems impossible that it will not be repossessed at some point this winter. The next payment, Paul knows, is due on Wednesday, and for the second consecutive month Murray will be unable to meet it.

Murray has always thought of himself as a Mercedes driver, the S-Class in particular – a serious, manly car for serious, manly men.

(Sir Alex Ferguson, for example, drives such a car, and Murray sees many similarities between himself and Sir Alex – both working-class Glaswegians who have made their way in the world; both hard men, generous and just, with a gritty inborn nobility.) But as fifty approached and he was still driving the second-hand Sierra, Murray had started to worry. He had started to lose sleep over the thought that he might *never* drive an S-Class – might never *be* an S-Class driver. Why it happened exactly when it did, he is not sure, but one ordinary day in July, on his way home, he stopped at Tony Purslow Ltd, the Mercedes-Benz dealer in Epsom. He was determined not to think about what he was doing – not until it was done – and everything was therefore slightly dreamlike. The salesman's smart suit and friendly, serious welcome. The shiny Mercs. The heated seats and leather-covered steering wheels and illuminated vanity mirrors. Forms were filled out, credit checks run, hands shaken. If the salesman was surprised at the impatient urgency of his client, he was too experienced a professional to let it show. And less than an hour after entering the showroom, Murray was motoring home in a long, wide S-Class – smiling down the A24 towards Leatherhead in its fragrant, insulated hush. The following week was one of the happiest of his life. At work, he was dreamy and absent-minded. He spent a lot of time staring out the window, or sitting on his own in the smoking room. At night, unable to sleep, he would get out of bed, and twitch the drapes, and look down at the car's silver bodywork in the steady greenish illumination of the street light. He would spend evenings sitting alone in the stationary car, occasionally going for a short drive. One night, he slept in the car, waking on the anthracite leather in the bright silence of the very early morning, surprisingly cold, a terrible pain in his immobilised neck, the windows frosted with condensation. He opened the heavy door – startling some crows who were strutting on the tarmac – and stiffly swung his legs out. The steering wheel seemed to have bruised his knees during the night . . .

'You all right, Murray?' Paul says. Murray nods. Paul starts to tell him about Mr Bannerjee. He does not seem interested – though he murmurs occasionally, he obviously isn't listening.

Leaving the pub at ten past two, they make their way back through Lincoln's Inn Fields, its massive trees, and the noise of Kingsway. The afternoon passes slowly (though less slowly than it would were he sober) until, when it is starting to get dark outside, just when he is standing up to go to the smoking room, feeling in his jacket pocket for fags and lighter, his phone rings.

It is Eddy Jaw.

'Hello – Rainey?' his blunt voice says.

'Yeah.'

'Where the fuck were you?'

The Old Cheshire Cheese is on Fleet Street, halfway from the High Court to Ludgate Hill. It is possible that Shakespeare frequented the old pub (it was rebuilt in 1667, following the setback of the previous year), a possibility somewhat oversold on the sign outside. It was, however, Dr Johnson's local, and Dickens knew its dark, creaking, wooden interior and cramped stairs. More recently, from the end of the nineteenth century and for most of the twentieth – until they decamped to less dear offices where the docks used to be – it was usually full of journalists. Now the only newsmen are from Reuters, over the road; the others have been replaced by investment bankers from Goldman Sachs, and lawyers from the Middle Temple, and tourists – lots of tourists – and salesmen.

Entering the narrow brick passageway where the pub's entrance is – under a huge old lantern with 'Ye Olde Cheshire Cheese' in Gothic letters on its milky glass – Paul remembers, with some nostalgia, how he and Eddy Jaw used to work together in offices nearby, the offices of Northwood Publishing, and themselves spend long afternoons in the Chesh. That was some years ago, and it came

43

to a sudden end when the contract they were working on was withdrawn. Which was a shame, because things had been very prosperous – 'fucking dial-a-deal' in the argot of the salesmen – and pushing open the pub's broad door, Paul smells again, in the distinctive woody scent of the interior – similar to that of a Wren church – the spectacular success that the withdrawal of the contract had interrupted.

He remembers where they used to sit, in the square, skylit room – himself, Eddy, the Pig, Murray and the others. This part of the pub, he is disappointed to see, has been divided into smaller spaces, now full of people, so he makes his way to where the wooden stairs go down, and steadying himself with a hand on the low ceiling, descends to the vaulted rooms below – the former cellars – and down yet more stairs, stone this time, into the loud, high-ceilinged basement bar. It is half past five and every part of the pub is packed. Eddy is not there, so Paul goes back upstairs to his favourite place, the snug on the other side of the panelled entrance hall from the Chop Room restaurant (which does not seem to have changed much since the late eighteenth century, except that the waiting staff are now mostly Antipodean), where there is a fireplace with orange coals in a black grate, and a muddy painting of a man wearing a wig, and a window of thick, imperfect glass – he used to while away whole afternoons under that window – and wealthy American bankers talking shop. He decides that he should settle somewhere, or he and Eddy will spend the whole evening wandering through the pub, saying 'Sorry, excuse me, sorry', without ever seeing each other, so he goes back downstairs to a sort of mezzanine between the two subterranean levels, where a few small tables are squeezed into the painted brick alcoves formed by the ceiling vaults. One of these tables is vacant, and there he sips his pint of Ayingerbrau, lights a cigarette, and looks over the laminated menu, as if it were something utterly mysterious.

44

'You're not going to eat, are you, Rainey? That would really fucking throw me.'

Eddy Jaw has not changed. Stooping more than necessary under the low vault, he is wearing, as he always used to, a three-piece Hugo Boss suit with very short, stubby lapels – he looks buttoned-up, encased in olive cloth. His big face is perhaps fleshier than it used to be, but it was always fleshy. His hair is blond and cropped. 'All right, Eddy,' Paul says.

'How the fuck are you, Paul?'

'I'm all right. How are you, Eddy?'

'I'm fucking brilliant. Do you want anything from the bar, another one?' Paul glances at his three-quarters-full pint glass. 'Course you do. What are you drinking?' Eddy smiles significantly. 'Prinz, is it?'

'No, it's Ayingerbrau.'

'For fuck's sake! What's the matter with you?'

'I'll have the same again.'

'No you won't. You'll have a fucking Prinz.'

Paul smiles, for a moment sincerely happy. 'All right then.' And Eddy's broad back disappears down the stairs into the clamour of the bar. It is strange to see him again. He looks full of himself, thriving – very different from how he looked when Paul saw him last. Excluding Friday, that is. It was a few months after Northwood had lost the contract with International Money Publications in the summer of ninety-seven – they had all scattered, at the height of that summer, and gone their separate ways. Eddy had come to Murray's barbecue, but after that he had disappeared, and none of them knew what had happened to him. Then, one wet November morning, Paul had seen him in Tottenham Court Road tube station. On his way to work at Archway Publications, Paul had been on the up escalator, and Eddy, a desolate face in the crowd, on the down, so it had been impossible to speak to him, and he had not noticed Paul. Paul has always remembered that sudden apparition of Eddy's face in the crowd, the undisguised wretchedness of its expression, as the escalators shunted them past each other. It had been a low point in Paul's own life – perhaps the lowest – and on the basis of nothing more than that glimpse, he has always assumed that for Eddy too that dank winter had been some sort of nadir. Perhaps it had not, but for Paul there is nevertheless a sense of shared experience – a sense sharpened to poignancy by their presence here in the Chesh; ensconced underground, unaware of the dark November evening above and able instead to imagine Fleet Street on a fierce July day. The taste of Prinz super-strength lager – unpleasantly spirituous and metallic – intensifies this effect. It was what they always drank then – except Eddy, of course. A Bacardi Breezer in his big fist he sits down opposite Paul, and clinks the neck of the bottle peremptorily on his pint glass. 'Good to see you, Paul,' he says.

'Yeah, good to see you, Eddy.'

From his long-cheeked face, Eddy's small eyes peer out, pale blue and smiling warily. Eddy is bluff and coarse, even brutal, but there is something else in his eyes – a slyness, for sure. Even an unexpected intelligence. He sits hunched forward, surrounding the Bacardi Breezer with his hands. 'Sorry about lunchtime, by the way,' Paul says. 'I completely forgot about that.' Eddy smiles. 'I thought you might, state you were in Friday.'

'Yeah, fucking hell . . .' Embarrassed, Paul sips Prinz. 'I don't think I've been here since we left Northwood,' he says.

'No, me neither.' Eddy looks around. 'Those were the days, eh?'

'They were.'

His smile widening, Eddy says, 'Fucking dial-a-deal.'

'Yeah, right.' And for a few minutes they unshutter a friendship with familiar stories about people they both know – Murray, Simon, who was their boss, the Pig – and about Northwood, the small company where they worked for a few summer months, and where everything seemed easy and exhilarating. Paul finds it strange that they worked there for only a few months. It seems like longer.

'You know why Simon lost the IM contract?' Eddy says.

Paul shakes his head. 'No.'

'He was trying to launch his own yearbooks. In competition with IM.'

'Was he?'

'Yeah. Trying to set up his own titles. They found out, and he lost the contract.' Simon. His empurpled face and loudly pinstriped bulk whelm into Paul's mind. His wavy white-and-grey hair, port-and-stilton accent, and habit of tapping the desk with his signet ring when under stress. It was all affectation, apparently. He was from the East End, though in the Northwood days he lived in Surrey. Or said he did. 'And what happened to him?'

'Topped himself,' Eddy says.

'He killed himself?'

'That's what I heard.'

'Why? When?'

Eddy shrugs. 'When he lost the contract, I suppose. He had kids in private schools,' he says, as though it explained everything. 'I heard he got really tanked up and drove the Jag over a quarry. Kaboom.'

'Fucking hell,' Paul says thoughtfully. They observe a moment's silence, then Eddy says, 'Saw *Glengarry Glen Ross* last night.' He says it with a strange, shy half-smile.

'Oh yeah?'

'It was on telly.'

'Was it?' Paul lights a cigarette. 'Haven't you got it on video or something?'

'On DVD. I always watch it when it's on telly though.'

'Fair enough.' Paul has never understood why some of the others, and Eddy especially, are so obsessed with that film. He remembers the first time that he saw it; not the film (he has seen it since) so much as the occasion – the end of a long night, one of those nights that has particularly stuck in his mind, though nights like it were

47

normal in the Northwood days. The stalwarts were Eddy, Murray and the Pig, and with them there was always, in the end, a gravitational pull to the east – the Pig lived near Brick Lane, and Eddy in Islington – and at about one o'clock, having stomped around Soho for a while looking for somewhere else to go, they shouted down a cab on the Charing Cross Road and piled in, telling the faceless driver to take them to Shoreditch High Street, where there was a lap-dancing place which Eddy and the others liked to go to. The cab rattled through the hot night. On the door, the bouncers had Eastern European accents. Inside, the young – and not so young – women performed on their little stages with the swift, precise movements of product demonstrators on the shopping channel. After each act someone went through the crowd of standing men with a pint glass, collecting pound coins. Later, Eddy and the Pig had the Yellow Pages out, and were leafing through it, looking for escort agencies. Paul was slouched, smoking, in the La-Z-Boy chair. Murray hovered by the door. They were in the Pig's flat, in a newish, hutch-like, secure development between Brick Lane and Bethnal Green. The idea of getting some escorts had been Eddy's, but it soon became clear that they had nowhere near enough cash for one girl each – not even enough for one girl between them – and when someone (Murray probably) asked the Pig where the nearest cash-point was, and the Pig said it was at Tesco's on Bethnal Green Road, the idea was quietly dropped. Extraordinarily, there was still some cocaine left, and for some reason the Pig had about ten litres of unchilled sweet cider, and then Eddy, who was looking through his video collection, found *Glengarry Glen Ross*.

Its depiction of their work is not, in Paul's view, inspiring, though some of the others seem to think it is. For him, the film's final line – 'God I hate this job', spoken by a salesman dialling a prospect's number – is not one which sends him out happy into the night, or in this case the deserted streets of Spitalfields at five o'clock on a cloudless summer morning. He and Eddy left the Pig's place together, and walked towards Islington. 'God I hate this job.' It is especially uninspiring in view of one of the film's other important lines – 'A man *is* his job.' On the other hand, it has to be admitted that Al Pacino and Jack Lemmon, Kevin Spacey, Ed Harris and Alec Baldwin were not assembled to make a film about, say, supermarket shelf-stackers; even depicted as sweatily desperate, duplicitous and soul-destroying, salesmanship is somehow made mythic by the film – stands in as a metaphor for a whole world's modus operandi – and some of its lines have come to define what many of Paul's fellow salesmen, and often Paul himself, like to see as the savage ethos of their profession. Their unmediated acquaintance with the stubborn realities of economic life is epitomised in the film by the terms of the monthly sales contest – 'First prize, a Cadillac Eldorado. Second prize, a set of steak knives. Third prize is you're fired.' Of course, most of them prefer to identify with Alec Baldwin's character – 'I made nine hundred eighty thousand dollars last year, how much you make?' – who delivers the terms of the contest, rather than the poor bastards listening to him. And – Paul has sometimes thought – it may be significant that he himself never *has* identified with Alec Baldwin, but always with the poor bastards, the losers, Jack Lemmon, Ed Harris, that other one – anonymous, not even played by a Hollywood star, the most loserish of them all in his unre-markable mediocrity. Murray, Eddy, he feels sure, do not identify with these men (and it is a film which smells intensely of men – there is only one woman in it, standing in the shadows behind a bar with no lines to say) even if the facts of their lives suggest that they should.

All these thoughts Paul had as he walked, still in his stale suit, back to the unfashionable part of west London where his flat was. A very long walk. He left Eddy at Old Street roundabout – silent at that hour – and made his way slowly down Old Street itself, and into Farringdon. Clerkenwell. Bloomsbury. When he passed Russell Square station it was open, just, and for a moment he paused. He decided that he would keep walking. He was in no hurry. Oxford Street was eerily empty – only a few delivery trucks and street sweepers, preparing for the day's massed, shopping hordes – and preceded by his sharp shadow, starting to sweat in his suit, he walked its whole length. There was something strange and sad about entering his sunny flat, everything exactly as it was when he set off for work twenty-four hours earlier. It seemed totally indifferent to him. He pulled the curtains (it was still light enough to set the alarm for noon) and undressed, and went into the kitchen for a glass of tepid tap water. He remembers lying down, his mind still fizzing exhaustedly, his heart knocking. Yes that morning, which he remembers so vividly – with its sunlight and sense of impalpable menace – he thinks of as the first intimation of what happened next.

When Simon took the call from Alan at International Money plc, one fresh and open-windowed morning a few weeks later, it was immediately obvious from his prolonged silence on the phone that something serious had happened. 'We've lost the contract,' he said, and smiled, and they all went to the pub. Not the Chesh – it seemed inappropriate – another one, which they did not normally go to, down by Blackfriars. When he was asked *why* they had lost the contract, all Simon would say was: 'I don't know. Because they're cunts.' They stayed in the pub until it was dark outside – Simon's gold card was behind the bar – and then, too drunk to stand or see properly, they dispersed. On his own, Paul was sick in the street. The next afternoon, Simon called them all individually and said that he was sorry about what had happened, and that he had 'something exciting in the pipeline' which he hoped they would be interested in working on. They never heard from him again. Paul didn't anyway. For a while, with money in the bank, he did nothing and during this short sabbatical, sitting in the hot sun on the balconette of his flat (which was just large enough for a straight-backed chair and an ashtray), smoking spliffs, he thought about doing something that he positively wanted to do. Nothing in particular occurred to him, however, and in early September – the school time, summer's end – he started to look for work. And work, of course, meant sales.

That his first stop was Archway Publications, and not one of the other multi-storey telesales factories that stud London, was down to nothing more than alphabetical order, and once he had arranged an interview with someone called James Grey, he shut the phone book and went back to his balconette to soak up some more of the Monday-afternoon sun. The interview itself was a formality. James Grey – a slick, oleaginous man who sat with his soft, manicured hands loosely interwoven, and whose tiepin, Paul noticed, featured the Playboy bunny – asked a few unsearching questions, the final one being when Paul would be able to start. Archway had a voracious need of salespeople. More or less anybody could walk in off the street and sign up for the next intake – a week of training starting every Tuesday. There was no salary, of course. Waiting for James Grey, Paul had been able to see the open-plan training area, the week's dozen trainees – it would be difficult to imagine a more varied set of twelve people, scooped from the sloshing population of London, and united only by their need of money – and the training manager saying, 'We are *not* selling advertising space. We are selling *sales*. The prospect will *only* buy space if he thinks it will increase the *sales* of his company – that is the only thing he is interested in. So you do not sell the *space* – you sell the *increased sales*. So, what are we selling?' Paul did not have to do the training week. He was put straight onto a team. It was, perhaps, only a month or two later, when he saw Eddy on the escalator at Tottenham Court Road, that he understood quite how unhappy he was.

Picking, with a heavy thumbnail, at the label of his Bacardi Breezer, Eddy says, offhand, 'So what you up to these days, Paul?'

'Oh . . .' Paul exhales vaguely. 'Did I say on Friday? I can't remember.'

'You said something . . .' Eddy says, equally vaguely.

51

'I'm working over Holborn way. Place called Park Lane Publications.'

'Yeah?'

'Murray's there as well. D'you see him on Friday?'

Eddy smiles. Whenever Murray is mentioned, people smile. 'Yeah, for a minute.'

Paul smiles too. 'I'm his manager actually,' he says.

Eddy laughs. 'Bet he's not fucking happy about that.'

'I don't think he is.' Paul lights a cigarette. That Murray may be even less happy about it than he seems sometimes troubles him. 'No, it's all right.'

'How did that happen, then?'

Paul shrugs. These things are, after all, always happening – people move from one job to another, and often find themselves being managed by someone they managed themselves a year or two earlier. Murray was Paul's manager for a few years when he started out at Burdon Macauliffe. Then they worked at Northwood together – Simon was the only manager there (though the Pig was his lieutenant, and on an override). When Northwood ended, Paul fetched up at Archway and Murray somewhere else – some place in Covent Garden that he found through a newspaper ad. Years passed. They more or less lost touch. Then, one morning, Paul – now a manager at PLP – picked up his phone, and it was Murray, looking for a job. Which was, of course, humiliating for him. 'I haven't done a pitch for fuck knows how long,' Eddy is saying. 'I miss it. Honestly.'

'I wish I never had to do another pitch ever again,' Paul says. And then smiles, to smudge the unintended sincerity of what he said.

'You'd miss it.'

'I doubt it. Maybe.'

'Is it not going well?' Eddy asks.

'It's going all right. Anyway, what are *you* up to, Jaw?'

Eddy takes out his wallet, and flips it open in his big hands. From

52

it he pulls a business card, which he holds out, mysteriously, to Paul. Paul presses his cigarette into the ashtray's glass notch, and takes the card. The first thing he notices are the words 'EDWARD FELTMAN, DIRECTOR OF SALES'. Then he notices the stylised elephant-head logo in the top left-hand corner, and the words 'DELMAR MORGAN' next to it. 'Is this you?' he asks.

'Of course it's fucking me,' Eddy says.

'Sales director?'

'That's right.'

Paul offers him the card back, but Eddy says, 'Keep it.'

'All right.' He puts it in his pocket. 'So how d'you get that then?' There is something sour about the way he asks the question, and, hearing this, he is slightly ashamed of the shadow of pique that seems to have fallen on him. Eddy is still smiling, and there is undoubtedly something smug about his smile. But then, perhaps in an effort to smooth over what has become an unexpectedly prickly moment, he leans back, and says, with a laugh, 'Oh, mate, I don't fucking know.' And if that was his intention, it works. Mollified, even smiling, Paul shakes his head and says, 'Fucking hell – *you*.'

'I know. It's mad.'

Having put the card in his pocket, Paul takes it out again. 'What's Delmar Morgan?' he asks.

'Sales place,' Eddy says, looking away with a sort of sudden shyness, and swigging the sweet, green dregs of his Bacardi Breezer.

'What sort of sales place?'

'The usual sort. Ad sales.'

'How long've you been working there?'

'A few years. Do you want another one?'

'It's my round, isn't it?' Paul says.

'Okay.'

'Same again?'

'Cheers.'

Standing, waiting at the bar, a tenner in his hand, Paul feels an unpleasantly keen sense of shortfall. That Eddy Jaw is director of sales somewhere . . . It suddenly puts things into perspective, makes him suddenly dissatisfied with his own life – even slightly ashamed of it – a shame deepened when he thinks of the flustered, envious shock with which he took the news of Eddy's unexpected success. And there, in the press of people at the bar, he experiences a savage twinge of panic, a dismaying sense that he has somehow overslept, that it is too late. It is his turn and he says, 'Pint of Ayingerbrau and a Bacardi Breezer.'

'What flavour?'

'Um. Melon.'

Eddy is more forthcoming when Paul returns to the table. He has a less edgy way of speaking now – the first Bacardi Breezer seems to have smoothed him out. 'Everyone thought I was mad when I went to Delmar,' he says. '*I* thought I was mad. It was going nowhere. It was going down. That old Chink with the Scottish name was running it then – Malcolm Kirkbride. *He* was MD. Five-foot-tall Malaysian bloke with a Fu Manchu moustache who could hardly fucking speak English and was called Malcolm Kirkbride. He was in charge in those days, and it showed. Morale was on the floor. People were leaving every day – whole teams disappearing overnight. But we turned it round – me, Tony Littleton and John Pascoe. We were just three salesmen, but we got together one day and decided to sort things out. I was sick and tired of fucking around, Paul. We all were. Since the end of Northwood I'd just been fucking around.' Paul nods in sympathy. Eddy smiles, and says, 'First thing I did was try to make money off the fucking horses. Can you believe that? I lost all the money I made at Northwood on the fucking nags. Lost it all in about two or three months. Then I went through a few sales jobs, here and there, just getting by. You know how it is. And I was *still* trying to make money out of the horses. I spent all my fucking time on the Internet, looking at tipsters' sites, looking at the fucking form and all that shit. Trying to put together the perfect staking plan . . .' He laughs. 'I never made any money from that. Everybody always thinks they can, they always think they're different. They're like fucking medieval alchemists, trying to turn base metals or whatever into gold, and the more they try, the more they believe it *must* be possible, because they've spent too much time and too much money to believe anything else, and it never is.' Eddy stops speaking for a moment and smiles, remembering all the hours he spent in smoke-filled bookies – and there's nowhere smokier – the little stubby plastic pens, blue in William Hill, red in Ladbrokes. He still goes in sometimes to have a bet – or just to taste the failure he no longer shares – enjoying the status he has in there, a big man in a suit, among the nervous unemployed, the dusty builders, the garrulous Chinese, the threadbare middle-aged men in overcoats who always sit in the same place, like it's their desk at work, their personal *Racing Post* spread out, their paper coffee cup, their dreams, their fags. 'And one day,' Eddy says, 'I thought, what the *fuck* are you doing? If it's money you want, you'd be making a fucking fortune if you put the hours, the dedication, the single-mindedness you're putting into the horses into selling ad space. You'd be making *more* than you'd be making off the horses even if your fucking system was *working*. That was the stupidest thing. You see, I'd always thought I was lazy, and that was just the way it was, but actually I wasn't. I was working evenings and weekends, working on the fucking horses – working on the *wrong thing*. So one day, when I'd just lost a couple of grand, I took all the fucking crap I'd accumulated, all the papers and pages of numbers and fucking spreadsheets and tipsters, and chucked it all. I chucked it all out, and wiped it off my hard drive, and cancelled all the subscriptions, and it felt fucking great. Like a fucking great load off my back. And obviously at first there was a void in my life. And nothing to hope for – that was the worst thing. *Nothing to hope for* – if you're trying to turn lead into gold, and you believe it can be done, and you think you're getting close, there's always something to hope for, something to dream about. Suddenly not having that is fucking hard. You've got to dream about something else, you've got to have something else to expend your energy on, to get you out of bed in the morning. And preferably something that will actually fucking get you somewhere.'

Pausing for emphasis, Eddy swigs green alcopop, and Paul lights a B&H. 'We were selling on a book called *International Pulp and Paper Yearbook*,' he goes on. 'Not a great book. A rubbish book, in fact. A basket case. Everyone knew it was rubbish, and no one expected it to make much money. So no one really bothered. We're all fucking good salesmen – John and Tony and me – we just weren't trying. And then one day, we just said, *Fuck this – there's just no point doing this like this*. And we really had a go. It's a shame you weren't there, Paul. I'd have liked you to have been there. Tony and John felt the same way I did – there's no point muddling through any more, faffing about. We wanted money, everything we needed was there, to hand, we just had to stop making excuses, and fucking get on with it. You seen *Taxi Driver*?' he asks, surprisingly.

Paul nods. 'Yeah, of course.'

'I love that film. There's a great line in it. I can't remember it exactly. It's that older taxi driver – remember him? – and he's talking to De Niro, and he says he sometimes wonders how he's ended up, at his age, still driving a company cab. You know, not having his own cab. And he says in the end it must be because he didn't really *want* his own cab. Because he didn't really *want* his own cab. I think that's brilliant.'

Paul nods slowly, meditatively.

'Isn't that brilliant? It's the only explanation he can think of, because if he really *wanted* his own cab, there was nothing to stop him having it. Nothing.' He watches Paul – who has gone quiet

– to see what effect his words are having on him. Then, with a smile, he says, 'Just going to point Percy at the porcelain. Back in a sec.'

When Eddy gets back, he continues his story. 'Once we started trying, once we started *working*, once we started only being satisfied with the max – it went through the fucking roof. Nobody else could believe it. And they weren't too happy about it either because it showed them up. Kirkbride was fucking happy, though.' Eddy does a crude, comedy Chinese accent – '"You boys de best! You de best! Me so horny!" Of course he was fucking horny – he got ten per cent of everything. When we finished *Pulp and Paper*, he put us on *International Project Finance*, which is a much better book, and we made much more money. More than at Northwood, Paul.'

'Yeah?' Paul says sceptically.

'Much more. And the books were rubbish, rubbish compared to what we were working on at Northwood. When I think about what we could have made if we'd actually worked those books *properly* . . .' He shakes his head. 'Anyway. We were making a fuck of a lot of money, and everything was hunky-dory. Then we said we wanted better terms, more commission – because if you're working that hard, you don't like to see eighty-five per cent of it go into other people's pockets – but Kirkbride wasn't so keen on that. "I see wha' I can do, boys. Ma-com see wha' he can do." And he did fuck all – so we asked again, said we weren't happy, *said we were going to leave.* That got his fucking attention. He got us into his office, very serious, very fucking sincere, and said he understood our concerns, and had an idea. He said he'd make us all managers, with a team each, and we'd get a special override, plus what we'd get anyway, if we improved the whole company's sales like we'd improved our own – which basically meant doubling them. The override was five per cent. Five fucking per cent!' Eddy drinks indignantly. 'So we got rid of Kirkbride. His sales director was a ponce called Pascal Olivier – we got rid of him too. We went to the chairman, behind Kirkbride's back – a bloke called Sir Trevor Cawthorne. A Geordie. I get on well with him. He knew *us* even then, because the three of us were making half the company's sales. We said to him, why don't you let us run the company? Get rid of Kirkbride, and we'll make you a lot more money than you're making now. It took him about two hours to think it over, before he called me and said, "All right." And I was in Kirkbride's office at the time, talking to him about some shit, and my mobile rang, and it was Trevor and he's saying, "I'm going to sack Kirkbride – you lot can take over." And I'm pretending it's someone else, and looking at Kirkbride, and thinking, "You don't know what's about to happen to you, mate. You don't realise that your life is in my hands." And I say, "Yeah, that's fine." And then a few minutes later, Kirkbride's phone rings and he answers it, and puts on his best arse-licking voice – "Ah hewow, Sah Trawah! How ah you, Sah Trawah?" And he waves at me to get out of his office, and whispers, "*Is Sah Trawah.*" And I'm thinking, "Yeah, I fucking know it is." So he went for a meeting with Trevor that afternoon, and Trevor sacked him, and then we had a meeting with Trevor – John and Tony and me – and he basically gave us the keys to the company, and said we had six months to show him what we could do. And we showed him. We turned things round. We changed the image of the company. I came up with the elephant logo,' Eddy says proudly. 'It's a new image. Honesty, integrity, long-term relationships.'

'Memory,' murmurs Paul.

'Yeah, of course. Our MD's an accountant. We nicked him from KPMG. He knows what he's good at and doesn't get involved on the sales side. Not at all. I deal with all that. And John and Tony run two super-teams. We wanted to cut out as many managers as possible – pare it down. We each get ten per cent of gross sales. The sales force gets ten to fifteen per cent. The rest goes to the company.

I made over a million quid last year, Paul. I'm not joking. That's more than *anybody* makes off the geegees. Even fucking Henry Rix.'

'Who's Henry Rix?'

'Doesn't matter. Now we're starting to think about an MBO.'

'What's that again?'

'Management buyout. The company's owned by a subsidiary of a subsidiary of a subsidiary of a shell company that's part of some fucking offshore investment vehicle. Fuck knows what else they're involved with. I don't really know much about it – Trevor's my only point of contact with all that. But whoever *does* own it isn't really interested in it, or they wouldn't have let Kirkbride fuck it up for so long, and they wouldn't leave an old codger like Trevor in charge. The point is, they'll probably sell if the price is right.'

'Sell to who? To you?'

'Yeah,' Eddy says, with a hint of impatience. 'A *management* buyout. We'd buy the company – me, Littleton and Pascoe.'

'With what money?'

'We're looking into that. A mixture of debt finance and venture capital probably. Mezzanine, maybe. We're looking to end up with about half the equity. Anyway . . . But that's not really relevant.'

'Relevant to what?'

'To what I want to talk to you about.'

'What do you want to talk to me about?'

'Should we get something to eat?' Eddy says. 'I'm starving. What about going to the Wine Press? For old times' sake.'

After two Ayingerbraus and a Prinz, Paul has no appetite. He feels settled in the warm low-vaulted space. 'All right,' he says unenthusiastically. 'If you want.'

'Excellent.'

Outside, fine light rain is falling in the alley. The Wine Press, a venerable pizzeria where they sometimes went in the Northwood days, is a little way along Fleet Street, near Fetter Lane. Paul is about to ask Eddy what he wants to talk to him about, but Eddy speaks first. 'How's your sex life, Paul?' he asks as they walk. Paul is evasive. 'It's all right.' He is aware of having described many aspects of his life as 'all right'. 'How's yours?'

'Very good actually. I think it was Henry Kissinger said power is the greatest aphrodisiac.'

'Did he?'

'He did.'

'You still with Kim?' Paul asks.

Eddy laughs. 'No.' He holds open the plate-glass door. 'After you.'

'Cheers,' Paul mumbles, and steps into the torrent of warmth under the heater inside.

'This place hasn't changed,' Eddy says.

Paul nods and lights a cigarette.

4

On the way to Blackfriars tube, Paul stops for a pint in the King
Lud. Eddy had waved down a black cab outside the restaurant,
and asked him if he could drop him somewhere, but Paul, to some
extent out of pride, more from a wish to be alone, had declined,
and walked slowly on up to Ludgate Circus, where – impressed
by the floodlit slice of St Paul's that can be seen from there – he
had looked at his watch, held his nose for a moment, and entered
the Old King Lud. They occasionally went there in the Northwood
days; it is not, however, a pub he knows well. A perfect place, then,
for sorting his head out, and settled at a small table with a pint
of lager he turns over his talk with Eddy Jaw. He wishes he were
able to think more lucidly. Everything seems jumbled up. He is
experiencing a kind of flaming excitement, and at the same time
– as if it disturbed him – trying to damp it down. It *does* disturb
him. He is not used to anything interesting or unexpected
happening; he is not used to opportunities, and he finds himself
instinctively shrinking from these things. Tomorrow, he feels – the
next few days – will be the time to think about *them*.

There is one thing, however, which he is unable to stop himself
from thinking about, which troubles his smoky torpor. 'No passengers.' Those were Eddy's words. 'No fucking passengers.' Paul had
half-heartedly tried to persuade him that Murray would not be a
'passenger', but Eddy had shaken his head and said, again, 'No
fucking passengers. Murray is just not good enough for this game.'
And of course, Paul had found the implicit flattery too pleasing to
want to jeopardise the mood by making an issue of Murray (of all

61

things) and he did not mention him again. Indeed, the vague, embarrassed sense of loyalty that had led to this short-lived quibble on Murray's part immediately seemed quaint and foolish under the Nietzschean stare of Eddy's small blue eyes. Despite which, it continued to trouble him. Eddy's proposal was that Paul join him at Delmar Morgan, as a manager, with those members of his team 'who can actually fucking cut it'. It was when Paul had asked what 'actually fucking cut it' meant in practical terms, that Eddy had cited Murray as an example of someone who could not. Seeing Paul's surprise at this, he said, 'And I've always thought that. I have always thought that.' It was essential, Eddy said, that the whole thing be kept secret. He wanted it to happen in the new year.

Paul's initial response, motivated mostly by pride, was a show – and it was only a show – of scepticism. Unfortunately, it set the tone for the rest of the evening. 'And why would I want to do that?' he had asked, lighting a B&H. A moment later the pizzas arrived and he had to put it out. 'Because,' said Eddy, when the waiter had withdrawn with his pepper grinder, 'Park Lane's contracts are shit, they're tired, they're fucked. You know they are.' Looking with undisguised disgust at the Margherita in front of him, Paul had said, 'It's a problem with the whole industry.'

'That's loser talk.' And Eddy, who had ordered a Capricciosa with extra olives and anchovies, started to cut it up. Paul silently refilled his wine glass. It *was* loser talk. That was undeniable. 'It's not even true,' Eddy had said, with his mouth full. 'I told you – things are going fucking well at Delmar. We need new people, at every level. Experienced people. For fuck's sake, Paul,' he laughed, 'I'm trying to help you. It wasn't by chance I was round last Friday. I heard on the grapevine where you were – I was looking for you.' Modestly, Paul drank some wine and toyed with his unlit cigarette. 'What do you mean the grapevine?' he asked.

'The grapevine. Someone from the old days who'd spoken to

someone. I was looking for you. When I heard where you were, I thought, Paul Rainey, there's a man you want on your side.' Perhaps feeling that this was flattery overplayed, Eddy had said, quickly, indicating Paul's untouched pizza, 'Are you going to eat that or what?' Paul shook his head. 'No,' he murmured. 'I'm not hungry.'

'So?' Eddy said.

'So . . . ?'

'Will you do it?'

They had only been talking about it for a few minutes, and it seemed premature to press him. Eddy, though, was always a loud, upfront salesman, succeeding through an unquestioning faith in the old tenets – the simple, time-tested precepts enshrined in *Glengarry Glen Ross* – of which there is no more perfect example than ABC. 'A, always. B, be. C, closing. Always. Be. Closing. Always be closing.' Which was what he was doing. 'I'll think about it,' Paul said flirtatiously, fully expecting Eddy to high-pressure him, but Eddy just nodded, and said, 'Okay,' and kept eating. It was disappointing – Paul wanted to talk about it more, and, after pouring himself another glass of wine, he said vaguely, 'So what have you got then? What contracts?'

Eddy's pizza was almost gone. 'You mean what contracts would you be working on?' he said.

'For instance.'

For a few moments he said nothing, then: 'I can't really say, mate. Not until you're on board. You understand.' He dabbed his mouth with his napkin, which he then tossed onto the table. Feeling rebuffed, Paul relit his B&H, and was relieved when Eddy, without further prompting, went on to say, 'They're fucking good contracts. People have seen what we can do.' He smiled. 'Nothing succeeds like success, Paul. We've got a whole lot of new contracts starting soon, and we're staffing up for them. That's why I'm talking to you. I'm talking to other people as well, obviously. We've got adverts in the national press.' Eddy was looking around, perhaps for the waiter. He seemed in a hurry to leave suddenly. It was as if Paul had disappointed him – that, at least, was Paul's impression – as if he had seen that Paul would be of no use to him. 'Got the first interviews this week,' he said. 'It's a fucking bore. What you working on these days?' Paul told him, but he did not seem to be listening. He just said 'Oh yeah?' several times, nodding mechanically. When he had the waiter's eye, he made a self-conscious scribbling motion in the air. 'I'll get this,' he said, taking out his wallet.

In the tiny toilet, washing his hands in the one-litre sink, Paul inspected his mottled face in the mirror. He was starting to feel like he had fucked something up.

There was a ridiculous amount of money in Eddy's wallet, and something about the way he rummaged through it defeated, without him having to say anything, Paul's half-hearted attempt to stop him paying the whole bill. He simply ignored Paul's mumbled words, put a big salmon fifty on the saucer and stood up, only then saying, 'Shall we go?' Outside on the pavement, he started to look for a taxi, and left it to Paul to mention the offer he had made him. 'I'll let you know about that then, Eddy,' he said, as the cab pulled round in the road.

'Yeah, do,' Eddy said. 'But soon, eh?'

'By the end of the week?'

Eddy smiled, as if amused by something. 'If that's what you call soon,' he said. 'See you, Paul.' He was already halfway into the cab when he turned and said, 'Oh, do you want a lift somewhere?'

Standing at the bar of the Old King Lud, Paul jingles the heavy mass of shrapnel in his suit pocket. He feels dissatisfied with the whole evening. He wishes – he can hardly admit it even to himself – that he had made a more imposing impression on Eddy, more symmetrical with the impression that Eddy had made on him. 'Fuck it,' he thinks, his pride wounded by the very fact of wishing this. 'He can stick his job up his arse.' Then, immediately, 'I'll call him tomorrow, to show I'm serious about it.' And thinking *this*, he is instantly uncomfortable – obscurely aware of his querulous conscience. He wonders how he would feel if Murray did to him what he is proposing to do to Murray. He imagines it – coming into work one morning, perhaps a Monday, to find that Murray and the team are simply not there. It soon becomes obvious, when there is no word from them, and they do not answer their phones, that they have left en masse. How would he feel? Something like that would have to have been planned – mass 'defections' (as they are known) do not just happen spontaneously. Probably for weeks they had all known about it – it would explain the knowing looks he had seen some of them exchanging on the sales floor; the embarrassed silence that had fallen that time he walked into the smoking room . . . And Murray, his friend – who had undoubtedly organised the whole thing – who else would? – had known about it for weeks, known about it every day as they sat together in the Penderel's Oak, known how totally it would fuck him up, how utterly humiliating it would be . . . Paul finds himself becoming more and more angry just imagining this scenario, and in the face of the great pulse of righteous indignation and wounded rage welling up inside him, he has to remind himself that it is not actually true. It does, however, suggest Murray's probable response.

Whatever his faults, Murray is supposedly his *friend*. If Paul does this to him, it would suggest – would it not? – that he, Paul, has a sadly hollowed-out sense of the meaning of the word. What, in fact, would its meaning be? He orders a pint of Foster's. Should he really pass up this opportunity, though? Make such a sacrifice for *Murray's* sake? What sacrifices has Murray ever made for him? He is still pondering this when he returns, with his new pint, to the table. The only significant thing he can think of is an occasion, years earlier – they were at Northwood at the time – when he stepped in front of a car, and Murray, instead of going on to the Sports Bar with the others, had accompanied him to A&E, and waited with him there until his head had been X-rayed, and then put him in a taxi home. He may even have paid for the taxi – Paul does not remember – but whether he did or not, his actions that night were surely only what was to be expected. They did not constitute extraordinary kindness, Christlike love, extreme Samaritanism, only a minimum standard of friendship – decency, even – standards by which Murray, it has to be said, quite often fell short. Nevertheless Paul had been touched by what Murray did that night. (Though he has never told him this, has perhaps never even thanked him.) It had, after all, been Murray and not Eddy or the Pig – any of them *could* have done it – who had travelled with him in the sickly greenish light of the ambulance. Paul does not remember why it was Murray. He only remembers lying on the black, abrasive tarmac, aware of his head having been knocked against it with terrible force, fear leeching through the haze of alcohol, and Murray's voice telling him not to move, and saying that he was going to be okay.

The need for secrecy, Paul sees, is the nub of the problem. If he were able to say to Murray, 'Eddy Jaw has offered me a job working for him. I'm starting next month and taking some of the team with me. I tried to persuade him to take you on as well. Maybe you should give him a call yourself,' Murray might be jealous, he might be hurt that Jaw had not asked *him*, but Paul would have done nothing wrong. Unfortunately, the secrecy is necessary – these things need to be done by stealth. And telling Murray in advance of a defection from which he was excluded would have only one outcome – he would go straight to Lawrence and, in the hope of a promotion, tell him everything. Lawrence. Imagining Lawrence's fury on hearing of the proposed defection, Paul takes surprisingly little pleasure in it. What he does experience, thinking of Lawrence, is an exhilarating sense of freedom – the sense that Lawrence no longer has any power over him. And without this power, he seems pathetic suddenly. How pathetic he seems. Pathetic. Yes, *pathetic*. In his mind, Paul lards the word 'pathetic' onto the word 'Lawrence'.

He even shakes his head sadly – sitting alone in the loud pub – and mutters it.

'Pathetic . . .'

And thinking of Lawrence, and of the wider implications, it occurs to him that this defection, were it to happen, might finally bring Park Lane Publications down. For some time it has been struggling. It is failing. Many of its contracts are in imminent danger of being withdrawn. Morale is at an all-time low. Single members of staff are already leaving, steadily, and filling the vacancies with people who 'can actually fucking cut it' is proving impossible. If a whole team were to disappear overnight, not only would it make it impossible to meet target on the publication involved – and while that happens every year, this time the sales total would be so derisory, the shortfall so indefensibly huge, that the contract would finally be lost – it might spark a general exodus. Trying to imagine the atmosphere if one of the other teams defected, and he were among those left behind – and for some reason he now finds this an almost unbearably depressing thing to consider – he pictures a scene of apocalyptic panic. People in large numbers pulling on their coats and heading for the lift. Others on the phone, openly looking for new jobs. Or just piling into the pub. The sense that everything was falling apart would have unstoppable momentum. This sense is so vivid to him that it is almost frightening. And he sees that he would take no pleasure in bringing the temple down, as someone in the Bible did. He does not feel fitted for that sort of task, and as well as fear at its enormity, he is already filled, imagining it, with pity for the innocents who would be smashed. Suddenly in a maudlin mood, he pours the warm lees of the pint down his throat, and goes to the bar for another. While he is waiting the barman says something to him. 'Sorry, mate?' Paul says.

'No smoking at the bar, please.'

'Sorry, mate.' Paul stubs out his cigarette, and jingles the coins in his jacket pocket. Turning to happier matters, he wonders who he would take with him, were the defection to happen. Not Andy. That is the first thing that occurs to him. 'Poor, bloody Andy,' he thinks. What would happen to him? Left to fend for himself, to face Lawrence alone, he would surely be sacked immediately, the same day. Even if he was not, everything would be different for him – the social aspect would no longer be there. He and Murray obviously hate each other. And what would happen to Murray? Even if the company as a whole somehow stayed standing, he would probably lose his job – he has been on the slide for a long time now. Emptying his throat, waiting for his pint, Paul points his thoughts once more to the question of who he would take with him. Not Andy. Wolé? Yes. Marlon? Yes. Elvezia? Maybe. Nayal? Probably. Dave? Probably not. Claire? He pauses. It is impossible to maintain, even in the privacy of his own head, that on the basis of her ability to sell the answer would be anything other than a brisk no. But.

But, but, but.

How happy it makes him to see her arrive every morning. To see her take off her coat. To hear her husky voice. To see her blush. To sit next to her, listening in on her calls, making helpful suggestions. To defend her from Lawrence, and make sure that she continues to receive her stipend of a hundred pounds a week long after it should have been stopped ... He has become increasingly aware of some people sitting at a table near his own. There are four or five of them, young, all in dark blue or black office clothes. He has noticed in particular the way that the two of them not facing him occasionally turn, smiling mirthfully. Once, his eyes met the aquamarine eyes of a very blond, white-skinned young man. Once there was muffled laughter. These things are making him unpleasantly self-conscious. And for the last hour and a half he has been sitting there without even a newspaper to hide his solitude. He has even, it occurs to him, been muttering to himself. He starts to work through his pint hurriedly, in big cold gulps, telling himself that he is being paranoid, that their laughter probably has nothing to do with him. He is unpersuaded by this, however, and when the blond boy stands up and starts to walk towards him – it is obvious that the others are watching – he is painfully unsurprised. Stiff-necked, holding his pint, he waits. The blond boy is very tall and thin, probably in his early twenties, with a bony face and pale eyes. He looks Nordic. He has an unlit cigarette in his hand, and is smiling. 'Sorry, have you got a light?' he says. The flimsiness of this pretext is underlined by the fact that one of his friends is actually lighting a cigarette at that moment. Nevertheless, Paul says, 'Yeah, sure,' and hands him his lighter. When he has lit the cigarette, the young man stays standing there loosely for a second. Then he says, 'Do you work round here?' He is still smiling, and there is something insolent about this question, put under the laughing eyes of his friends. 'Yes, I do,' Paul says.

'What do you do?' the young man asks immediately.

Fuck off, Paul feels like saying. However, in a hoarse voice, he says, 'Media sales.'

'Ah,' says the young man.

'What do you do?'

'Media, what sort of media?'

'Why do you want to know?'

'Just curious.'

When he sees that Paul is not going to volunteer anything further, is in fact staring furiously at him, the young man says, 'Do you live near here?'

'No, I don't.' Said with such obvious impatience that the young man's smile wavers for a moment. Then he says, 'Thanks for the light.'

'That's all right.'

'See you.'

Paul just nods, and the young man returns to his table. When he sits down, there is an unnatural lull in the conversation – though in low voices they *are* talking – then loud laughter, which suddenly stops with an emphatic 'Shh!'

Slowly Paul finishes his pint. He will not let them force him out. He feels, though, as if the whole pub, having witnessed the short exchange, is turning away from him to hide its knowing smirk. People seem to look at him slyly. Time itself seems to have slowed. When, at last, he has finished, he stands unsteadily and leaves. Outside in the wind, poised to walk down to Blackfriars, he pauses. The prospect of the train journey seems unusually onerous, and he turns and starts to walk down Fleet Street. He is heading for 'Dr Johnson's', the quiet little courtyard where the erudite doctor lived, and where, in the Northwood days, they would smoke their spliffs in the white depths of the afternoon. Now, in the tousled darkness, he stands next to Hodge's memorial, skinning up. There is no one around. No one at all. The elegant Georgian houses are all solicitors' offices and barristers' sets, and the whole area is empty in the evening. He is still smarting painfully from the incident in the King Lud. A strange misery fell on him when the Nordic young man, with his insolent tipsy smile, started to question him, a misery which will not be shaken off. He does not know why it made such an impact on him. He lights the spliff. The first inhalation triggers a volley of flinty coughing, doubling him over, squeezing water from his eyes. 'For fuck's sake,' he mutters, when he is finally able to. He fiddles with his lighter. Smoking the spliff makes him feel unpleasantly light – even a bit queasy – and he throws it away unfinished.

He starts to walk. Not, however, in the direction of the tube station – not Blackfriars, not Temple, not Chancery Lane. He is walking towards the Penderel's Oak. Underestimating the distance, however, it takes him more than ten minutes, and he even starts to wonder whether it is worth it. Michaela might not even be working tonight, and he feels deeply fuddled, what with everything that has happened. Washed- and whited-out with drink and dope. He has allowed an idea to form in his mind, an idea of his status with Michaela which has little or no foundation in the observed world. While with Claire, for instance, his imaginings are tempered by the melancholy knowledge that nothing is ever going to 'happen', the idea that he has formed of something secret and mysterious involving Michaela and himself permits him to hope that, in spite of everything, something might. He has no memory of when exactly this idea formed – she had been working in the Penderel's Oak for weeks, or even months, when it did – but it has been there, never far from his mind during his waking hours, and intense and immediate when he drinks, for over a year, a year in which she has split up with one man, and started to see another. (Paul's smile, when she told him *that* particular piece of news, was probably the least expressive of happiness ever to shape his face.) Sometimes, in the bruised, unforgiving reality of a hangover, he sees the folly of his imaginings, sees that they *are* only imaginings – that she is fifteen years younger than him, and that her lovers (extrapolating from the two he has met on various occasions in the pub) seem typically to be handsome young men, strong-jawed outdoors types – not much like him. Usually, however, he manages to overlook these things. And if *she* sometimes sees, when he is very drunk, the intensity and scope of Paul's preoccupation with her (once, worryingly, he squeezed her hand and would not let it go for several minutes), it may be unnerving, but she prefers not to dwell on it. She is able to pretend – very successfully to pretend, to herself – that she suspects nothing, that he is simply nice.

He peers through the windowed front of the Penderel's Oak into the dim, carpeted interior. The pub is not very full. Quiet, even. She is there. He sees her behind the bar, and with a sudden sense of uplift, as well as an enjoyable nervous quickening of his pulse, he opens the door and goes in. She is talking to someone, someone sitting on one of the high stools . . . And suddenly recognising the squarish head with its dirty bronze hair, the shapeless back of the blue suit, Paul stops. He had not told Murray that he was meeting Eddy Jaw because Jaw had specifically told him not to. (It had seemed strange at the time.) He had said that he was tired, and going home.

Murray, too, had said that he was going home, and yet here he is, at almost ten, in the Penderel's Oak, talking to Michaela. Normally it is obvious to Paul that Murray, in his own preoccupation with her, is pitifully mistaken if he thinks that it might lead anywhere. She is obviously quite scared of him. (When, several hours earlier, Murray had entered the pub alone, she had watched him approach the bar with dread, which intensified when she asked if Paul would be in, and he said, 'Not tonight, my love. It's just you and me tonight.') Paul's shock at seeing him there unexpectedly, however, tips him into total paranoia – the idea that he and Michaela might actually be lovers suddenly takes on a sort of horrific plausibility. It is like a nightmare. From where he is standing in the shadows he watches Michaela's face, small and white, slightly pinched, her ski-jump nose – she seems to be listening intently to what Murray is saying, staring into his eyes, nodding. He feels as if he is seeing something that has been specifically hidden from him. And he is sure that Murray must not see *him*, must not know that he is there – in his fuddled state he would be unable to explain why he is not in Hove. For a few minutes he watches them. Then suddenly sickened with himself, he leaves, lighting a cigarette as soon as his feet hit the pavement outside. Still in turmoil, he walks quickly away. He needs another drink, he needs to get his whirling thoughts together, so before descending to the tube at Chancery Lane, he goes into the Cittie of Yorke. The long, high, loud interior is surprisingly full. There is hardly room to move. Sweating, Paul struggles to the bar. Some sort of event – a graduation of some kind – seems to have taken place nearby because the pub is full of young people in black academic gowns and older people who are obviously their parents. Lots of photos are being snapped, and looking around disorientedly he is hit full in the face by a flash and dazzled. He shuts his eyes, squeezing them shut, and opens them again. 'You being served?' someone yells at him over the din. He orders a pint of lager, and only then notices that he has a headache.

5

In the great grimy cavern of London Bridge station, facing a soiled wall, a finger in his left ear to block out the roar of bus engines, faintly aware of the smell of urine, Paul phones Eddy. It is five to nine on Tuesday morning, and he is not feeling well. He did not get home until nearly two o'clock, on the filthy, forlorn eleven fifty from London Bridge, stopping at East Croydon, Gatwick Airport, Three Bridges, Haywards Heath, Brighton and, at twenty-five past one, exhausted and empty, the silent little station at Hove, where Paul tumbled alone onto the ghostly platform. The air was sharp and cold. In their dark bedroom, Heather was already asleep (he had phoned, hours before, to say that he would be late), and he undressed as quietly as he could, losing his balance as he pulled his trousers off, dismally tormented by the knowledge that in five hours he had to get up and go back. And, of course, it was torment. Hypnotised by fatigue, he was in the train again – the train full now – as daylight started to appear through the drizzle, over the dark fields and estates and industrial parks. He knew now that he was going to take Eddy up on his offer. The decision seemed to have been made overnight, while he slept. Or perhaps it had never really been in doubt. It seemed possible that his moral tussle of the previous evening had been nothing more than a hypocritical show, hastily staged at the insistence of his mouthy but ultimately ineffective conscience, and that having seen the show, it had been more or less satisfied – as if the show itself were enough, were all that was morally required. Distantly aware of this, in a detached, indifferent state, he had waited for the train, and sat slumped in a corner at the back of the carriage, with small lip movements husbanding the moisture of his mouth. His eyes closed, his bad head bumping lightly against a schematic representation of 'London Connections', he remembered, in a hazy, dreamlike way, walking in on Murray and Michaela in the Penderel's Oak – and, with a pang of private embarrassment, the feelings and ideas that seeing them together had stirred up in him. In the sober morning light, he no longer thought it a serious possibility that they were lovers – though the awful idea would not now be entirely dispelled, and he was still angry with Murray for seeing her in secret, no matter how deluded and futile his intentions.

The train got in to one of the outlying platforms and he had to walk – part of a huge unspeaking herd – through a network of wet, dingy tunnels to the main station. There, he took out his phone, and Eddy's number.

'Hello, Eddy, s'Paul,' he says, leaning into the foul wall in front of him.

'Paul. Morning.' Eddy sounds businesslike, perhaps slightly surprised.

'I've thought 'bout what you, we, were saying yesterday.'

'And?'

'I'll do it.'

'Excellent,' Eddy says, without excitement. 'That's good news, Paul.'

'So what do we do now?' Paul asks after a few moments. Eddy says they should meet again later in the week. He asks Paul how many people he thinks he'll be bringing with him. Paul says he is not sure. Eddy says he'll phone him to arrange a time to meet on Thursday or Friday.

Pocketing his phone – an old, heavy model – Paul lights a cigarette, his first of the day. He is shaking – he presumes with excitement, though it might, of course, be delirium tremens. It is not so much that his hangover has disappeared than that it has been pushed into the background. Feeling too energised to take the tube, he looks at his watch and then walks out, past the red rain-streaked logjam of buses, into the open air, towards the river. He is stopped, immediately, by the traffic of Tooley Street, and waits in the Scotch mist with a crowd of suits and umbrellas, sober raincoats and briefcases, for the lights to change. On the bridge the pavement is blustery. Spots of rain flick his face. The khaki river looks slow and old, but wherever it encounters an obstacle – the piers of bridges, the prows of moored vessels – its unsuspected momentum is visible in rushing vees of turbulent water. He walks with his head turned, looking downstream. The distant towers of Canary Wharf are little more than immense, pale silhouettes, illusive under their winking hazard lights in the poor visibility of the day.

He takes the tube from Bank, and arrives late at Park Lane Publications. It is very unusual for him to be late; everyone else is already there. Everyone, that is, except Murray, and seeing his empty seat, Paul experiences a short, unpleasant encore of the previous night's paranoia, seriously fearing for a moment that the explanation for Murray's lateness might lie in his having spent the night with Michaela. He feels relieved – and then immediately ridiculous – when in answer to his worried question, 'Where's Murray?', Andy says, 'In the smoking room.' This sorted out, however, he is still tense. He is especially tense at the thought of Murray's return to the sales floor, of the moment when they first see and speak to each other. Taking off his jacket, sitting down at his desk, he is desperate for a cigarette. Not wanting to meet Murray in the smoking room, though, he waits, purposelessly shuffling papers. Normally, he would have shouted 'Get on the fucking phone' more than once – only Nayal and Marlon are making calls – but the more time that passes without him having shouted it, the more he seems unable to do so; and the more, he feels sure, his team sense that something odd is happening. (In fact, they are used to his moodiness, and do not see much unusual in it today.) Sunk in this preoccupied lethargy, it suddenly occurs to him how extraordinarily difficult it is going to be even to pretend to care, for the next two weeks, about the fate of *European Procurement Management*. But he will have to pretend – and suddenly steeling himself, shunting Eddy's proposal out of his still-hurting mind, he sits up and says, 'Come on, you lot, get on the fucking phone.' And as he says it, Murray walks onto the sales floor. There is, Paul thinks, picking him up in his peripheral vision, something shifty about him. He takes his seat without speaking. 'All right, Murray?'

'All right, Paul.'

'Good night, was it?'

'What?'

'You look like you were out on the piss last night.'

'No.'

'You weren't?'

'No, not at all,' Murray says.

'Oh, I thought you were for some reason.'

'No.'

Surreptitiously, Paul spends the long morning watching the members of his team, his eyes moving from one to the next. There are a few definite 'yeses' – he knew immediately who they would be. Wolé, large and shambling, with a slowness and patience unusual in the profession, but nevertheless a natural salesman, possessor of a weighty, charismatic pitch, his voice almost hypnotically deep and imposing. Nayal, the precise technician, with his headset and smoke-blue sports jacket, also patient, quiet, unflappable, not a high-pressure merchant. That's more Marlon's style. All that standing on the desk stuff. 'Power selling'. Paul doesn't like it much, but Marlon somehow makes it work. Those three, the definite yeses. (And incidentally, Paul makes a mental note, the three hardest-working members of the team. *The harder I work*, he thinks, *the luckier I get*.) Then there are the noes. Andy. Murray. Dave Shelley, an odd, morose young man with lank, greasy hair and a motheaten suit, who never speaks to anybody and spends most of his time in the smoking room. Sami, the affable, smiling Saudi Arabian, who only joined a week ago, and is obviously destined for failure. And Richard, a small man in his mid-fifties who always latches on to the new people – Sami is the latest – and follows them everywhere, telling them how wonderful it is to work for John Lewis. On the phone, it is obvious that he is speaking from a script; so obvious that it seems to be his intention to sound like he is. And indeed Paul has known this to happen, known people who are just unable to stop sending signals to the prospect dissociating themselves from the words they are saying.

Finally there are the maybes. The women on the team. Claire he sets to one side; she is a somewhat special case. Which leaves Elvezia, and Li, a youngish Chinese woman – it is difficult to estimate her age – with horrible yellow teeth and alarmingly thinning hair. To Paul she doesn't seem clean somehow, like she hasn't washed for weeks. In spite of this, she is being assiduously courted by a ruddy nerd from another team, who comes to eat his sandwich at her desk every day. She pitches in Chinese, calling the Far East, and because of this she works unusual hours, getting in at five in the morning and leaving at lunchtime, after the visit of her suitor. She makes sales, but Paul is suspicious of them, of the strange ideogrammic signatures and notes on the agreement forms – those flimsy, non-legally binding bits of fax paper – of deals closed when no one else is there. He does not entirely trust her. She could be telling these people anything, he thinks, listening to the weird gurgling sounds that emanate from her as she pitches, half turned to the wall. It could all be some kind of scam. (A few years earlier, two well-dressed, polite young Russians had joined the sales force, and they had done well, making sales to Russian and Ukrainian companies. They earned thousands of pounds of commission. Then, one morning, they were gone. And when the companies were invoiced for the dozens of ads they had bought, they turned out not to exist.)

Paul supposes that he will not involve Li in the move to Delmar; her English seems so poor that he is not even sure he would be able to explain it to her.

Which leaves Elvezia. A stout, mannish Italian lady in early middle age, still known for the massive deal she made, over two years ago now, with Fiat (she sells in Italian), for a series of ads in a number of different publications. It was something of a sensation at the time, the talk of the smoking room, and Elvezia – to her flustered delight – became a company celebrity, an unlikely star salesman, like 'Beer' Matt Riley and Pax 'the Fax' Murdoch. Yvonne Jenkin, the managing director of PLP International Ltd, who the salespeople do not normally see, put in an appearance on the sales floor to present her with a magnum of champagne; it was the biggest single sale in the company's history. Despite her denials, Elvezia had enjoyed all this, and was never entirely able to suppress an impish smile when people expressed wonder, as they often did, at her achievement. Her moment of fame did not last. Her successes since the Fiat deal have been numerous enough, though mostly very small – she is really a specialist of the micro-deal, the quarter-page ad, heavily discounted – and she has long since lapsed into the familiar, tetchy, plodding obscurity that was always her lot in the past. The photo of herself and Yvonne Jenkin and the magnum of champagne, still Blu-tacked up on the wall near her desk, is discoloured and starting to curl. *Sic transit gloria mundi* – it is the only Latin tag Paul knows. In his mind, he moves her halfway to the yeses. He is worried, though, what Eddy will make of her.

The first person he lets into the secret is Nayal, phoning him from the train home. 'Hey! Nayal!' he says. 'It's Paul.'

Politely, Nayal tries not to sound too surprised. 'Paul. Hello.'

'How's it going, mate?'

'Um. Fine.'

Paul says he wants to talk to him about something, and suggests they meet for a coffee, somewhere not too near the office. They meet the next morning in an Italian café on Museum Street.

It is, for both of them, a strange situation. Nayal – smart, fortyish, with a neat moustache – never mixes with other members of the team out of work, and away from the safe, familiar environment of the sales floor he and Paul are strangers. He notices how different Paul is – how solicitous, how serious – and thinks, 'What does he want from me?' smiling mildly and stirring his coffee. When he has lit a cigarette (having first asked Nayal whether he minds), Paul comes to the point. He prefaces it with, 'This is between you and me, mate.' And Nayal nods. He is, Paul knows, nothing if not discreet. 'I'm going to be leaving PLP,' he says. Nayal pulls a surprised face. 'I've been offered a job somewhere else. Somewhere quite a lot better actually.'

'Well,' Nayal says. 'Congratulations.'

'Yeah. And I'm hoping you'll come with me. That's what I wanted to talk to you about.' When Nayal hesitates, Paul says, 'I'm not asking everybody. Just the best people.' First smiling to acknowledge the flattery, Nayal says, 'The thing is, Paul, I'm planning to leave PLP too.'

'Oh.'

'So . . .'

Though he knows that it is unfair, and tries, unsuccessfully, not to let it show, Paul finds he feels extremely let down. It had not occurred to him that members of his team might have their own secrets, their own plots. Perhaps seeing his expression darken, Nayal says hurriedly, 'I'm planning to finish *EPM*, of course.' Paul ignores this. 'So what are you going to do?' he says.

'Well, it's supposed to be a secret. I've just bought a hundred thousand minutes of talktime between the UK and Pakistan.'

'You've bought a hundred thousand minutes of talktime?'

79

'Yes.'

'Why?'

'Oh. To resell it. Yes. So if you ever want to call Pakistan . . .' The levity is misjudged. Paul does not even seem to notice it. He says, 'So you're not interested in . . . ?'

Nayal shakes his head sincerely. 'I'm afraid not,' he says. 'I'm sorry.'

'Don't be sorry, mate.' In his frustration, Paul says this with an unintended edge. There is a tense silence while he stubs out his cigarette. The situation is unnervingly similar to a blowout – *is* in fact a blowout, an unexpected one – and they are both more familiar than they would like to be with the feelings of impotence and humiliation associated with *them*. Even Nayal – his famous sangfroid notwithstanding – is often twisted into noiseless fury by them, usually expressed in a slight cold smile. 'So where are you going then?' he asks, delicately.

'Oh, another sales place, you know.'

'Well, I'm sure it's a wise move.'

'I think so. Park Lane's fucked.'

Nayal smiles.

They walk back to the office in silence.

It has not been an encouraging start.

Later, seeing Wolé Ogunyemi stand up and head for the smoking room, Paul waits for a minute or two, and then follows him. When he opens the door, Wolé is at the window, leaning out. There is no one else there. Wolé looks over his shoulder. 'All right, Paul,' he says. 'All right, Wolé.' Paul sits down wearily on one of the low chairs, and lights up. 'How's it going, mate?' he asks. Wolé turns. 'How's it going?' he says. 'How is it going? Shit.' He laughs, and Paul laughs too. 'I wanted to have a word with you, actually,' he says. And lowering his voice, 'Strictly between ourselves.'

'Sure.'

'I'm serious. Tell no one.'

'I won't. Sure.'

Paul lowers his voice further, almost to a whisper. 'I'm leaving PLP, mate. I've been offered another job. A better one.'

'Yeah? Lucky you.'

'And I'm sounding some people out, seeing if they want to join me.'

Suddenly Wolé's face takes on a more focused, serious look. He too lowers his voice. 'Where?' he asks.

'It's a place called Delmar Morgan.' Paul is whispering; the words 'Delmar Morgan', in particular, he more or less mouths in silence. 'It's a very good place,' he says. 'They've got excellent contracts. Much better than here. This place . . .' With a small gesture he indicates their immediate environs. 'This place is in serious trouble, mate. That's obvious.' Wolé nods thoughtfully, and after pausing for a moment to let the morbid prognosis sink in, Paul murmurs, 'So, would you be interested – in principle?'

Wolé looks thoughtful. 'In principle, I suppose, yes.'

And violating the hushed, smoky seriousness of the room, the door whoops opens. It is Murray. 'All right, Murray,' Paul says immediately in an overloud voice. Sensing something odd – he may even have heard Wolé's 'In principle, I suppose, yes' – Murray hesitates. Then he says, 'What's up?'

'What do you mean, "what's up"?'

Perplexed at Paul's intensity, Murray shrugs and simply says again, 'What's up?'

'Nothing's fucking up. Nothing's ever fucking up, is it, Wolé?'

Wolé just smiles. Stubbing his cigarette out on the inner surface of the metal bin, he opens the door, and says, 'I'll see you gentlemen back up there.'

When he has gone, they sit in silence for a while. Nothing unusual in that; the smoking room is a place of licensed silence. But this silence seems, to Paul, to tremble with tension. Murray himself seems tense and suspicious, as if aware that something hidden is happening. In the Penderel's Oak at lunchtime, Paul had found himself unable to stop needling him with sarcastic quips and insinuations. For the past two days, in fact, whenever he has spoken to Murray, his words have emerged tinged with sarcasm, sneering. And now, sitting in silence in the smoking room, he wonders what Murray suspects – because he must suspect *something*. 'I'll see you upstairs,' Paul says, pressing out his cigarette, and not looking Murray in the eye. Murray watches him as he stands up. 'Have you got a problem or something, Paul?' he says.

'A problem?'

'Yeah.'

Paul assumes a puzzled expression, and shakes his head. 'What sort of problem?'

'I don't know. That's why I'm asking you.'

'No.'

'Okay.'

Paul stands there for a moment, and then without knowing why he says, 'I saw you the other night, Murray.'

'What night?' Murray does not seem to understand.

'Monday.'

'Monday? What are you talking about?'

'You know what I'm talking about. You were in the Penderel's.'

'Yes. And?'

'You said you were going home.'

'So?'

'You didn't go home.'

'No, I didn't.' Squinting suspiciously, Murray says, 'So what?'

'You went to the Penderel's,' Paul says. 'I saw you.'

'I know. I saw *you*.' Murray sees the surprise on Paul's face – it is suddenly mottled with surprise – and waits for him to speak. He does not. 'I saw you walk out the door,' Murray says. 'I was sitting up the bar, and Michaela said to me, *There's Paul*. And I turned

82

round and saw you walk out the door. And by the way,' he adds, 'you said you were going home as well.'

'I *was* going home,' Paul says. 'I got a call from an old friend. We had a drink.'

'Who was that?'

'You don't know him.' He says this looking Murray straight in the eye, and then, 'You and Michaela seemed to be getting on pretty well.'

'Yes we did seem to be getting on pretty well.' There is something about the way Murray says this – with leathery squinting defiance – that Paul does not like. 'Do you often go in there on your own, then?' he asks.

'No, I don't,' Murray says shortly. 'What's this about?'

Paul sees that he is only making things worse. It would be absurd for him to start levelling accusations at Murray, when he himself had said he was going home, and was also in the Penderel's Oak. And absurd, as well, for him to play the jealous lover over Michaela. He is suddenly depressingly aware of the absurdity of *that*. 'Forget it,' he says quietly. 'I'll see you up there.'

On the way back to the sales floor, he tries to put the whole thing out of his mind, and to the surprise of his team, throws himself with unprecedented energy into the hopeless cause of *European Procurement Management*. For what is left of Wednesday afternoon, and the whole of Thursday morning, he yells and storms, scolds, encourages and exhorts, with a maniacal energy they have never seen in him – an energy which seems to have exhausted itself by the time he gets back from the Penderel's Oak, drunker than usual, with Murray and Andy, in the middle of Thursday afternoon, and on Friday morning he is deeply morose and untalkative. The previous evening, he met with Eddy Jaw.

Since Paul had insisted that the meeting take place as far as possible from Park Lane Publications, Eddy had suggested that he visit the offices of Delmar Morgan itself. These were in Victoria, and Paul took the tube there after work, standing on the train with his neck folded sideways, his face in an armpit, pressed against the door by the human stuffing of the carriage so firmly that when it sprang open at Tottenham Court Road he was forced out onto the platform, and halfway along it, by the flood of people leaving the train. Unable to fight his way back on in time, he waited for the next one, which was so full that to make space he had to shove some other passengers further in, something which initially seemed physically impossible. 'What are you doing?' one of them shrieked. Another told him he was a 'fucking twat'. 'You can fuck off,' Paul murmured, his face smeared against the dirty Perspex of the in-sliding door. At Oxford Circus, where he had to change to the Victoria Line, things were worse. And when he finally emerged into the evening at Victoria station, part of a moving mass of people pressed together, a sullen aggregate pouring out of the Underground, hurrying and pushing, it was of course already dark, and raining.

In the downstairs lobby, he was told to take the lift to the fifth floor, where he stepped out into a quiet cream space, where a young woman, half hidden by a huge vase of white orchids, was sitting behind a walnut desk. She was on the phone. On the wall were the words DELMAR MORGAN, and Eddy's elephant-head logo. She acknowledged Paul with a quick look and a half-smile, and held up a single finger, presumably to indicate that she would be with him in one minute. He stood there, looking around, pretending not to listen to what she was saying. She was very pretty, with black hair. And he thought, soon I will work here, and she will know me. It was quite exciting to think of himself working there. It occurred to him how important surroundings are, how it would be natural to work properly in a place like this. Working in a place like this, he thought, would give you confidence and self-respect. You would value yourself if you worked in a place like this. Paul has heard about offices with bowls of fresh fruit (peaches and stuff, not apples and bananas), and Gaggia espresso machines, and fridges full of Evian, and he wondered if they had those things here.

He said, 'I'm here to see Mr Feltman.'

'And what's your name, please?'

'Paul Rainey.'

'If you'd just like to take a seat, Mr Rainey.'

'Thanks.'

Clearing his throat – his voice had been rather hoarse – Paul sat down. There was a glass coffee table strewn with newspapers – the *Financial Times*, *The Times*, the *Telegraph* – and some low modern leather chairs. He took the *FT*, and had started to look at the stories on the front page, when the receptionist said, 'Mr Feltman will be with you in a minute, Mr Rainey.'

'Thank you,' said Paul, and cleared his throat again.

It was in fact ten minutes before Eddy appeared, wearing a complicated raincoat with epaulettes and carrying a tan leather briefcase. 'All right, Gwyn,' he said to the receptionist with a smile. 'See you tomorrow, sweetheart. Paul. Sorry to keep you, mate.'

'That's all right.'

'Let's get out of here. Fancy a drink?' His smile widened. 'Course you do.'

They went to a pub nearby. The Cardinal. Late Victorian in style, with funereal mahogany everywhere and elaborately frosted windows, it was full of office workers, and loud with their voices. Everyone was damp from the rain. 'I don't think there'll be anyone from Delmar in here,' Eddy said. 'Discretion – you know.' Paul nodded, looking around, without much hope, for an empty table. There was only one, occupying the short stretch of wall between the doors of the Ladies and the Gents, deep in the pub. He sat there, smoking, his back against the wall, studying the burgundy honeycomb of the ceiling, while Eddy got the drinks. 'So, how's it going?' Eddy said, sitting himself down on the maroon leather seat of a stool. Paul was slurping his pint. 'How's what going?' he asked.

'You've been talking to people? Interesting them in making a move?'

When, after answering in the affirmative, Paul told him that he had so far signed up only one salesman to come with him, Eddy frowned and said, 'One? What do you mean?' Paul started to explain about Nayal's talktime idea. Eddy interrupted him. 'You're going to have to do better than that, mate.'

'There's a couple of others,' Paul assured him. 'A couple of others I haven't spoken to yet.'

'A couple? Two?'

Paul nodded.

'For fuck's sake, mate! You're supposed to bring a whole team. I was thinking eight or ten people.'

'I thought you only wanted the best people,' Paul said, reddening. He coughed.

'Well, I was hoping you could get together eight or ten decent salespeople.'

Paul murmured, 'There's probably not eight or ten decent sales-people in the whole of PLP.'

'You can't come with two or three people, mate.' Eddy was smiling with a kind of sorrowful incredulity. 'I'm sorry. You must be able to do better than that. I wanted you to bring your own team – that was the whole fucking point.'

Paul nodded. 'All right,' he said. His voice was hoarse again. 'What would be the minimum?' he asked.

'The minimum?'

Tapping the ash from his cigarette into the big glass ashtray, Paul nodded like a naughty boy. 'Yeah.'

Eddy said he needed at least six people. On the way home Paul thought about this. If – *if* – Elvezia and Marlon agreed, that would make three. Li, four. Claire – under the circumstances there were no more doubts about whether to include *her* – five. And one more. Who? Dave? Paul frowned and shook his head. But it would have to be him. Andy had made one sale, months ago, and Sami and Richard had never sold a thing. As the squeaking train pulled out of East Croydon, he was suddenly aware of how stressed he was. The stress, the worry, the pressure, the subterfuge, he saw, were inevitable. And he started to wonder whether it was all worth it. What, after all, was the point? His job would still be to marshal muppets – the *same* muppets, for fuck's sake, minus Andy, Richard, Sami (whose physical resemblance to a muppet was overwhelming) and Dundee. He thought about the line Eddy had mentioned from *Taxi Driver* on Monday night, and wondered whether he in fact sufficiently wanted whatever he was hoping to get from this move to make it worthwhile. And what *was* he hoping to get? He asked himself this as, rocking gently from side to side, the train whistled along its rails through the darkness between Croydon and Gatwick. He was not entirely sober. After only one drink Eddy had said he had to go somewhere, and they had parted, as on Monday, with him clambering into a black cab. Paul had walked to the station. There, impulsively, he had stopped in the Shakespeare, the transients' pub opposite the main entrance, where he had had a pint or two while thinking things over.

Later, still thinking them over on the train, he wondered what he was hoping to get from this move. The extra money was not the main thing. Unusually for a salesman, he is not principally motivated by money. He needs it, of course. Quite a lot of it – he spends perhaps two hundred pounds a week on alcohol alone. For a long while, though, he has been living within his means. For all their ubiquitous efforts, for all the money they have thrown at him in an attempt to make him want things, modern marketing and brand management have ultimately failed with Paul Rainey. (Perhaps it is simply his alcoholism that makes him more or less immune to them.) No, what he hoped to get from this move, he thought – as the train slowed, and an automated female voice announced its imminent arrival at Gatwick Airport – was what he had imagined while waiting for Eddy: a more positive sense of himself. Money played an essential part in this, of course; money, however, not principally as something to be spent. Money as pure success points, as an ultimate index of personal progress, of his very own economic expansion. What other trustworthy indices did he have? What he hoped for – he spelled it out it to himself as the train slid away from the pinkish glow of the platforms at Gatwick, and once more into the darkness – what he hoped for was simply a sense of progress. That, surely, was what he wanted. It was frightening to think how little progress he had made in the past five years. That was what his doomed attempt to stop the Felixstat had been about. And also an even more ambitious September attempt to quit smoking, an attempt which had lasted one long – very long – Monday morning. As soon as he entered the Penderel's Oak at twelve, he had known for sure that it would fail. And if failure was inevitable, what was the point of struggling? It did occur to him that this was sophistry, that failure need not be inevitable, that he was simply *allowing* himself to fail, but by then he was already sweatily feeding his quids into the machine, muttering the usual stuff about it not being a good week for it and, as the fine shiny pack dropped into the tray, promising himself to quit the following Monday. And the following Monday, on the point of lighting his first of the day, a terse interior dialogue had taken place:

'Um, aren't you supposed to be giving up today?'

'No.'

Yes, a sense of progress. That was what he wanted. So why, when his thoughts turned to the things that he had to do tomorrow, did the questions keep putting themselves so insistently: Was it all worth it? What was the fucking point?

6

It was not true that the past five years had seen *no* progress. The children had progressed immensely, and although they were not his own, their furious progress, their non-stop growth and development, their leaps of intellectual achievement, the regular obsolescence of their very clothes, had distracted him from the more plateau-like nature of his own life.

He remembers the first time that he met them – one Sunday afternoon, at Heather's parents' house in Hounslow, where she was living at the time. Nervous, he took the tube from Barons Court. The train galumphed past the yellow-brick backs of terraced houses. It intersected with major roads, and traversed spaces full of a summer's green growth. The sky was low and overcast. From Hounslow Central the walk along the Staines Road was longer than he had expected (perhaps because, despite being late, he was walking slowly) and he had started to wonder whether he might have missed the turning when he found it – a quiet road of hawthorn bushes and speed humps. On one side, hidden behind trees and hedges, was the heath. From the other, from one of the cul-de-sacs that curved between the houses, he heard the crackling jingle of an ice-cream van, which was immediately obliterated by a heavy mass of aircraft noise as another plane went over.

Later he would sit tipsily in the garden, watching them. They were low enough for him to see the white eddies of turbulence on the trailing edges of their wings. Heather's father, Mike Willison – an immigration officer at Heathrow – said that he could tell from its noise alone what sort of plane each was. Laughing, they tested him – he put his hands theatrically over his eyes. To Paul they all sounded more or less the same, except the jumbo jets. These seemed lower than the others, and to be moving more slowly – it was frightening when he first saw one, the way it seemed to hang over the houses as it hauled its palpably enormous weight into the cloud-blanket. Warm and fuzzy with wine, and swirling in its glass the whisky that Mike had pressed on him, Paul meditated on the sound of the planes as they went over at one-minute intervals. The sequence was always the same. Thunder, emerging quickly from the depths of the scale until it started the drinks tinkling on the tray, then the harsh sound of a circular saw set to sheet metal, and finally, when the plane was overhead, a loud whistle or wail or scream. 'Amazing when you think of all those people off to America and God knows where, isn't it?' shouted Joan Willison, holding a cigarette and looking up – an observation that, like her husband's aeronautical party trick, was offered to all first-time visitors.

Joan had answered the door – appearing to Paul first as a tall, wavering, marigold shape in its frosted-glass panels. Her smile was sunny and spontaneous, her hair pale greying gold, her face strong-featured and handsome – and Paul saw immediately where Heather took her slightly thick features from, though in her mother they were more successful, more well proportioned perhaps, or more fully and easily occupied. They shook hands in the narrow hall, and he took off his jacket. Perhaps her tallness had something to do with it – Heather had not inherited that. Mike Willison was shorter than his wife. A lively, paunchy man, with blue eyes, he came into the hall wearing a novelty apron, its design based on Michelangelo's *David*, openly impatient to see his daughter's 'other half'. He shook Paul's hand enthusiastically and said, 'Hi, Paul. We've heard a lot about you.' Then they went into the lounge. Paul had hoped that Heather would be there. She was not. There was only a small, blond child, hiding most of himself behind the settee's low velveteen arm, and staring at them with eyes as blue as his grandfather's. He did not say hello to Paul, despite Mike's entreaties and the fact that Paul had said hello to him, addressing him, with awkward embarrassment, as if he were an adult – almost extending a hand for him to shake, and saying, 'Hello, Oliver. How are you?'

'He's just shy,' said Joan, smiling. 'What do you want to drink, Paul? Heather'll be down in a minute. She's upstairs with Marie.' Paul noticed that she was nervous, and when Mike said, in a loud voice, 'I'll get the drinks, I'll get them,' and went into the kitchen, she lit a cigarette and offered him one, which he took, though it was a Silk Cut Ultra and smoking it seemed to him like inhaling through a hollow tube. 'Let's go outside,' she said. 'Shouldn't smoke round the kids, should we?' And she smiled again. With an uneasy look at Oliver, who had not moved and was still watching him, Paul followed her into the garden. Like the house, it was tidy and well arranged. 'This is nice,' he said, self-consciously taking in the minuscule lawn, the water feature, the table and chairs; a garden that refused to acknowledge its own smallness, adopting instead – to Lilliputian effect – the airs of a spacious acre. 'Very nice.' And it was at that moment that, visibly startling him, the first jumbo jet appeared, shockingly low in the sky overhead. Humbled by its noise, he stared at it in awe as it powered over. When it had passed, and no longer obliterated their voices, he found himself laughing nervously, and Joan smiled and shook her head, as if to say, 'I know, I know.'

It was strange for him to see Heather holding Marie, who at the time was a pale, plump toddler, still in diapers. 'Hi,' he said, making an effort to seem normal. 'We're just having a look at the lovely garden.' Heather nodded. He saw that she was much more nervous than he was, which immediately made him feel less nervous himself. 'You must be Marie,' he said. And smiling at the child, he took her tiny, dimpled hand and gave it a jocular shake. She seemed intrigued, but after a moment turned away from him and pressed herself into

91

her mother's breasts. Paul said, 'I met Oliver a minute ago.' Heather looked at him with a hard, intense expression, an expression that he did not understand – they had only known each other a few months – but what had been near-panic in her when she stepped into the garden was to some extent, it seemed, defused.

It was an English barbecue. There were sausages and burgers and minted lamb kebabs. Australian wine and Belgian lager. It was not cold, but the sky was solidly overcast. They talked about house prices. Mike was very pleased with how little the house had cost him because of its proximity to the airport – 'I can drive to work in five minutes!' – and insisted, quite hotly in the face of very tentative scepticism from Joan – scepticism anticipated in fact, because she had hardly started to speak when he interrupted her – that they did not mind the noise. 'You just don't notice it after a while. You really don't.' 'Then why are there always those people going round with microphones?' she asked. He waved this away. 'The thing is,' she said earnestly, turning to Paul, 'you just can't let it get to you. If you let it get to you, if you become obsessed with it, it becomes a nightmare. Doesn't it? You hear about people who just *crack up*.' Paul nodded seriously, and wondered, with a sudden flutter of panic, if they knew of his own 'crack-up'. The previous November he had met the hard floor of the plummet that had started with the dissolution of Northwood. He had stopped turning up to work, and then stopped leaving his flat entirely, when even a trip to the shops was full of indefinable terrors. And when his brother Chris, over from Rotterdam, found him behind the drawn, dusty velour of the living-room curtains, he had insisted on taking him to a doctor. The doctor had put him on Felixstat.

They were talking about the awfulness of public transport, and when Mike expressed surprise that Paul had come on the Piccadilly Line, Joan said, with motherly vehemence, 'Don't be silly! He wanted to enjoy a drink.' They were all quite tipsy, even a bit squiffy – the

Famous Grouse had been brought out for the gentlemen – by the time Mike started to show off his knowledge of aircraft noise. Later, he and Paul, Heather and Oli went for what he called a 'yomp' on the heath, which was low-lying, with cracked concrete paths and a derelict atmosphere. The planes went over steadily from the airport's implied location to the west. When Paul put his arm round Heather, she seemed to stiffen – perhaps aware that Oliver, who was walking with Mike a little way ahead, kept turning to look at them – and after a minute or two, without either of them saying anything, he let her go. Some people went past on horseback, and Mike, who was an enthusiastic student of local history, told Paul that in the olden days the major road into London from the west had struck across the heath, which was notorious for bandits and highwaymen – which is, he informed him, why one of the highwaymen in Farquhar's *The Beaux Stratagem* is called 'Hounslow'. People used to stop for the night, Mike went on, at a coaching inn nearby, the Crown, and continue on to London in the morning. They wandered through the nature reserve, and when they returned to the house – Joan was in the kitchen reading the *Mail on Sunday* – they had tea, and sat in the low-ceilinged lounge with the telly on.

Opposite Paul on the tube as it travelled through the long dusk of that Sunday in July were two JAL stewardesses, one Japanese, the other Scottish. They looked exhausted, had obviously just flown in from Tokyo or somewhere. Their suitcases were small, mere overnight bags; and their looks – the Japanese girl flat-faced, her legs short and plump, her hair pure black, and the Scot tall, blonde and pale-eyed, with a prominent nose – seemed designed to emphasise how far apart they had started life, how infinitesimally unlikely it was that they would one day sit together on a suburban train in London making tired small talk. Paul had been thinking about fate as he waited on the empty platform at Hounslow Central, and when,

93

sitting down in the train, he noticed the stewardesses, they seemed set before him as a living embodiment of his thoughts. Made unusually pensive by the afternoon's drinking, and the quiet melancholy twilight of the station platform (the lights had just flickered on, turning the surrounding sky a deeper evening blue), he had been thinking how easily he might *not* have been there, in the extreme west of London, where London finally ends, waiting for the train which eventually pulled in with a protracted sigh. He found it frightening to think how easily he and Heather might not have met; how easily either of them might have ended up somewhere other than Archway Publications. Nothing is fated, he thought, but most things are so improbable that once they have happened it seems they must have been.

His small flat was somewhere in the sleepy labyrinthine limbo south of Talgarth Road, where the horizon, showing through holes in stretches of terraced housing, was often low. There were derelict open spaces, insomniac highways, acres of rusting track. Private tennis clubs and municipal cemeteries. From his balconette he could hear the metallic mutter of the tube trains, down in their damp cutting two streets away.

7

The heavy beats of the music from upstairs are only faintly audible in the Gents – and not at all when the automated rinsing of the urinal starts. It is Friday night in the Penderel's Oak, and alone at the tin trough, Paul is drunk and feeling dissatisfied with himself. He has done nothing today. It had been his intention to get in early – say, eight o'clock – when he would find Li alone on the sales floor. This had not happened though. When the stuttering alarm had started to peck the quick of his head at five forty-five, the whole idea had seemed like nonsense, and he had ignored it. (Though he spent the next hour in a fretful, unsatisfying half-sleep.) Elvezia and Dave he had intended to speak to in the smoking room, as he had spoken to Wolé. This had not happened either. He would, he had thought, quietly arrange to meet Claire for a coffee somewhere, perhaps offer to take her to lunch, or for a drink. After a drink, he could suggest dinner . . . No, he had not spoken to Claire, though they had been alone in the smoking room for several minutes. He could simply have explained the situation to her there, of course – but then there would have been no reason to have lunch or a drink with her next week, and he had no intention of forgoing *that*. Presumably, then, he had at least made the arrangements for this little tête-à-tête? No, he had not. He had mistakenly, naively, presumed that it would be a nerveless matter to suggest such a meeting to her. It was not. In his mind he was now more or less asking her out on a date. And might it not look that way to her too, this mysterious invitation? And what would she make of *that*? He felt squeamish even to imagine such a misunderstanding on her side. Perhaps it *would* be better just to speak to her there, in the smoking room. That was what he was doing with the other smokers, wasn't it? And he had been about to do this, to say something, when like a shoal of fish suddenly changing direction, and in doing so seeming to change colour (he has seen such things on TV), his thoughts reversed themselves – why pretend that she was not a special case? Why pass up this opportunity to spend some innocent time alone with her? That would be perverse. There was nothing wrong with it. He had done the same with Nayal. What he had not done in Nayal's case was spend hours worrying over the precise form of words he would use to extend the invitation . . .

There is a sudden short surge in the volume of the music as the outer door of the Gents is opened. Paul zips himself up and turns to the sink. In the dull metal mirror, he sees Marlon enter the low room. 'All right, Marlon?' he says without turning.

'All right, Paul?'

It is strange that Marlon should still be in the pub. Strange and, Paul feels, providential. Usually, if he comes to the Penderel's after work on Friday at all, it is for a quick half, or even a soft drink of some sort, and yet here he is at nine, cheerfully whistling at the urinal. Casually, Paul checks the wet, graffitied stall. 'I wanted to have a word with you actually, Marl,' he says, looking in the metal mirror again.

'Oh yeah?' Marlon might even be drunk, which is unheard of. 'What about?'

'Don't mention this to anyone, mate, but I'm leaving PLP.'

'Oh yeah?'

'I've been offered a job at another place, a better place. I'm asking around a few people, seeing if they want to join me there.'

'Oh yeah?'

'Would you be interested at all?'

'What's the place?'

'It's a place –'

96

'Excuse me.' Marlon has finished, and wants access to the sink. Paul stands aside. 'It's a place called Delmar Morgan,' he says.

'I've not heard of it.'

'It's a top-quality place.'

Washing his hands, Marlon seems unenthused. 'A lot better than PLP,' Paul affirms throatily, looking at the pigeon grey of Marlon's broad, suited back, and the dingy yellow ceiling light shining on his skin-coloured pate.

'Who else have you asked?'

'Does it matter?'

'Just curious.'

'I'm not asking everyone.'

'I'm sure you're not.'

Arrogant sod, Marlon, Paul thinks. 'Only the top people,' he says. Without reacting to this, Marlon starts the hand dryer. Paul raises his voice. 'PLP's not in good shape, mate, that I *can* tell you.'

'It's not going to be in better shape when you take the top people, is it?'

'No it's not,' Paul says, after a moment. 'You should get out while you can.'

'I'll think about it.'

'All right.'

For a few seconds the only sound is the shouting of the dryer. Paul is about to leave. Then Marlon says, 'When would this happen?'

Paul smiles, very slightly, at the obvious buying signal – obvious not only in itself, but as an attempt to prolong a pitch that had seemed about to end. He had been worried by Marlon's evasiveness. Now he sees that he simply considers himself too grand to say yes straight off, or even seem interested – the sort to savour, as if on principle, the power of the prospect. 'Um, soon,' Paul says. 'In a few weeks.'

'Oh. That soon.'

'Yeah. We'll start after Christmas basically.'

'Okay.' The hand dryer shuts up suddenly. 'I'll let you know in the next few days.'

'Cheers, Marl,' Paul says. 'And keep it quiet, yeah?'

They leave together and go up the dim, carpeted stairs. The pub is full – 'heaving' as Andy would say. The music thuds and the bar is four-deep. Marlon has some friends in, outsiders, not salespeople, which is why he is still there. Pushing through the mob with Paul in his wake, he moves towards them, but as he passes Murray and Andy and some of the others, he shouts over the music, 'Paul just tried to proposition me in the toilet.' Emerging from the thick press of people, Paul – who did not hear him – sees everyone smiling. 'What?' he shouts. 'What did you say?'

'I'm just telling them,' shouts Marlon, 'that you just tried to proposition me in the toilet. See you later.' And he moves off, shouldering his way towards his friends.

'Rainey, you fucking bender,' shouts Murray Dundee.

And furious, Paul smiles.

On Monday morning, Paul is in by eight. It is strange to see the sales floor so silent – the messy, misaligned desks unoccupied, semi-darkness still outside. And the smell of cigarette smoke – that is strange too. Li has obviously been smoking at her desk – has in fact just put a cigarette out – there are still blue veils floating in the air around her, visible in the sharp light of her desk lamp. He sees a saucer, smeared with black ash and holding a number of butts, among her papers. She is surprised to see him, her mouth open, half smiling. Her narrow shoulders hunched. Instead of saying anything she nods – a miniature bow. 'Morning,' Paul says. 'Have you been smoking here?' It is simply undeniable, and she smiles, showing rotten yellow teeth. 'You shouldn't,' he mutters – and then, taking out his own cigarettes, lights one, and says, 'Don't tell anybody.'

'No, I won't,' she says, and laughs as if he were mad.

This is a strange situation, Paul thinks. 'How's it going?' he asks, indicating the mess of papers on her desk.

'Fine.'

'Any deals?'

'I think so.'

'Who?'

Unnervingly, her initial answer is a laugh. Paul is not sure why, or what this means. He smiles uneasily. 'Who?' he says again, with more emphasis, raising his eyebrows.

'Chinese company.'

An obviously inadequate answer, vague to the point of deliberate evasiveness, and simply to accept it would surely make him look like a fool. Seeing that he is in need of it, she hands him her ash-saucer, and for a minute he stands there, smoking in silence. He is surprised that she has not asked him why he is in so early. 'I wanted to have a chat with you, Li,' he says. She maintains her smile, but it becomes worried, even panic-stricken. Which disturbs him – why should she be so terrified? What does she think he has discovered? If he takes her to Delmar Morgan and she perpetrates some kind of scam there . . . 'Are you okay?' he asks. 'Is something wrong?' She laughs and shakes her head. 'Nothing wrong.'

'You sure?'

She nods.

'Okay,' Paul says, uncertain whether to proceed. 'Yeah, I wanted to have a chat with you,' he says slowly. 'Don't tell anyone, but, um, I'm leaving.' She nods again, as if there were nothing surprising about this. 'Going to another company,' he adds, waving his cigarette. 'Another sales company.' Another earnest, respectful nod. 'A better one. Better than this one. It's called Delmar Morgan.' This time the nod is eager, as if she recognises the name and is impressed. 'You've heard of it?'

She shakes her head.

'It's a good company.' An emphatic nod. 'And,' he goes on, 'yeah – I'm asking some people if they want to join me there.' He stubs out his cigarette on the filthy porcelain of the saucer, and sets it on the edge of her desk. 'Would you be interested in doing that?' She nods, but he wonders whether she has really understood. 'You would?'

'Would I be interested?' she says.

'Yes.'

She nods again.

'Yes, you would be interested?'

'Yes.'

'Yes?'

'Yes.'

'Yes, you would be interested?'

'I would be interested.'

He is still not entirely sure that she knows what he is talking about. With a look at the dark entrance, and in a low voice, he says, 'You would be interested in coming to work at Delmar Morgan? Leaving this company and going to the other company, Delmar Morgan.'

'Yes,' she says.

Paul smiles insincerely. 'Okay. We're planning the move in a few weeks, if that's okay.' Why am I asking her if it's okay? he thinks. He feels uneasy – the uneasiness that often follows an apparently effortless sale, the sense that something has not been properly understood. In these situations, in his efforts to establish the situation as sound, the salesman often finds himself seemingly trying to talk the prospect out of it. Paul says, 'We'll start work at the other company, Delmar Morgan, after Christmas.'

She nods, smiles. 'Okay.'

'That's okay?'

'Yes.'

'Okay. Fine. And don't tell anyone, okay? No one.'

'I won't tell.'

Paul smiles, more warmly this time. 'Not even what's-his-name – you know, your beau.' She is not familiar with the word 'beau', but she guesses – perhaps from the way Paul is smiling – who he is referring to, and laughs. 'No, I won't tell,' she says.

The Kingsway Benjys is jammed with the bleary-eyed, the grim-faced, the harassed, the hurried. This is its peak time, eight thirty, and behind the long counter a line of pallid, green-T-shirted East Europeans hustle frantically with hot drinks and money. It takes Paul ten minutes to get his coffee, and when he re-emerges onto the loud grey pavement, he is surprised to see Li there, waiting, wearing her round-shouldered coat, which resembles a soft, mousy dressing gown. 'All right?' he says. She throws away her cigarette. 'Paul, I just wanted to ask you – can Justin come too?'

'Justin?'

'My beau.'

'Oh.' He smiles at her use of the word. 'Um . . . Yeah, maybe. I'll think about it.'

'Okay, thanks,' she says, and together they walk round the corner to PLP's tinted-glass door.

Adding more than an hour to its front end makes the day difficult. Paul's head is not working properly, and coffee – he has had five – has no effect, except to stir up a faceless potent fear, and percolate nauseously through his innards. Cigarettes seem poisonous. The windows seem too light. And the January 2005 edition of *European Procurement Management* is terminal – there is no hope for it – only ten more selling days until Christmas, and it is not even halfway to its target. Lawrence, however, still stalks the sales floor like a fatally wounded animal with no understanding of death. And, struggling with lassitude and indifference, Paul must promise this animal, with spittle-foam in the corners of its mouth, with a messy, volu-minous crown of hair, that everything is all right, that there is 'a lot out there', that the target will, in the end, be met, or only slightly undershot – the first time that even *that* has been admitted, though the target has never – not *once* – been met before. 'Insane,' Paul thinks, sloping off to the smoking room for the umpteenth time. 'Insane.'

Justin Fellowes, Li's beau, is on the Pig's team, and on his way to the smoking room, Paul stops off, as he sometimes does, to say hello to Dave Mortished – the Pig. Filling his executive seat, he looks like a ginger Buddha with a fake tan, his mild eyes on the working salespeople of his team. They are not doing quite as badly as Paul's people, but *International Finance and Financial Policy Review* will not make target either – though unlike *EPM*, selling extends into the new year. Perched on the edge of the Pig's desk, Paul tunes his ear to Justin Fellowes' pitching voice. (He has already found his name on the whiteboard, and seen with satisfaction that he is someone who actually sells – a salesman, not one of the transient desperadoes who make up at least half the workforce at any one time.) The voice is nasal and dully earnest, but he is able to project enough authority over the phone for this to be, if anything, an asset. He sounds trustworthy, simple – someone who, with unimaginative persistence, sticks to the pitch. A plodder, but apparently an effective one, and Paul is pleased. And wondering whether to jettison Dave Shelley in favour of Justin Fellowes, he experiences an enjoyable frisson of power – of deciding the fates of others' lives as if hesitating between two products in a supermarket aisle.

The Pig is not a talker. He nods a lot, and occasionally mutters a few words, his eyes fixed elsewhere. Today, Paul finds him particularly unforthcoming. He wonders, has often wondered this past week, whether Eddy has an arrangement with the Pig similar to the one that he has with him. And why wouldn't he? He and Mortished know each other well from the Northwood days, and the Pig's team – Paul has to admit it – is stronger than his own. When he asked Eddy if he was talking to anyone else from PLP, he was knowingly evasive – 'You don't need to worry about that, Paul,' he had said, with a smile, as he swigged his Bacardi Breezer. Paul had, of course, taken this as a 'yes'. And the Pig's more than usually taciturn mode, and distracted lack of interest in verbally eviscerating Lawrence, suggest that he, too, has something momentous on his mind.

'S'my birthday on Friday,' he says. 'We're having drinks and a meal, if you want to come along.'

'Sure,' Paul says. 'Sure. That'd be nice. How old are you going to be, Dave?'

Of the same generation as Murray Dundee, Mortished has been in sales-based publishing longer than any of them except Lawrence himself. He ignores Paul's question. They go to the smoking room. One of the buttons of the Pig's white polyester shirt has come undone and, as he sits, a shape of colourless, hairless flab pours heavily through the gap. The fake tan, Paul realises, must be restricted to his hands and head, with its soft wispy copper hair. The cigarette, as he brings it to his mouth, looks puny in his fat hand. After the failure of Northwood and the subsequent diaspora, he spent some time in Thailand and the Philippines, living cheap off his savings, sweating a lot. And when the money ran out, he returned to the UK, and sales. He and Paul joined PLP at about the same time, the Pig first by a month or two. And then Murray showed up . . .

Later, in the seemingly endless reaches of the afternoon (and it is only *Monday*), the sky over Kingsway darkening for a downpour, Paul gets Elvezia alone in the smoking room. As he is starting to outline his proposal, the door opens and Dave Shelley walks in, holding a single unlit cigarette. Finding the room occupied, he seems to hesitate for a moment, his long face unsmiling – he knows exactly when the smoking room is most likely to be empty, as he prefers it, and is displeased to find people there. Paul had decided not to include him in the move, now that Justin is involved, but he cannot be bothered to find another opportunity to speak to Elvezia – he has been following her down to the smoking room all day – so he says, 'Dave, mate, sit down – I wanted a word with you as well actually.' And quietly, he puts the plan to them. They both seem flattered, and sign up on the spot.

By close of business on Wednesday, and despite several openings, he has still not spoken to Claire. On Tuesday, Marlon had confirmed his interest in the move. And returning from the pub on Wednesday afternoon, Paul had found a letter from Li in his desk drawer (he had asked her to speak to Justin herself) which he read sitting in one of the luxurious stalls in the Gents, and which unexpectedly confirmed his suspicion that the Pig had his own arrangement with Eddy Jaw. The letter said: '*Paul, I have spoken to Justin. He said he has already been invited to the other company, Delma Morgan. So that is fine. Kind regards, Li.*' It made Paul feel powerful to have unearthed this information, even inadvertently – made him feel in a position of strength, though there was no obvious practical use that he could make of it. *Knowledge is power*, he said to himself, stuffing the letter into his pocket and, for the sake of appearances, flushing the toilet. He knew things that others did not know he knew – Eddy, the Pig, Murray. Things that they thought he *did not* know. So only he, Paul, had all the facts. He stared at himself impassively in the bright mirror. *You fucking shrewdie*, he thought, and needlessly washed his hands. With two teams defecting – and, who knows, perhaps more – it really would be the end of Park Lane Publications. And this knowledge increased Paul's sense of Olympian elevation as he walked back to his desk – all these salespeople, and like the sinful inhabitants of some antique city (he thought) about to be smitten by the immortals, overwhelmed by water, and still they toil on the phone and fret and bicker, unaware of what was about to befall them. Lawrence, in particular, presented an image of poor, deluded humanity. He will be swept away in the impending flood, and yet here he is, strutting around, lisping orders – an absurd, doomed king.

He feels so fortified by these thoughts, that when, at the very end of the afternoon, he once more finds himself alone with Claire, he invites her for an after-work drink without hesitation. Except that he visits the smoking room first. She is staying to make a call at five thirty, and as the others leave, he lingers, pretending to have things to do. Slowly the sales floor empties. At twenty past, except for the two of them – and near the exit, Tony Peters, in his coat but still detaining two members of his team with stories that they pretend to find amusing – it is deserted. Claire is reading a newspaper. His heart thumping – Why, he thinks, am I so fucking nervous? This is *business* – Paul slips off to the smoking room. It is obvious that he will never have a more perfect opportunity than this. If he does not speak to her now, he surely never will. He must ask her to join him for a drink *now*, today. And if she can't – or won't – he must simply put the plan to her on the sales floor. Though he seemed to light it only moments ago, his cigarette is already over. He considers smoking a second, then with a grunt of self-contempt, stands up – slightly unsteadily – and leaves. Slowly he mounts the silent stairs. Tony and his lickspittles have left. She is alone. As he approaches the desks, she looks up from her newspaper for a moment, and they smile shortly at each other. He sits down, and is about to speak, has actually opened his mouth to do so, when she picks up the phone and, consulting an index card, starts to enter the numbers. 'Yes, hello,' she says in her polite, husky voice. 'Is Mr Gross there, please?' There is a short pause, then she says, 'Sarah Scotland. I'm calling in association with the International Federation of Procurement Management.'

Paul pretends not to be listening. He slides open one of his desk drawers and looks through the obsolete papers it contains. He does this to be helpful. It is harder to make calls on a silent, vacant sales floor than on a teeming one. The whole exercise can seem unreal, weird. 'What, he's left?' Claire says sharply. 'But he said I should call at six thirty.' She is blushing – Paul notices – with irritation. 'No,' she says. 'No, I'll call back tomorrow morning. Thank you.' She hangs up and says, primly, 'For fuck's sake.'

'He's gone?' Paul asks, sympathetic, still staring into his desk drawer.

'He specifically said I should call at six thirty, his time.'

'Yeah, it's fucking annoying when that happens,' he says vaguely. 'When you stay behind for one call, and then that happens.'

She has started to ready herself for leaving, is putting things hurriedly into her bag. She ties her scarf around her neck, pulling her hair from its woolly loop at the back. Now she is pushing her slender arms into the sleeves of her coat. In a few seconds, she will be gone. 'Um,' Paul says, sliding his desk drawer shut. 'I wanted . . .' He clears his throat. 'I wanted to have a word with you, Claire.' His voice, unintentionally, was heavily ominous, and she stops, a look of worry on her high-cheeked face. 'Nothing to worry about,' he adds, seeing this.

'Okay,' she says.

'Do you want to get a drink or something? Maybe you're in a hurry.' He rushes these words out, and immediately feels he has made a mistake. She looks uneasy. He must clarify what this is about. 'Just a quick one. It'd be nicer than talking here. I've got a proposal for you. A work proposal.'

'What proposal?' she says, still uneasy. Perhaps more so.

'Um. Well.' He wavers for a moment, and then, painfully abandoning the idea of a drink, says, in a low voice, 'The fact is, I've been offered another job. At another company. And I'm asking some of the team if they want to join me there. It's a better company.'

'Oh,' she says. 'Right.'

'Um. So that's it. That's the proposal.' He smiles. 'Interested?'

'Another sales company?'

'Yeah. A better one.'

She looks uncertain.

'You don't have to give me an answer now,' he says.

She shakes her head and laughs sadly. 'No, it's not that. It's just that I don't think I'm very good at this.'

106

'Good at . . . ?'

'This. Sales.'

'I think you are,' Paul says. And she smiles, pinks, in spite of everything enjoying the praise. 'But I haven't *sold* anything,' she protests half-heartedly. 'I've been here two months and I haven't sold *anything*. It's embarrassing . . .'

'It's normal.'

'I just don't think . . . it's really me.' She smiles apologetically. 'I've been wanting to talk to you about it, actually.'

'About?'

'About leaving.' Experiencing a quiet sense of inner disintegration, Paul waits for her to go on. For a week he has been imagining this conversation. Not once did he imagine it like this. She is now saying how helpful he has been, how it's not his fault . . . 'It's just really not me,' she says again, looking at him with sincere, uncertain blue eyes. He takes out his cigarettes, offers her one, and lights it for her. 'Thanks.' He lights one for himself.

'It's normal, you know,' he says, after a few moments. 'You shouldn't give up on it so easily. I think you could be very good. I honestly do,' he says. 'I wouldn't just say that. And this new place we're going to, it's much better. Much better publications. Much better leads. It'll seem easy after the stuff we've been working on here.' She does not say anything. He can see that she does not want to be persuaded, is set against it, and when he goes on it is without vehemence – 'This would be the worst time to stop.'

'It's not just that.'

'What is it?'

'I don't really enjoy it.'

'You're not supposed to enjoy it!' he says jokingly. 'We're not doing it for a laugh. Do you think I enjoy it?'

'No, I know.'

They smoke in silence for a few moments. 'Anyway,' he says softly, 'think about it.'

'I have thought about it,' she says. 'I can't do this. I've tried, but I can't.' She pauses. 'I'm sorry.'

He laughs. 'Sorry for what, why?'

'I don't know. I feel I've let you down.'

'Not at all. Don't be silly.'

'I've been wanting to tell you for a couple of weeks. I don't know why I've kept putting it off.' Her latest plan, formulated that very afternoon, had been to stay until Christmas, and then simply slip away in the new year. And instead she will slip away now. Today, it turns out, has been her last day, as he understands. He had not meant to precipitate *this*. 'I gave it a try,' she says, with a smile.

'Yes.'

They leave together, ride down in the lift, slightly uncomfortable in its dim, confined space. Together, they wait at the lights, and cross Kingsway. 'Okay,' she says, halting at the entrance to the tube.

'Okay. Well . . .'

'Good luck in your new job.'

'Yeah, thanks. And good luck with whatever you do.'

'Thanks.'

'Okay . . .' There is a moment of slight confusion. 'Well, don't be a stranger, Claire.'

'I won't,' she says, though they both know that they will never see each other again, and for a moment they wonder, both of them, whether a peck on the cheek would be appropriate here. In the end they shake hands quickly, and she turns and goes through the grey barriers.

Wearing a pair of frameless glasses that do not suit his big face, Eddy Jaw looks over the list of names – *Wolé Ogunyemi, Marlon Smith, Elvezia Buonarroti, Dave Shelley, Li Zhang, Justin Fellowes*. It is Thursday again, and they are again in the deep red interior of the Cardinal in Victoria. Paul is drinking Ayingerbrau. 'All right,'

Eddy says, putting the list down on the table's dark mahogany. 'Well done, Paul.'

'No problemo,' Paul mutters, and feeling pleased with himself – though also prickly at receiving such a condescending pat on the head from his old co-equal – he lights a cigarette. He has not yet really come to terms with the fact that Eddy is now – there is no ambiguity about it – his boss.

'Tell me something about these people,' Eddy says.

Paul indicates the list. 'About *them*?'

Eddy nods. 'Yeah.' Taking his time, Paul sips lager while he looks through the names. 'What do you want to know?' he says. Eddy laughs. 'Something about them. Who the fuck are they?'

'All right. Um. Wolé, yeah, fucking brilliant. Really top salesman. Marlon too. Um. Elvezia – she pitches in Italian. She's good. Reliable. Li pitches in Chinese. Mandarin, I think. Or Cantonese. The same – good, reliable . . .'

'What about, you missed out . . . Dave Shelley?'

'Dave? Yeah, he's good. Not as experienced as the others. But good. Yeah . . .'

'And Justin Fellowes?'

Paul wonders whether Eddy has had an equivalent list from the Pig, also featuring Justin Fellowes. Something about his smile, almost imperceptible – perhaps imagined – suggests that he might have. 'I recruited him from another team,' Paul says.

'Oh?' Eddy nods, apparently impressed. 'Great.'

'Yeah, there was nobody else good on my team.'

'That's great, Paul. Well done. So this Justin Fellowes is good, is he?'

'Yeah, pretty good,' Paul says.

Eddy takes a pull of alcopop. The liquid – WKD Original – is a strange, fluorescent blue, and at this trigger, like some programmed Sirhan Sirhan, the strapline of an advert pops into Paul's head: *Have you got a WKD side?*

109

'So,' Eddy says, 'they're all ready to go?'

'Yeah.'

'And you?'

'I'm ready. Of course.' Paul stubs out his cigarette. He is not sure, suddenly, that he wants to work for Eddy Jaw – he has not until now, until this meeting, thought about it in precisely those terms. He has thought about it in terms of what he is *leaving*. Now he starts to think – in more specific, solid detail – about what he is going *to*. And he finds he is not sure about it.

'And it's all been kept quiet?' Eddy says. 'No one knows who's not involved?'

Paul shakes his head. 'No.'

'Not Murray?'

'Definitely not Murray.' He lights another cigarette. Eddy, sitting on the other side of the table, studies him almost sympathetically. 'I know it's a bit of a shit thing to do to a mate,' he says.

Paul says, 'Well . . .' Then stops, and shrugs, and looks Eddy in the face. The face is long, and despite some flab on the jowls, still quite youthful – narrow-mouthed, small-eyed, with fair brows and lashes. Eddy is smiling. 'It's business,' he says. 'That's all.' Paul says nothing. 'He'll understand that. Wouldn't you?'

'I suppose.' Though Paul does not think he *would* understand. Not in the sense that Eddy means, anyway – a sense which seemingly sought to isolate 'business' from everything else in life, as though it were an entirely separate sphere – as though, in each sphere, we were not the same person.

'I want to make the move on Monday,' Eddy says.

Paul is stunned. 'Monday?'

'Yeh.'

'*This* Monday?'

'Yes.'

'But it's Thursday . . .'

'It is, yes.'

110

'It's just . . . I thought we were going after Christmas.'

'No.'

Paul shakes his head, as if trying to wake himself up. 'Why?' he says.

'If everything's ready, why wait?' Eddy smiles. 'Tomorrow's your last day at PLP, mate. I thought you'd be pleased.' Paul is speechless. While it was safely on the far side of Christmas, of the new year, it all seemed somehow hypothetical. Now it is *Monday*. And suddenly it is something that is actually happening. He is aware, in an entirely literal sense, of his feet turning cold under the table. In a sterner tone, Eddy says, 'You said you were ready.'

'Yeah, I am.' He has had no time to prepare himself psychologically though.

'Then what's the problem?' Eddy seems impatient.

'There isn't a problem.'

'Fine.'

'So,' Paul says hoarsely, 'so what do we do?'

8

Three thirty, and Paul is standing in his cotton boxers outside the bedroom door – that centrally heated inky cave, smelling of human breath – having left the bed in protest at his brain's obstinate refusal to close down. Aware of the carpet's nap under the slightly sweaty soles of his feet, he stands there, in the sleepless stare of the street light, the window's shadow on him like a cross hair, knowing that there is nothing for him to do. Nothing. He is itchy-eyed and headachy with fatigue. He has been standing on the same spot for several minutes, and it seems that he has more chance of falling asleep standing there – his head occasionally nods involuntarily – than in the hot darkness of the bed. This is always the way. He is not angry any more. That was an hour ago. The tears, too, have been shed. Poor, imploring tears. He moves silently down the stairs, and turns on the light in the lounge. It assaults his eyes, and he squints – and when that is not enough, covers them with his hand. He has not got his contacts in, and the room, when he can look at it, is soft-focused. It seems desolate, dishevelled. Sad. Especially the dour, coniferous shape of the unilluminated Christmas tree. Crouching on his white hams, he plugs in the coloured lights. (They bought the tree on Saturday. It was too tall for the room – as he had said it would be – and he had had to labour in the garden for an hour with a saw.) He snaps off the oppressive overhead light and sitting on the sofa wearily starts to make a spliff. His fingers are swollen. It is Monday morning.

For Paul, Sunday is typically the least toxic day of the week, and this one was no exception. He had woken with an erection, an increasingly unusual occurrence, and inveigled Heather into sex for the first time in over a month. Then he had pulled on some clothes and gone out into the morning, which was frosty, to buy the paper and a pack of cigarettes. Returning to bed with tea and an ashtray, he and Heather had read the paper. He started with the sports section, studying every word of the snooker and taking a passing interest in some of the other sports, such as motor racing and rugby. Then he moved on to the business section. Not all of it – mostly pieces on companies whose products and services he purchases himself. Diageo, for instance, and BAT. J. D. Wetherspoon and SouthEast Trains. He started to read one of the economic analysis columns before noticing, halfway down, that he literally did not understand what it was *about*, let alone the specifics of what it was trying to say. He had started on it out of a sense of obligation – a sense that he *ought* to understand these things. *But why?* he wondered, untidily folding the business pages and dropping them onto the carpet. *Why?*

He turned his attention next to the news section, which Heather had just finished with. (She was now reading the travel section.) Wearily, he ploughed through national and international news and various op-ed pieces. A lot about house prices. He liked the almost irreverent little graphics which this particular paper always uses to illustrate its news articles – little men jumping out of an exploding truck to show how an escape had occurred, statistics presented as a series of different-sized oil barrels, a picture to show exactly how, in several numbered stages, a light aircraft had become tangled in power lines and crashed in a field. Finishing the news, he hesitated between the News Review and the travel section, which Heather had discarded (she was now looking through the Culture magazine). Neither of them particularly appealed to him. In the end he decided on the News Review, but only after leafing quickly through travel. The News Review kept him occupied for quite a while, and he followed it with a flip through the glossy Lifestyle magazine (shite, he thought, as always) and a half-hearted study of the personal finance section, before searching through the mass of paper everywhere on the bed to make sure that he had not overlooked anything. He found a special property pull-out – an 'Essential Guide to Buying and Selling' – which he perused for a while. ('Appointments' and the kids' section he never bothered with, and the Culture magazine, because it contained the TV listings, would be around all week – there was no hurry where that was concerned.) By this time it was dark outside. At various points during the day he had made trips to the kitchen for food – cheese toasties, crisps, biscuits, a French stick defrosted in the microwave, pâté. More tea. Later, in the waist of the afternoon, while he was reading the News Review, he had gone to get a beer. The detritus of all this surrounded them. Heather, smoking guiltily, wearing glasses and her dressing gown under the duvet, was reading the Lifestyle magazine. His head full of fresh information, most of which he was already forgetting, Paul went downstairs in his towelling dressing gown and socks, turning on the light in the dark hall. The measured sounds of televised snooker could be heard through the sitting-room door.

The only other thing to happen on Sunday was that Martin Short came round. Sitting on the sofa, watching the snooker with Oliver, who for some reason had his cue with him, Paul was irked when the doorbell rang. Oliver had been there all afternoon. It was about five o'clock when Paul joined him, during the second frame of Ebdon's third-round match against Lee, and sixish when the doorbell rang. *For fuck's sake*, Paul thought. 'You expecting someone?' he shouted up the small stairs. 'It's probably Martin,' Heather shouted back. 'He said he might come round to do the drains.' Paul opened the front door, and there was Martin Short, somewhat inappropriately six foot four, his breath vaporous in the evening's iciness, holding clobber. The clobber, a mass of hoses and metal coils and pumps, was a professional drain de-blocking machine. What kind of fucking idiot, Paul found himself thinking – and he was aware

114

of the implicit ingratitude – has his own professional drain de-blocking machine? 'All right, Martin?' he said.

'Thanks, Paul,' said Martin, smiling warily. 'And you?'

'Yeah, I'm all right.'

A manager at the West Hove Sainsbury's, Martin lives a few houses down with his wife, Eleanor. She is eight years older than he is, and his lean and youthful thinness stand in ever more tragicomic opposition to her increasing obesity and evident middle age. Wearing a blue tracksuit that had obviously been ironed, he lugged his machine into the hall, while Paul mumbled, 'Cheers, Martin. Lucky for us you've got this thing.'

'Yeah it is,' Martin said. 'Well. Should we get started?' Paul helped him move the machine into the kitchen, where the sink now took several hours to drain and the imperceptible slowness of the receding water left an unpleasant greasy scum on the stainless steel. 'Let's have a look.' Martin opened the cupboard under the sink, where the cleaning products were kept, and clearing them out, knelt on the floor's fake terracotta tiles and half crawled into the musty space. Feeling it his tiresome duty to stay there while Martin worked, Paul watched his fleshless tracksuited arse – the outline of his underpants visible – and the white soles of his trainers with unsmiling disdain. 'Got a bucket?' Martin said.

'Um, yeah.' Paul found it and put it into his waiting hand.

'I'm just going to take the U-bend out.'

'Fine.'

There was a short sloshing sound, like someone being sick. Paul lit a cigarette and looked on, bored, while Martin backed out of the cupboard, his hands black with foul-smelling sludge, and started to set up his equipment. Kneeling again, he inserted the long flexible bladed rod of his machine into the waste pipe. 'Give it a few minutes,' he said. Paul nodded. 'Do you want a beer or something, Martin?'

'No, thanks.'

'You sure? I'm going to have one.'

'Thanks.'

In silence, Paul opened the fridge and took out a can of Foster's and opened it. The disdain with which he regarded Martin was mirrored more or less exactly in Martin's opinion of him, as he looked at him now, in his dressing gown and socks, unshaved, smoking, a slob. Neither of them quite suspected the extent to which the other looked down on him – it would have seemed an Escher-like impossibility. There was some tense silence, then deciding that he had to say something, Paul said, 'Been watching the snooker, Martin?'

'Not really.'

'No? Fair enough.'

A short conversation, and neither of them even tried to pretend that he had enjoyed it. After a few moments, though, Martin seemed to feel that it was his turn to make an effort, and said, 'It's very restful, isn't it, though. The green. That's what they say.'

'Yeah, I suppose it is. I suppose it is,' said Paul. And then the silence reasserted itself until, damp-haired and dressed, Heather joined them. 'Hi, Martin,' she said, smiling widely. 'How are you? Do you want a cup of tea? Do you want a mince pie?'

Martin did want a cup of tea, and a mince pie, and a cloth to wipe his hands.

There are several hundred luxury mince pies in the house. Heather has already started to stock up on wine and champagne, brandy and port and cigars. The fridge and the freezer are overfilled, and the children are longing for objects they have seen on TV, or in the hands of envied mates at school. Their longing is clamorous, whiny, sometimes tearful. An ultra-hard sell. They have been brought up to long for objects, Paul reflects sleepily. To believe that having things brings happiness. Look around you, he thinks, holding the lighter flame to the brown hashish, turn on the TV, open a maga-zine, walk down a street – see the pictures of happy people. Paul himself is lukewarm on the subject of Christmas. It is expensive, of course – that's the whole point – and this year both his parents and Heather's are coming to Hove for the lunch. He knows that Heather has bought a new TV, an enormous flat-panel thing. It is hidden in the garden shed – he hardly ever goes in there, but he found it when he was looking for a saw. It must have cost thousands, that TV. It was covered with old blankets in a crude attempt to conceal it or keep out the damp, and at first he thought it was a piece of furniture, a massive flat-pack from IKEA. Oh well, he thinks, with weary tolerance. In two weeks it will all be over for another year. And Eddy's promised 'golden hello' should take some of the strain off the finances.

In the warm gules of Christmas-tree light, Paul crumbles the fragrant hash. Yes, the 'golden hello'. That should cover Chrimble, even if Heather seems determined to overwhelm her parents and in-laws with superfluous luxury. All the products she buys have that designation. And, it seems, anything with that designation, she buys. Questioning these arrangements would see Paul condemned – by Heather, with the tacit support of the children – as a kind of hateful Scrooge. A joyless puritan. Yes, an awful person. He knows this, and will not question them. And if he is worried about the amount of money she is spending, he probably ought not have told her that he was starting a new job at a place where they have bowls of fresh figs in the office and order in lunch from Carluccio's. For two weeks, he has been telling her that he is on the point of being deluged with lucre, and now he frowns at his own foolishness.

Briefly rubbing his fingertips across each other to remove the clinging residue of the hash, he feels, like a sudden blow, the leaden exhaustion in his head. After this spliff, he is sure, he will be able to sleep. Perhaps here on the sofa. He hates to think about what will happen at PLP in the morning – finds it almost literally unbearable to imagine. His imaginings focus on Murray. As he fashions the roach, he sees Murray arrive, take off his coat, and say something like, 'Where the fuck is everybody?' Only Sami, Nayal and

Andy are there, uneasily occupying their desks. (Richard was sacked last week.) Sami shrugs. Nayal, of course, knows what has happened, but he too shrugs, and says nothing. Andy still has that stupid smile on his face. And Murray, sensing imminent humiliation, will be enflamed, tense, aggressive. He will phone Paul. And when he finds his phone switched off – Paul has already decided to have his phone switched off all morning – he will know, somewhere inside him, he will know what has happened. But at first he will not want to believe it. He will phone several times. Leave messages, terse and shaking with horror. Or perhaps he will be too horrified, too humiliated, to leave messages. That Dave Shelley, in particular, should have been included, and not him, will seem impossible. Just too insulting, too humiliating to be true. It will take him time to understand that it *is* true. And it will be a great sensation – like a huge heist. People will flock to peer at the empty desks – somehow sinister in their sheer normality. When Paul thinks of his fellow managers in particular – of Tony Peters, Simon Beaumont and Neil Mellor – he wishes that he were able to be there to take the plaudits of their hypocrisy. And Lawrence. When he imagines Lawrence, Paul experiences pity, of all things. And a strange sort of shame. But his imagination keeps focusing on Murray – on the moment when Murray understands what has happened. What he, Paul, has done.

He has stopped making the spliff, and is simply sitting on the couch, his spine a dejected curve, his white forearms resting on his white knees. The possibility of sleep seems to have been driven away by his dwelling on these things.

He did not tell them, his six recruits, until Saturday afternoon that the move was on for tomorrow – today. He phoned them when he had finished with the tree, still out in the cold, dying garden, with wet sawdust on his shoes. His forehead was frosted with sweat. There was an excitement about it. He felt like Hannibal, or whatever his name is, in *The A-Team* – the one who loves it when a plan comes together. He had intended to phone them on his way home

118

after seeing Eddy in the Cardinal, but at Jaw's suggestion had waited until the weekend. As Eddy pointed out, if he told them on Thursday, some of them might not show up for work on Friday, which would have led to unnecessary suspicion. He licks the adhesive strip of the paper and, without finesse, rolls the joint. This done, he compacts its contents with the blunt point of a plastic chopstick kept specifically for the purpose, and twists the paper at the end. He snips off the resulting bow with a pair of nail scissors.

Though he has been doing so sporadically all weekend, he has still not entirely sifted his memories of Friday night – the Pig's birthday, and inevitably, under the circumstances, a strange occasion. Murray, in particular, had been grotesquely drunk. All afternoon in the Penderel's Oak he had been drinking determinedly and, too far gone for anything else, he kept trying to start renditions of 'Happy Birthday'. For a while people sang along, but eventually they just stopped joining in, and on the final occasion – perhaps the fifth – he found himself singing solo. Once he had started, it would have been more embarrassing to stop – that was obviously what he thought – but it was painful, unpleasant, to watch him press on alone, slurring and out of tune, in spite of the horror of the situation, which was visible in his eyes, though his mouth was still trying to smile.

Later he vomited on the floor of the toilets in the Indian. Paul saw him suddenly white out, and stagger from the table. When he sat down again, he was a more normal colour. 'That's fucking disgusting,' he said, not making eye contact with his curry. 'Someone's sicked up in the toilets. On the floor.' Everyone must have known it was him. They had all, surely, seen the urgent way he staggered to his feet, felling his chair. But the Pig was still engrossed in his food, mopping out a metal bowl with a naan, and his wife Angel, who was almost as drunk as Murray, seemed to take what he said at face value, expressing voluble, almost hysterical disgust. Andy did not seem to hear, seemed to be thinking about something else. They had been in the restaurant – a small, old-style Indian, dark, with barely audible sitar music, and a heavy, soporific atmosphere – for a long time. It seemed like hours. They were practically the only people there, and their conversation, what little there was of it, could be effortlessly overheard by the two unoccupied waiters standing near the kitchen door. The obvious weary boredom of these waiters did nothing to enliven the atmosphere. When Murray announced that 'someone' had thrown up on the floor of the Gents, Paul saw them glance at each other. Then one of them went into the toilet. A moment later he emerged, looking shaken.

Paul did not feel well himself. He felt bloated with beer and curry. No longer drunk, though not sober either. Quite downcast, in fact. To be there, at the end, with Murray and Andy, both of them oblivious to what was looming, was not what he had wanted. He wished that Murray was not so drunk. Why *was* Murray so drunk? There was something dark and miserable about his drunkenness. Andy, too, was strangely silent and withdrawn – smoking sullenly, he stared at the exit. And Paul was aware that he himself must have seemed preoccupied and morose. (It had appalled him how he had been unable, all morning in the office, to act normally – people had been asking him if he was okay.) Only the Pig and Angel seemed their ordinary selves. The Pig untalkative and indifferent, and Angel, wearing a pink T-shirt with *Angel* picked out in rhinestones, her face pockmarked, motor-mouthing on her own for minutes at a time. She had an American accent with a tangy Hispanic twist. The Pig had brought her back from the Philippines, and must – Paul thought, as she talked and talked – weigh several times more than her. What were those monstrous things he had seen on television? *Elephant seals* . . . The celebrations, the festivities, had begun hours before, in daylight, in the Penderel's Oak, and she had been drinking vodka Red Bulls since noon – at one point flirting drunkenly with Andy, sitting in his lap, unbuttoning his shirt and putting her hand inside it. This was not unusual.

Embarrassed, Andy tried to stop her, while the Pig looked on with apparent indifference.

It had been a long, smoky, beery afternoon, and Paul had not been in the mood for it. He had worked his way joylessly through the pints and a whole pack of B&H, occasionally trying to make conversation with the Pig, who showed no sign of nervousness or sentimentality in view of the fact that this was, as he must have known, the last day. The only time a melancholy note entered his voice was when he murmured, staring after his wife as she minced to the Ladies, 'She used to have an arse like a little boy.' He then told the story – which they had all already heard – of how, when she had been out visiting her family in the Philippines, he had sent her a photo of himself being fellated by her, which her father, a devout Catholic, had found. He had no way of knowing that the man in the photo was Mortished – only a central tranche of his doughy Caucasian body was shown – but even if he had known, it is unlikely to have made a difference. When he threw her out of the house (seeing her emerge from the Ladies, the Pig wraps the story up quickly, in a low voice) she returned to London, and fellated him in the toilets of the arrivals lounge at Heathrow, as she had promised she would if he met her at the airport. Andy laughed heartily and said, 'Excellent,' as though he had never heard the story before. Paul merely smiled.

Whenever he saw Michaela's little ski-jump nose – and he often turned his head to look for it – he experienced a surge of sentiment, triste and soggy. It saddened him that he would not see her any more. Sometimes it seemed to undermine the whole point of the move. It was already dark outside when he found himself facing her – he was buying a round, having to half shout to make himself heard. And he found himself telling her that he was moving on – it was madness, *madness*, Lawrence was in the pub – telling her that he was moving on and *up*, and inviting her to join him for a drink at Number One Aldwych. 'We should go for a drink sometime,

Michaela,' he was saying, trying to sound as if the idea had suddenly occurred to him, sorting through the coins in the palm of his hand. She laughed – a slightly forced, uneasy laugh. 'What about the bar at Number One Aldwych? I hear that's quite nice.'

'Yeah, I hear it is.' Her eyes were on the filling pint pot. 'Quite pricey, though, isn't it?'

He shrugged, as if to say, 'What of it?' And she laughed again – exactly the same slightly forced, uneasy laugh. 'Well?' He was not joking. She turned and stretched her key out to spring the till (the key was attached to the waist of her skirt with a tight flex like that of a phone's handset) and as she did so she dropped one of the coins. She stooped, and Paul saw a narrow ellipse of ivory skin open between her black skirt and white blouse. She seemed to be able to feel his eyes on it, and put her hand over it for a second, until she stood up. She passed him his change with a short smile, and immediately started to serve someone else. Did she not understand? he thought, manoeuvring his way through the Friday-night mob. Did she not understand that *this was it*?

Unless – he thought later, in the dripping peace of the Gents – unless of course it was *not* it. Unless he returned next week, even in the new year, pulling up in a taxi outside, entering the pub in a pinstriped suit and ordering a bottle of champagne – they keep a single bottle of Dom Perignon, he has noticed, in the window-fronted fridge under the till . . . He would be transformed then – that transformation the whole point of the move he was making – a new Paul to present to her, to take her away from this unpleasant place. And he smiled and washed his hands.

Only when they left the pub, at about eight thirty, in search of a restaurant, did the meagreness of the party become apparent. While they were still in the Penderel's Oak, and especially after five o'clock, various people had attached themselves, temporarily as it turned out, to the occasion – Simona, Neil, some members of the Pig's team whose names Paul did not know, even Lawrence – giving the impression that there would be a sizeable group going on to the meal. In the end there were only five of them. They waited for a few minutes on the pavement in front of the pub, as if expecting others to follow, but when it became obvious that this was not going to happen – Andy went in to hurry them up, and came out, still alone, shrugging and shaking his head – they wandered off. The Pig and Angel walked ahead, Paul following with Murray and Andy – forced until the very end, he thought, to live out a hypocritical show of mateyness. It was exactly what he had not wanted. They walked in silence – and Murray, Paul felt, was pointedly ignoring him. So much so that he wondered whether he knew something – had someone told him what was going to happen? Had Michaela said something? It had been stupid – so stupid – to tell her. For whatever reason, *something* seemed to have changed that day, because since the sharp exchange in the smoking room, the past two weeks had been more or less normal. 'Where the fuck are we going?' Paul muttered. Neither Murray nor Andy made any reply. They were trudging up Gray's Inn Road, trailing Angel and the Pig. Murray did not look well – though he strode with drunken assurance, his world was disconcertingly fluid. Andy was smoking a spliff, which he passed first to Murray, whose face turned noticeably paler with each inhalation, and then to Paul. The traffic poured past. Ahead of them, the others had stopped, and were waiting at the cola-coloured glass front of an isolated curry house.

Paul looked at his watch. It was quarter to eleven. They had been in the dead, velvet interior of the Indian for nearly two hours. Having finished, the Pig slowly reached into the pocket of his suit jacket, which was slung over the back of his chair, and withdrew his cigarettes. He opened the pack and extracted one, and then reached into the other pocket of his jacket for his lighter. Unhurriedly, he lit the cigarette, and savoured the grey smoke. 'Should we go then?' Paul said, twitchy with impatience. The sitar music, though almost inaudible

– or perhaps for that reason – had long been playing havoc with his fragile nerves. The Pig shook his head, and said, 'We can't.' And there was something about the way he said it – the immovable grim finality – that took Paul to the edge of panic. 'What do you mean, we *can't*?'

'We've got to wait for Jaw.'

'Eddy Jaw? Is coming here?'

'Yeah,' the Pig said.

Andy seemed to be falling asleep. Murray, too, was vacant – inscrutable with post-emetic exhaustion. Even Angel had stopped.

'When?' Paul said, moving in his seat. He had, he noticed, lit a cigarette.

'He said about eleven.'

The waiter started to go round the table, piling up plates and metal balti dishes in the crook of his arm. The Pig ordered another pint of lager, and another vodka and Coke for Angel. The waiter nodded humbly. 'And then what?' Paul said.

'And then what? What do you mean?'

'Have you got any plans for later?'

The Pig just shrugged. No doubt there would be a taxi. Eddy might have some coke. There might be pole dancing. A dark, airless, deafening club. Murray was staring with bloodshot eyes at the shadowy right angle where the floor carpet met the wall carpet, as if wanting to lie down there and sleep. 'I might go, mate,' Paul said. 'I've got to get back. You know.' Again the Pig shrugged. 'Whatever,' he said.

'Yeah, I'm gonna go.'

'You gonna leave some money then?'

'Of course.' Paul took out his wallet. 'How much is it going to be? Let's just split it. Could we have the bill please?' he called, with some urgency, to the waiter loitering by the kitchen door, who nodded and disappeared somewhere. For a few minutes, they waited in silence.

'You don't want to stay and see Jaw?' the Pig said.

Paul looked at him irritably. 'What?'

'You're not interested in seeing Eddy Jaw?'

'I've got to go, Dave.'

'All right.'

Then, a minute later, the Pig went on, 'It's just that you've not seen him in a while, I don't think. And who knows when you might have a chance to see him again.'

Why are you doing this? Paul thought. He stared at him – stared for a few moments into his mild blue eyes, trying to understand. He must surely have known that Paul would see Eddy on Monday, that he would be seeing him every day for the foreseeable future. Was this an act, then, played for the benefit of Murray? Or Andy, half asleep, his head fallen forward, his eyes taking in the grease-stained, rice-scattered tablecloth? It occurred to Paul that the Pig might *not* know that he too had been approached by Eddy Jaw. Whether he knew or not, he must suspect it – and there was something strange, knowing, not entirely innocent, about the way he had mentioned him. 'I saw him a few weeks ago,' Paul said.

'Oh, did you? Fair enough.'

The waiter approached with the lager and vodka-Coke.

'The bill, please,' Paul said firmly. He had a pressing sense of hurry, did not want to be there when Eddy arrived.

'Where'd you see him?' the Pig asked.

'Where did I see him? I saw him in the Penderel's Oak. I think you were there, weren't you?'

'When was this?' Murray said.

'Three, four weeks ago. I can't remember exactly.'

'Jaw was in the Penderel's?' The situation, Paul felt, was suddenly threatening. He thought he sensed some sort of understanding between Murray and the Pig, and told himself not to be paranoid. He was under stress. Exhausted. Irritable. Not sober. 'You know he was,' he said to Murray. 'I saw you talking to him.'

Murray shook his head. 'I don't remember. When?'

'It was the day you had that bust-up with Marlon.'

Murray did not like this being mentioned – especially as Andy, though semi-conscious, seemed to smile. Murray smiled himself, in a pained, nervous way. 'Yeah, well . . . I was fucking pissed that night,' he said. 'I don't remember much about it.'

'There's not much to remember. Jaw was there and you spoke to him. That's all.'

The waiter set the folded bill down in front of him, on a saucer with several mints. 'Thanks,' Paul said, pleased to be able to change the subject without seeming overly keen to. 'So, the damage . . .'

'He's here,' the Pig said grimly.

Paul, who was sitting with his back to the entrance, turned and saw a large figure, who had just entered, being accosted by one of the waiters, and asked if he wanted a table. He heard Eddy's loud voice saying, 'No, I'm here to meet some people.' The waiter stepped aside, and Eddy advanced over the noiseless carpet into the shadows of the interior, making for their table, which was now the only one to be occupied. 'This is a bit fucking miserable,' he said, smiling widely. 'All right, everyone? Happy birthday, Dave.' The Pig nodded in acknowledgement of this, and Eddy made a great show of kissing Angel's hand, while she tittered. Then he turned to Paul. 'All right, Rainey? Last time I saw you, you were so pissed you could hardly stand up. You were leaning against the wall of a fucking toilet drooling down your front. I hope it was drool.'

'All right, Eddy?' Paul said. 'How you keeping?'

'Very well. And you?'

'Yeah, not bad . . .' Eddy was not listening to him. He had placed a large hand on Murray's suited shoulder and was saying, in a way that suggested he hadn't seen him for years, 'Murray Dundee – how the fuck are you?'

Murray, who had always been intimidated by Eddy Jaw, seemed unwilling to look him in the eye, and said, 'Yeah, I'm well, Eddy. Well. Not bad. And you?'

'I just said. I'm very well.' He extended a hand to Andy. 'I'm Eddy,' he said. 'Which of these losers do you work for?'

Andy shook his hand, and then pointed at Paul, saying, 'That one.'

And everyone laughed.

In the sombre rose of the Christmas-tree light, the hour approaching four, Paul sparks the spliff he has made. He had left, hurried out of there, said he had to get the last train. And the others – Murray, Andy, Eddy, the Pig and Angel – the others had piled into a black cab on the Gray's Inn Road. The goodbyes had thus been rushed. And they were all the wrong way round. With Eddy, who he would see on Monday, it was a sincere 'Yeah, good to see you, mate, hope to see you again sometime, stay in touch'. And with Andy and Murray, who he might well never see again, 'See you Monday, lads.'

'See you, Paul,' Murray had shouted, as he entered the taxi. His voice was insouciant – why would it not be? Then, however, from the back of the cab, through the window as the others were getting in, he had shot Paul a strange look. Several times over the weekend Paul has revisited that look. And as the inhaled smoke starts to soften and seduce the part of his mind that has been so intransigently resisting sleep, he does so again. At first it seemed straightforwardly accusatory. Angry. Then he thought that there might have been sorrow in it too. And, most strangely – he has been thinking about it all weekend – unless he is mistaken, a trace of pity. It lasted only a moment. Then the shivering taxi was gone, and he walked alone down to Chancery Lane. To part like that was sad. To part like that from a friend . . . What did that say about him? He shied away from the question. Anyway, he and Murray were not *really* friends. Not really. Still, to part like that was sad. And it occurred to him that there were, perhaps, people who had proper friendships – not ones that were provisional, insubstantial, illusory – and who would not do what he had done not because they had such friendships, but had such friendships because they would not do what he had done. He was feeling quite depressed.

The effect of the spliff seems to make his whole being vibrate slightly. He wonders if Eddy might have told Murray, yelling in the pandemonium of some club, what was going to happen on Monday. Today. Drunk, after a line or two of coke, he might have told him. Paul hopes that he did. It would spare him the worst. The desire to lie down, to sleep is becoming overpowering. He struggles to finish the spliff. It is pathetic – he thinks – how unnatural he was in Eddy's presence on Friday. He is useless at subterfuge. And there had been something odd about Murray too. Preoccupied with his own performance, he had not noticed it at the time. As he stubs out the unfinished spliff, however, he has a distant, unsettling sense of this oddity, but it is lost in dark, swirling clouds, and seems unreal.

9

Alcohol drinks as a way of life started for Paul, he supposes, in the Northwood days. Simon was a serious drinker. They would get drunk at lunchtime every day, and then go back to the Cheshire Cheese after work. That the pub was so quaint made it seem unserious somehow. And everything was going well – money was being made – the boozing was exuberant, not morose. Now, when he is sober, there is always a sense that he is waiting for something.

Walking out of Delmar Morgan, Paul's first thought had been of alcohol drinks. It was eleven, and the pubs had just opened. In truth, part of him had started thinking of alcohol drinks the moment Eddy had said, 'There isn't a job for you here, Paul.' And a part of him had – if he is honest – even been *pleased* to hear those words. He had immediately felt licensed, permitted, almost obliged, to go out and drink until he was very drunk. There was nothing to stop him doing that anyway, of course – he had money – but he was not the sort of uninhibited alcoholic who pours a beer, or mixes a Bloody Mary, first thing in the morning. He did not have – as George Best is said to have had – a wine bar by his bed, so that waking in the middle of the night (probably still in his clothes, lights burning silently all over the house) he could top up his blood-alcohol level before passing out again. Paul's alcoholism still operated within limits – very substantial limits – but limits nonetheless, and to exceed them he had to have, he himself insisted on this scrupulously, a *reason*. Of course, he could always find a reason – and he always did –

but it was nevertheless a sort of luxury to have a *real* reason; and terrible misfortunes, disasters, vicious setbacks and disappointments, were superbly fit for purpose. His shock and humiliation, his stunned sense of collapse as he walked down Victoria Street, were entirely unfeigned. His legs were trembling under him. He felt awful, weepy, as if he'd been beaten up, and he entered the first pub he saw, which was the Albert.

'There isn't a job for you here, Paul.'

All he had said then, lamely, was, 'You're joking.'

'No.'

There was an awful silence. Then Paul said, 'I don't understand.'

'What don't you understand?'

'What do you mean there isn't a job for me?'

'I mean – there isn't a job for you.'

He had stared at Eddy for some time, simply unable to believe the turn that things had taken. And surprisingly, he found himself thinking of a sexual fantasy which Eddy was said to have often played out with Kim – the Pig had told him about it – in which he would pretend to be 'a whole rugby team'. How, Paul had always wondered – and, for a few moments, he wondered again – does one man pretend to be 'a whole rugby team'? And he was thinking of this – involuntarily, it just popped into his mind – as he stared at Eddy with persistent disbelief.

'I'm sorry,' Eddy said, eventually.

Though it was the pivotal point of these events, Paul remembers little of what was said in Eddy's office. The earlier part of the morning, however, he remembers well. It had been his intention to take the seven forty train from Hove, which would have got him to Victoria at eight forty-eight. As it was he had come to consciousness, sunk in the seat cushions of the sofa, on the unfamiliar fabric, at about seven thirty. At first he thought it was still the middle of the night – the wide silence, the darkness (except for the glowing Christmas-tree lights) and the steady, intense, sleep-deprived ache in his own head all told him that it was. Then he heard the radio start, overcheerful as always, but this morning horribly, insanely so – the gabbling DJ actually seemed *insane* – and lifting his head, he saw through the ajar door that the lights in the kitchen were on. Heather was in there, moving around. It must have been her arrival downstairs that had woken him. Sitting up in numb agony, he listened to the blood singing in his ears.

He missed the eight eleven by a few minutes. The next train was not until eight fifty-five. He might have tried to get the eight forty-four from Brighton, via Haywards Heath, Gatwick Airport, East Croydon and Clapham Junction, getting in to Victoria at nine forty-three, but he did not understand what the well-meaning Network Rail employee was saying to him. In a state that might be described as 'static hysteria', he stared at her through the thick plastic of her window, hearing but not comprehending her conscientious, electronically mediated voice. That he had to wait for forty minutes seemed especially vindictive. He had showered, shaved and dressed – hardly able to master his tie – in frantic haste. With wild-eyed emergency, he had commandeered Heather, still in her dressing gown, to drive him to the station. And there he waited, singeing his mouth on an overpriced coffee, sitting on a red metal bench.

At nine twenty-three the train left Gatwick Airport, and while it was somewhere between there and East Croydon – travelling through a landscape that seemed confused about its own identity, the closes and shopping centres plonked down in ploughed fields, the dormitory towns overspilling their valleys – Murray would have arrived at Park Lane Publications. Certainly, by the time the train stopped at the expansive platforms of Clapham Junction, at nine forty-nine, the scene that Paul had spent the weekend imagining would have started to play itself out. He looked at his mute, unpowered phone. There would be missed calls from Murray. From Lawrence enraged howls, tirades of horrid abuse. He would have to listen to them later. He felt slightly sick, as the train stood in Clapham, to think of what was happening in Holborn. The train was moving on, through the roofy chaos of south London, through Battersea, past the late-autumn trees of the park, trundling over the river where it curves by the disused power station with its four cream chimneys. It was exactly ten when it wheezed to a halt alongside the platform at Victoria. The station was so much more pleasant, he thought, in a moment of flat tranquillity as he crossed the spacious concourse under the cast-iron mock-Gothic of its translucent vault, than London Bridge or Blackfriars. Of course, normally he would be there earlier, in the thick of the rush hour. He was very late, and hurried through the streets, agitation and exhaustion wrestling in him to set the overall tone.

He wished he was looking better. In the lift, on the way up, he surveyed himself in the mirror. His hair, short, greying and parted in the middle, was somewhat fluffy. His skin waxy and inhomogeneous. His eyes set in deep empurpled recesses. And a zit or a cold sore was starting to appear at one end of his lipless mouth. He is used to receiving discouraging news from his reflection, but this was very bad – the awful night heavily imprinted in his face. Installed on the cream leather of a Mies van der Rohe chair, screened by the orange-pink expanse of an unfurled *FT* – he had been appalled by his inability to understand *anything* of the newspaper's text, until he realised, after a few moments, that it was in *German*, an edition of *FT Deutschland* – he tried to prepare himself for his meeting with Eddy Jaw. When he had announced himself to Gwyn – 'I'm here to see Mr Feltman. I'm a bit late. Paul Rainey' – she had looked at him sceptically, and phoned through. She herself was extraordinarily healthy-looking, the skin of her face flawless and rosy, her green eyes shining as if polished, her black hair taut, with a surface like watered silk. She looked, Paul thought, like something out of

132

an advert. 'Mr Rainey's here,' she said quietly. When Eddy had finished speaking she put down the phone. 'Mr Feltman's busy just at the moment,' she said. 'He'll be with you as soon as he can. If you'd like to wait here.'

'Thanks,' Paul said, though something went wrong with his throat, and almost no sound emerged.

'That's okay.' He did not like the smidgen of pity he thought he saw in her smile. And he sat down, and hid himself behind *FT Deutschland* in shame. After a few minutes, he lowered it. There was no ashtray on the table in front of him. 'Um, I'm just nipping out for a smoke,' he said hoarsely. 'I'll be back in a minute. If Mr Feltman . . .'

Gwyn nodded, but did not speak.

Outside on the pavement there was a little hollow pillar, waist-high, for cigarette butts, and he stood next to it, in the traffic noise, smoking and trying to pull himself together. Movement, the struggle to get there, had to some extent distracted him from the fact that he was in a truly terrible state, and sitting behind the German newspaper, he had felt himself quite quickly falling apart. He had thought he might have to be sick, but that had passed. He definitely needed to get out of there though. To move, to get some fresh air into his frowzy, hurting head. He looked at his watch – it was ten thirty.

When he stepped from the lift, Gwyn said, 'Mr Feltman was here a minute ago. I told him you'd just popped out.'

'Oh. Er. What did he . . . say?'

'He said he'll be back in a few minutes.'

'Okay then.'

Paul sat down wearily on the leather seat and waited. He was sweating – waves of grimy sweat oozing from his scalp, his fore-head, the backs of his hands. His clothes, fresh that morning, seemed stale and smelly. A day that had begun with such intemperate speed had turned into a day of endless, stupefying waiting.

He had just picked up *The Times* – though he had no interest, none at all, in what it might say – when the door opened and Eddy came in, not wearing a jacket, his torso sheathed in a long waistcoat with stubby lapels, his shirtsleeves full and blouson. His trousers were in the same mild plaid fabric as the waist-coat. He seemed to have had a haircut since Friday, a severe crew cut that emphasised the fleshiness of his face. To Paul's surprise, he did not seem at all angry. In fact he was smiling. For a moment he looked at Paul, as if sizing him up – there was something odd about this look – then he said, 'Paul, mate. Step this way.'

'Sorry I'm late, Eddy,' Paul started gruffly, getting to his feet.

'Don't worry about it.'

'I am sorry.'

They went through the door – Eddy, the perfect gentleman, letting Paul precede him with a tight smile. The sales floor on the other side was very large, very open, very light, the walls on two sides being floor-to-ceiling glass; nevertheless it was a sales floor like all the others that Paul had worked on. Eddy led him through the hubbub of pitches. The atmosphere was perhaps more serious, more focused than at PLP, the suits perhaps, on average, slightly smarter, but essentially it was the same. The same scrawled-on whiteboards, the same messy work surfaces, the same dog-eared directories of leads. And Paul experienced a sinking of his spirit, a sort of tired sigh, seeing it all.

Eddy held open the pale oak door of his office. 'Come in,' he said. His manner had altered markedly. He seemed tense. One of the walls of his office, the one opposite the door, was glass, but the room was not particularly light because it faced, at close quarters, the blind side of another building. It was huge, though, with a dark, corporate three-piece suite in one corner, a massive desk, a smaller desk with two computers on it, one of them switched on, a screen saver frantically scribbling. There was a widescreen TV. Photos of Eddy's children in silver frames. An old-fashioned hatstand on which his raincoat and jacket hung. On the desk was a little sign which Paul, waiting to be invited to sit, leaned in to read. It said: *If you don't smoke I won't fart.* He smiled. Eddy moved round the desk to his black leather throne. 'Have a seat,' he said tersely. He was obviously nervous about something.

'So . . . ?' Paul tried to sound upbeat.

Eddy looked at him. The look seemed furious, and Paul did not understand why. He shook his head. 'What is it?'

What happened next, exactly, he does not remember. Eddy may have said, 'I've got bad news for you, Paul.' He does remember that among the objects on Eddy's desk was a miniature bronze cannon – chosen for its resemblance to the one on Michael Corleone's desk in *The Godfather Part II* – and that Eddy was holding it, as if trying to draw strength from the cold brown metal. He put it down. 'Sorry,' he said. 'Really. I'm sorry, Paul.'

'You're sorry?'

'I am.' Eddy had picked up the cannon again.

'Why? What are you talking about?'

Petulantly, as if irritated with him for not having heard what he seemed unable to say, Eddy said, 'For fuck's sake, Paul, why would we want you here?'

Paul only restated the question, as if he had not understood it. 'Why would you want me here?' he said.

'*Yes.*'

He shook his head. 'I don't know.'

Eddy laughed, horribly. 'No, I don't know either. Look, Paul . . .' he said, but then stopped, leaning forward, and laughed again – or was it a sigh? – in the same quiet way, as if helpless, shaking his head and lowering his eyes.

'What's funny?'

'Nothing.' Eddy's face was suddenly serious, but a persistent smile still seemed to be trying to force its way in, through his lips. 'Nothing's funny,' he said. 'It's really not funny at all.'

'What isn't?'

'This. This situation.'

'What situation?'

'*This* situation. This situation in which we find ourselves.'

'What is that?'

'There isn't a job for you here, Paul.'

'You're joking.'

'No.'

And Paul remembers asking, 'Why isn't there a job for me?' His voice was quiet, level, slightly hoarse.

'Look at you!' Eddy was saying. 'You look terrible. Probably up all night drinking.' With a pained sense of injustice, Paul silently objected to this, shook his head – he had specifically *not* been drinking the night before. 'You show up an hour and a half late! I'm trying to run a serious business. You're a mess. All over the place. A fucking alcoholic. I don't need that here. You've got to try and sort yourself out. I mean it.'

'Look, I'm sorry I was late,' Paul said. His face was suffused with embarrassed, submissive heat. The situation was hellish, bewildering – far worse than any envisaged worst-case scenario. 'Are you sacking me because I was late?' he asked – the question straightforward, humble and seemingly without anger. It was Eddy who seemed angry. 'No I'm not sacking you because you were late!' he shouted. 'I'm not *sacking* you. You never had a job here.'

Seeming slow and stupid in his shock, Paul said, 'I don't understand.'

Eddy had not wanted Paul to come to the office. He had left a message on his phone soon after eight o'clock telling him so – an awkward, peremptory message (he had intended to leave it on Sunday but had procrastinated) telling him that the job had 'fallen through'. He understood that Paul must be in shock, and even found himself feeling sorry for him. 'Look, Paul,' he said, after a long pause, his tone suddenly softer, 'this wasn't really my idea.'

'Whose idea was it?'

Eddy waited, as if wondering whether to say. Then he said, 'It was Dundee's.'

'Murray's?'

'Yes.'

'What do you mean?' Paul seemed puzzled.

'Murray's going to come and work here. He'll be looking after the people you recruited.'

'Murray's going to work here?'

'That's right.'

'And the people I recruited?'

'Yes, if they're good enough.'

Paul does not remember what he felt on hearing this. Probably nothing. The situation had already numbed him.

He remembers Eddy saying, in answer to some question he had asked, 'He said he couldn't. He thinks they don't like him. He said they liked you. If you recruited them, there'd be a better chance they'd come. That's what he said. And he said if *he* approached them, they'd probably talk to you.'

'Murray approached *you*?'

'Not really. I just bumped into him . . .'

'That night in the Penderel's?'

'In that pub, yeah.'

When he asked why it had been necessary to *exclude* Murray, Eddy said that it was because Murray had wanted to know whether Paul *would* exclude him. If he wouldn't, Eddy said, the whole thing would not have happened. Murray would only do it, so he said, if he first saw that Paul would be willing to do the same to him.

137

'Murray's very upset, actually,' Eddy said. 'He feels like you've stabbed him in the back.'

'*I've* stabbed *him* in the back?'

'That's what he feels.'

The conversation ended with Paul saying, matter-of-factly, 'I need a fag.' Eddy just nodded, grim but sympathetic, as if he, an ex-smoker, understood. As he got up to leave, it was not clear in Paul's mind that this was it, that he would not be coming back to Eddy's office after his cigarette to continue their chat. But as soon as he was on the noisy sales floor – Eddy did not follow him out – it was obvious that there would be no reason to return. Eddy would certainly not expect him to – there was nothing more to be said, and that solemn nod, it was now clear, had been his way of saying goodbye.

Only on the pavement did things seem lifelike again. He was shaking, and unable to remember much of what had been said in Eddy's office. Without thinking where he was going, he started to walk. It had all been done to secure PLP's contracts, Eddy had said. He said that he had been negotiating with the various contractors for a while – if PLP did not make target on them they were going to withdraw them. 'And they're not going to make target now, are they?' he had said, unable to hide his exultation. 'Half the fucking company's just walked out.'

Amid the Albert's faded Victoriana, fortified by a drink or two, Paul turned his phone on. There were three messages – not as many as he had expected. The first was from Eddy. He sounded embarrassed, fumbling, as he explained that the job had 'unfortunately fallen through'. The next message, from Lawrence, made it very plain that if Paul had been thinking of a return to PLP, he would not be welcome. It was unpleasant, especially today, after what had happened – and moreover in a fervent, suggestible, sleep-deprived state – to hear such a message, to get such an earful of poisonous hatred, to know that someone out there really *hated* you. The final message, which he had expected to be from Murray, was Lawrence again. More of the same. There *was* no message from Murray. He had not even tried to call, and it was this, more than anything, that seemed to verify – though Paul had never actually doubted it – what Eddy had said. Suddenly he felt very low.

He started to smoulder when he thought of his performance in Eddy's office. How pathetic he must have seemed, sitting there, putting quiet, polite questions, seeming to take what had happened as if it were simply his due. He did not understand *why* he had acted like that. Why had he not shouted, smashed, hit? And as if to make up for it, he imagined himself – silently, as he sat in the Albert – he imagined himself trashing Eddy's commodious, battleship-grey office. And then, when Eddy tries to stop him, he transfers the violence – more fantastically – to Eddy himself, hitting him, unleashing on him a wild savagery of infinite strength. He snapped out of this only when a member of the pub staff, entering his field of vision, said, 'Excuse me', and emptied the ashtray. Lighting another cigarette, he was ashamed of his fantasy. Not of the fantasy per se. Not at all. What he was ashamed of was the vast discrepancy between *it* and what he had actually done. And if he pretended, for a moment, to think that he might go back and mete out some real violence, he was still undrunk enough to see, from the start, that that was simply not going to happen. Instead, he meandered to the bar and asked for another pint of lager.

While he was waiting, he noticed a Chelsea pensioner, sitting on his own with a thrifty half. There is a man, he thought, who has probably known mortal danger, machine-gun fire, shelling. Who has waded ashore past the bobbing dead bodies of his friends, into a storm of bullets and explosions and seemingly endless barbed wire, and slithered up an open beach towards thousands of heavily armed men whose only implacable aim was to kill him. How would *he* have reacted to what had happened to Paul? With immediate surrender, as Paul had? *With polite questions?* It seemed unlikely.

Had he punched Eddy in the face (and quite possibly Eddy would have punched him back, much harder – that didn't matter), had he punched Eddy in the face he would undoubtedly have been feeling less venomous and self-pitying now, even nursing a flattened nose. But perhaps the pensioner, he thought, still waiting for his pint, perhaps the pensioner would talk about violence never being the answer – these pensioners often did, in TV interviews. When they said that, though, they meant wars, surely, not smacking a man in the face who had purposely wrecked your life with lies. The set of the old man's mouth, his hard eyes on either side of his great nose, were not such as would lead anyone to believe he was against *that* sort of violence. As a sergeant (he still wore the three stripes on his soft, scarlet sleeve) he must have dealt out plenty himself, in feral bars from Portsmouth to Singapore.

It made Paul sick to think how Jaw had spoken of Murray as if he were some kind of saint. He *knew* Murray. Paul thought of a seagull swallowing a hatchling duck alive, gulping it down, its eye a staring orange horror. And a fresh sense of injustice flooded him with silent fury. He had been drinking for a few hours, and in a fierce mood he suddenly stumbled on a sense of pure righteous-ness – everything else, he felt sure, was just sophistry – nothing more than ploys to lure him into a moral murk, where everyone was equally sullied. The truly sullied always tried to do that. In fact, it was simple – he had been wronged, lied to, tricked into professional suicide in someone else's selfish interests. That was what had happened. And Murray, supposedly his friend, had been fully involved. Impulsively, he tried for the first time to phone him. Murray's mobile, though, was switched off. 'Hello,' the familiar, nasal voice intoned, 'this is Murray Dundee. I cannot take your call at the present time. Because I'm busy. Please leave a message. Er. Cheerio.' The high-pitched note invited Paul to speak, but he did not. He realised that he had nothing to say. Unlike Lawrence, his fury seemed insufficient to sustain such a one-sided showdown.

What he had wanted was to hear Murray's voice – to listen for the guilt. Murray had always been bitter about working for him, his former protégé. Bitter, bitter, bitter. He had worked for Paul at Park Lane Publications for two years. Had he spent *all* that time plotting something like this? Waiting for an opportunity like this? It was entirely possible. Murray, let us not forget, is a shit.

Paul noticed that it was two o'clock – the time he had told the others to arrive at Delmar Morgan. Vengefully, he imagined intercepting them outside, telling them that the whole thing had 'unfortunately fallen through' . . . But it was too late for that. By the time he got there it would be five, ten past. They would already be in a meeting room with Eddy Jaw, being told that unfortunately he, Paul, would not be joining them. Essentially, he thought, settling in his chair, in some ways pleased that it was too late, essentially it had been a *coup d'état* – after Christmas they would start work on the new, June edition of *European Procurement Management*, but instead of Paul, Murray would be managing the team. That was all that would really have changed – everything else, from Murray's point of view, if not Eddy's, was just mechanics. And what would the salespeople make of it, the overthrow of their erstwhile manager? Would they mourn? He found it difficult to think that they would. Would they even pity him? Probably not. They would be surprised, then shrug, and start their new jobs. What else can the little people do? They have their own livelihoods to worry about. Only Elvezia, perhaps, would spare him another thought. Secretly, silently, she might give him a single sad, pitying thought. They had worked together for several years, and got on quite well. He had once asked her to help him find a birthday present for Marie – he had had no idea what to get – and they had gone to Superdrug and picked out some sparkly hair clips for her. She had been delighted with them.

And would *Murray* be in that meeting room? Stationed up by the flip chart, sitting with his arms folded in his shapeless suit? Of course he would. *That* would take them by surprise, to see him sitting there – their new manager! He knew for a fact that they all disliked him. What would *Marlon* make of it, for instance? The thought led Paul to laugh out loud in the sun-filled pub. And Wolé, Elvezia – neither of them could stand Dundee. There would be dismay when they saw him sitting there, with that frozen smile on his grey face, squinting at them, unable to hide his nervous tension. He was not a likeable person, the Croc. And the salespeople, Paul thought, would hold him in contempt. Would they refuse to work for him? Not immediately. But they would soon be restive, resentful, openly disrespectful. Marlon would simply not be able to stomach Murray in a position of authority for long. And he would fall, like many another usurper, to popular anger, hung up by the heels, his face pissed on. Eddy would soon understand what a mistake he had made. With deep satisfaction, Paul lit a cigarette. No, Eddy would not be pleased with Murray's performance. He had been sold a pup, and he would soon realise it.

Well, good luck to them! Paul thought with joyful spite. *He* was out of it. And he felt a punch of elation. Yes, he was out of it. Out of the whole thing forever. He thought of the sinking feeling, the terrible obscure disappointment that he had experienced walking onto the sales floor in the morning, when he still thought that he would be working there. The sense of liberation was exquisite and heady. Time and space – the afternoon, the city's thoroughfares – suddenly seemed opened to him. *His*. Wonderful. He stood and went to the bar. Standing in the pub's warm mid-afternoon stillness – he and the Chelsea pensioner were the only ones there – he was almost euphoric.

10

Geoff Rainey, a heavy, saturnine man, stands alone in the lounge, holding a flute of effervescing champagne. He looks tired. For many years he worked for ICI, in the end managing a small plant in Buckinghamshire where nylon thread was manufactured. When it shut, it was difficult for him to find work, as a fifty-four-year-old with no experience of anything other than the textile industry, and for a decade now he has been a coach driver – mostly ferrying public schoolboys to and from sports matches and the theatre in Stratford-upon-Avon. Waiting in the hot coach, with his sleeves rolled up and his tie loosened, while the moneyed teenagers sit through *King Lear*, he eats his packed sandwiches, shaking the crumbs out of the Tupperware when he is finished, and reads the paper, or – for the last year or two – works on his poems. (One, 'Sanatorium', has been published in the *Bucks Advertiser*. Angela is threatening to read it out after lunch.) In two years, the mortgage will be paid off, and he will take the coach back to the depot in Aylesbury for the last time. From then on in, his ICI pension should suffice. He hears his wife's loud voice on the stairs with Paul. Paul – as Geoff noticed when he opened the front door – looks tired and pale. He does not look well. Nor does he put much effort into the pretence that he is actually listening to what his mother is saying – an occasional nod or listless 'Oh' being the sum of it. When, a few minutes later, she stops speaking for a moment to take a sip of champagne, Geoff says, 'So how are you, Paul? All right?'

'Yeah, I'm well,' Paul says. His mother smiles, her mouth drawn back from her long pink gums. She is a short woman, with a large head. Ever since the winter of his 'crack-up', questions such as 'How are you?' have become unpleasantly loaded – inescapably mementoes of that dark guilt-sodden episode, never openly spoken of – and to neutralise this they are put by his parents, especially his father, as now, in an exaggeratedly offhand tone. They still have a strange, spiky intensity. 'Everything okay at work?' Geoff follows up, his eyes fixed on the overdecorated Christmas tree, sadly lost under the weight of tinsel and empty boxes wrapped in gold paper and baubles. Under it there is a drift of presents, and standing apart – far too large to fit under the tree – a substantial oblong in shiny blue paper. On first entering, everyone notices this object, and wonders what it is.

'M-hm,' Paul says. 'Um, I'll just get the bubbly.'

Flushed with heat, sweating, Heather is heaving the huge half-cooked turkey from the oven. Paul smiles tensely, and opening the fridge, faces a wall of food. He stares at it for a few moments, in no hurry to return to the lounge. He has told no one, not even Heather, what happened. For a whole week, every morning at the usual time, she took him to the station. On Tuesday and Wednesday he actually went to London (Blackfriars, not Victoria) and spent the day in pubs there – indulging in a maudlin orgy of nostalgia and self-pity. On Thursday, he only got as far as Croydon, and on Friday he spent the morning at Gatwick Airport, boozing in the Red Lion, the pub-by-numbers in the departures area, before passing the afternoon in Three Bridges, mostly in the Snooty Fox. When Heather asked him about his new job, he was vague, but said it was going well. Unable to sleep, he spent much of the night smoking spliffs in the lounge. And in the morning had to haul himself out of bed and put on an otiose suit.

His thoughts turned uneasily to a news story he had once seen. It was set in France, and was about a man whose wife and children were under the impression that he was an eminent surgeon, when in fact he was unemployed and had no medical training whatsoever. And how had that situation started? Had he simply lied to a woman in a bar to impress her, and then, when they saw each other again, and started to go out, and later got married and had children, never told her the truth, found that it was too late to stop lying, just not possible because the lie was now an integral part of the very foundation of his life? He kept up the pretence for years, and in the end, when for some reason – probably something to do with money – it could no longer be sustained, he found it easier to kill his family, and then himself, than to admit the truth to them. Thus an apparently insignificant fib – perhaps even meant, in the first instance, as a joke, not intended to be taken seriously – ended in quadruple murder, in infanticide.

With the cold green champagne bottle, Paul returns to the lounge. He understands with unpleasant immediacy how a situation like that might turn into a living nightmare. When he got home on Monday, half sobered-up, and Heather asked him how his first day in the new job had gone, he hesitated for a moment. Then he smiled, and said, 'Fine.' He had not decided to hide what had happened from her. He had not decided anything. In that infinitesimal moment of hesitation things might have fallen either way. As it happened, they fell the way they did, and in just one week he has piled lies on lies – it is terrible the way they are proliferating. He has found it more and more difficult to keep track of them, to keep them in line. But at every point – and this was the truly pernicious thing – it was, in the short term, much easier to maintain the pretence than to admit the truth. Had it been thus for the unfortunate, foolish Frenchman? What extraordinary lengths he must have gone to to maintain the illusion. And how awful those years of pretence must have been for him. Paul remembers reading that while his family thought he was at work, the man simply spent all day sitting in his car. He did that every day for *years*. Sitting in his car. The stress of it. The boredom. The sense of waste. Of entrapment. A weird pretend life. And then, for everyone, death.

'Well, merry Christmas,' Paul says, with a wry, lopsided smile. Angela holds out her glass to be refilled. Her white hand is hard and fleshless. There are stony rings on some of her fingers. 'Thanks, darling,' she says.

Everything in the house has been altered in honour of the season. Even the windowpanes have had their corners sprayed white to suggest snow, though outside it is quite warm and grey and damp. And where did the money come from? (He is still thinking about the Frenchman, while his mother talks.) That was never properly explained. Perhaps an inheritance. Or stolen. Most probably just mountains of debt. And as has happened frequently over the past week, Paul suddenly sees with tilting vertiginous terror the depth of his own financial emergency. Most of the time, he is able to ignore it, but more and more frequently he is experiencing these moments of vertigo. When he does, his face becomes totally expressionless. 'What is it?' his mother asks worriedly. She must be worried – she was in the middle of telling him about Patrick's new angora rabbit. 'Oh, nothing,' he says, smiling. She looks at him for a moment, and then, full of tedious zest, and as though nothing has happened, keeps telling him about Patrick's rabbit. Patrick is a favourite of hers, a neighbour in Amersham, 'openly gay' – always the first thing she tells anyone about him. She is demonstrating how the rabbit wiggles its nose, while Geoff looks on impassively, holding his champagne. Paul's smile is starting to get sore. He is trying to work out when, exactly, he will run out of money, when overdraft limits and credit-card limits will be hit, and how he will pay the January rent.

He notices that his mother's mood has changed. She seems tetchy, and he listens for a moment. 'There's just not much in it compared to before,' she is saying. 'And if the local press aren't providing local news, where else are we going to find out what's going on around us? This week they didn't even print the Amersham Community

Voice column. *Or* Little Chalfont. It's all about Wycombe. Apparently, the head office for the *Advertiser* is in Uxbridge, which is why there's so many adverts for the Uxbridge shops, but since they joined forces, there's been sweet Fanny Adams about Amersham . . .'

'There is an Amersham edition,' Geoff mutters impatiently.

'Yes but it's usually exactly the same! Only the front page is different. Sometimes. And not *very* different.'

Geoff shrugs and turns his old rugby-player's head to the window. Someone is parking in the street outside.

Mike and Joan look nervous. Their jollity is a little tense and over-played. Mike is wearing a Father Christmas hat. When Angela sees it she smiles snowily. She and Geoff have never met Mike and Joan, and Paul makes the introductions while Heather goes to get the children, who are upstairs. The men shake hands warily. Fleetingly, the woman kiss each other. It then takes about five minutes for the Willisons to unload their presents, Joan taking out the wrapped parcels and handing them to Mike, who squats by the tree, placing them on the papery pile already there. Paul notices his parents look at each other in alarm when Joan takes out a bottle-shaped thing and, handing it to Mike who is waiting impatiently, says, 'And this is for, um . . . Geoff.' Angela, flushed and agitated, whispers something to her husband, who touches his tonsure and purses his lips. Paul says he is going to get more champagne. In the kitchen, he lights a cigarette and starts to remove the heavy foil from the next bottle. His hands are shaking. He does not feel well. When he returns to the lounge, his mother is speaking, everyone else listening in silence. 'And it's because all the reporters, I think there are four of them, work out of Chalfont St Peter or Uxbridge. Not a single one in Amersham . . .' That she is nervous is obvious from the speed and volume of her voice, and the flushed points in her slack cheeks. Joan and Mike look tired. His father, Paul notices, keeps glancing at Joan, who is listening with a patient, though increasingly strained, smile. Mike, if he was smiling before, has stopped. Seeing Paul come in with the bottle, though, he perks up. 'All right, Paul?' he says. 'How's tricks?'

'Very well, thanks, Mike. Very well. Champagne?'

'I think I need a refill, darling,' Angela says.

Mike stands aside. 'Ladies first.'

'Of course.'

'Have you got an ashtray somewhere, Paul?' Joan asks, holding an unlit cigarette, her forehead furrowing apologetically. 'Sure, I'll just get you one.' He sets the bottle down, happy to be able to leave the room again. As he leaves, he hears his father and Mike tentatively start talking about the traffic.

They do not sit down to lunch until two thirty, and everyone is quite tipsy when the order finally comes to move to the table, which is lost under silver-sprayed pine cones, candles, and a twinkling mass of polished cutlery and glass. Smoked salmon and cold toast, posh-looking white wine and some sort of dill sauce are slowly ferried out. Heather sits down last, at the head of the table, flushed with heat and alcohol, and dabs her brow with one of the new linen napkins. Mike, who is sitting next to her, pours her some wine. 'Thanks,' she says, and takes a quick sip. 'Mm!' She seems pleasantly surprised. 'Merry Christmas, everyone.'

There is something slightly insane about the way that Angela is still talking about the *Bucks Advertiser*. 'Since they joined forces,' she's saying, 'there's been less and less about Amersham every week. I can't believe nothing's happening. It's that the paper only has satellite offices now. They've closed the old offices, and that's because they're only interested in advertising revenue, rather than local news ...' Paul helps Heather take out the small starter plates and washes the wine glasses. It is obvious that his mother and Mike hate each other. When he returns to the table, she is wearing her half-moons and holding a piece scissored out of a newspaper – a letter to the *Bucks*

Advertiser. 'I have a friend who is a journalist on the south coast,' she is saying, 'who once had someone complain to her about their event not being covered. When she asked them who they had contacted at the paper, the person complaining admitted they hadn't told anyone ...'

'Paul, where's the toilet, mate?' Mike says loudly, standing up.

'My friend jokes people think she has a crystal ball on her desk,' Angela presses on, markedly increasing the volume of her voice. 'Considering the amount of stuff which appears in the papers, I'm sure the *Advertiser*'s quartet of reporters put a lot of work in and find out what they can and then tell us the readers.' She is almost shouting now. 'But why assume, just because you know something, that they have been told, or would know. Yes, they're supposed to inform the masses, but someone has to tell them first. Or maybe someone knows a repairman who can fix their crystal ball?' She laughs delightedly.

Joan, too, politely laughs.

'Haven't we heard enough about the *Advertiser*, Mum?' Paul says.

She ignores this, but the atmosphere is momentarily icy.

Joan says, 'I sometimes read the *Hounslow Chronicle*.'

'Oh, don't you start!' Mike says, standing in the doorway. Then he laughs, to pretend that he was joking.

'Do you need any help, darling?' Angela asks Paul, putting a hand on his arm. 'No, I think it's all right actually,' he says.

'Are you sure?'

'I'll ask Heather.'

'Let me know if you need help carving the bird!' Mike shouts after him as he leaves.

Heather is in the kitchen. She looks upset. She says, 'I think it needs another ten minutes. At least. It's still a bit pink inside.'

'That's okay. Why don't you go in there? I'll keep an eye on it.'

'I don't want to go in there,' she whispers, laughing.

'Where are the kids?'

149

'Upstairs.'

Paul opens the door and steps out. It is wonderfully still outside. An empty Christmas silence hangs over all the dead gardens. Though no yuleophile, Paul normally has no problem with Christmas. He is usually able to take it for what it is – which is, for him, primarily a sort of obligation to drink more than usual. This year, though, he has felt oppressed by it – by the unending hysterical imprecation to purchase things; by the tired, insincere imagery of snow and reindeer and holly (none of which he ever sees in real life); by the empty jauntiness of the advertising jingles, and the Christmas singles, and most of all by the sense, screaming out of the TV, in newspapers and magazines, on illuminated bill-boards in the street, that if you are not happy with all this stuff – *look how happy the people in the pictures are!* – there must be something wrong with you. Yes, the festival of shopping oppresses him this year.

There is no one in the kitchen. Saucepans bubble quietly on the hob, and the hot oven hums. Everything is eerily quiet. It is as though everyone has left – only a CD of carols still playing in the empty lounge. (Paul recognises it as *Carols from King's*, sung by the choir of King's College, Cambridge – one of a number of Christmas CDs that Heather purchased the previous week.) Wondering where everyone is, he is shocked to see Heather's parents and his own still there, listening to the prim pre-pubescent voices sing 'God Rest Ye Merry, Gentlemen'. 'Oh,' Paul says, unable to hide his surprise. 'All right?' Something seems to have happened.

'Where's Heather?' he says, after a moment.

Joan answers. 'Um, I think she's upstairs.'

'I think we're going to eat soon,' Paul says. 'The turkey needed a few more minutes.'

It takes a long time to serve the meal. Finally, they sit down. Just as they are about to start, Angela tings her glass and launches into a pious, long-winded toast – several minutes, including tributes to both Paul's elder brother Chris, who lives in Rotterdam with his Dutch wife, and Geoff's sister Jennifer, who lives in a nursing home near Cambridge – ending with the words, 'So, to Heather.' Everyone echoes this with drunken gusto, and they start to eat.

Outside, the dusk is leaden.

An hour later, and in the dark Heather is presenting the pudding, under its diaphanous blue ghost of flame. Her father made it himself. There is applause. Paul, now very drunk, wolf-whistles. Then the lights are switched on and it is served. While the plates are passed round, Angela – who quietly refused a portion herself, saying, 'No, thank you, I can't stand it' – says, 'Well, Geoff's too modest to mention it, but he's a published poet now.'

'Published?' Mike says. 'Where?'

She ignores him. It is as if her face and Mike were magnets of the same polarity – wherever he is, her nose turns the other way.

'*Where?*' he says, and Geoff himself mumbles, '*Bucks Advertiser.*'

Mike laughs.

'Yes,' Angela says. 'He had a poem published in the *Advertiser.*'

'Did you?' says Joan. 'How impressive.' She smiles at Geoff, whose eyes are gloomily following the boat of brandy sauce as it circles the table. He knows that his wife will speak for him, and she does. 'He did,' she says. 'And I'd like to read it to you.'

'Oh God, can I go now, Mum?' Marie says, in a petulant whine.

'Don't be so rude,' Angela says.

Marie scowls at her. The children do not quite understand how they and Paul's parents fit together – a perplexity that is entirely mutual.

Though expressionless, Geoff's heavy face, with its prominent dark eyebrows and five o'clock shadow, has turned brick red. An embarrassed wall. 'Really,' he says, 'I don't know if this is the right time . . .'

'It *is* the right time.'

'Mum,' Paul says, 'if he doesn't want you to . . .'

'He *does* want me to.'

'Do you?'

'I don't think it's the right time,' Geoff says moodily. His arms are tightly folded.

'Why not? It's a lovely poem. I'm sure everyone would love to hear it.' And Angela looks particularly to Joan, who, with her 'Did you? How impressive', had shown such a kind interest in Geoff's work.

'Well . . .' Joan says. 'Of course, but . . .'

'If you're going to read it, just read it. Get it over with,' Geoff says, pouring himself a full glass of red wine. He is, in fact, quite proud of the poem. Angela was not wrong when she insisted that he *did* want her to read it out. 'It's called "Sanatorium",' she says proudly. And in a slightly – only slightly – strange, otherworldly voice, she starts to read.

White, rectilinear,
on a green alp.
From the terrace –
white mountains.

Vegetable soup.
Fresh loaf.
Water from out of
the white mountains.

Glacial lake
in a bowl of rock.
Cowbells echo
from the white mountains.

> *High summer pasture –*
> *lying in the grass*
> *with closed eyes.*

'That's really very nice,' says Joan, following a well-mannered silence.

'Thank you,' Geoff mutters. He starts to eat his pudding. 'This is very good,' he says.

In the downstairs loo Paul blows his nose. The tiny frosted window is open a little and the temperature is more or less the same as outside. It smells of air-freshener, chemical cleanliness, a plasticky approximation of pine. He looks at himself in the mirror. His eyes are still slightly pink. Why had it happened? The tears. He does not know. He just feels unstable, easily upset. Perhaps that is why the poem touched him so unexpectedly. His father had listened to it without expression on his brick-red face. Paul had not known, or suspected, that he wrote poetry. And he would not have suspected, either, the feelings which the poem timidly tried to express. It had made him sharply aware of how little he knew his father. As he stood up, murmuring, 'I'm just going to the loo,' he had heard him say, in answer to a question of Joan's, 'Well I think I'm quite influenced by Japanese haiku.' *I think I'm quite influenced by Japanese haiku!* Who was this man? Paul did not know him, whoever he was. He knew his father as a tense, distant, empirically-minded headmaster. The laughterless driver of a black Rover (property of Imperial Chemical Industries) who liked snooker and political memoirs and watching the news. A seventies manager with a hairstyle like early Arthur Scargill and a collection of cardigans the colour of autumn leaves. A former pipe smoker, resentful at not having had a university education. This was the man Paul knew. Haiku had nothing to do with him.

Nor lying in a high-summer pasture, listening to the lazy clatter of cowbells. Though the poem's longing was pathetically naive, Paul sees – still sniffling in the nippy loo – that he too is in love with the idea of hiding himself somewhere. Somewhere impossibly pure. How he would love that. It shocked him, though, that his father would even imagine such things. *Why* had it shocked him? He does not know why he found it so upsetting either. He blows his nose a final time, and flushes the toilet.

In the lounge, Mike's CD is playing loudly.

> *So here it IS, merry Christmas,*
> *Everybody's having fun . . .*

'*There* you are,' Heather says. 'We're opening the presents.'

'Okay.'

Paul sits at the table and lights a cigarette. In his dark, anxious, weepy, drunken mood, the thought of unwrapping presents depresses him. With something approaching disgust, he watches his father claw inexpertly at the paper wrapping of his present from Mike and Joan. It is a bottle of Johnnie Walker Black Label. 'Thank you so much,' Geoff says, holding it and staring at it as if it were a newborn baby. Then he looks up, meeting the eyes of Mike and Joan in turn with an innocent, small-toothed smile. 'Thank you.'

'It's our pleasure,' Mike says, magnanimously. 'Where's Angela's present, Joanie?' Joan searches through the stuff. 'Um. Here.' She holds it out to her.

Not enjoying herself, but with a chilly little smile, Angela unpicks the bright paper. Inside is a box of mint chocolates. 'Thank you so much,' she says, setting it aside. 'You really shouldn't have.'

'It was our pleasure,' Mike says. He is enjoying himself. 'To give,' he says, 'is better than to receive.'

Most of the presents have now been opened and the room is ankle-deep in crumpled husks of wrapping paper. The children have squealed with joy at the mini iPods they received from Mike and Joan, and said unsmiling thank-yous to Angela and Geoff for the old-fashioned paperbacks their impatient fingers found. Paul has tried on the crimson Pringle jumper his in-laws offered him. (It was too small – the scrawniness of his arms, the soft lumpiness of his torso cruelly exposed in the clinging lambswool.) Heather said, 'This will be useful,' when she saw that her present from Paul's parents was a food blender, and went misty-eyed with delight when she unwrapped the tall, oxblood leather boots her mother had selected for her. From Paul, she received a huge bottle of Chanel N° 5 – not imaginative, but she did not expect that from him. Her thank-you kiss was perfunctory. Paul himself seemed out of sorts, withdrawn, depressed. He sat at the table, not even feigning enthusiasm when presents were handed to him. When he opened the one from his parents, it was so inappropriate that he laughed sadly – a pair of hiking boots. Very expensive ones. He nodded, trying to understand, while his mother went on about Gore-tex and breathable fabrics and ankle support. And he felt a painful resurgence of his earlier sadness when he reflected that by presenting him with these boots his parents had betrayed a profound, and perhaps wilful, failure to understand who he was. At this moment of sorrow, Mike is trying to get his attention, bobbing in front of him as he sits with the boots – one of them still wrapped in tissue paper in its box – on his lap. He wants to take a picture using his new digital camera, and when Paul looks up the blue-white flash immediately hits his stunned retinas. He starts to smile, but it is too late.

'What about that?' Mike says, indicating the huge blue box, while erasing his image of Paul in pain. 'Whose is that? What lucky ess aitch one tee gets to open that?'

'It's Paul's,' Heather says quietly. She has just lit a cigarette and is smoking – uneasily in front of her parents. She seems nervous and holds her lower lip with her teeth.

'Go on, Paul.' Mike puts the viewfinder to his eye.

Paul stubs out his cigarette, and slowly standing, says, 'I know what it is.'

'How do you know?' Heather says.

'I saw it in the shed.'

'But you never go in the shed!'

'I was looking for a saw.'

'Why?'

'To cut the tree down to size. It was too big, remember? I had to borrow a saw from Martin.'

Everyone watches – except the children, who are upstairs, downloading tracks for their iPods – as Paul approaches the blue present. He sighs, and touches its shiny surface, looking at it as a sculptor who has lost his enthusiasm for his art might look at a new block of marble – yet another bloody block of marble – bored and demoralised. 'How the fuck am I going to open this?' he mutters. He is aware of the extreme loutishness of his demeanour – his determined, obtuse failure to evince even the slightest excitement, the least hint of enjoyment – and he finds it offensive himself, distasteful, selfish, ugly. Yet he is somehow unable to stop himself, which only intensifies his distress. As he faces the horizontal blue monolith, he feels the silent disapproval of the room behind him. His mother and Mike, despite their instant loathing for each other, have largely sat on their writhing animosity and smiled, so as not spoil things for everyone else – and yet here he is, joylessly unimpressed by his huge blue gift, and making not the slightest effort to hide it. Quite the opposite – sourly, he seems to be exulting in his unpleasantness. Finding a taped seam with his finger, he starts to tear, pulling the paper off in strips, slowly revealing the box. 'It's a TV,' he says, in the tone of someone finding a ticket under their wiper. The camera unleashes its sheer flash and, wearily, he finishes pulling off the paper. 'Is it one of the flat-screen ones?' Mike asks, and Joan says, 'How on earth did you get it here from the shed? It must weigh a ton.'

'One of the neighbours helped me.'

'You'll enjoy watching this, Heather,' Paul says.

'So will you.'

'Oh, yes. So will I.' His voice is openly sarcastic and sneering, and he knows as soon as he has spoken that it was too much. 'Hea-*ther* . . .' he hears Mike say, and turns, just in time to see her leave. 'Oh, God,' he mutters, and shouts half-heartedly after her – 'Heather . . .' Somewhere upstairs a door slams.

As he trudges, sighing, up the narrow stairs, his performance already seems strange and inexplicable to him. Shameful. Why had he been so determined to spoil things? And he has spoiled them. They *are* spoiled. Despite his shame, however, he is still angry. In this state, he knocks on the bedroom door and opens it. It is dark, and he fumbles drunkenly for the light switch. When he finds it, the scene is desolate – the windows black, the morning's mess of unwanted apparel on the floor. Heather is lying on the unmade bed, her skirted haunches turned to where he stands in the doorway, her small feet drawn up under them. 'Heather . . .' he says. She does not move. 'I'm sorry.' Still she does not move. 'Look . . . You'd better come back downstairs. I'm *sorry*.'

He is halfway down the stairs when he stops and, with a whispered 'For fuck's sake', turns and stomps back up. To his surprise she is not where she was. She is standing up, looking at herself in the mirror. 'Oh,' he says. 'You're coming down?'

'Piss off, Paul.'

'What do you mean, piss off?'

'You don't deserve anything,' she says gnomically, still not looking at him.

'What are you talking about?' She ignores this question. 'The TV? Are you talking about the TV?' He finds he is shouting, and makes

157

an effort to lower his voice. 'It's true you'll watch it more than me. That's fucking obvious . . .'

'Only because you're never here. Always pissed,' she murmurs.

'Well, don't try and pretend the fucking TV's a present for *me* then!'

'It's pathetic.'

'You're pathetic. *You* are. Buying a TV for yourself and then pretending it's a present for me. I don't mind. Fine. But don't expect me to be fucking grateful.'

'I don't,' she says.

'You don't? You seem to. You seem to. Why did you come upstairs then? Why this fucking scene?'

'Because you were being a twat.' Her voice is level and quiet. 'As usual. I should be used to it by now. Excuse me.' She has finished, and he is in the doorway. He stands there, twisted with fury. 'Excuse me,' she says again.

Downstairs the TV – the old TV, itself not small – is on. Geoff and Angela, Mike and Joan, are watching it – some fifty-year-old film with matt, artificial-looking colour and mannered acting. Sentimental orchestral music. Their faces are expressionless. Geoff keeps yawning. Mike has finally taken off his Santa hat. 'Do you want a hand clearing the table?' Joan says quietly when Heather comes in.

'No, it's all right. I'll do it later.' She sits down on the arm of the sofa.

'Where's Paul?' Mike says.

'I don't know. Upstairs.'

'Is he all right?'

Heather seems distracted. 'I don't know.' Despite what she has just said, she stands up and starts to clear the table. Joan immediately starts to help her. 'It's okay, Mum,' Heather says impatiently. 'I can do it.'

'I'll just give you a hand.' Joan is stacking dessert plates.

'It's okay.' Joan seems not to hear this. '*Mum!*' Two annoyed sylla-
bles. 'Go and sit down. I can do it. You sit down.'

'Are you sure?'

'*Yes,*' Heather says emphatically.

She takes the stack of plates to the kitchen. There, in the pasty
neon light she puts them down, and lights a cigarette. Was it
inevitable, she wonders, that the day would end like this? If so, what
was the point? And she had been truly looking forward to today.
When she sees the fine cigars that she picked out, still in their
aluminium tubes – she had imagined presenting them after dessert,
with the port, part of her perfect Christmas meal – for a moment
her vision fogs with tears. She shuts her eyes to squeeze them out,
and wipes her face with a tea towel. Then she pours the dregs of a
bottle of wine into a used glass, and drinks them down. The straw-
yellow wine, though warm, is rich and buttery – much better than
the stuff she usually drinks. It is all so sad. When she has finished
her cigarette, she stubs it out in the little foil base of a half-eaten
mince pie, finally sinking it into the dark mincemeat with a tiny
hiss.

Though still apparently watching the film through the open door
of the lounge, Geoff is standing in the hall, with his hands in his
trouser pockets. He is wearing a dark blue round-necked jumper
with the lump of a tie knot just visible at the throat. He seems to
be waiting for something, and Heather says, 'Do you want a coffee
or something, Geoff?'

He looks at her as if startled. 'What? No, no thanks, Heather. I
think we're off actually,' he adds vaguely, after a moment.

'Yes, we're going,' Angela says, emerging from the downstairs loo,
adjusting the belt of her high-waisted trousers. 'We've got to drive
back and everything. Thank you so much, Heather. It's been a
wonderful Christmas.'

'I'll just get Paul,' Heather says. 'I don't know where he is.'

She goes upstairs, into the bedroom, where the lights are off. In the dark, she can see Paul lying on his back, with his hands behind his head. 'What are you doing?' she says sharply. 'Your parents are leaving.' He does not move or speak. She turns on the light. Though it has slipped back on his head, he is still wearing the mauve paper crown, and seeing it, she puts her hand up and snatches off the yellow one that she had forgotten she was still wearing herself. 'Your parents are leaving,' she says again. 'What should I tell them? You're not coming down to say goodbye?'

'How much was that TV?' Paul asks, still staring at the ceiling.

'What?'

'How much was the TV? How much did it cost?'

She frowns. 'Um. About two thousand pounds.'

'Can we take it back?'

'What do you mean? Why?'

'To get the money back.'

'I don't know. Why?'

'Shut the door.'

'What is it?' She looks worried now. She shuts the door. 'What is it?'

'I'm in trouble, Heather.'

'What trouble?' She is not entirely surprised. He has been behaving strangely for weeks. And there was – this she especially noticed – there was something odd about his answers whenever she questioned him about his new job. She feels sure it must have something to do with that. 'What trouble?' she says again. He seems unable to speak. His eyes are fixed on the off-white ceiling, where the light-shade is surrounded by perforated, concentric shadows. Irritated by his stalling, and starting to panic, she says, '*What –*'

This time he interrupts her: 'I've lost my job.' After he has said it, moving only his head, so that the paper crown almost slips off, he turns to look at her. He seems to look out of simple curiosity, to see what her reaction will be. Initially, she shows no reaction, except that her nose seems to twitch. Once, twice. Her large blue eyes stare at him. Her face is perhaps pale. She is shocked, despite all the premonitions. 'Why are you telling me this now?' she says. And he notices that she is trembling with a strange intensity of feeling. A sort of fury. It startles him. 'I know I should have told you before. I wanted to. I tried.' He sits up, inelegantly, with an effort of his muscleless trunk, eventually having to use his arms. 'Sweetheart, I tried.'

'Your parents are leaving,' she says. And she leaves herself, and goes downstairs.

11

Vaguely Paul remembers kissing his mother, shaking hands warmly with his father in the hall.

The next morning he wakes very early. It is only just starting to get light outside, and Heather and the children are still asleep. The silence is so strong, so settled that the house itself seems to be asleep. He feels strangely clear-headed, though shivery and fragile, and wonders what time he went to bed. It cannot have been later than eight or nine. Perhaps earlier. He does not remember Heather's parents leaving. What he *does* remember, suddenly, sharply, standing amidst the piled-up, encrusted wreckage of the kitchen, is his own performance, and from that his mind instantly flinches. Did he . . . ? Surely not. Yes. *Yes*. Searching the lounge for cigarettes, assailed by an urgent need to atone, he knows that he will have to *do* something. Private sorrow, even sincere words, will not be enough. Something will have to be *done*. Of course, he has been in this situation before. Innumerable times. It is almost a weekly event – the grey-faced penitent in his terrycloth dressing gown, engaged in psychic self-flagellation. That is easy – essentially painless. Nothing more, in fact, than self-indulgence, self-pity. No, that will not be enough . . . And how many times has he said *that*! How many times has he said solemnly to himself, '*That will not be enough*'? It is simply part of the hypocritical show, a well-established element of the snivelling self-disgust, something which he quickly permits himself to forget, usually by mid-afternoon, as soon as the physical pain recedes, and even in the worst,

the grimmest cases, within twenty-four hours. It is not easy, therefore, for him to take these feelings seriously. Their very familiarity
is deeply demoralising and, like the ashy half-cigarette he is
smoking, makes him feel significantly worse. That he is not actually in physical pain, and yet still has such feelings is, however, a
positive sign. So perhaps is his unusually intense and moody aware-
ness of his failure to follow through on previous occasions.

He is impatient for it to be light outside, so that he can leave the
house. He does not want to be there when Heather wakes up. A
soft greyness is in possession of the street when he sneaks upstairs
to dress. He takes some clothes – whatever is to hand – and puts
them on downstairs.

Outside the uncertain grey has hardened into daylight – white
and flat, cloud-light – and unsurprisingly, the streets are empty.
They are sound asleep.

The Hove seafront is prosaic – modest blocks of flats peep over
the weathered line of locked swimming huts to the waves, the
pebbled shore. Pausing for a lone lorry to sweep past towards
Brighton, Paul crosses the road and goes down the brick steps to
the beach. It is only now that he smells the sea – wet wool, salt,
sodden wood, mussel shells. The beach rises in a steep hump.
There are bald patches of sand further down. The air is cold, and
the sky, though still clear over the Channel, is starting to cloud
over, as it often does in the morning. Orange buoys are dark dots
on the tinfoil water. He stands there, his hands in his pockets,
while the wind inflates his jacket and flutters his trouser legs. The
waves fall lazily, unhurriedly, each looking for a moment like an
imperfect barrel of green glass until it falls and expends itself in
a sigh of the shifting flints and shingles. Hugging the wall of the
esplanade, making slow progress over the pebbles underfoot, he
starts to walk towards Brighton, and its grander line of seafront
wedding cakes.

*

He opens the front door with trepidation. Heather, he hears, is in the kitchen, doing the washing-up. He is tired, and the boots are hurting his feet. He sits down on the second carpeted step and eases them off, then hovers indecisively in the hall for a few moments, holding in one hand the milk he has bought, and in the other the cigarettes. When he finally goes into the kitchen – she ignores him. He puts the milk down on the table, and taking a tea towel, without saying anything, starts to dry the things that she has washed. This goes on for some time, the only sound the sloshing of the water in the sink. It goes on, in fact, until the washing-up is finished, almost an hour later. At which point, Heather pulls off the pink rubber gloves and, still without having spoken to him, walks out. 'Heather,' he says. She immediately turns in the doorway. She is wearing her dressing gown and slippers, her hair a Sunday-morning mess. 'What?'

'You all right?'

She seems undecided how to respond, and hesitates. Then she says, 'I think we need to talk, Paul.'

'Yeah, I know.'

'I'm going to have a bath.'

'Okay.'

She goes upstairs, and full of foreboding, he refills the kettle.

The talk takes place a little later, when Mike and Joan – who spent the night in a hotel in Brighton – take the children to McDonald's for lunch.

At first, they seem to misunderstand each other. Paul assumes that the primary topic will be his offensive stunt of the previous day, his successful attempt to spoil Christmas, but, while Heather is angry about that, her main worry – and it makes sense to him as soon as he thinks about it – is the fact that he no longer has a job.

She is, he thinks, surprisingly sympathetic. However, when she asks him – her eyes serious, worried, yet full of a desire to understand, to take his side – why exactly he lost his job, he finds himself unable to tell her the truth. He says that the new job – the one he has been talking about for weeks – 'unfortunately fell through' ('I thought it sounded too good to be true,' she sighs), and that he was sacked from his old job for not making target on the publication. She looks at him – he looks wretched – and says, 'Everything's going to be fine. It is. I know you'll find another job. And you're brilliant at what you do.' She says that they are 'in this together', and even that she will do a few more hours a week at Gumley Rhodes.

Her mood suddenly shifts, however, when he says that he does not want another job in sales.

She says, 'But you always said one of the best things about your work is you can always find another job, just like that. Just walk in somewhere and start working.'

'Yeah, I know . . .'

'So you should just do that then.'

Her tone suggests that this should be the final word. For a few moments, he says nothing. And he might, at this point, have simply nodded, and said, 'Yeah. Okay.' It is what she expects, and her implicit scorn for the idea that he should do anything other than sales seemingly having worked, she is about to stand up and ask him if he wants some tea, when he shakes his head.

She stays on the sofa. 'Why not?' Her voice is quiet. The tone of the question, though, throws the onus on him entirely to justify himself, makes it more or less impossible for him simply to say, 'I don't want to.' So first he hesitates, and lights a ciga-rette, and looks at her. Her face is very still. 'I just don't want to,' he says.

'Paul,' she says, 'the January rent is due in about a week.'

'I know. I've got money for that.'

'You've got money for that?'

'Yes . . .'

'What money?'

'There's . . . I've got . . . An old savings account.'

For a moment, she seems flustered by the existence of this *deus ex machina*, this 'old savings account', and she stares at him. 'How much have you got in it?' she says. She seems suspicious, displeased.

'Enough for the January rent.' Though he is not even sure there is that much.

'And after that? What's going to happen after that?'

'I'll get another job.' His voice, however, is limp and uninspiring – low on steely will.

Hers is not. '*What* other job?'

'I don't know . . .'

'*Pau-aul!* This is ridiculous.'

'What?'

'*This.*'

'Heather,' he says.

'How can you be so selfish?' She seems furious suddenly. 'You can't just do what you want. *Selfish!* What about me? What about the children? You're not on your own. You can't just do what you want as if other people don't exist.'

'What are you talking about? I'm not saying I'm not going to work.'

'So what are you going to do? And don't say "I don't know"!'

'I *don't* know. You're worried I won't be able to pay the rent. I know –'

'Not just the rent! The council tax, the bills . . .'

'I'll pay them.'

'*How?*'

'Well, the January rent's covered –'

'I hope so.'

'Yes.'

'Because it's due in about a week.'

166

'It's covered. I told you.'

'I hope so.'

'It is,' he says impatiently. 'And I'll start looking for another job straight away.'

'WHAT job?'

'I don't know. I haven't really thought about it.' He is well aware that this is not a satisfactory answer. 'Anything, initially.'

'You *haven't really thought about it*?' She wails the words. 'Paul,' she says, as if imploring him, 'I don't understand. Really.'

'What don't you understand?'

She does not understand why he would want to leave sales.

He does not fully understand it himself. It is a job that has served him well, more or less, on and off, for over fifteen years. It is all he knows, the only thing on his CV, aside from a lower second in English language and literature from the University of East Anglia. He *is* a salesman – 'a man *is* his job'. And it is his job. Yes, he is tired of it. And yes, there is the hypocrisy of being an advertising salesman whose interior monologue increasingly fulminates against advertising whenever he sees it. And yes, lately he has not been doing well. Lawrence had been losing patience with him. And not without reason. These ups and downs, though, are simply part of what it is. He knows that he could walk into any of the major commission-only outfits – Silverman, for instance, or Oliver Burke Clarke – and, as Heather said, just start working. Sit down at a desk and pick up the phone. The new scenery would probably freshen him up, and the sales would be there. He *would* make money. So why not? Why is there such an immovable bar of opposition to it in his mind? And there is. He himself is surprised at the strength of it.

It has been there since his afternoon in the Albert, when it occurred to him that he was *able* to leave sales. He had simply to walk out. And stay out. The immediate sense of freedom had been overwhelming. It was something intensely felt, and utterly unthought-through – something thus not unusual in the throes of drunkenness. What *was* unusual was his endorsement of the idea when he was next sober. And even now, when it is hopelessly occluded with practical problems, he feels that whatever else he might do, he must not ignore it and professionally pick up a phone. Faced with Heather's intransigence, however, he might well have done so, were it not for the fact that only that morning, sitting in the lounge, he had seen – or thought he had – that no process of self-improvement he might initiate would have any hope of success, would fail like all its predecessors, unless it involved him leaving sales. His way of life – he had thought, using an overlooked wine glass as an ashtray – was embedded in sales. 'A man *is* his job.' It forms his way of thinking, of living. If he quit sales, it seemed to him, everything else would become unfixed, malleable, able to be re-formed in a more satisfactory way – an idea which seemed to bring moral and intellectual respectability to the beery rapture of the Albert.

He is unable, or unwilling, to explain this to Heather. 'I just can't do it any more,' is all he says, slumped, his head nodded forward, as if he were pushing onto his posture the unwelcome weight of explanation.

'But I thought you liked it.'

It has been years since they have spoken seriously about his work. He sees that now. 'I used to,' he says. 'I suppose. Not any more.'

'And do you think I *like* working at Gumley Rhodes?'

'I don't know.'

'Do you think I *like* it?'

'I'm going to get another job. I don't see what the problem is. Why is that a problem?'

'*What* other job? What job?'

That is the question.

And he does not have an answer for her. He has not thought about it himself. He had been too taken up with maintaining last week's masquerade. He offers her this – if he has not found another job 'soon' . . . 'What do you mean "soon"?'

'I mean, you know, soon.' This does not seem to satisfy her. 'A few weeks,' he says.

'In a few weeks! In a few weeks it'll be almost February!'

'Yes.'

'And what about the *February* rent?'

He finds it extremely stressful to think so far ahead. He screws his face up, and puts a dry hand over his eyes. 'We're going to have to borrow money for that anyway,' he says. 'Whatever I do. Even if I started a new sales job the first week of January I wouldn't have enough money by then. Unless you can pay it. I'll pay you back, obviously.'

'No, I can't.' She sounds upset, aghast.

He does not want to open his eyes. He says, 'We'll have to mortgage the car.'

Turning, then, to specific jobs he might do – what is there? He looks through the jobs section of a week-old paper, the *Argus*. Estate agent? No. One of the things that he is sure of is *no sales*, not in any form. He does not even want to work in a shop, the whole retail sector is out – *no sales in any form*. He does not want to mingle professionally with the money-spending public. Any non-sales but phone-based work – call centres, principally – he also excludes. It is thus a dispiriting experience to leaf through the jobs pages of the *Argus*; his *no sales* and *no phones* policies put a line through many of the jobs on offer, and his lack of any non-sales skills does for most of the others. There seems to be a number of openings for chefs, for instance. Not much use to him. Nor the vacancies for prison officers, driving instructors, typists, database analyst developers, dental nurses, roadside patrol mechanics or financial consultants. This last he looks at more closely, but it is not for him. Not only does it turn out to be a straightforward sales job – a 'target-driven environment', as the text of the ad delicately puts it – but it requires him to have 'plenty of drive and a proven track record in selling financial products', to be 'a great communicator and relationship-builder', and to hold 'qualifications FPC 1–3 or equivalent'.

More or less the only job which he feels would be suitable – and that only because it does not specify *any* necessary qualities, skills or qualifications, except in the very vaguest terms – is 'Purchase Ledger Clerk'.

> We are currently recruiting an Accounts Assistant to join the small and friendly finance team of this busy public sector organisation. Reporting to the Finance Manager you will be responsible for purchase invoices. A minimum of a year's experience in a similar role is desirable. Applicants should be enthusiastic and have good attention to detail. The client offers an excellent basic salary and an attractive benefits package as well as the opportunity to work in a positive and supportive environment.

Heather, who was not at all satisfied with the outcome of their talk, is on edge and suspicious, and prods him with pointed looks and impatient sighs whenever she sees him doing anything other than finding a job – watching the tail end of Christmas TV, for instance, or putting his jacket on to take Oli to the snooker club. Several times a day she seeks progress updates, and he tells her, with increasing irritation, not to expect anything to happen before the new year. 'But you're not even *trying*,' she says, a shrill, despairing note to her voice.

'I am. I've already applied for a job.'

She shakes her head incredulously. 'What?'

'Purchase Ledger Clerk,' Paul mutters, walking out the door and telling himself that he must send his application tomorrow.

Life is pervaded by a sense of financial emergency. The new

television was taken back to Dixons. 'God that was embarrassing,' Heather said, as they emerged from the shop onto Western Road, which was thronged, like North Street and Churchill Square, with impatient shoppers, struggling for their share of the sales. She had spent the whole twenty minutes they were in the shop under a crimson blush, her hair curtaining her face as she filled in the forms. She said that the money from the TV would be reserved for the February rent, the council tax, for bills – for all of Paul's liabilities going forward. They went to Sainsbury's. No luxury products were on the menu now. Instead the trolley was piled with *basics* in their no-nonsense livery, extra value multipacks and special offers. It was almost fun – like an old-fashioned game show – trying to pile up as much food for as little money as possible. The children, in particular, participated with enthusiasm, even questioning the necessity of many items, until they started to get on the adults' nerves. And having at least a week's supply of food stashed in the house seemed to stabilise the situation. There was something atavistic about the way that the food made everything seem more secure. Even Heather seemed to feel relaxed – she gently green-lighted a four-pack of Carling for Paul, and it was at her insistence that they bought a bottle of cava for New Year's Eve.

What is it about 'Purchase Ledger Clerk' that fills him with fear and despondency? As he haltingly types a CV on Oli's computer, wondering how many years of previous clerking experience to bestow on himself, Paul feels a massive lack of enthusiasm for the role. Filing invoices, filing bills – despite the vision of secure public-sector drudgery, there is something wrong with it. It is not the drudgery he minds. The drudgery is fine. More than fine – he is in a state in which the thought of it elicits strange little pangs of ecstasy. No, it is not that. It is the *environment* of 'Purchase Ledger Clerk' which depresses him. It will certainly take place in a grey-carpeted office with desks and ceiling panels and office equipment in neutral plastic tones. He will wear his suit. And somehow the fact that he will be filing invoices troubles him too. Leaving his half-made CV on the screen, he goes downstairs for a cigarette.

The children do not seem to understand what has happened. Or if Oli does, since it has nothing to do with snooker, it does not seem especially of interest to him. He has not said anything, or asked any questions. Of course, that may be because he senses that Paul does not want to talk about it – that it would be painful and embarrassing for him to do so; which it would be – he *is* embarrassed, the sense of ignominious failure is sharp, and he knows that it will be worse in the new year when instead of returning to work, he is still haunting the house in jeans and a jumper, typing CVs, and poking around in the kitchen for some lunch. He thinks of his own father – how he lost his managerial job and became a coach driver. Paul did not think less of him. Of course not. Or did he? Did he in fact, in some way, think less of him? Perhaps he did. Did he suddenly seem pitiable, impotent, *small* in a way that he had not until then? That he took his fate with stiff dignity did not make him seem any less diminished. Yes, he seemed *diminished*, and Paul senses that Oli's perception of *him* is already drifting in a similar direction. The boy's sense of status, of society, is sufficiently sharp – it is that after all, more than anything else, that he is learning at school – to notice that, in those terms, Paul has taken a knock.

Oli is watching television. 'Have you finished with the computer?' he says huskily, still staring at the screen.

'Er, not yet,' Paul says. 'I'm taking a break. Go ahead and use it if you want.'

Oli shakes his head. 'S'all right.'

Paul stands there for a few moments, pretending to follow what is on the TV, then goes to the kitchen and takes one of the Carlings from the fridge. He has thought a lot, since Boxing Day, about the Buddhist monks of Dharamsala who live by repairing motorbikes and cars. *That* is the sort of thing he has in mind. Useful simple manual work. Is it important that it is *manual* work, physical labour? Somehow it is. That seems to be part of the problem with 'Purchase Ledger Clerk'. He wants no involvement, not even the most menial, with the workings of the money machine. That is precisely what he does *not* want. Though he had promised himself not to do so until the CV is finished, he breaks open the can of Carling and swigs at it thirstily. He does not want a *job*, he thinks – pleased with his precise semantic distinction – so much as *work*.

Perhaps it is simply the specificity of 'Purchase Ledger Clerk' that has extinguished his eagerness. Might not any such work, in all its dreary specifications, have the same effect? And more menial jobs, even more so? The old edition of the *Argus* is on the kitchen table, and to test this, he sits down with his lager and looks at it again. If he is really so keen on something of utter meniality – if 'Purchase Ledger Clerk' is too serious, too white-collar – then let him see how he responds to what is on offer for the semi-literate. There seems, however, to be very little on offer for them in the *Argus*. The jobs advertised there include secretaries and receptionists and sous-chefs and sales assistants, but nothing in the way of unskilled manual labour. Disappointed – more than that, starting to get depressed – he sits back and lights a cigarette.

He is drinking the second can of Carling when Oli comes into the kitchen. 'Have you finished with the computer now?' he asks.

'Yeah. Yeah, I have, Oli. Thanks.'

Oli spins on his heel and leaves.

He will finish the CV in the morning. There will be time to do it then. It is early evening, dark outside. Though it is Wednesday, it feels like Sunday. He drops the empty can into the bin and goes to the fridge for the next.

In the morning a letter snaps through the front door. He recognises the handwriting. It is from his mother, and he knows what it will be – a thank-you note for Christmas. It was, she says, 'wonderful', its setting his 'lovely home', where she had 'so much enjoyed' meeting Heather's 'wonderful' parents. He smiles, touched. Also perturbed. It makes him sad, this sense that his mother is just a little insane. Why does she always have to overstate everything? It just makes it all seem even worse than it is. There is a PS – 'I enclose Dad's latest PUBLISHED work!' He looks in the envelope. There is a narrow strip of newspaper with a Post-it note stuck to it – *Bucks Advertiser, 30 December 2004*. Presumably a slow day for local news.

'Gardens'

A few stalks of corn.
A cherry tree.
Muttering sprinkler.

Deep shade in the botanical gardens.
All the exotic flora
looks quite ordinary.

Window –
the garden looks dreary
on a wet December afternoon.

Pigeons feeding,
rustling unseen
in the foliage of the big tree.

Why had he not thought of it until now? All his life, he has watched with envy from the insides of schoolrooms, of offices, while gardeners tasked outside in the fresh.

12

December, of course, is not the most opportune time to be looking for work in the horticultural sector. This does not even occur to Paul as he strolls to the newsagent for the *Argus*. It is a sunny day, seagulls wheeling clamorously overhead, and he wishes that he could immerse himself in some planting immediately, without delay. He imagines surveying the finished work with healthful satisfaction, enjoying a well-earned smoke. Or some tree surgery – harnessed high up the great trunk, wearing earmuffs and goggles, making delicate adjustments with a chainsaw . . . The feeling of freedom, this time from the unsatisfactory world of 'Purchase Ledger Clerk', is almost equal to what he experienced in the course of his afternoon in the Albert. 'It's a fucking nice day,' he says to Heather, smiling. She looks at him strangely, perhaps suspicious of his unaccountably happy mood. 'Yeah it's nice,' she says, returning her attention to her magazine. She is sitting at the kitchen table in her dressing gown, an empty coffee cup before her. Paul starts to unload his shopping – Danish bacon, eggs, sliced white bread, a large can of baked beans. Her head still bent over the magazine, Heather watches him with slight anxiety. When he starts whistling, she says, 'Are you all right?'

'Yeah. Do you want a fried breakfast, full English?'

She shakes her head. 'No.'

He takes out the frying pan and cuts a large wedge of butter into its shallow Teflon base, then, setting it over the gas, starts to open the bacon. He has decided that, after applying for all the gardening jobs in the paper, he will go out and take his own little garden in hand – he does not know why he has not done it before. For that – for a morning's work in the sharp air – he will need a good breakfast. While everything is cooking, he opens the *Argus*. Unsurprisingly, on the last day of December, the jobs section is extremely slim, and that there is even one gardening job advertised in this midwinter limbo is extraordinary, providential. Paul is nevertheless disappointed. When he has searched through the whole section several times, he comes back to the lone horticultural vacancy. The employer is Brighton and Hove Council. '*We are seeking to appoint a permanent gardener to undertake duties such as grass cutting, hedge trimming and street sweeping using a variety of powered hand tools and light plant (ride-on mowers). Successful applicants will also provide assistance to higher graded gardeners in more skilled tasks.*' The salary, he notices, is inadequate even for his minimal needs, but he ignores this for the time being. What troubles him more is the mention of 'street sweeping', which does not seem to square with the sort of work – the sort of life – that he is imagining.

The newspaper directs him to a website for further information, and after breakfast and a rolled cigarette, he goes upstairs and knocks on Oliver's bedroom door. In his pyjamas, Oliver is listlessly surfing the Internet. 'Um, Oli,' Paul says. 'Mind if I use the Net quickly? It's quite important.' Without saying anything, Oli stands up and leaves the room. 'Thanks, mate,' Paul says. Two-fingered, he types in the address from the *Argus*. There is a PDF document several pages long about the gardener job, and he opens it and scrolls through it on the screen. The opening statement sounds promising – '*Overall purpose of job: to undertake grounds maintenance/horticultural work in public parks, playing fields, cemeteries and crematoria, landscaped areas and similar open spaces.*' There follows a list of specific duties. Some of these he likes the sound of, such as '*grass cutting, hedge trimming, clearing of leaves, planting, pruning, and seeding*'. Others he does not – '*patrol and attendance duties, including the issuing of tickets and the maintenance of orderly conduct by the public*'. And some he does not understand – *'to ensure that all relevant aspects of the documented quality system are followed in practice and that the defined standards and level of performance are consistently complied with'*. Still, he understands that they have to spell everything out, even if the job is mostly simple gardening. There are, however, some other potential problems. Although not an essential requirement, applicants with a full driving licence and 'previous experience of triple-mower driving' are particularly welcome, and he has neither. Then there is the importance of 'basic horticultural experience, ability and knowledge'. Also, technical skill in the use of tools and equipment. Starting to sweat, he scrolls on.

The next page – *'ALL OF THE FOLLOWING ARE PRESENT IN THE NORMAL WORKING ENVIRONMENT'* – seems specifically designed to dissuade fantasists and other frivolous applicants from taking things any further.

ALL OF THE FOLLOWING ARE PRESENT IN THE NORMAL WORKING ENVIRONMENT

- EXPOSURE TO ALL TYPES OF WEATHER. Exposure to the weather is constant, from freezing cold and wet conditions to dusty and dry, and working in the heat of the sun. In the summer there is risk of sunburn, and in winter blisters, falls and respiratory problems.

- HAZARDOUS EQUIPMENT. Constant use of hazardous equipment. Examples are mowers, strimmers, hedge cutters, saws, etc.

- TOXIC CHEMICALS. Regular work with toxic chemicals such as pesticides, marking fluids, herbicides, etc.

- LITTER/WASTE. All litter must be removed from public areas prior to and whilst gardening. NB This may include handling contaminated waste, dirty syringes, animal excrement, etc.

- MEMBERS OF THE PUBLIC. Members of the public can also be a potential risk should they become abusive or violent. The possibility of violent or aggressive behaviour.

- DOG ATTACK. When working in parks or other open spaces there is always a risk of dog attack.

Stony-faced, he stares at the screen.

No. No, this determined miserabilism does not provide a true picture of the normal working environment – which is not an unending nightmare of dogshit and hooded youths, plastic tubs of poison and fatal triple-mower accidents. These things feature occasionally, of course – it would be naive not to understand that. But he has *seen* council gardeners at work, seen them lazily clipping hedges and mowing lawns unmolested in the sun. The page is obviously a sort of test – and also, of course, a near-hysterical attempt to head off future litigation.

He scrolls down to the final page. This is a table of, in one column 'essential' and in another 'desirable', experience, qualifications, skills and 'personal qualities'. First, he looks quickly through the 'essential' column. Everything seems to be in order there, with the possible exception of 'basic horticultural experience and knowledge'. He turns then to 'desirable'. Here he does not fare so well. 'Experience of using and maintaining small mechanised plant.' Unfortunately not. 'Full driving licence (covering vehicles up to five tonnes).' No. 'Horticultural qualifications.' None to speak of. He hopes, however, that his strong showing on the only other item in the column – 'Conversant with the geographical area' – will to some extent offset his weaknesses elsewhere.

And with the strong sense that things could have been worse, he starts to fabricate an apt CV.

Doug Woburn, who occupies a position – Paul is not sure what – in the parks and open spaces section of the council environment directorate, was not initially an intimidating figure. With the shapeless khaki bag of his suit, he wore a burgundy shirt and a turquoise tie, and even Paul thought it a strikingly unsuccessful ensemble. Though probably not much over forty, Woburn's hair is entirely white, styled like a Roman emperor's, and his face unusually soft and pink.

'And,' he is saying, 'what do you think you would do in the event of some sort of mechanical problem?' He leaves a pause before adding, 'What would you do in a situation like that?' He asks the question, and waits for the answer, with his eyes fixed on Paul's application form. They are in the underground staff canteen of the town hall – which is emptying as the lunch hour ends – sitting at a round table, each with a plastic cup of coffee in front of him. Paul clears his throat. 'Mechanical problem?' he says. Apparently engrossed in the application form, Woburn nods. The interview has not been going well. Paul wonders, in particular, whether he should have dressed differently. He spent hours – literally hours – deciding what to wear. In the end, he went for jeans, green jumper, suit jacket and hiking boots – only to jog back to the house from the end of the road, and change into a full suit. It would look bad, he had thought, to show up *not* in a suit if that was what was expected – worse than the other way round. Now, though, he is not so sure. His suit seemed to have an instantly unsettling effect on Woburn, and seeing this – and seeing also how Woburn himself was dressed – he had realised, too late, already shaking his interviewer's soft hand, that it was probably not appropriate. He was applying for a job as a *gardener*, for fuck's sake, not deputy manager of the finance directorate. Downstairs, they did not speak while they waited, standing side by side, for the machine to dribble coffee into their plastic beakers. Woburn, in particular, seemed intent on not looking at Paul, as though this in itself would constitute some sort of insult, as though half his face were a loud mulberry birthmark.

When they were sitting down, still refusing to look him in the eye, Woburn said, shuffling the mass of papers in his hands, 'So, er, what, er, what is it that interests you about this job?'

Paul said, 'Um.' He took a sip of coffee, though it was still too hot, and for an infinitesimal moment, Woburn looked at him. 'Well, I've always been interested in gardening,' Paul said. 'I worked as a gardener for a few years before I went into . . . went into, you know . . .' Woburn nodded – the CV had Paul working as a 'private gardener' from 1987 to 1991. 'And now,' Paul said, already losing momentum, 'now I just want, you know . . .' He stopped, and again Woburn looked at him, this time for a whole second. 'You know, I was just getting tired of sales. Being stuck in an office all day. I love the outdoors. You know. And.' He left this 'and' hanging as he took another sip of coffee. Then simply said, as if everything had been explained, 'Yeah.'

'Okay,' Woburn said nervously. 'But what, um, what was it that attracted you about *this* job in particular?'

'About this job?'

Woburn nodded, and made a sort of affirmative murmur – 'Hn.'

Wasn't that the same question, Paul thought, the one he had just answered? 'Well, I just said. Um. I want to get back into gardening. That's it really.' He had not thought his *motives* would be an issue. (They never were in sales – there, no one ever even pretended that anything other than money played a part, and questions such as these were unnecessary.) Woburn was obviously not satisfied with his answer, but seemed slightly intimidated – or perhaps just indifferent – and nodded, still leafing through papers. 'So your previous experience . . .' he said vaguely.

'Yes.'

'A few years . . . From eighty-seven to ninety-one?'

'That's right.'

'Um. Perhaps you could tell me a bit more about that?'

'Yes, of course.' Paul had spent the previous five days preparing this, and had it down pat. He had worked, he said, for a firm in London, Alfred Gold Ltd – 'I don't think it exists any more, actually' – doing 'all sorts of things', mostly 'in the London area', including some 'quite complex plantings' and 'sizeable hard-landscaping commissions'. Woburn nodded, seemingly impressed. The firm had prospered in the late eighties, but then the property market slump – so Paul said – had hit it hard, and he had had to look for work elsewhere. So it had never been his intention to leave 'the horticultural sector'. (He said the pompous phrase with a wry smile, which Woburn, however, did not see.) Economic imperatives had forced him out. He said that he had always intended to take it up again, and ended by saying, once more with a wry smile, 'Better late than never, I suppose.'

Woburn looked up at this and smiled milkily himself, and Paul felt, for a moment, that he might have turned things round.

Then Woburn said, 'What sort of equipment have you used in the past?'

'Equipment? Er. What sort of equipment? Pretty much what you'd expect, I think.' Apparently at ease, Paul drank the dregs of his coffee.

'But specifically . . .'

'Oh . . .' It was odd – his mind seemed totally empty. 'Just the usual stuff.' Suddenly, he remembered some words, and said them. 'Lawnmowers. Strimmers.' He shrugged. 'Um. Maybe if you could give me an example of what . . .'

'What sort of strimmers have you used?'

Without hesitation, Paul said, 'Different ones.' He tried his coffee cup again – it was empty. Woburn was waiting for him to say more. 'I can't remember exactly,' he conceded after a few moments. 'It was quite a long time ago.'

'Sure. But what sort of power were they?'

'Oh, quite powerful.' He almost reached for his empty cup, but caught himself in time.

'Like . . . what . . . ?'

Paul stuck out his lower lip and shook his head.

'What sort of wattage?' Woburn said, looking at his papers.

'I'm sorry. I really can't remember.'

'That's okay.' Woburn wrote something down. 'Have you used a triple mower before?'

'Um. I don't think so.'

Woburn nodded, and wrote. 'What would you say,' he said, still writing, 'was the most important factor in prioritising your work-load?'

For fuck's sake, Paul thought, shifting in his seat, literally scratching his head. It was obvious that – though phrased as if it were – this was not a matter of opinion. Woburn was looking for something specific. That Paul did not know what this was was already evident – if he did, he would simply have said it. 'Um,' he said. And then, unable to keep a slight interrogative twinge out of his voice, 'The, the weather conditions?'

This evidently *was* the answer – the nature of Woburn's nod said as much – so there was something sinister about the lack of follow-up questions. Woburn said, 'Are you familiar at all with the relevant health and safety procedures?'

Picking up his empty cup, Paul said, 'Yeah – yeah, that should be fine.'

'Okay. And what do you think you would do in the event of some sort of mechanical problem? What would you do in a situation like that?'

'Mechanical problem?'

'Say with a piece of plant.'

'Plant?'

'Yes.'

183

'Mechanical problem with a plant?'

Woburn nods, his eyes on the form that he is slowly filling in, ticking boxes – or not – as Paul struggles with his questions.

'Sorry, I don't understand,' Paul says. He shakes his head, squinting. 'Mechanical problem with a *plant*?'

'With a piece of plant. A lawnmower, for instance.' There is a tiny edge of impatience in Woburn's voice.

'Oh, plant, yeah.' Paul laughs. 'Sorry. Um. Well. If there was a mechanical problem . . .' He wonders what to say. 'I would inform my supervisor?'

At first Woburn says nothing. Then, 'You wouldn't attempt to repair the problem yourself?'

For some reason – perhaps something odd in Woburn's tone – Paul thinks that this is a trick question, that he is being set up to say that he would, only to be told that it is against the health and safety procedures. This would obviously undermine his earlier suggestion that he was familiar with them – thus, of course, undermining *everything* that he has said. 'No,' he says, 'I don't think so.'

'Why not?'

'Well . . .' He is hesitant, terribly unsure now.

'You wouldn't even perform a preliminary investigation?' Woburn says. Paul is uneasily silent. 'To establish whether it is a minor difficulty before referring it to the workshop?' He seems to be quoting from something.

'I suppose, I would, yes,' Paul says. 'I mean, I thought you meant, once I had established that. Yes.'

He tries to see what Woburn is writing on the form, but Woburn is left-handed and writes with his wrist wrapped secretively around the pen. 'Would you say you were physically fit?'

'Quite. Yes. Quite.'

Woburn seems unconvinced. He does not even nod. 'I'm going to read you a list of things,' he says. 'I want you to tell me, in each case, whether you think they'd present a problem for you.'

'Sure.' Paul clears his throat.

'Walking,' Woburn says.

'Walking?'

'Up to ten miles a day.'

'Fine. No problem.'

'Okay . . .' There is no doubting the scepticism in Woburn's voice. 'Digging,' he says. 'For example, bedding. Or graves.'

'Graves?'

'Or bedding.'

'I don't think that would be a problem.'

In the same sceptical tone, Woburn says, 'Okay.' He presses on: 'Spraying. For example, carrying twenty litres of pesticides.' And he looks at Paul, looks him in the face, as if defying him to say that he would be able to do *that* without difficulty.

'In a kind of backpack?' Paul says. 'Sure. That would be okay.'

'Lifting small plant and machinery. For example, hedge trimmers, mower boxes, bags of fertiliser, *tree branches*' – he seems to emphasise that – 'et cetera.'

Paul nods. 'M-hm.'

'You wouldn't have any problem with those sorts of activities?'

'No.'

Once more, Woburn pauses pointedly. And Paul thinks that he detects a snide amusement in his voice – is sure that he sees a mocking smile quiver on his dainty mouth – when he says, 'Climbing trees.' He looks up for a moment. 'Climbing trees with ladder or hoist.'

Paul nods. 'Yeah,' he says.

'Yes?' Woburn's eyebrows – which are still dark despite the white mop – have actually ascended.

'Yes.'

'You're sure?'

'Yes, I am.'

'Okay. Do you do regular physical exercise?' Woburn says,

offhand, writing something down. 'I hope you don't mind my asking.'

'I don't mind. Yes I do.'

He is looking quickly through Paul's CV. 'And you don't have a driving licence?'

'No.'

'Okay.' For a few moments he says nothing, scanning the CV, one hand loosely holding his turquoise tie. 'And your date of birth *is* 12th of June '65? That *is* right?'

'Yes.'

Woburn nods. He seems to suspect Paul of being a man well into his forties trying to pass himself off as thirty-nine. 'Okay,' he says with an insincere smile on his soft pink face. 'Well, thank you very much for coming in.'

'That's all right.'

They stand up. Woburn's handshake is limp. He starts to follow Paul upstairs, so Paul says, 'It's okay, thanks. I can find my own way out.'

'No, I have to meet someone else in reception.'

'Oh. Okay.'

The awkward silence in which they walk slowly up the stairs does not suggest that the interview has been a success.

'Bye,' Paul says.

'Yes, bye,' says Woburn.

A young man is waiting there. His head is a mass of bright piercings – nose, ears, eyebrows, lip, tongue. He is dressed in tracksuit bottoms and a hoodie and sturdy trainers. 'Michael Fry?' Woburn says.

'Yeah, that's right.'

They shake hands.

(And months later Paul happens to see Michael Fry in Hove Park, on a ride-on mower, smoking what appears to be a spliff as it drones slowly over the lawn.)

186

It never occurred to Paul that he might not be *able* to work as a gardener. Even after such an obviously unsatisfactory interview, it is a shock to him. And having allowed himself to become infatuated with an idea of professional horticulture, he is uninterested in anything else. In desperation, he applies for a job at the Wyevale Garden Centre – thus violating his own ban on the retail sector in the interests of spending the day among plastic sacks of compost and terracotta planters. He does not even get an interview. And for several days after that he does nothing – spends much of the time in bed, or asleep on the couch under lingering blue veils of cigarette smoke, Heather increasingly freaked by his lapse into total inertia. And it is then, in mid-January, that he flirts one dark afternoon with the idea of becoming a tramp. It seems to him, as he lies on the couch, nothing more than a logical extension of his failed plan to become a gardener, inasmuch as that had grown out of a wish to secede from sales, money, status. Well, if he wished to secede, why not do it properly? And lying on his back in the dim room, he experiences a surge of dark, fizzing excitement, a sudden twinkling sense of freedom. Part of the appeal, of course, is simply that it is *possible* – always possible. All he has to do is walk out. And stay out. He can transform everything, his whole life, as simply as that. He will relinquish all his possessions except for the clothes he is wearing, and wander the streets, seeking wisdom . . . His mind sparkles with excitement at the thought of this. He has recently started to take an interest in ascetic and anti-materialist figures – St Francis of Assisi, Sundar Singh, Michael Landy, men who embody notions of success specifically opposed to the piling-up of pelf – and as he muses on his, perhaps quixotic, understanding of their tenets (essentially, that it is only by possessing nothing, *nothing*, that we can hope to see, to understand, who and what we are), the idea of simply walking away from the burden of his material and financial problems seems irresistible. Why not? Why not just walk out – and stay out? And with a sudden energetic movement, he sits up.

He is upstairs, sitting on the edge of the bed to tie his bootlaces, when it starts to rain. He has slept outside twice in the past. Once as a student, when he and some friends went to Amsterdam for the weekend, and too tired and stoned to sort out somewhere to stay, had simply lain down on the floor of the station, where Dutch policemen kept prodding them with their steel-toed footwear. It had been a sort of torture – especially as they had spent the previous night on a coach, and partly on a ferry, watching with itchy, exhaustion-fogged eyes as obese truck drivers ate roast dinners in the seesawing ship's hot canteen. When dawn started to seep through, they were back on the coach, moving slowly north through a flat agricultural landscape. So by the time they lay down on the stone floor of Centraal, they had been up for forty hours. Yes, a memorably bad night. But not as bad as the other one. It was not so much the discomfort that made this one undoubtedly worse – it was how he had felt in the morning. It was very cold, and he had woken many times during the night – possibly every five or ten minutes – instinctively pressing himself further into the soft rubbish that kept him slightly warm. When he woke for the last time, it was daylight and he had never felt so cold. He did not understand *why* he was there. A refuse truck was approaching along the street – a street of the blind backs of buildings. He could hear the coarse shouts of the men, and the hissing and crunching of the machine's operation. Never has he embarked on a day more unhappily, and with less hope, than he did then.

And as if to underline this, he imagines – framing the horrors to himself with the energy of a medieval painter depicting hell – what would happen if he were to walk out, and stay out. What would he do? Wander around. Shelter from the rain somewhere – a bus stop, the station, under some trees. And as night fell, and the temperature dropped? What then? A bench? A doorway? And in the morning? He would want coffee, food. He would be hungry. Would he sit outside Churchill Square, then, with a cardboard face, an angry plea written clumsily across it? What other options *were* there? Still, the idea of passing each day in meditative inaction, watching the busy legs stride past, amassing a few quid for a bun, a sausage roll, a cup of tea, is not without appeal. (He thinks of the Buddha, sitting under his tree, waiting for wisdom.) Perhaps it would be possible to find a bed in a hostel somewhere . . . But, of course, it would be far, far more vicious and desperate than that. A pitch outside Churchill Square, he knows, is highly prized – as is any prime stretch of pavement. (And in winter the places where warm air pours out of office buildings.) It is not possible simply to show up with your cardboard announcement and start soliciting coins. Someone else would already be in possession of that spot, and almost certainly prepared to fight for it. It would, after all, be the *only* thing they were in possession of, apart from the filthy togs they were standing up in. And the strangled shouts of fighting tramps speak of a life in which the mundane material struggle, though simplified, is not in any way eluded.

And there is another problem. He knows that he would not be able to walk out on Heather and the children. In this there seems to be little positive volition on his part. He even finds it slightly shameful. And thinking about it, he experiences one of his periodic storms of jealousy and ill-will towards the man who *did* walk out, and stay out – though presumably never homeless – Dr John Hall. Still a potent absence after so many years. He can never be forgotten, of course – through the children he maintains his profile in the household; *literally* maintains it in Oli's high forehead, in Marie's wide inelegant mouth and curly black hair. It troubles Paul sometimes, this ineradicability of Dr John Hall.

He knows little of him, or of Heather's life with him. What he does know is that in her early twenties Heather was a healthcare assistant at the West Middlesex Hospital in Isleworth. This hospital job was, he thinks, her father's idea; and it was there that she met John Hall. When he finished his internship and said that he was

189

moving to Brighton, where he had a job lined up, she went with him. They lived in a flat on the top floor of a shabby Victorian villa (Paul has seen it from the outside) on a steep street near the station. They went on holiday to Turkey one summer, and Italy the next, on that occasion with another doctor from the surgery and his wife. They had a second-hand car – it was then, Paul knows, that Heather learned to drive. She did some secretarial work. He knows that they moved house once or twice, once while Heather was pregnant with Marie. Oliver was named after John Hall's father.

Paul does not know exactly what happened next. The way he understands it, one day Dr John Hall just disappeared.

So many years later, however, he is, inevitably, *still* here. It is even possible that Heather is still in touch with him – Paul suspects that he sends her money for the children. It is probably piling up in a savings account somewhere, or invested in sound financial products – Heather would be sensible like that. She has never spoken to him about this money. She has never really spoken to him about John at all, and he has only seen a few photos of him, stumbled on when searching for something else in an obscure drawer.

Paul often supposes that, in spite of everything, Heather is still in love with John Hall, or with an idealised memory of him. (It was her idea, for instance, that they move to Brighton, where he had left her – and troubled by its associations with him, Paul, though wanting to leave London, had insisted on Hove.) And during these periods of jealousy especially, he finds himself objecting to the way in which he helps to support the doctor's children, while at the same time never being allowed in any way to supplant him as their acknowledged father. There is, Paul sometimes feels, something humiliating about this. And far from improving with time, it seems to have become worse.

When he goes downstairs, once more in stockinged feet, the rain is falling steadily through the twilight outside, puddling the old tarmac and uneven pavements of Lennox Road. Soon Heather will be home from work, and the children from school. And while, standing at the window, he is thankful to be inside, out of the weather, this is tempered – more than tempered, almost entirely undermined – by the depressing, inescapable sense that he is a prisoner, unable to walk out, and stay out.

13

He has not hitherto been used to having the house to himself. They have not, that is, spent much time alone together – Paul and the house – and soon they sit in awkward silence, the small talk exhausted, the situation odd. The house, in particular, is a shy, taciturn presence, and just to lift the hush that hangs so heavily in its interiors, Paul finds himself telling it whatever pops into his head. He has hardly thought, since the week of make-believe when Heather dropped him at the station every morning and he had no work to go to, of his former fellow salesmen, his erstwhile mates. The Christmas holidays ensued, and he never thought of them when he was on holiday. So it was not until well into the second week of January – when the sense of an extra-long Christmas was slowly shading into something else, something disquietingly shapeless and open-ended – that, lying on the sofa somewhere in the level afternoon, he found himself telling the empty house about them. About Murray, for instance – Murray Dundee, the Croc. Paul explains to the house that Murray's nickname in fact predates the 1986 film usually taken to be its inspiration. (Though, of course, a new and extraordinary element of hilarity was added when posters for something called *Crocodile Dundee* suddenly started to appear.) No, the nickname was inspired, he understands, by Murray's *smile* – a long, cold, crocodilian thing. His memories of Murray in the early days, when he worked for him at Burdon Macauliffe, are murky. It is strange, though, to think that Murray was younger then than Paul is now. He has a memory – he tells the empty house – of watching a rugby match in a pub on the river somewhere. Putney or somewhere. Rain falling into the grey river. The terraces of the pub wet and deserted. Raindrops beading the outdoor furniture. Murray was there, and Lawrence, and Eddy Jaw . . . The house seems unimpressed by this plotless little fragment, and Paul moves on.

Years later. Northwood. Fucking dial-a-deal. It was fun – everyone making so much money in the smart little office overlooking Fleet Street. To listen to the men who were there, you would think that every pitch was a deal. It was not like that, of course. Still, there were undoubtedly more deals than usual. Made twelve thousand pounds in a single month, Paul says proudly. (Perhaps the house is impressed, perhaps not.) Murray had had enough money to find four thousand for a personalised number plate for his Sierra. What was it?

M56 RRA.

And Paul remembers laughing – farting with laughter in the shadowy interior of the Chesh – and Eddy screaming in Murray's unsteadily smiling face, 'You could have got a better fucking *car* for that!' There was – though it was obviously something to do with the money, there seemed to be more to it than that – there was an air of insouciance about that time. They could do what they wanted – *that* was the prize of success. There were long liquid lunches in the Wine Press, and later spliffs in Gough Square, in the vibrant stillness of the shade.

In those days all the work was done in the mornings – and work *was* done. The mornings had a frenetic, wild-eyed quality. Eddy, Paul, Murray, Mundjip – all shouting into their phones.

. . . *calling from International Money Publications* . . .

. . . *is Mr Jadoul there? I need to speak to Mr Jadoul* . . .

. . . *the world's leading banks and insurance companies* . . .

. . . *that's very good news, Mr Nicelli* . . .

. . . *so if I could just confirm that* . . .

Some of them standing on their desks, some sitting *under* their desks, the strong draught from the windows dispersing the cigarette smoke, the numbers on the whiteboard multiplying all the time. They had the togetherness, the loudmouth mutual self-assurance of a winning sports team. Tuesday was payday – when the trophies were handed out. In turn, they would go up to Simon's office to collect their cheques – written in front of their eyes with his gold fountain pen – for two, three, four thousand pounds. And Simon himself was not a negligible ingredient in the extraordinary savour of that time. He was like a pig in shit – buying champagne, paying for taxis, five-hundred-pound bottles of Pomerol at El Vino, dinner at the Ivy. He was munificent – and no wonder – he was making as much money as all of them put together. He wanted them to love working for him, and they did. For two months.

Then the fateful phone call from Nigel at IM.

Then the Diaspora.

And then . . .

Yes, *that*.

Paul sighs (the house is tactfully silent) and, swinging his feet onto the carpet, sits up. He moves through to the kitchen. The house is still listening – mildly, like a mental-health professional. For a while he says nothing, lost in his own numb non-thoughts. He opens the fridge. Shuts it. The green digits of the oven clock say that it is two. That was always the pivotal point of the day, he mentions. Two o'clock. The point at which, in the various pubs of his sales life – in the Duke of Argyll, in the Greyhound, in the Prince Albert, the Windlesham Arms, the Red Lion, the City Darts, the Ten Bells, the Seven Stars, the Gun, the Crown, the Golden Heart, the White Hart, the White Swan, the Perseverance, the Nag's Head, the Devonshire Arms, the Punch Tavern, the Captain Kidd, the Coach and Horses, the Prospect of Whitby, the Old Bell, the Tipperary, the West Wall, the Printer's Devil, the King and Keys, the Masons Arms, the Edward VIII, the Cheshire Cheese, the Old Bank of England, the Old King Lud, the Cittie of Yorke, the Finnegans Wake, the Tom Tun, the Shakespeare's Head, the Fitzroy Tavern, the W. G. Grace, the Castle, the Chequers, the Prince of Wales, the Ellesmere Arms, the Stage Door, the Sherlock Holmes, the Carpenters Arms, the John Keats, the Head of Steam, the Rose and Crown, the Prince Rupert, the Lord Clyde, the Colonies, the Cricketers, the Adam and Eve, the World's End, the Bag O' Nails, the White Horse, the Marlborough Arms, the Green Man, the Bunch of Grapes, the George, the Dolphin, the Duke of York, the Saracen, the Blackbird, the Hand and Racquet, the Blue Posts, the Barley Mow, the Belgrave Arms, the Dover Castle, the Golden Lion, the Goose, the Bull, the Eight Bells, the Two Chairmen, the Constitution, the Duke of Wellington, the Northumberland Arms, the Blind Beggar, the Feathers, the Beehive, the Phoenix, the Bear, the Sussex, the Crown and Anchor, the Anglesey Arms, the Oxford, the Windmill, the Fox and Hounds, the Three Compasses, the Cask and Glass, the Crossed Keys, the Lamb and Flag, the Man in the Moon, the Cock, the Stag, the Builders Arms, the Hour Glass, the Wheat Sheaf, the Windsor Castle, the City Tram, the Lord High Admiral, the Morecombe Arms, the Grenadier, the Queen Anne, the Catherine Wheel, the Bell, the Angel, the Rising Sun, the Robin Hood, the New Moon, the King's Arms, the Star and Garter, the Mitre, the Magpie, the Flag, the Ship, the Plough, the Melton Mowbray and the Penderel's Oak – two o'clock was the point at which they had to make up their minds what to do. Until then, there was always a sort of tension, a tension which peaked on two o'clock; and when, at two o'clock, Paul imagined *leaving* the pub – stepping out onto the pavement and walking back to the office – he would usually dismiss the idea as impractical. Pointless. Naive. Imagining, for a moment, stepping into the rain that he saw was starting to fall outside, the hurrying people, the thrusting black taxis with their headlights on for the early gloom, he would inwardly shudder. So they would usually stay, especially in the second half of the week; and the first post-two o'clock pint produced an imme-diate sweet easing – a sudden luxurious expansion of time, 'all sense of being in a hurry gone'. (A phrase he remembers from somewhere.)

Later, however, it might start to seem that perhaps it would not have been *entirely* impractical, or pointless, to have put in a few hours' work – hence the penitential tinge so typical of four forty-five.

On the sofa – his feet on one of its arms, his head propped on the other – smoking a cigarette, he addresses the silent house like a shrink. Yes, the penitential tinge, in the warm, low light of the Penderel's Oak – the moving light of the fruit machines, the heat lamps of the food servery, and the illuminated front of the cigarette machine – a picture of a rabbit or a hare, he never knew which, squatting vulnerably in American scrubland, and in big blood-red letters, the single word, LUNCH. They never ate lunch, he and Murray.

Lying on the sofa, he finds himself thinking of one particular afternoon – the afternoon of Murray's salesman's tiff with Marlon. It was two o'clock. Murray was smiling, and somewhere in his smile he was issuing an imploring plea. Paul was not sure what it was about exactly, Murray's tiff with Marlon. He knew, however, that Murray wanted to stay away from the office. That was what he was silently pleading for. Paul looked at his watch. With a series of soft impacts he stubbed out his cigarette. Murray, the smile still fixed in the folds of his face, must have thought that Paul's hesitation was simply a form of sadism. Paul even wonders, supine on the sofa, whether it was. He thinks not, however. That day – he informs the house – the penitential tinge had appeared early, while there was still time to leave the pub and put in a few hours' work. So it was out of kindness, out of a sort of softness – which, he was sadly aware, must somehow put him at a disadvantage in life – that he had finally said, 'Well . . . What you having then?'

And that night – *that very night* – Murray had spoken to Eddy Jaw.

Why? Was it because he had taunted him about his Merc? Yes, he had taunted Murray about his Merc. When he landed the post-two-o'clock pints on the table, he saw that Murray had taken one of his cigarretes – Murray never had his own cigarettes – and seating himself, he said, his voice full of sympathy, 'Still having trouble with the car finance people?'

'The finance people?'

'Yeah. When's the next payment?'

'Um, it's in, er . . .' Murray looked up at the ceiling, which was the colour of pie crust. 'Two weeks, something like that.' Paul knew that that was a lie. The next payment was due on Monday. Keen not to talk about it, Murray said, 'You got anything out there?'

'Parking's a bit of a nightmare, though,' Paul said. 'Isn't it?'

'Not at all.' Murray shook his head. The word 'parking' was unpleasant for him to hear, provoked a stab of pain – his long silver S-Class being at that moment immobilised in Little Russell Street, as he had found when he went there mid-morning to put another twenty quid in the meter. 'So you got anything out there?' he said. 'Or what?'

For a moment Paul was silent. 'This and that. You know. This and that.' And Murray immediately started to talk about something else – something that *he* had 'out there'. 'There's this goldfish breeder,' he said. 'Fucking Singaporean goldfish breeder. His name's . . . It's spelt . . . N G. How the fuck do you pronounce that?' Paul shook his head slowly. 'How the fuck do you pronounce that?' Murray said.

'I don't know,' said Paul. Murray said, 'How the fuck do you pronounce that?'

'Dunno,' said Paul, staring at the green illuminated exit sign.

'I said to him, I said to him, it's the latest fucking big thing. Did you not know that? I'm talking about corporate HQs. Fucking fish tanks. Fucking aquariums . . .'

Paul was not listening.

Lying on the sofa, eyeing the off-white ceiling, he wonders what sort of friendship was expressed in that not untypical slice of time. Is it normal, he wonders – seeking the opinion of the silent house

– for friendship to be such a mesh of irritations, of sly wounding stabs, of one-upmanships, of tedium? Surely not. There would seem to have been little, then, for either Murray or himself to traduce when they made their symmetrical pacts with Eddy Jaw. And there *was* a symmetry there. Though not a perfect one, of course. Nor, obviously, was the outcome symmetrical. But would he swap places with Murray now?

He imagines Murray, now, on – what is it? – *Wednesday* afternoon. Two thirty. Marooned on a wide grey sales floor, lying for a living. Struggling to sell space in pretend publications. Trying to talk impatient strangers into doing what is not in their interests. Losing sleep over notional sales targets. Smarting at the slap of blowouts. Marshalling muppets. Being bossed by Eddy Jaw. And seeing what a mistake he has made – two weeks into January, and not one sale – Eddy will be starting to lose it, starting to fly into eye-popping storms of anger, the veins on his neck standing up, his face the colour of sunstroke. And Murray sitting there, making small munching movements with his mouth, feebly trying to smile – trying to make light of it – while Eddy, in a plaid Hugo Boss suit, smashes the white plastic handset of Dave Shelley's phone against the plasterboard wall.

Paul stands up – is woozy for a moment – then searches for his plastic pouch of tobacco and king-size papers. Once more sitting on the smooth floral fabric of the sofa, he starts to make a spliff. He had promised himself not to smoke one until five o'clock. However – he spells it out, though the house has made no objection – he has nothing to do, so there seems no point *not* being stoned. Stoned, everything seems further away, quite far away – as if seen from on holiday, or in hospital. And the tedium of the level afternoon is numbed. The house is tolerantly silent. Or does he – as he dusts the hash from his fingerprints – does he sense a hint of disapproval? A slight sad shake of the head? An almost inaudible sigh?

*

He is half asleep when a key scratching at the front-door lock prefaces the noisy ingress of Heather and the children. Oliver, in his school uniform, looks into the sitting room. He sees Paul lying on the sofa, like a hieroglyphic of a sleeping man – his legs tucked up, his hands under his head. Lazily, he opens his eyes. 'All right, Oli?' he mumbles. 'Was just having a little nap.'

14

In the end it is Heather who finds him a job. From the kitchen, she hears him enter the hall – there is something exhausted about the way the front door shuts.

He has been in Brighton, talking to a street sweeper named Malcolm. It is mid-January – the 20th in fact – 'almost February' – and he had found, advertised in the *Argus*, 'a vacancy in this high-profile operation for street sweepers'. The 'operation', once again, was Brighton and Hove Council. The only requirement of the job was 'being able to stand up for eight hours a day'.

We are looking for hard-working, conscientious people who can work on their own with minimal supervision. Being able to stand up for 8 hours a day in all weather conditions is essential. Does this sound like you? If so, you could be who we are looking for.

The problem was that Paul was not sure if he *could* stand up for eight hours a day. And after his failures with Woburn and the Wyevale Garden Centre, he knew that he would not survive failure here. He had no experience of 'cleansing', had never undertaken a 'litter pick' – things which would surely weigh against him. The only other job he had even made enquiries about was a grave-digging post at Hove cemetery. Immediately excited by the possibilities of this – its rich nihilism, its ghoulish glamour, its echoes of *Hamlet* – he had phoned to ask if it was absolutely necessary that applicants be licensed to operate a mini excavator, and had been told that, yes, it was absolutely necessary. That *was* the job.

Or at least the most important part of it. There would be some hand digging as well. Some of the other duties – they might have been off-putting to other people, or to himself at other times – positively attracted him. To work outdoors 'to depths of seven feet in confined spaces', to 'lift grave shuttering boards', to 'locate graves for interments', to 'reopen graves', to 'assist at exhumations'. It had been disappointing about the mini excavator. Very disappointing. And moreover he was sure that it was Woburn he had spoken to when he phoned to ask about it. It was the same department – cemeteries, parks and open spaces.

Prudently, Paul decided to find an existing street sweeper and have a word with him. See what the job involved – there was no point trying for it if he did not think that he would be up to it, if it was pie in the sky. And it was thus that he found himself in conversation with Malcolm on the Brighton seafront opposite the conference centre – he had walked into town, where he wasn't known – one sunny afternoon. 'We don't just sweep up chips and condoms,' Malcolm was saying. 'I picked up a bra the other day.' He was leaning philosophically on his barrow, with stained fingers bringing the last damp, smokable centimetre of his roll-up to rocky lips. The exhaled smoke was accompanied, lower down, by a guttural shifting of phlegm. He cleared his throat. His face was delicate, russet-bearded, bespectacled, some grey hairs in the beard. There was something childlike about him, Paul thought. Also something of the intellectual – he had a self-conscious, thoughtful, measured way of speaking. 'There's this habit of public "grazing", isn't there?' he said. Paul nodded sombrely. 'When I started, twenty years ago, there was just the one fast-food outlet, a fish and chip shop in a back street. Now there's takeaways everywhere.'

'Yeah, there is,' Paul agreed sadly.

For a few moments, the two of them stood there, looking out to sea, squinting, moist-eyed for the wind. The air was cold, brilliant.

Though his voice was frail, Malcolm obviously liked to talk, to muse aloud. Paul had told him that he was thinking of a street-sweeping job (he had expected Malcolm to find this surprising – he did not seem to) and wanted to know what it was like. 'Well . . .' Malcolm had said, still slightly wary. 'You've got to keep your patch clean.'

'Your patch?' Paul said.

'Your patch, yes. This is my patch.' He outlined the limits of his patch – a stretch of seafront, and a hinterland of little streets. 'It's a good time to join, actually.' Saying this with earnest enthusiasm, his narrow, smiling face seemed innocent and kind. 'There's more money coming into the service.'

'Oh, is there?' Paul said.

'And we've got the brooms and barrows back.' Malcolm smiled, and patted his equipment. 'Machines are okay for some areas, but in the city centre they can't get into corners. You know. Behind tele-phone boxes, for example.' Paul nodded. He was experiencing a sort of joy. He felt that he had found – in this mild man, who, though intellectually vital, seemed satisfied with his simple honest life – a sort of ideal. The monks of Dharamsala had suggested how it should look. They, however, were no more than the flickers of his imagina-tion and now here it was in flesh and grubby saffron overalls. 'Shop doorways,' Malcolm was saying – only one item in a long list of spaces inaccessible to street-sweeping machines. 'Especially when they've got a step.'

'Sure.'

There was a moment's lull – the traffic went past, the waves hissed, the gulls mewled. The long dun beach stretched deserted between the two piers. Then Malcolm said, 'There's a hell of a lot of satisfaction in this job.'

'Yeah, I bet.' Paul was wet-eyed – was it only the wind?

'You see the city wake up. You're responsible for your patch. You feel part of the community. In spring, the birds are singing.'

'Yeah,' Paul said. 'Yeah.' He was smiling.

'Mind you, in winter it's cold, wet and depressing.' Malcolm laughed. He had a shy, quiet laugh. 'Your toes get cold and don't warm up all day . . . But I couldn't work indoors. And we're the council workers most people meet. They like moaning to us about council services, just like they used to moan about British Rail.'

Paul chuckled. 'Yeah,' he said.

For a moment, Malcolm looked out over the wriggling, glittering sea. 'There's a new sense of optimism though.'

'Is there?'

'Yeah, I think so.'

'Why? How come?'

'Well . . . we merged parks and street-cleaning last year.'

'Parks and street-cleaning?'

'Which means the crisp packet,' Malcolm went on, 'or the cigarette packet, which blows from the street into the park is our problem now, not someone else's. Which means the gardeners can get on with the horticulture basically.'

'Right.'

'It makes sense.'

'Yeah, I'm sure.'

'And one of the reasons it's worked is because our director of services put a lot of effort into involving the staff in decision-making. In fact, we're more involved in decision-making than ever before. And it was a real challenge integrating two separate sections that were working under – it was actually *three* different contracts . . .'

Paul was unsettled by the turn that things had taken, by the *terms* Malcolm was using, and the mental landscape they seemed to manifest. It was this mental landscape – which had appealed to him so exquisitely only moments before – that he thought of when he imagined what the job *was*. 'Three?' he said, trying to maintain his enthusiasm.

'He's very positive, our director of services,' Malcolm was saying. Paul nodded. 'He's always trying to find solutions to take the staff with him. I really respect him a lot. Every month there's a meeting between front-line staff – that's myself and my colleagues – with Mr Woburn and the management team, to talk to the consultants. They're validating the new process –'

'Mr Woburn?'

'He's our director of services. Since the merger. Do you know him?' Paul responded with a perfunctory shake of the head. 'I really respect him a lot. He's changed things since the merger. There are more teams in the city now – they're based on the political wards now. We call them "tidy teams". That was his idea.' Malcolm smiled, somewhat feebly. 'I know – it's a bit corny. But it's working well. We had an outside audit commission do a CPA a few weeks back, and the report was really positive. And we had a really constructive best-value review as well.'

Paul was about to drop his fag-end onto the pavement, but suddenly remembered who he was speaking to, and held onto it. 'What's that?'

'Well, we spent two days, and created a framework that allows continuing dialogue. But some best-value reviews seem to be CCT all over again. I'm fed up with hearing about bloody Richard Branson!' Malcolm laughed shyly, and Paul laughed too, and said 'Yeah, right,' though he did not understand the joke. He did not really know what Malcolm was talking about any more. He was suddenly struck, however, by his physical resemblance to Richard Branson – the same reddish hair, the same face, beard and blue eyes, even the same strange mingling of self-assuredness and diffidence in his manner; but of course, Richard Branson as he would look if – rather than having spent the past twenty-five years high-altitude ballooning and skiing in the nude – he had spent them sweeping the streets of Brighton in all weathers. That is, less silky, less in the pink, less like the cat that got the cream. A lot less.

'You hear ministers talking about help for key workers, but they always mean teachers and nurses and so on . . .' Paul was aware of

Malcolm's voice again. 'And they all earn ten thousand pounds a year more than street sweepers, or dustmen, but we're equally as crucial.'

'Of course.'

'I'm lucky – my wife works and we've got no children. We bought our house twenty years ago. But none of my younger colleagues can afford a house round here. One of them has to cycle twenty miles to work. Twenty miles! And remember we start at six a.m.'

'You start at six a.m.?'

'They need to include street sweepers and dustmen, otherwise the city'll be buried in rubbish.'

'Sure.'

'Six a.m., yeah. It's an early start. But it can be lovely early in the morning. In summer, that is.' Timidly, Malcolm laughed. 'In winter it's not so good. Total darkness. Icy pavements. We just start gritting the pavements when we arrive – don't wait for a manager to tell us – you can't sweep an icy pavement.'

'No.'

Even were it not for Woburn's presence at the apex of the power structure in which Malcolm toiled – and that in itself put an end to his practical interest in the job – Paul now found that, in his mind, it no longer seemed to have anything to do with the monks of Dharamsala. The work had not changed, of course. However, his estimation of Malcolm had been in free fall for several minutes, and from the height of some sort of holy fool or idiot savant, he had plunged, in that short time, to the level of institutional brown-noser, stupidly infatuated with the pompous vapidity of management-speak. Paul thanked him, and when Malcolm said that he hoped to see him on a litter pick sometime soon, said, 'Yeah, I hope so. See you, mate.'

'Do you want a cup of tea?' Heather shouts from the kitchen as soon as he steps into the heated house, immediately starting to stew in his jacket. Her offer surprises him. He knows that something must have happened, because usually she welcomes him home with impatient questions about where he has been, and what he is doing to find a job. It had been his hope that she would still be at work; in case she was not, he had, as he walked from the bus stop, prepared a short statement. On entering the kitchen he starts to say it – something about the jobcentre. She seems uninterested. Then he notices the plate of biscuits and stops. 'What's up?' he says.

'What do you mean?' She is in her work clothes, a grey trouser suit. Not very flattering – it makes her legs look shorter than they are. The top half is better, the wide cream collar of the blouse highlighting the freckled solarium-tan of her face.

He waves limply at the table. 'I don't know. The biscuits . . .'

'What about them?'

'Nothing,' he says, with a shrug. He takes one. 'You seem in a good mood.'

'Do I?'

'Have you been on a sunbed?'

'I spoke to Martin.' She has her back to him, is pouring hot water into the teacups. 'You know – Martin. Martin Short.'

'Yeah of course.'

'Well, he says they're always looking for people to do the night shift. At Sainsbury's.'

'Oh. Yeah, well . . .' He sits down. 'Is that why you're in such a good mood?'

She puts his tea on the table. 'Paul,' she says matter-of-factly, 'it's almost February. You promised me if you didn't find something else soon you'd get another sales job.'

For a while he stares out of the window. It is twilight – cold, deepening twilight. Over the roofs of the opposite house-backs, two garden lengths away, the sky is gelid, luminous, sad. A quiet albescent yellow. Everything is very still. 'Yeah,' he says. She has been waiting for him to say it.

'And we agreed,' she goes on, 'that "soon" meant three weeks from the new year.'

He nods – it was agreed.

'That's tomorrow.'

He nods again.

'Maybe you've found something else?' she says. He shakes his head – he has not even told her about the street-sweeping. Or the grave-digging. He has become very secretive, turned inward. And he had thought that, with the TV money taking care of the February rent, she was simply waiting for twenty-one days to elapse before sending him out to find work in sales. For this reason, he is surprised by her suggestion of shelf-stacking in Sainsbury's. Surprised and touched.

'I think there's a job there if you want one,' she says.

'Is there?' He sounds vague. 'Why? What do you mean?'

'Martin gave me that impression.'

'What did he say?'

'Oh . . . Just . . . He said they always needed people. I said you were looking for a job. He said if you wanted one, he couldn't see it being a problem.'

'You told him I was looking for a job?'

'Well, you are.'

'I wish you hadn't.'

'Why?'

That is the only problem. That he would be working with Martin Short – the fresh-produce manager, lean and hungry, swanning around the shop floor in his Next suit. Except that, working nights, Paul would presumably never see Martin, would never even be in the shop at the same time as him.

'What did you tell him?'

'I didn't tell him anything. If you don't want the job, fine. I'd rather you went back to your old job. Something in sales. It's ridiculous. You shouldn't be working in supermarkets, garden centres!'

'Why not?'

'I mean, stacking shelves . . . What do you mean, *why not?*'

'I mean, why not . . .'

'It's ridiculous. And *I* find it insulting. It's an insult to *me*.'

'An insult to *you?*'

'Yes.' Said emphatically – though with a slight hesitant wobble.

There is a strange superficial stillness. 'I don't understand,' Paul says. 'An insult to you?'

'Look, Paul . . . I don't want to have an argument about this . . .'

'Nor do I.'

'If you're interested in the job, you're supposed to call someone . . . I've got the name – the personnel . . . The human resources lady. If not . . .'

'I am interested,' he says.

'Okay.'

'But I want to talk to Martin about it.'

'Why?'

'I just do. What's the problem?'

'It's not a problem,' she says. 'I just don't know why you want to talk to him.'

Why *does* he want to talk to Martin? There is, it seems, nothing to talk about. Martin has given Heather Sally Marshall's number, and said Paul should phone her if he is interested. Paul, though, does not want Heather to be his intermediary with Martin. He does not want things to be furtive, only to meet his smirking pentagon of a face in the street one day. So full of purpose, after smoking a spliff, he puts on his jacket and leaves the house. The two-storey Victorian terraces of Lennox Road are moonlit and shadowy. Although the houses are identical there is immense variation in their states of repair, from the frankly derelict, through the merely tatty (Paul's is one of these), to the ostentatiously souped-up – the Shorts' house being perhaps the most souped-up of all. In its small front space, separated from the pavement, as they all are, by a low brick wall, is an illuminated, 'Japanese'-style water feature – a zinc slab with a sheet of water perpetually sliding down it into a basin of round white stones. There is also some dead bamboo. A wall light next to the door is covered by a convex strip of metal, so that the illumination spills onto the painted brickwork above and below it. The brickwork, the whole house, is painted a shade of pale avocado, or lime sorbet. Paul opens the dinky gate (unlike his own, it does not squeak), and covers the three paces of salvaged York stone to the front door, which is the same colour as the bricks, but glossy with a big brass knob. He is nervous. He knows that the slightest pause, the slightest opportunity to think, will see him turn and slip away, so he shoves the brass bell push into its socket before he has even stopped moving, and then waits, while his heart beats thickly. He is not calmed by the continuous burbling of the water feature. The ground-floor curtains are drawn, but he can see that the lights are on, and Martin's yolk-yellow Saab – how often has Paul seen him washing it, seen his tight tracksuited arse as he stoops into it with a dust-buster of a Sunday morning – is parked a few metres along the street.

He has just tilted his head back to inspect the upstairs windows when the door opens. Martin seems slightly out of breath. He is wearing jeans and a baggy green jumper, and even more than usual, his face looks as if it were being subjected, at that very moment, to enormous G-forces, the shallow flesh stretched tight over the prominent underlying bones. His skin is pink and dry – it looks painfully so in places. He does not hide his surprise on seeing Paul – perhaps he is unable to. 'Oh,' he says. And then, for several moments, is speechless.

'All right, Martin.'

'Paul – hello.'

And since Martin is still simply standing there, smiling extremely uneasily, Paul says, 'I'm not getting you at a bad time, am I?'

'No, not at all. Of course not. What . . . Do you want to come in?' he suddenly blurts.

'Um, yeah, sure. Thanks. If that's okay?'

'It's okay. Of course it's okay. Come in.'

The interior of the house feels strange to Paul, being a mirror image of his own. The stairs, instead of being on the left, are on the right. The front room is on the left, instead of the right. He cannot get his head round it. It makes him feel queasy. Everything is brightly lit. 'Come in, come in,' Martin keeps saying. He seems to be encouraging Paul to go straight ahead, towards the back of the house where, as in Paul's own, an extension has been built on. In Paul's house this extension is a modest, flimsy addition, entirely functional, containing the kitchen and, above it, the bathroom. Here, though – and Paul is unable to suppress an awestruck, mumbled 'Cor' on entering – it resembles some sort of Viking hall, timber-framed with a high pointed roof – like something, Paul thinks, remembering his university days, out of *Beowulf*, except that it holds a pool table with raspberry baize, a TV even larger than Heather's ill-fated purchase, and a black leather three-piece suite with red leather scatter cushions. Wherever he looks there seem to be discreetly positioned speakers, and warm pools of halogen light. There is a small bronze statue of a woman, naked, lying on her back.

'This must take up half the garden,' Paul says. 'How'd you get planning permission for it?'

Martin is watching him with smiling satisfaction. When he smiles, his mouth seems in danger of widening beyond the limits of his face. 'Like it?'

'It's great,' Paul says. He stares at it for a few more seconds – longer than is natural, in fact, out of politeness. 'Can't be cheap to heat.'

Martin smiles steadily – his smile even widening, as if to say, 'No, it isn't. Why?'

'Is Eleanor in?' Paul asks.

Which literally wipes the smile off his face – though it reappears instantly in a much more muted, diffident form. 'Um, no, she's out,' he says. 'She's away, actually.'

'Oh. Where? If you don't mind my asking.'

'Visiting family.'

Paul nods. It is obviously a sore point, and while it would not be socially unacceptable to ask one or two further questions, he desists.

The state of the Shorts' marriage is a subject on which he and Heather often speculate – it is a subject which makes them feel warm and secure in their own togetherness. That people who do not know them would probably assume that Eleanor was Martin's mother must be a strain, Paul thinks. He is under the impression that they have been married a long time – since Martin was a student, perhaps twenty-one or twenty-two – and suspects that she might even have been his first girlfriend. Sadly, with her huge, utterly pendulous breasts, her swollen limbs, her natty grizzled hair, she has not aged well. Her face retains some feminine prettiness in its features, but between them the flesh has lost its tension. When Paul sees her in the street – and even more when he sees them together – he feels sorry for Martin. Embarrassed for him, too. And Martin himself – it is obvious – is embarrassed. Paul finds it a depressing situation to think about. Whenever he and Heather talk about it, he says – hopefully – that he is sure it won't last, while Heather warbles dutifully about love, and insists that it will. Well, it seems that she was wrong. It had always been Paul's assumption, of course, that when it ended, it would be Martin who ended it. He looks shell-shocked though. Perhaps, after twenty years, Eleanor has walked out on *him*.

Martin interrupts his musing – Paul is actually quite stoned – to say, 'What, what can I do for you, Paul?' He still seems nervous.

'Oh, it's just about this job,' Paul says, snapping out of his stupor. 'The job you told Heather about, didn't you?'

'Yes, um.' Martin seems to flounder for a moment. Why is he so flustered? 'On the night shift.'

'Yeah,' Paul says.

And Martin, embarrassed, says, 'Yeah.'

It strikes Paul how pathetic, how humiliating his situation might seem – *must* seem – to Martin, from whose perspective the shelf-stackers of the night shift are down in the murk somewhere, so low as to be out of sight. They do not even have names. Martin in fact finds it painfully distressing even to imagine himself in Paul's position. And suddenly understanding this, Paul is dry-mouthed with embarrassment himself. It happens instantaneously, strikes him suddenly – Martin's dismay is on account of . . .

HIM.

This dismay, this embarrassment of Martin's – which overwhelms, without quite obliterating, his well-meaning struggle to hide it – is infinitely worse than the sort of sly sneering that Paul had prepared himself for. It has such sincerity – a naturalness which sneering, any sort of nastiness, would never be able to have. It is involuntary. And it is not without sympathy, which is perhaps what makes it so peculiarly painful. As soon as he sees this, Paul wishes that he was not there. 'So . . . ?' he says, feeling the heat flaring in his face.

'So, um . . .' Martin is making an effort to be ordinary, level, his hands trapped in the tiny pockets of his jeans. 'Did . . .' He hesitates on the name. '. . . Heather give you Sally's number?'

Paul nods. 'She did, yeah.'

'You should just call her,' Martin says. 'Just call her.'

'Sure. And . . .'

But there is no 'and'. There is nothing else to say. There never was anything to say.

'And you reckon they're looking for people?' Paul says.

'They are. I know they are.'

'Okay.' It is obviously time for him to leave, but Paul feels he has to explain. 'I just need some money to tide me over,' he says.

Martin smiles. 'Sure. Of course. I understand.'

And as if it were his duty, Paul looks again at the lofty space of the extension. Only for a second or two. 'Well, cheers, Martin,' he says, turning.

'That's okay.'

Martin leads him to the front door and holds it open for him.

'And say to hi to Eleanor from me,' Paul says, stepping into the cold. Did he say it, he wonders, out of spite? Or just unthinkingly? He is not thinking straight.

'I will,' Martin says.

Paul hesitates, expecting him to reciprocate and offer his regards to Heather, but he does not.

15

Alone in the bedroom, under the yellowing ivory scattered by the ceiling bulb, light the colour of his teeth, Paul pulls on the blue trousers of his uniform. He tugs the polo shirt over his head, and shoves his arms through its little sleeves. He is nervous. It is twenty-five to ten. Seeing the light still on in Oliver's room, he slips over the landing and tiptoes downstairs. In her coat, Heather is sitting on the sofa, with a magazine. 'Should we go?' Paul says quietly. The car has a damp smell, and seems irked when she wakes it with the key. They drive in silence to the Old Shoreham Road. Heather's silence is so weighty, so pointed – she sometimes holds her lower lip in her teeth, as if something were *imminent* – that Paul says, 'You all right?'

'M-hm,' she nods, staring straight ahead through the wipers' sleepy to and fro.

'Thanks for driving me, by the way,' he says a few minutes later.

There are few other people out – unsurprising on a rainy Sunday night in January – and it only takes five minutes to get there. It seems to take no time. Paul leans over, his left hand opening the door – the kiss is a formality – and says, 'See you in the morning,' with a weary shot at a wry smile. He is early, and sitting alone at a table in the staff canteen, he feels odd in his ill-fitting uniform. He is also surprisingly tired – and it is only ten o'clock. Downstairs, he identified himself to Graham, the night-shift manager – a short, obese black man with a medicine-ball-sized head and fat-lensed spectacles that magnified his eyes.

Wearing a leather jacket, he sat on the rubber conveyor belt of a dormant checkout, singing quietly to himself, and tapping his clipboard with a biro.

Paul cleared his throat. 'Hi, um. I'm Paul Rainey?'

'All right, Paul,' Graham said, with unwavering, wide-awake smiliness. 'Why don't you go and wait upstairs with the others? Do you know where the canteen is?'

'No,' Paul said.

Graham looked around, his jacket creaking as he twisted his squat trunk. One of his feet – in a petite leather shoe with two buckles – maintained tenuous toe-contact with the floor. 'Someone'll be along in a minute,' he said. Unselfconsciously, he resumed his singing, while Paul stood there. The last stragglers of the day shift were trickling out in their coats, going home to late dinners and TV.

'Gerald,' Graham shouted. 'Gerald!'

A tall, espresso-skinned man of about forty-five lifted the headphones from his ears with leisurely slowness, a sloth-like absence of haste. They were very old-fashioned, the headphones, linked by a narrow steel band over the crown of his woolly hat, and padded with orange foam. 'This is Paul,' Graham said. 'He's starting tonight.'

The two shelf-stackers nodded at each other.

'All right,' Gerald said.

'All right, Gerald.'

'Gerald'll show you where to go,' said Graham.

In silence, Paul followed Gerald over the shop floor. Pushing through some heavy translucent rubber strips, they were suddenly in a grey, utterly functional space. The walls, undressed breeze blocks. The floor, concrete. The lighting, high overhead, greenish and cold. They went through fire doors, and up the linoleum stairs. Most of the shift were present in the canteen. Paul seated himself at an empty table – and was sitting there, moronically ogling its grey surface, when a voice at his shoulder said, 'What the fuck you doing here?'

Whose is that voice? He knows it. He looks up.

Rashid.

Paul says, 'What ...'

He remembers going to Rashid's fairly magnificent pad – it was in a brilliant, high-ceilinged Regency terrace – to pick up freezer bags of grass. The palatial appointments of the flat were a little worn and knocked about, but there was, nevertheless, always a sense of turning up at court. Rashid's courtiers were various male relatives, all shorter, hairier, fatter and uglier than he was; and there were always a few (usually quite unattractive) girls hanging around. Charlie – Rashid's burly, ochre dog – was always sprawled somewhere, taking the weight off his stubby legs, and panting with a pink, smile-shaped mouth. Rashid himself never answered the door – one of his cousins always did that – and he was often not in the sitting room when Paul came in, murmuring salutations to the courtiers, who murmured them back. Towards him, the cousins were deferential, the ugly girls haughtily indifferent. In no hurry, Rashid would emerge, presumably from some sort of boudoir, always wearing, if it was before eight p.m., a short silk dressing gown – so short that it did not reach his knees – and after some friendly, informationless small talk, business would be transacted in gentlemanly fashion – no counting of money, no checking of merchandise – and one of the cousins would show Paul out.

Now, seeing Rashid, Paul is mystified. He says, 'What ...' And then, 'What are you doing here?'

Rashid is smiling; his face shows no sign whatever of his own surprise and mortification. 'What happened to you, man?' he says. 'Why *you* working here?'

Paul shrugs. 'I . . . I am. I don't know . . . What happened to you?'

'What you talkin' about?' The question is put in an intimidating tone, and the message is obvious. Rashid pulls up a brown plastic chair and sits. 'So what the fuck you doing here?' he says. Paul fobs him off with a vague suggestion of personal tragedy. 'Oh, I don't know, mate,' he says. 'Things have just been ... You know.' Unhelpfully, Rashid shakes his head. 'Things have not been great.' Paul does not want to elaborate any more than that. He does not think Rashid would understand. Suddenly desperate for a cigarette, he feels in his pocket for his tobacco, and at that moment, Graham's voice summons them to work over the PA system.

As they troop down the stairs, someone – Paul does not see who – shouts out, 'Oi Rashid! Apparently you' on pet foods again.'

Rashid half turns, continuing to descend, and says, 'Pet foodz? *Pet foodz*? No way, man! I did that yesterday. How d'you know that?'

'That's what I heard. Apparently.'

'What, Graham told you?' Rashid shakes his head. 'No way. Not fuckin' pet foodz. No way.'

Graham does not seem to have moved. When he reads out their postings for the night, Rashid is indeed on pet foods. 'Aw, man,' he wails. 'Not *pet* foodz! I did them yesterday!'

'Do them properly this time, all right,' Graham says, without lifting his goggled eyes from the list.

'I *did* do them properly!'

But Graham is already saying, 'Mark, non-foods. Alex, refrigerator compartments. Dewayne, wines and spirits ...'

And Rashid, in his Timberlands, stomps away sighing to pet foods.

'How was it?' Heather says when he enters the kitchen in the morning, self-conscious in his uniform. It has been a long night. Two hours into the shift, Graham's wide shape had appeared at the end of the cereals aisle, where Paul was working. 'How's it going – all right?' he said. He seemed displeased about something.

'Yeah, fine,' Paul said. 'Fine.'

Graham nodded fatly. He was about to move on when he added, apparently as an afterthought, 'Try and hurry it up, will you?'

'Oh. Yeah, sure.'

Paul had stowed about half the cereal on the shelves when Graham appeared for a second time and, without hesitating, waddled purposefully into the aisle. 'Look, mate, you're going to have to get a move on,' he said. He looked impatiently at the shelves that Paul had already done. 'It doesn't have to be perfect,' he said. 'Just neat and tidy, you know.' And with surprising swiftness, and a cavalcade of creaking from his leather jacket, he suddenly dealt with a crate of All-Bran. It took him about twenty seconds, and his exertions brought out a bright sweat on the dark, porous surface of his forehead. 'There, you see,' he said, out of breath. Paul nodded sleepily. It was quarter to one, and he was very tired.

From two o'clock onwards he did not understand how he was still working. The worst hour was six to seven a.m.. This hour nearly left him a sobbing, head-shaking wreck, talking nonsense as he was led away. Then, suddenly, things no longer seemed so hopeless. For one thing, people started to arrive from the outside world. And these people – first the bakery staff, then others – seemed to rese-cure the supermarket, which in his mind had slipped its moorings, in time and space. Their faces pink from the cold air outside, they seemed to him like rescuers. He felt like kneeling and tearfully plas-tering their newspaper-holding hands with kisses. Then there was daylight – he saw it first from the smoking-room window, off to the left on the rim of the sky, like a ship on the horizon.

In the last minutes leading up to eight o'clock, the duty manager – a Mr Watt – started to fret about the presence of the night shift on the shop floor, as though they were stage hands and the show was about to start. There was a final frenzy of activity. And then it was too late – the shop was opening – they had to disappear. And they disappeared. They went upstairs to the locker room, put outer garments on over their uniforms and slipped out, unnoticed by the money-spending public as it poured in. Outside, it was blearily sunny. Grey splinters of sun stuck in his shrinking eyes, coming at him off puddles, distant roofs. The drone of the A270 was overlaid by the temporary clattering of a train. And in shapeless blue trousers, black leather jacket, Paul Rainey lit a pre-rolled cigarette in the numb morning air.

Heather is still waiting for an answer to her question.

'Yeah, fine,' he says, trying to sound upbeat. 'It was fine.' Seeing the kitchen table, however, he has an unsettling flashback to the small hours, to the breakfast cereals aisle, its dry odour, its garish topography, its absurd fauna – Honey Monster, Tony the Tiger, the chocolate-addled monkey on the Coco Pops . . . In fact, for the first hour the cereals had fascinated him. There were cereals for the would-be athlete, for the weight-conscious, for the sophisticate, the nature lover, the hedonist, the Spartan. Each seemed to be striving to transcend its simple, essentially standard flakes of starch, and offer a short cut to a whole way of life, of self-definition.

Marie is examining him with intense interest. (Oliver, though, is staring into the chocolate milk of his Coco Pops; and there seems to Paul to be something sullen in his not looking at him.) 'Have you been working *all night*?' Marie asks, with a sort of wonderment.

'I have.'

'*Have* you?'

'Yeah, I have.'

'In Sainsbury's?'

'Yeah.'

He explains how all the products she sees in the supermarket are pulled out onto the shop floor on wheeled pallets, and how he and a dozen others spend all night putting them on the shelves. 'It takes *all night*?' she says. 'Just to do that?'

'Yeah, it does,' he says. 'There's a lot of products. A lot of products . . .' Oliver is showing no interest. 'All right, Oli?' Paul says.

And though he says, 'Yeah,' he will not look him in the eye.

To finish work at eight in the morning was, in a way that was difficult to define, quite depressing. In the sunny, suddenly vacant house

– silent, except for the liquid drops of the kitchen tap, dripping into the crockery of three breakfasts that had been hurriedly dumped in the sink – Paul would sit on the sofa, still in his uniform, and start to make a spliff. The first morning – the morning of Oli's sullen silence – as soon as he lay down he had plummeted into unconsciousness, waking four or five hours later in the early afternoon and a state of total disorientation. The bland daylight was hateful – he felt like a vampire; eventually, though, turning his back to it, he managed to sleep, on and off, until the others got home at fiveish. Half waking from this shallow slumber, he heard them come in, shouting and crashing about downstairs. And with a ringing in his ears, resigned to getting no more rest, he had pulled on his jeans. It was not like getting up in the morning – it was less wholesome – and though, over the weeks, it did start to seem more like that, it never entirely shook off the sense of something amiss. Sometimes he thought of Gerald, who had been working nights for years – for as long as Paul had worked in sales – and wondered what it was like for him. He, surely, no longer suffered from this sense of being out of sync with the world. How could he survive otherwise? Perhaps he lived on his own – that might be easier (though of course not without its own tribulations) – because Paul's vague sense of displacement was forcefully verified when, mooching downstairs with a fuzzy morning head, he found, not only the sad, late-afternoon light, but beings with a whole day of wakeful incident behind them. He was unable to communicate with these beings. He ate his breakfast – he had started to eat Highland Porridge Oats for breakfast, a bowl of porridge every day at about five p.m. – while the children, still in their school uniforms, watched TV, and Heather started to think about supper. Though they inhabited the same physical space, through some sort of temporal slippage they seemed aware of each other only as phantoms, with whom it was impossible to interact. So Paul sat there, eating his porridge like a ghost, while Heather, still in her work clothes, waited for some burgers to defrost in the microwave.

On a positive note, he was drinking less than he had for years. (One effect of which was the sudden, startling resurgence of his libido. Heather – though she had for a long time placed its sluggishness high on the list of reasons why he should stop drinking – seemed impatient with this development, turning over with a *tsk* when, on his nights off, he took up her morning tea with a hard-on, and shooing him away when he surprised her towelling herself after her bath.) Perhaps he was inhibited by a sense that, no matter what hours he was keeping personally, the morning was off-limits to alcohol. There had been one testing night during his first week on the shift when he was assigned to the wines and spirits aisle. To be surrounded by all that liquor, to handle it for hours, had been hard; his thirst – his desire to open one of those bottles and have a swig, a *taste* at least – had been increasingly urgent. Hour after hour. The heavy glass bottles. The bright liquids. He came very close to pilfering something – a quarter-bottle of Scotch, rum, anything – and slipping off to the Gents to add it to his dumbly hungering blood. As he worked, he imagined in extraordinary detail the way the seal of the cap, its frail connections, would break with a soft crunching click. He imagined that over and over again. The taste of the auburn liquor, the mild fire in his throat . . . Yes, that had been hard. When he finally finished the aisle, his jaw was so tightly clenched that he could not open his mouth, and his temples throbbed. Perhaps, though, it was his successful emergence from that ordeal – into the morning light – that persuaded him that he would be able to do without alcohol after work. Whatever the reason, he *was* able to do without it, and that pleased him.

Heather, on the other hand, seemed to be drinking more and more. Paul noticed, from the way the bin filled up with bottles, that she was putting away an unprecedented quantity of wine. And she was going out more than she used to. In the past, she had not had much of a social life. She went out perhaps once a fortnight. Now she was out twice a week. She was usually tipsy when she got home, and sometimes worse. On one occasion in particular, she was so drunk that she was unable to open the front door. For several minutes, while he finished making his spliff, Paul listened to her scraping at it with the key. When he finally went to open it himself, she more or less fell into the hall, her face a glassy mask of confusion. It was half past one, and he had been worried – he had even phoned her. She had not picked up. When he asked her where she had been – he was himself entirely sober, if quite stoned – she just shook her head and pushed past him, moving with inept purpose towards the kitchen. He watched irritably as she walked into the wall. She did not look well. Her face was unpleasantly chop-fallen, and blotchily red, as if it had been rouged by a blindman; there were particularly handsome crimson flares on either side of her nose. 'Why didn't you answer your phone?' he said. She did not seem to hear. Apparently losing interest in the kitchen, or perhaps simply forgetting where she was going, she sank down onto the floor in the hall, still in her coat, as if she intended to sleep there. 'Where were you?' Paul said. She was curling up on the floor. For a few moments he stared at her, wondering what to do. Was he like this, he wondered uneasily, when *he* got home at the oblivious end of a big session? Surely he was never *this* drunk. She was blotto. It was, he thought, incredible that she had made it home. 'How did you get home?' he asked, without much hope of an answer. 'Did you take a taxi?' Surprisingly, she seemed to shake her head. 'You *didn't* take a taxi?' Another ambiguous head movement, most probably a shake. 'So how did you get home? Did Alice drive you?' It seemed unlikely. 'Did Alice drive you home?' he said. He was keeping his voice down – the kids were asleep upstairs.

Heather murmured something.

'What?'

She mumbled something.

'I can't hear, Heather. What did you say? "Nothing"?'

She made the noise again, a sort of two-syllable moan.

'Marvin?'

'Muh'n.'

'Marvin? What? *Martin?*'

At this she seemed to pull herself into a ball – a coat ball about her hips, only her dry leonine hair spilling onto the carpet and oxblood booted feet protruding.

'Martin drove you home?' Paul said, not sure whether he had understood. When he tried to make her stand up ('You can't sleep here, Heather') she fought him off with misdirected fisticuffs, until he muttered, 'Suit your fucking self,' and went into the kitchen to make his lunch. He was puzzled, and fractious. Later, passing through the hall to empty the ashtray – it must have been about four – he saw that she had gone.

In the morning when she came downstairs her face was grey and immobile, her eyes a bloodshot mess in their hollows. He was still in the lounge, of course, reading the early edition of *The Times*, just emerging from the obits – *fascinating*, the obits – into the looser prose of the sport. He was surprised to hear her on the squeaky stairs – he had not expected her down so early, though in fact it was the usual time. He waited a few minutes, then folded the paper and went into the kitchen. She did not at first acknowledge that anything unusual had happened. He said, 'You were quite drunk last night.'

'I wasn't that drunk . . .'

'Yes, you were. You were . . .' She interrupted him. 'I'm sorry, Paul,' she said drily. And knowing that he was in no position to exercise any sort of sanctimony, he just shrugged. 'Well,' he said. 'Whatever. How did you get home?'

She seemed to sigh. 'Martin drove me,' she said.

'Martin? Martin Short?'

'Yes.'

'I thought you were with Alice.'

'I was.'

'So what was Martin doing there?'

'He wasn't there. I asked him to come and get me.'

'You what, you called him?'

'I know – it's ridiculous.'

'You called him, at one o'clock or whatever, and he came to get you?'

'Yes.'

'Where were you?'

'Some wine bar in town.'

'Wasn't he asleep?'

'I think he was, yes.' For a moment – nervously, naughtily – she laughed. Then she made a pain face.

That Martin would do this was not in itself surprising. His seemingly unlimited willingness to do things for her was a joke that even the children were in on. This, however, seemed excessive.

'The poor fucker probably had to go to work today.'

'I think he did.'

'You can't use him as a taxi service just because he'll do it.'

'I know,' she said.

For a moment, Paul wondered whether to say the words. He had himself drunk next to nothing for weeks. 'Well, you shouldn't drink so much,' he said.

Holding the mug over her mouth, she shot him a sharp look.

'You shouldn't,' he said. And then, 'I've more or less stopped drinking, Heather. I don't know if you've noticed.'

'No, I have,' she said. 'It's good.'

'It'd be a shame if just when I stopped, you started.' He paused. 'Why were you so pissed anyway?'

She shrugged. 'We were just having a good time. You know.'

16

Since leaving prison, Rashid has been living with his aunt and her husband, an accountant – staying in their spare bedroom, and working four nights a week, for a tenth of what he used to make. It just isn't worth it. What sort of life is *that*? When he and Paul are alone he often expatiates on this subject. What sort of shit life is this? Why is a life like this worth living? What's the point? In the dry air of the smoking room – greenish with neon light and bruised with exhaustion – Paul listens patiently.

More or less the whole shift is in the smoking room now – in ten minutes the lunch hour will be over – and the presence of the others subdues Rashid. He despises them. He does not understand why Paul puts up with them so tolerantly. Though he despises Paul too, it is a less pure feeling, and in fact he feels a sort of kinship with him – a kinship of misfortune, if nothing else. There is no misfortune involved in those others being here, he thinks – the blacks, the paedophiles – this is their natural element, what they were always destined for. He and Paul on the other hand – he and Paul should not be here, this is not for them. 'Take it easy, yeah,' he says.

'Yeah, see you later.'

Rashid passes Gerald in the doorway and, standing aside to let him in, shakes his head with a sort of weary disdain. Gerald is the senior worker on the shift – the oldest and the longest-serving. He is trained to use the hydraulic pallet truck, and trusted with the cigarettes, and once Paul saw him, dressed startlingly like an arctic explorer, wheeling trolleys of meat from the misty frozen vaults of the warehouse. Sometimes he says strange, mystical-sounding things. One night, when Paul met him on the shop floor, for instance, and told him that he had been put on fresh produce, Gerald said, 'Oh yeah? Goin' out in the garden?'

And to be amid the fresh produce – the damp leaves of the lettuces, the cool scent of the soil in the punnets of cress – *was* a bit like being in a garden. As well as the presence of vegetable matter, the space was more open than the limiting narrowness of the aisles. If it suggested a garden, however, it did so extremely faintly – there was, after all, almost no soil in the punnets, and the lettuces were each in their own plastic bag. So faintly, in fact, that it was intermittently sweet and sharply frustrating. Nevertheless, Paul's senses and imagination strained to enjoy what was there. Gerald had inspired this exercise, and at such times he seemed the purveyor of a subtle wisdom.

Most of the time, however, Paul thinks that years of nocturnal living have made him slightly mad. He is obsessed with the mineral waters. He often points out – with nostril inhaling exhilaration, as if he were actually in the Alps – the pictures of 'nice clean mountains and stuff' on their bluish bottles. He is obsessed too with supermarket politics, a subject on which he often holds forth in the smoking room. Paul usually ignores him – focusing his mind instead on the smouldering tobacco in his hand, staring at the grey wall, and shutting everything else out. So he was doing tonight – until he heard Gerald say, '. . . you know, *that Martin Short.*' Then, still leaning forward wearily, with his elbows on his knees, he started to listen. Gerald is speaking mainly to Mark, a whey-faced forty-five-year-old with colourless hair and eyes who is sitting next to him. Mark's eyes move furtively from Gerald's face to the linoleum floor, he nods a lot, and sometimes, like someone taking instructions, he murmurs something to show that he is listening.'

'Watt is going out his mind,' Gerald says. With the exception of Mark, his listeners do not seem interested; they smoke in vapid silence.

This despite the fact that the political situation in the supermarket is more interesting than usual, owing to the imminent stepping-down of Jock Macfarlane, the store manager. For a long time – for years – it has seemed obvious that his successor will be Roy Watt, his deputy. Gerald's point seems to be that Watt's inheritance is suddenly under threat. And the source of the threat – he has just said it – is the fresh-produce manager – 'you know, *that Martin Short*'.

It is a sort of seminar – with Gerald steering – and now he wonders, in his nasal Estuary English, *why* Martin is such a threat. Mark nods, as though it were a question that has been troubling him for some time. Gerald's own theory is that it is the unusual profitability of fresh produce that makes Martin a threat. He says that with the exception of wines and spirits it is the most profitable section of the supermarket. (People are starting to leave, to wander downstairs, where Graham is waiting.) And this, of course, leads to the next question – *why* is fresh produce so much more profitable than one would expect? How does Martin do it?

Gerald, Mark and Paul are the only ones left in the smoking room. Gerald looks at his watch, and stands up with a sigh. He is extremely tall, with a small head the colour of wet coffee grounds. 'So how *does* he do it?' Paul enquires huskily as they leave. Strangely, though he spends so much time holding forth, whenever he is asked a specific question Gerald seems indisposed to speak. He laughs quietly, and shakes his head. 'I don't *know*,' he says, as though it were naive of Paul to have expected him to.

Then, however, turning away, he mutters, 'I only know what I been told.'

Paul follows him to the water cooler.

'What have you been told?'

Gerald slowly swallows two cups of water. 'What have I been told,' he says.

'Yeah.'

Perhaps not used to people taking such an interest in what he has to say, he seems suspicious. He and Paul are alone in the canteen – Mark has vanished. Gerald peers at Paul for a moment, perhaps wondering what his motives are.

'If you don't want to tell me . . .' Paul says, with a shrug, and pours himself a cup of water, tilting the cooler's blue plastic tap. 'Is it a secret?'

'I don't know, my friend. I don't know.'

'Fair enough.'

And in silence, side by side, they descend the stairs to the shop floor.

In the morning, Paul is waiting for the bus. Suddenly aware of someone standing near him, he turns. It is Gerald, trussed up in his donkey jacket. He is wearing his woolly hat even though it is not cold. 'Oh, all right?' Paul says. And in a quiet voice, looking off to one side, Gerald says, ''Cos of the perishable and seasonal nature of the produce, the fresh-produce manager's got a certain degree of autonomy in purchasing matters.'

'Oh yeah?'

'Yeah.'

Starting to fear that Gerald is a muddled and lonely man looking for someone to latch on to, Paul is not listening properly. He tries to seem uninterested. His eyes fixed emptily on the horizon, he hears only isolated phrases. 'Budget for discretionary purchases . . . To take advantage of short-term availability . . . Temporary price troughs . . . Unexpected surges in local demand . . . You're talkin' about produce that's decayin' all the time . . . Once it's gone its value is nil, right?' Paul says nothing. 'Fink of the stock as perishable money . . . Everyfing happens *fast* . . . That's why he's got to have more autonomy.'

A bus is approaching, and Paul squints to see the number. Half a dozen different buses stop there. It is not his, and he stands aside

228

to let people on. They jostle him, and he hears Gerald say, 'He's supposed to go through the approved suppliers only.'

'Is he?'

'That means from the list. To add a supplier to the list takes time. He's got to send the information up to head office. They got to investigate . . .'

'Yeah.'

'So he's got some autonomy, but he can only use the approved suppliers.'

'Sure.'

'Well, what I heard . . .'

Paul sees his own bus, pulling in behind the one that is there. 'Sorry, that's my bus.' He starts to move towards it, and is surprised – and perturbed – when Gerald follows him and waits while he pays for his ticket. He is even more perturbed when Gerald purchases a ticket himself, and sits down next to him. Paul, squashed in the window seat, stares through the soiled glass as the bus pulls out into the road. 'What I heard,' Gerald says, steadying himself.

'Is this your bus, mate?'

He waves the question away. 'S'okay. I can take it. *What I heard is –*' his voice sinks to a whisper – 'Short's been usin' suppliers who've not been approved.' More preoccupied with the possibility that someone mentally ill is following him home, Paul says, 'Oh? Why?'

'That's the question.'

Still staring out the window, Paul says nothing as the bus turns onto the Old Shoreham Road, and the low morning sun hits it full in the face. 'Could be the suppliers we're talkin' about wouldn't *be* approved,' Gerald says, in an offhand sort of way, turning to look out of the windows on the other side of the bus. Wheezing, it stops at the lights.

'Why not?' Paul's voice is equally offhand. He is wondering whether to get off in Portslade. 'Why wouldn't they be approved?'

Gerald just shrugs.

The bus has started to move again. It is turning into Boundary Road, the streaming low sun showing its filthy windows for what they are, when he says, 'Might be they use illegal immigrant labour. Might be they don't pay taxes. Who knows.'

'So why does he use them?'

Gerald laughs. 'Why d'you fink?'

They cross the railway line, and for a moment, with the sun in his eyes, Paul looks straight up the white tracks. 'Dunno,' he says.

''Cos they're cheaper, innit.'

'Are they?'

'Course. And if they're cheaper . . .' For the first time he looks at Paul, with a small teacherly smile of encouragement.

Paul says, 'Fresh produce makes more profit?'

'Exactly.'

The bus is scudding down Portland Road, towards the sun. Perpendicular streets flash past on either side – down some of which, in the distance, it is possible to glimpse a small glitter. The sea. 'Exactly,' Gerald says again, tapping his foot. Paul turns to the window. He jumps off two stops too soon, and is thankful when Gerald stays on the bus.

They wait in the alley, Paul and Oliver, in the stare of the security camera, outside the metal door. Paul yawns. One evening the previous week, he was eating his porridge in the kitchen. Oliver was there, in his pyjamas. 'How's your job, then?' he said, with his face in the fridge. The question was surprising because since Paul started his job Oliver has never mentioned it. There has in fact been a frostiness between them since the morning when Paul got in from his first shift and Oli, staring into his Coco Pops, seemed to ignore him. It is something that has quietly depressed Paul for the past two months. 'Yeah, it's fine,' he said. Working through his porridge, he tried not to show how pleased he was. 'It's fine.' And a few moments later – 'Thanks.'

'That's all right,' Oli said.

They talked snooker for a while, and Paul suggested a visit to the club. 'How about Saturday?'

'Won't you be too tired?' Oliver – not one to be fobbed off with empty promises – was openly suspicious.

'Nah,' Paul said, 'I'll be all right.'

And so they wait on Saturday morning until Ned shows up, whistling, with the keys. He seems surprised to see them. 'All right, Paul?' he says. 'All right, mate? All right, Oli? You're here nice and early.' It is ten past twelve. 'Yeah, well . . .' Paul says. Ned smiles. His small, friendly eyes seem to search Paul's face – which is, he thinks, unusually pale and tired-looking, with several days' stubble. 'You all right, mate?'

'Bit tired.'

'Are you? *Are* you? Big night, was it?' He starts to unlock the door. It takes him a minute – there are four stiff locks. 'Not seen you two for a while.'

Oliver says nothing, so after a few moments Paul mumbles, 'No, not been around for a while.'

'Why's that then?'

'Just . . . Been busy. You know.'

'Busy?' The door opens, and Ned stands aside for them to enter.

'Well, I'm working nights at the moment,' Paul says, starting up the damp concrete steps. In the echoic stairwell, his voice sounds huge.

'Nights?' Ned shouts, following. The word is drowned out by the boom of the door as it closes. 'You're working nights?'

'Yeah,' Paul shouts, without stopping or turning.

'What you doing then?'

'Supermarket. You know.'

'What?'

'Supermarket . . .'

The snooker hall is in darkness – velvety darkness, with a mouldering

231

smell. Paul and Oliver wait while Ned walks into the void. A few seconds later neon tubes flicker where the bar is. Even when they have established themselves, their unwholesome bluish light is very localised. Most of the hall is still invisible. In this sickly light, Ned is stirring. He switches on the illuminated taps – Foster's, Guinness, Carlsberg, Coca-Cola – and then a warmer tungsten filament in the bar. 'What you say you were doing?' he asks, putting the pint of milk that he has with him into the fridge with the alcopops and bottled beers. Paul, who was hoping that the subject had been dropped, says, 'What?' Now leaning on the bar, he seems engrossed in rolling a cigarette.

'What you doing nights?'

What is irritating is that Ned, still preparing for the day's trading, is obviously not *that* interested in what Paul is doing nights. When he asks the question he is hidden from sight, fiddling with something at floor level.

Oliver seems to have wandered off into the darkness.

'You know. Supermarket work.' Paul says this simultaneously with licking the cigarette paper, and it seems unlikely that Ned would have heard it. Nevertheless, standing up and dusting off his hands he says, 'Oh yeah.' And then, 'Too early for a pint?'

'Not for me, mate,' Paul laughs hollowly.

'No, I s'pose not.'

Ned starts to pour a Foster's – the tap quickly sputters, spitting out only foam. He sighs, and withdraws.

Sleepily, Paul turns to the hall – now that his eyes are more used to the darkness, it is full of shapes. The tables and the large hooded lights that hang over them. 'Oli?' he says.

Oli's voice, from somewhere out in the hall – 'Yeah?'

'All right?'

'Yeah.'

'Ned's just changing the barrel.'

Paul tries to shrug off his sleepiness. The darkness and dusty silence of the hall do not help. He wishes that he could lie down under one of the tables, on the filthy, mildewed carpet – its colour is something of a mystery – and sleep. He empties his throat, loudly – as if to startle himself into wakefulness – and steps over to the rack where the club cues are kept. They are a miserable, motley crew – some grotesquely warped, some unweighted, their tips knocked down to splintery mushrooms. One is even cracked. Surely no one ever uses it, yet it is still there in the rack . . .

He hears Ned return from his 'office' saying, 'Sorry about that.' It is nice to see Ned – he has not seen him for two months. And with all that has happened, old Ned for one is still the same. 'No problemo,' Paul says.

Ned transfers several pint pots of foam to the little stainless-steel sink before the lager starts to flow. 'As fresh as it gets,' he says, pushing the pint towards Paul.

'And a Coke for Oli.'

'Yeah, sure.' Ned has just poured himself a quarter pint of Foster's and slung it down his throat. He wipes the foam from his mouth. 'Which table you want?' he asks, taking a can of Coke from the fridge.

'Whichever,' Paul murmurs, still yawning in front of the cues.

'Whichever. Right.'

When he has poured the Coke into a pint glass, Ned turns to a panel of sixteen brown light switches with a marker pen number next to each one. 'Number eight then.'

And suddenly the table is there.

Staring at the cues, Paul wishes that he had not smoked that last spliff, an hour ago. That had been a mistake. It had flattened him, made him want to slither upstairs and lie face down on the bed. That was what he would normally be doing at this time – and tomorrow, tomorrow would be the same as today – they were going up to London to have Easter lunch with Heather's parents. It would be hell for him, of course – sitting down to a steaming roast dinner in the middle of the night – but Heather was insistent. He takes one of the cues and weighs it in his hand. Then he shuts one eye and looks down it. It is fucked. He is faintly troubled by something that happened at about eleven thirty last night, when he was on his way home from the twenty-four-hour shop. Turning into Lennox Road, he saw Heather emerging from Martin's car. She had been out with Alice. When he walked over, she explained that Martin had been meeting someone in the same place, and had offered her a lift. 'Where was that?' Paul had asked. They were standing next to the yellow Saab. Martin was still strapped into the driver's seat, with his hands on the wheel. When she told him where it was – the bar of the Metropole – Paul said, 'Oh, very swish,' and stooping to peer into the car, he had thanked Martin for driving her home . . .

'Here the balls,' Ned says, wiping some foam from his mouth.

Without exchanging the fucked cue, Paul walks to the bar for the pitted plastic tray. Oli has emerged from the darkness and is waiting in the penumbra of the table's light, swinging his cue impatiently from side to side. 'Set the balls up, will you, Oli,' Paul says, putting the tray down on the baize. It is what he always says – a sort of liturgical utterance, words that hallow what follows and set it apart from the usual fare of life.

He has met Martin several times over the past two months. None of these meetings has been pleasant. Leaving the supermarket one morning, he walked into him – muttering, 'Sorry, mate,' and only then seeing who it was.

'Oh, Paul,' Martin said.

'Yeah. All right, Martin?'

Peering past him into the shop, Martin said, 'Um . . . How's it going?'

'Fine.'

'Great. That's great!'

'And you?'

Martin nodded. 'Fine.'

'All right, well . . .'

'Yes, I . . .'

'See you soon I hope, Martin.'

'Of course. See you soon, Paul.'

He had been immensely troubled by this meeting. It had upset him for a week; sent him scurrying for whisky, ending the era (how short it had been!) of teetotal Paul. It seemed to pop open questions that he had hoped were shut and put his small, private sense of satisfaction under strain.

The doorbell sounds – the snooker players have started to arrive – and Ned, wiping foam from his mouth, switches on the security camera's grey-and-white screen.

It sometimes happens that, when unusually tired or stoned, Paul produces snooker of a semi-professional standard. On these occasions – his muscles strangely limp, his mind vacant – he somehow makes the balls move exactly as he wants them to.

So it is today.

Initially, however, while Oli starts (and is at the table for some time), Paul – sitting under the brass score sliders – struggles just to stay awake. Several times, Oli has to tell him to keep up with the scoring, and once his cue slips from his hand and smacks the carpet – just as Oli is taking on a tricky black. He misses. Paul tells him to take it again. Oli shakes his head – he looks displeased. With a sigh, Paul stands. Oli sits with his arms folded, frowning. When he sips his Coke, it is with a furrowed brow. He does not feel that Paul is taking it *seriously* – with a sort of negligent laziness, he stoops to the first shot he sees, one that does not require him to move from where he is standing. It is not an easy red. It is as if he *wants* to miss it, Oliver thinks, so that he can sit down again, and sleep.

Slapdash, nonchalant, Paul pots it.

And yawns.

*

Oliver is a sulky loser, and vanishes from the hall while Paul is settling up with Ned. 'There's something I've been wanting to talk to you about, actually,' Ned says.

'What's that?'

He lowers his voice. 'I've had a word with Jack Oakshott.'

'Oh yeah?' Jack Oakshott, the president of the Brighton and Hove Snooker Association. Paul has met him once or twice.

'About young Oliver.'

'Sure.'

'Jack thinks he could go far,' Ned says, wiping foam from his lip. 'He's very enthusiastic.'

'What about?'

'About putting him in for the Youth Championship. It's in Bristol, in September –'

'The Youth Championship? At his age?'

'I know what you're thinking,' Ned says. 'You're thinking –'

'What about the Juniors?'

'Yeah.'

'Wouldn't that be more realistic?'

'Listen.' Ned is whispering. Why, Paul does not know. 'Jack's thought this out. If we put him in for the Juniors, he might win. Sure. But winning the Juniors – it's no big deal. Listen. Jack can reel off a list of Junior winners that never went on to go pro. It's a sort of kiss of death. The Juniors. That's what Jack says. Now the Youth Championship. Well, I don't need to tell you all the big names have won it in their time. It is *the number-one* springboard to professional status.'

'But he's not going to win the Youth Championship,' Paul says tiredly.

'Not this year.'

'And not next year.'

'Not next year. But in three or *four* years, when he comes up against lads his own age, he'll have three or four years' experience of the tournament. And they'll be coming from the Juniors. D'you see?'

'Well,' Paul says, 'yeah.'

'Jack's seen this done with other players. He knows what he's talking about.'

'Sure.'

'I want to get you two together for a drink sometime – have a chat about it.'

'Yeah, let's do that.'

'I'm excited about this boy,' Ned says. He taps Paul – who does not look excited – on the arm. 'Aren't you excited, mate?'

'Yeah, course.'

Suddenly solicitous, even worried, Ned says, 'You all right?'

'I'm fine. I'm tired, that's all.'

'Jack's thinking about the *Argus* for sponsorship.'

'The *Argus*?'

'Well, they know him, don't they?' They do know him – he was in the paper last November, in an article headlined HOVE SCHOOLBOY MAKES MAXIMUM BREAK.

'Where is he, by the way?'

'He's gone. He's left.'

'Why? What's his problem?'

'Dunno. He doesn't like losing.'

'Who does? And he's a winner.'

'He is indeed.'

Paul finds him loitering sulkily in the alley outside. 'All right?'

'When can we play again?' he says.

'Dunno. Next week?'

'Okay.'

'Okay?'

In silence – one sullen, the other sleepy – they walk back to Lennox Road.

17

Staring fixedly at the oncoming motorway, Paul is trying to stay awake. The swishing hum of the engine as it toils, the monotony before him, the fact that it is more or less his bedtime – quarter to twelve, a.m. – all weigh heavily on his eyelids. In the back of the car, the children have stopped making noise, are probably asleep. Nor is Heather in a talkative mood – she has said hardly a word since they set out. And next to Paul, at the wheel, Martin's jaw – like the air in the Saab's cramped cabin – is tensely, nervously tight. It is Easter Day, and they are off to Heather's parents' house for lunch.

She did not mention to Paul until last night that Martin had offered to drive them. She told him as she was going up to bed, leaving him to spend the next few hours in uncomfortable wonderment at the lengths to which Martin would go to be of service to her. Was there *anything* he would not do?

'What, he's coming to the lunch?' Paul had said in disbelief.

'No, of course not.'

'What's he going to do then – wait in the car?'

She was standing in the doorway in her dressing gown. She yawned. 'I don't know,' she said. And they both laughed uneasily.

'But he *can't* do that!' Paul said, suddenly feeling that it was in fact too much. For Martin to regrout the shower, to unblock the drains was one thing. To do *this* though . . . 'Come on . . .' There was something weird about it. Was it not slightly insane? And should Martin not be *dissuaded* from such insane actions? Paul was surprised, even shocked, at Heather's willingness to make use of him.

'He wants to,' was all she said.

For a few moments Paul was speechless. Then he said, 'It's not right.'

The doorbell's urgent exclamation sounded on the stroke of eleven. Heather was still upstairs. She seemed unusually on edge, was yelling impatiently at Marie. The doorbell sounded again. Though it was, of course, too late – he was able to see Martin's tall shape splintered in the frosted glass panels of the door – Paul wished, as he went to open it, that he had done something to forestall this situation. He found that he was humming to himself, out of nervousness. Nobody's dignity, he thought, twisting the mortise, is going to survive *this* intact. Martin was wearing a blouson jacket of greenish-blue suede, jeans and moccasins. Also sunglasses – iridescent teardrop mirrors – which he whipped off as Paul opened the door. He was blushing, his grey-blue eyes subtly evasive. 'Morning, Martin,' Paul said.

'Paul.'

'It's really very good of you to offer to do this.'

'It's no trouble.'

Paul laughed – a single, flinty *Ha!* 'I'm glad you think so. I'm glad you think so. Come in.'

Martin stepped warily into the hall, looking around with the air of someone who had never seen it before; with the strange air, in fact, of someone entering a famous space, the Sistine Chapel say, for the first time – there was something of the well-behaved tourist in the way he moved his head from side to side, systematically taking in his surroundings – the beige hall, the small steps, the framed print of Salisbury cathedral. 'Um, come through,' Paul said, holding out a hand in the direction of the sitting room. There they stood in the residual haze of the spliff smoke; and there too Martin seemed to think that he was in a museum, piously inspecting Heather's knick-knacks, and keeping his hands safely in his pockets. 'Coffee?'

Paul said. He hoped that Martin would want one, if only to give him an excuse to leave the lounge, where the atmosphere stung with discomfiture, with a kind of dumb imbroglio, the social ineptitude of a botched and sinking date. Martin shook his head immediately and said, 'No, thanks.' There followed perhaps a minute of silence, and then, unable to think of anything else to say, Paul asked him what he was planning to do while they had lunch. Martin just shrugged and said, 'I don't know.' Paul was still nodding, as if weighing up this answer, his lips held in a thoughtful moue, when – preceded by the children with their newly brushed hair – Heather tumbled down the stairs. 'Hi, Martin,' she said, with the merest skimming look in his direction. (Paul thought her embarrassment entirely understandable.) Martin did not even say hello to her. Excited by the prospect of travelling in the yellow Saab, it was the children who did most of the talking.

Low in the sporty leather seat, Paul struggled to stay awake as they sped up the A23, through its innumerable chalky cuttings, towards London.

The traffic is light, and the sun shines through intermittently, dumping its metallic brightness on the monochrome hues of the road. Martin stares straight ahead. In the back, the children are quiet, as if drugged by the scent of leather and – used to the sluggishness of Heather's old Vauxhall – the smooth impulsive acceleration of the vehicle. Near Reigate, still in uneasy silence, they join the M25. The stiffly generous banter of the first fifteen minutes of the journey, as they disentangled themselves from Brighton – Paul had made a particular effort, Martin was more monosyllabic – is a distant memory now. No one has said a word for an hour. At some point between junctions eight and nine, Paul finally nods off – and wakes with a start in a quiet, residential street, to the patient, measured tick of the indicator. Aware of him in his peripheral vision, he wonders how Martin must feel. Their presence in Hounslow makes the situation seem even stranger than it did in Hove. They are on the Staines Road . . . His head flops loosely on his exhausted neck as the synthetic voice of the GPS system says, 'Turn. Right.' And Martin turns the wheel. He lets them out in front of the house. Standing on the pavement, Paul fears for a moment that Heather will invite him to join them for lunch. She does not. She says she will phone him when they have finished, and – still strapped into his seat – he smiles tensely (feeling quite foolish, Paul imagines) and drives away with a defensive brusqueness, a dash of turbo, as if he has things to do.

It is the first time that Paul has seen Mike or Joan since starting his new job – initially its precise nature was kept from them – and he finds, to his irritation, that they now treat him as if he were seriously ill. 'I've worked nights,' Mike says sympathetically, sad-eyed, as they sip their aperitifs. 'It's not as bad as all that. It's not so bad.'

'That wasn't in a supermarket, Dad.'

'No,' he says, judiciously. 'No, it wasn't.'

And it is not mentioned again, even when Paul dozes off over his crescent of melon and rag of Italian ham.

In the sweltering room, everything seems so slow. The successive procedures of the meal. There is an extended, inexplicable lull between the starter and the main course, during which he goes out into the garden for a cigarette to try and wake himself up. On his own, watching the planes scream over, he sees them all sitting there one cloudy Sunday, Mike with his hands over his eyes, smiling; Heather holding Marie; himself, somewhat younger, listening politely to Joan. 'The thing is,' she is saying, 'you just can't let it get to you. If you let it get to you, if you become obsessed with it, it becomes a nightmare. Doesn't it?'

He falls asleep with a plate of roast lamb in front of him, and it is then that he is told to leave, and wanders upstairs. And he wakes, several hours later, in Heather's old room, on her old single bed, wondering what time it is. Through the window the sky is listlessly ambiguous. Descending the stairs in his socks, he hears voices indistinctly from the lounge. And then, when he is halfway down, he hears Martin's voice. He stops. The drive from Hove – though he knows of course that it happened – had seemed, when he woke and sat for a few fogged minutes on the edge of the bed, like an unpleasant dream. Now Martin is *there* – he is in the house – and Paul feels that this finally is too much.

When he appears in the doorway, frowsy and thunder-faced, Heather says, 'Oh there you are. I was just about to wake you up. We're going.' She sounds drunk.

'Well, I'm up,' he says. 'All right, Martin?'

Martin just nods. He is looking through some photos.

Joan brings Paul a coffee, and he sits down. Martin is looking through the photos – which are of Mike and Joan's narrow-boat holiday – as if they were the most interesting things he has ever seen, examining each one for ten or twenty seconds. Paul enjoys his obvious unease and embarrassment. He should not have showed up there. It turns out, however, that Heather more or less invited him in. She phoned to say that they were leaving soon, and since he was sitting in his car two streets away, she suggested – with voluble encouragement from her parents – that he join them.

It is nightfall when they leave. Heather, Paul notes, is totally drunk. When they finally slip onto the M25 near Staines, it is night. Not long after this, however, they have to pull over onto the hard shoulder. Heather falls out. In silence, Oliver and Marie watch her stagger towards the undergrowth, while Paul and Martin sit in their seat belts, staring straight ahead. She has not made much of an effort to hide herself, and waves of headlights wash her squatting form. 'Sorry about this,' Paul mutters. Martin – keeping an impudent eye on her in the mirror – says nothing. This offish silence, and the way in which he is openly staring at her, make Paul furious. In a quiet voice he says, 'What did you get up to this afternoon then?' Still staring at Heather as she wobbles towards the car, Martin just shakes his head.

Thereafter, an icy silence sets in until he parks the Saab in Stoneham Road. Heather is asleep, and when Paul tries to wake her, she shrugs him off. As soon as Oliver and Marie were out, she slid into a horizontal position, and now seems intent on staying there. They wait on the pavement looking nervous while Paul, in an increasingly savage whisper, tries to persuade her to disembark. Standing next to them, Martin wears a look of extreme, sober seriousness, like a politician on TV in the midst of a natural disaster. Squashing herself into the leather of the seat, Heather shoves Paul with a stockinged foot – her shoes have fallen off – and he hisses, 'For fuck's sake, *get out*.' He takes her arm and tries to pull her into a sitting position, but she wrestles it free and slithers further in. He sighs and stands up, with a sort of shrug. For a moment, humiliated and at a loss, he just stands there. Then he fumbles the house keys from his pocket and hands them to Oliver. 'Mum's not well,' he says. 'We'll be along in a minute. Go inside.' Without a word, Oliver takes the keys, and he and Marie walk away – Marie looking over her shoulder.

In the few seconds that this has taken, Martin has insinuated himself into the situation – perched on the ledge of the seat, leaning into the car, he seems to be whispering something to Heather. Paul wonders what to do. It does not seem to be Martin's place to try and wheedle her out – except that it *is* his vehicle and he, Paul, has already tried and failed – and the impulse to seize his suede shoulder and say, 'What the *fuck* are you doing?' quickly evaporates in the face of these observations, and of Paul's weariness and wish to end this situation as quickly as possible. He looks along the quiet, terraced street.

Something seems to be happening, some sort of movement, and for a nightmarish moment he thinks that Martin is *kissing* her. Then he withdraws slowly from the interior and sighs. 'She's been sick,' he says.

They stand there.

'Look, I'm sorry, Martin,' Paul says. Martin, touching his palms tenderly together, seems to be pondering something. Paul assumes – wrongly – that it is something to do with the vomit in his spotless Saab. 'I really am,' he says. 'We'll pay for it to be valet-cleaned. You know . . .' Seemingly lost in thought, Martin shakes his head. Paul wonders whether he is dismissing the offer. Martin sighs again – a great heaved sigh; he is shaking his head with a sort of weighty sorrow. Suddenly wanting a cigarette, Paul takes one out of his pocket, and is about to light it, when it occurs to him that Martin's pensive, sorrowful immobility may just be a matter of waiting for *him* to deal with the situation, so he shoves the cigarette into his pocket and hurriedly inserts his head into the now sourly unpleasant-smelling interior of the Saab. 'Come on, Heather,' he says. 'Let's go. You've puked up in Martin's car.'

Very pale, she sits up. For a moment she does not move. Her face is expressionless and at the same time utterly miserable. Slowly, in silence, she manoeuvres her way to the open door and steps out, moving past Paul as though he were not there. 'Your shoes . . .' he says.

She is already walking away, tiptoeing with drunken single-mindedness in a wavy line up Lennox Road. It is Paul's turn to sigh now, fiercely. He stoops into the car and takes her shoes. One of them has vomit in it. While he is doing this, Martin is watching Heather walk away. And he is about to speak, to say something, when standing up, holding her soiled shoes, Paul speaks first. He says, 'I'm sorry, Martin. I really am. We'll be in touch, all right?'

Martin just nods, and Paul starts to walk away.

'Paul.'

He turns. 'What?'

Martin is not even looking at him. He is staring at a spot on the pavement, with a strange little smile on his face.

'Look, we'll be in touch,' Paul says, and walks on, only stopping momentarily when he is some way off to turn and shout, 'Thanks for the lift.'

He waits for Heather in the kitchen from first light. In fact, he is in the garden when she emerges. Through the window, he sees her enter the kitchen with her tawny hair trailing over her face. Her face is lifeless and ugly. With a final leaf through the notes in his head – fizzing with indignation, he has spent the night preparing this talk – he opens the door and steps inside.

'I'm frightened of him, Paul,' she says.

'Sorry?'

'I'm frightened of him.'

'Who?' She says nothing. 'Martin?'

'Yes.'

'What do you mean you're *frightened* of him?'

'He won't leave me alone,' she says, her eyes shining. This is not what he expected. 'He won't stop pestering me! I don't know what to do. I told him he shouldn't take us to London. He wouldn't listen. He's mad.'

Paul steals a look at the text of his speech; it seems to have been overtaken by events.

'He just won't leave me alone. He won't stop phoning me.'

'You shouldn't encourage him.'

'I know. I know.' She starts to sob.

'You encourage him.'

'I know. I don't know what to do.'

'What do you mean he won't stop phoning you?'

'He phones me ten times a day. I have to switch my phone off. He wants to see me all the time . . .'

'He wants to *see* you?'

'Yes!' She is tearful. 'Why do you think he took us to London? He just wanted to see me. I said I couldn't. So he said he'd drive us to London. He insisted.'

'Why didn't you tell him you didn't want him to?'

'I did. He wouldn't listen. He's mad. He's mad . . .'

'What about Friday night?' Paul says.

'Friday night?' She doesn't seem to follow.

'He drove you home from the Metropole.'

'Yes?'

'You said he was there with someone else . . .'

'No, that's not true! He wasn't there. He phoned me. He wanted to see me. I told him he couldn't. He asked me where I was – he said he'd come and get me when I wanted to leave. I told him not to. But he came anyway. I'm frightened of him, Paul.'

'What do you mean you're *frightened*? Why are you frightened? What's he done?'

'It's not what he's done . . .'

'Why are you frightened?'

'He's . . . He's . . .' She is shaking her head.

'Has he threatened you?'

'No. No.' She wipes her eyes. 'Maybe I'm just being silly.'

'You should just ignore him,' Paul says.

'I know.'

'Stop encouraging him. Tell him you don't want to see him.'

She nods.

'And if he still won't leave you alone . . .' She is staring at the floor. 'Well,' he says, 'we might have to . . .' Hearing one of the doors open upstairs, he stops. 'You know.' She looks up haggardly for a moment. Then, wiping her eyes on the rose towelling of her sleeve, starts to take things out of the fridge and transfer them to the table.

'You should just ignore him,' Paul says.

She ignores him.

'Do you want *me* to have a word with him?'

She says nothing.

Smoking in the garden once more, he feels shamed and furious with himself for ignoring his instinct, throughout Sunday, to punch

Martin in the mouth. Yes, he should have punched him in the mouth, and sod the consequences. Should have done *something*. Next time, he promises himself, he will.

18

'Hello, Paul?'

The voice is very familiar, but he does not immediately recognise it. 'Yes?'

'It's Martin here.'

'Martin . . .' Paul is unable to hide his surprise. For a moment he is perplexed, and Martin says nothing. There was something strange about his voice – an urgent, suppressed intensity. Still he is silent. Paul suspects that this is about the vomit. Tiresome. He says, 'Um . . .'

Simultaneously, though, Martin starts to speak. 'I really hope you're strong enough to take this, Paul,' he says.

I'm going to be sacked, Paul thinks.

So when Martin says, 'I've just been with Heather,' it seems a puzzling non sequitur.

What? Paul wonders. *Heather? Why?*

He quickly surmises that something must have happened to her. Even – his mind makes the sickening leap – that she is dead. *I really hope you're strong enough to take this, Paul.* And how will he tell the children that their mother is dead? 'What is it?' he says quietly.

'Paul, we're having an affair. We're in love.' A pause. 'Yes.'

Paul says nothing.

'Yes,' Martin says again, in a more sadly sympathetic tone, though still unable entirely to suppress the note of satisfaction. 'For a few months now. Since, um –' said as though looking it up in a diary – 'since January.'

Expecting Paul to have something to say at this point, he waits for a moment, and then – when Paul still does not speak – his voice tilts unsurely, and he evinces for the first time a hint of embarrassment. 'So, um.'

Standing in the lounge in his uniform, Paul is tempted to hang up and pretend that nothing has happened. Make his supper, watch television . . .

Martin is impatient. 'She told me things haven't been going too well between you,' he says. 'That's what she told me. Is that true?'

'I don't think that's any of your business, Martin,' Paul says. It seems like a long time since he has spoken, and he is surprised to hear his voice – its stony, perfectly level tone.

'No, I know.' Martin seems to take the point – until a moment later, when he says, 'It's just that she told me –'

Paul interrupts him. 'I don't think it's any of your business.'

'No,' Martin says. 'No.' And he sighs, obviously peeved.

'Why are you calling me?'

'Why am I *calling* you?'

'Yes.'

'Well, I wanted to tell you,' he says, as though it were obvious. 'I thought you'd want to know. This is . . . It's a fucked-up situation,' he says. 'I don't like it. I'm sure you don't. I want to see if there's any way we can sort it out. It's a fucked-up situation.' Swearing is not like him – he is using the expression to show how serious he is. He is silent for a moment. He does not seem satisfied with the way things are going; and as if deciding to tear up what they have said so far and start again, he says – not without petulance – 'Look, if I could just ask. What's going on with you and Heather? I mean, what *exactly* is going on? Because she told me –'

'Look, it's none of your business, Martin. Thank you very much for your call. Thanks. I appreciate it. Thank you.'

He puts the phone down.

He is trembling. Trembling quite violently. In a form of trance – with an absent-minded expression on his face – he steps into the hall and quietly shuts the front door. (In his hurry to pick up the phone, he had left it open.) The situation, of course, does not feel particularly real. It was important for him to hang up on Martin, to be the one to end their talk, on his terms, ensuring that he had the last word, but now he is dissatisfied. Perhaps *he* should have asked *Martin* some questions – his head is loud with them now. Distractedly, in the middle of this mob of questions, he undertakes a first skimming survey of the previous few months, and finds them solid with evidence. The only strange thing is his surprise. Or perhaps not. It is, he thinks, strange that it should be Martin. *Martin*, of all people. Still trembling, he finds himself wandering through the house. He steps into the garden. He stands in the lounge.

It seems like some awful joke. Of course, Martin has long taken an obvious interest in Heather – making an obliging handyman of himself at the slightest murmur of need; lugging in the unwieldy apparatus for unblocking the drain; regrouting the shower while Paul watched snooker downstairs; passing hours in futile tinkering under the bonnet of her car. And Paul had quite liked having Martin as his handyman. He had always understood his motivation, of course – even Heather had stopped pretending that she did not see *that* – and to be so openly and extravagantly helpful to her some-times seemed to verge on insolence, to be a direct expression of desire at which Paul might be expected to *do* something. If he did not, it was because he never saw Martin as any sort of threat. He was a joke. They all laughed at him – even the kids, even to his face sometimes – and Heather laughed most of all. In fact, laughing at Martin seemed to have become one of the mainstays of their own life together, one of the subjects to which they were able to turn for affirmation of what they shared – a way of asserting that they were akin, homogenous, members of a tiny tribe; because what they mocked in him were the many ways in which he seemed to differ from *them* – his obsession with high-tech novelty, his fondness for soft rock, his ineffably holier-than-thou aversion to alcohol, his love of whitewater rafting ... And they had laughed – how they had laughed – at his smitten willingness to perform services for her. Paul even found his efforts to please quite touching. They seemed maladroit, naive, innocent, harmless – and because of this, incidents which would otherwise have made him suspicious met with no more than an indulgent laugh. Martin's tie turning up in the sofa, for example. Paul did not know at first that it was his – he simply found a mysterious tie in the sofa. When Heather said, without hesitation, that it was Martin's, everything seemed fine. If it had been someone else's – Nigel the solicitor's, say, for whom she worked at Gumley Rhodes – Paul would have spun all sorts of suspicious scenarios from its silk and polyester mix. As it was, he just laughed. Over tea, Martin had taken off his tie, and forgotten it. Paul handed it back to him himself while they waited for Heather on Easter Day. The sudden jump in the number of her evenings out might also have raised questions in his mind (and indeed he *had* questioned this sudden surge in her social life), but he did not suspect, ever, that the explanation might lie in her having an affair *with Martin*. Not even when he saw her, last Friday night, getting out of his car. How was it possible that he had not seen what was happening? And Easter Day ... A 'fucked-up' situation indeed – one that was in front of his face, and that he had still somehow failed to see. Is he really such a fool? When he thinks about that day now – and he goes through it with the minute care of a chimp going through another chimp's hair for nits – he understands that Martin, in his own mind, would already have taken possession of Heather, and that from his point of view it would thus have been *Paul*, paunchy and half asleep in the seat next to him, who was the interloper, not himself. And Paul *had* had an unpleasant premonition of the truth, shambling downstairs that afternoon, to find Martin in the Willisons' lounge; he had seen them together – Heather, her parents, the children, and Martin – and had felt for a moment, with a frisson of exclusion that he, and not Martin, was the outsider there.

He tries Heather's phone.

It is switched off.

Then, feeling a terrible need to leave the house, he walks out into the trembling streets. He does not see where he is going. Later, finding himself leg-weary, he waits for a bus on the Old Shoreham Road. He has walked as far as Mile Oak.

He is intensely impatient to hear what Heather will have to say for herself. *What will she have to say for herself?* In the lounge, still trembling a little, he punches her number into the phone.

She picks up immediately. 'Hello?' she says. She sounds frightened.

'It's me.'

'Hello.'

'I've spoken to Martin.'

Silence.

'He told me everything.'

When she still says nothing, he says, matter-of-factly, 'Where are you?'

'I'm in town. I'll come home. Paul . . .'

'Okay, I'll see you at home.'

And for the second time that day he indulges in the satisfying violence of putting the phone down on someone as they speak. For a long time, he does not move. He looks lost in thought. In fact, his mind is empty. The Claymore seems futile somehow, but he takes it out – with its underdesigned, over-Scottish label, thistles and fluttering tartan – and pours himself some anyway. It tastes of watery alcohol with sharp overtones of sour vomit and a desultory smokiness, its lukewarmth somehow slightly sickening in itself.

It is twelve o'clock. High noon in Hove. Hearing Heather come into the hall, Paul is immediately aware that she is sobbing. She seems to snatch at her sobs as she shuts the front door. 'Paul?' she says, and there is a plaintive, almost desperate, note to her voice. 'Paul?'

He does not move, though his heart is sprinting, and his failure

252

to answer seems to trigger a quiet doubling of her tears. He hears her go into the kitchen and put something down. There follows an odd delay, and he has started to wonder – with a smear of dark rage – whether she is actually going to join him in the lounge at all, when he hears the muffled flush of the downstairs loo. The sound of the flush, though diminishing, becomes more defined as the loo door opens, and he leans forward and starts to fiddle with his spliff-making materials. He does not look at her when she appears in the doorway.

She is blowing her nose on a square of toilet tissue. 'Paul,' she says.

And absurdly, he says, 'Yes?' as though he does not know what she wants to talk to him about.

'What did he tell you?' she asks.

'Martin?' The name, he hears, has an entirely new sound.

'M-hm.' She is nervously working a little plastic lighter.

He seems to think for a few seconds; then he says, 'Why don't you tell me yourself, then I'll tell you what he said.'

When he looks up, however, she is staring at the carpet, using her upturned hand as an ashtray. Looking at her, she seems a stranger. He thinks of the first few times that he saw her – when he had still not steeled himself to speak to her, and did not know her name – in the secretaries' pool of Archway Publications, or peering through the Friday night mob in the Finnegans Wake – now he sees her like that again, sees what she looks like, her solid nose, powdery face, cornflower eyes. He notices her mannerisms, her posture. It is, for a moment, as though the intervening years have been unlived.

'So?' he says.

She still does not speak. She is staring at the carpet's tired oatmeal nap.

'Were you going to tell me yourself?'

They are both smoking. The room is full of slowly swirling smoke. His whole life of the past few months, perhaps longer, now seems like a fiction; something in which he was participating without understanding that it was not properly real. Perhaps this is partly why he has such a strangely theatrical sense of the situation. Leaving the room, he feels, will be like leaving a set. Slowly, he stands up. There are still so many questions, and he is leaving. The inquest has only just started and he is sick of it. It seems wearisome, pointless . . . He has forgotten to stub out his cigarette, and leaning down, he makes a quick, unthorough job of it – it is still smouldering in the ashtray when she says, 'Where are you going?'

'I'm going to bed. I'm tired.'

'Okay,' she says softly. Then, 'Sleep well.'

'Yeah, I'll try.'

She is suddenly in tears. 'Paul,' she says, 'I don't think you're well.'

'Why not?'

Putting one hand over her face, she shakes her head. 'What is it?' He stands there. 'What is it?' She sniffs a few times. 'Sorry,' she says. 'I'm sorry.' She is wiping her face with what is left of the paper tissue. 'All this crap . . .'

'What crap?'

'Working at the supermarket. It's mad.'

'Is it?'

She blows her nose. 'I mean, it must be pretty awful.'

'It's all right,' he says. 'I'm tired, Heather.'

She nods, and moves aside to let him pass. 'Sleep well.'

'Yeah, I'll try.'

'Paul, I'm sorry.'

Everything seems unsatisfactory. He does not think he will be able to sleep. He even wonders whether to go back downstairs. His head is still seething with weary, insistent questions – questions he has asked so many times in the last few hours that they seem tedious, even unimportant to him now. With nothing else to do, he lies down, still in his clothes, and as soon as he does this and shuts his eyes, he knows that he will be able to sleep – that sleep, surprisingly, is pouring in on him, erasing everything.

When he wakes, earlier than usual, for an hour or so he lies in bed, wondering where he stands. His placid assumption – it is eerily placid – is that Heather is going to leave him. He is not sure how he feels about this. As he lies there exploring the soft shadows of the ceiling with his eyes, there are moments – only moments – of intense sadness and anger. Mostly there is just a numbness. He hears Oliver and Marie, hears Heather stomping up and down the stairs, her supervisory voice impressively ordinary. These muffled sounds seem to find him from the past; they are like memories of an earlier part of his life, mysteriously fresh in his mind on waking. Swinging himself out of bed, in his underpants he tiptoes into the bathroom. The equanimity with which he has been outstaring the situation for the past hour has suddenly vanished and he wishes he were able to get it back. To this end, he fumbles with the box of Felixstat, and thumbs one of the pills from the blister sheet; each is labelled with the name of a day of the week. They are not fast-acting, but in moments of stress to take one is to know, at least, that psychoactive reinforcements are on the way, and having swallowed 'Tuesday' he feels less frightened.

Downstairs, Heather is waiting in the smoke-filled lounge, in the macabre sulk of the silence. Sitting in the kitchen, Paul seems to be doing nothing. In fact he *is* doing something – he is *not going* into the lounge; and this *not going* is so engrossing that he forgets his porridge until summoned to the odour of scorched milk. He is not hungry, and spoons it into the bin, wondering – dispassionately for the most part, with only occasional minor needles of pain – what the mechanics of the affair were, how they worked things. Then, stopping his imaginings when they wander too far – towards a vision of Martin, naked, pipe-cleaner limbs and mousy pubic hair – he washes out the saucepan in which he made his porridge, scouring the brown burn-mark with unexpected ferocity. Then he smokes a cigarette, and in a hurry now, pulls on his jacket in the hall. On his way out, as he passes the open door of the lounge – the fact that the TV is not on lends the house a miserable air of emergency – he says only four words to Heather. 'Do the children know?'

'No, of course not,' she says.

He waits alone at the bus stop on Portland Road. The spring evening is mild; ink-blue with cold, wet depths. Only in the last week have vestiges of daylight still lingered in the sky as he makes his way to work. The road is quiet, the shops shut, the many take-aways seemingly untroubled by customers. A few preoccupied cars whizz past. He takes a pre-rolled cigarette from his pocket and lights it – and as soon as he has done so, he sees the lights of the bus as it crests the rise, and snags briefly on each of the two stops visible higher up the road. In the dry peace of the non-foods aisle it is easy to imagine that nothing has happened – that nothing *is* happening. There, even when it occurs to him – as it frequently does, unpacking dishcloths or spray-headed bottles of shower cleaner – that they might be together, he is strangely untroubled.

A week later, things seem suspended in a sort of limbo – since they do not use the bed at the same time, it has not even been neces-sary for someone to move to the sofa; since they seldom see each other, the new situation has had little scope for showing up in the transactions of everyday life. It has started to seem as though things might go on as they are indefinitely.

Then one morning Heather suddenly opens final settlement nego-tiations. She has the bruisy circles under her eyes, the queasy pallor, the long-haul look of someone who has been up all night with her troublesome thoughts. 'The house,' she says. It is ten a.m. – Paul is microwaving a curry for his supper. 'What about it?'

She sighs, slightly impatient. 'Well, what are we going to do about it?'

'I don't know.'

'Are you planning to keep it?' she says.

'Of course not.'

'Well, nor am I. We've got to write to Norris.'

Norris Jones – the landlord. Paul nods. He wants to ask her where she is planning to live . . .

'Where are you planning to live?' she says.

He just shrugs.

'You must have thought about it.'

'No.'

'You haven't?'

'No, I haven't.'

This is true.

There is a sad pause. 'Do you want me to write to him?' Heather says. 'Norris.'

'If you want.'

'It's not what I want . . .'

'Yes, write to him. Where are *you* planning to live?'

'I don't know. Martin wants me to live with him.'

'Does he?'

'I don't know what I'm going to do,' she says. And then, 'I'll write that letter.'

Slumped in the blue flicker of the twenty-four-hour news, Paul wonders whether to write a letter of his own.

When he woke up, he had not moved for a while, spat out by oblivious sleep, and unwilling to leave the limited warmth of the bed. (Which was very stale and human-smelling – discoloured, discomposed, with sulphur-grey shadows on the pillows.) It was only his need to urinate that eventually pulled him into a sitting position – stage one of his self-extraction from the sweaty sheets; the heating was turned up too high, and he had been sweating into his sleep all afternoon. He was on the verge of performing stage two – standing shakily – when he was suddenly aware of an engine ticking over in the street outside. The sound had been discreetly present for some minutes. Standing shakily, he twitched the drape and looked out. The yellow Saab was waiting in the road. As he watched, Heather walked into view – she had shut the front door so quietly that he had not heard it. He saw Martin's head turn in the shadowy interior to follow her with his eyes. Then he leaned over and opened the door; she said something as she lowered herself into the seat. The door slammed. With a snarl the car surged forward, and was immediately out of sight.

Silence.

Silence except for the low muffled noise of the television from Oli's room.

Paul let the drape swing shut, wiping the street light from his face. He wondered why he was so painfully stunned. He had seen nothing surprising. It was, however, the first time that he had seen them together. He slipped into the bathroom. He has upped his dose of Felixstat, and taken the subsequent dopiness, the moth-balling of most of his mind, without demur. Having swallowed the pills, he turned to the toilet, and making water stared at his face in the mirrored door of the medicine cabinet. It was expressionless, yet somehow the despair – which did not seem too strong a word – was obvious; it seemed to seep out through the pores, through his dead, sad eyes. He flushed the toilet. On his way downstairs he knocked on Oliver's door, and said, 'Time for bed, Oli.' The thought of being separated from the children hurts him surprisingly. Though he and Heather have not spoken of it, there seems no question of his seeing them in the future – why would he? – yet she implicitly expects him to babysit while she is out with Martin. Sometimes – on his own in the lounge while they sleep upstairs – this seems an emasculating imposition. More often, though, he finds himself holding onto the illusion of normality that it lends things. However, what he saw from the window, on top of Heather's writing to Norris Jones, seems to have kyboshed that illusion, and in the blue flicker of the small hours he wonders whether to write anonymously to Watt; to set in front of him what Gerald said, and see what happens. While he is wondering what to write, he hears the Saab stop in the street outside. He waits, motionless, for several minutes until he hears one of its doors open and slam; it does not move on until Heather is inside, and the squeaky step squeaks under her weight.

19

In his blue uniform, Paul is towing a pallet of products onto the shop floor. The pallet is wrapped in cling film, so thickly that the whole thing is shiny, white, opaque. It crashes and rattles as he pulls it over the uneven concrete of the warehouse – then is suddenly quiet, only whispering on the smooth shop floor. He shoves it into its aisle, and wanders unhurriedly back to the warehouse. Passing from the shop floor to the warehouse always feels to him like exiting a stage; it must be even more like this, he supposes, during the day when the shop is open and the customers, like an audience, are there.

The warehouse is parky enough to turn olive oil opaque in its bottles. In the loading bay it is parkier still. The four-metre-high folding doors are open to the night sky, and outside a fine drizzle is falling through the orange light. The pallets, unloaded from the lorry, stand around and quickly Paul tries to estimate their weight. He does not want one full of pet foods, or detergent, or bleach. Heavy things. (The heaviest ones, of course – the wines and spirits, the mineral waters – cannot be moved without the hydraulic pallet truck, which makes them light work, like pulling an empty; but only Gerald is trained to use that.) Through a tear in its film wrapping, he sees that one of the pallets is loaded with packet soups and noodles – not too bad. His gloved hand grasps the side grille, and with a brief strong tug to start it moving, walking sideways with his pulling arm outstretched, he steers it noisily out of the warehouse. The shop floor seems warmly lit by comparison. Temperate, and almost plush. Posters over the aisle tops show pictures of tasty-looking food and happy-looking people. Everything here is presentation, and precisely fabricated effect.

On Wednesday morning Watt is on duty. From seven o'clock, Paul spies him on the shop floor, wearing a grey suit – a suit the colour of a dark miserable dawn. Looking harassed and slightly irate, he prowls the aisles with one hand stuffed into his suit pocket. Watt never speaks to the night-shift staff himself; whatever he has to say he says to Graham, who passes it on in his squeaky voice. Paul is not in non-foods – he has been sent to help a novice in trouble with the pasta. And he is there, slinging penne onto the shelves, when Watt and Graham walk into the aisle, Graham's leather jacket shining like wet tar. Watt whispers something to him, and Graham shouts, 'Move it, move it.' Looking up, Paul nods – and for a moment, his eyes meet Watt's. Stuck in his irritable stare, Paul is suddenly unsure of himself. The letter is in his hip pocket – it was dawn when he finished it, and switched off the electric light, leaving the lounge ashen. Watt moves on. Of course he moves on. Why *wouldn't* he move on? Nevertheless, the moment unsettles Paul. Watt does not seem the sort of man to take seriously improbable tip-offs; nor to suffer nonsense sympathetically. He seems an unimaginative institutional type to his sturdy bones. Most probably, he would pass the letter straight to Macfarlane, and suggest a thorough investigation to unmask the sender.

Mounting the linoleum stairs on eight o'clock, Paul is more or less persuaded of the wisdom of taking it home and disposing of it. Then he notices who he is following. Ten steps further up, he sees the square heavy-seated form, one hand still stuck in his suit pocket. Quietly, Paul follows him along the windowless corridor – past the locker room, where he had been headed. Past the notice-boards. Past two girls, teenagers, laughing in their blue uniforms, smelling of cigarette smoke. Watt mutters good morning to them. Then he pushes through the swing door into the staff canteen. Paul stops. Through the pane of strengthened glass in the door, he can

261

see that the canteen is quite full. Watt goes over to the managers' table – it is exactly the same as all the other tables, and its status is entirely unofficial, but no one except managers ever sits there. And managers never sit anywhere else. Taking off his suit jacket, Watt places it over the back of one of the moulded plastic chairs. Then he moves to the food servery, takes a brown tray, and in an egalitarian spirit joins the line of staff queuing for breakfast. There is no one else sitting at the managers' table, which is in the sun, near the windows.

Paul waits outside in the corridor. He does not know what to do. (In the queue, Watt is laughing with some hair-netted girls from the bakery.) The jacket is *there* – he simply has to stuff the letter into one of its pockets. There will never be a more propitious opportunity. (Now Watt is talking to the serving woman, telling her not to give him too much scrambled egg.) Paul seems unable to move. Some people – men from the meat counter with brown bloodstains on their aprons – stand up from a table, tucking their tabloids under their arms, and walk towards him. He will have to move, one way or the other . . . The door swings open. The men are pushing past him, and at the same time, without thinking what he is doing, he is pushing past them, into the canteen. It is the first time that he has been in there in the morning and it feels foreign to him, the levels of light and noise much higher than he is used to. Taking the letter from his pocket, he forces himself towards the managers' table. The thing is not to try and be too subtle about it – is just to do it *quickly*. Quickly, and then walk – at an ordinary pace – straight to the smoking room. No one will notice if he does it like that. He is already there. He feels very prominent in the white sunlight. And already he is fucking it up. He has stopped. He is standing next to the jacket, looking out of the window. *Why?* No one ever looks out of the canteen window; there is nothing to see except car park and sky. And then into the car park slides the yellow Saab.

With quickening urgency, Paul turns, and sweating freely starts to fumble with the jacket. He cannot find the pockets . . . *He cannot find the pockets! How is that possible? How is it . . .*

He finds one – it is heavy with objects – and shoves the damp letter in.

Then he sees Watt. Preceded by his tray, he is only a few metres off, his face fixed in an expression of incredulity. No longer smiling, standing stock still in the warm sunlight, Paul is mute. 'What are you doing?' Watt says. 'What have you taken?'

Paul shakes his head.

There is a strange quiet in the canteen.

Watt puts his tray down on the table, and with his eyes still on Paul stoops slightly and pulls his jacket from the back of the chair. Still staring at Paul he searches slowly through the pockets. 'What did you take?' he says again.

'Nothing.' The sun is surprisingly strong. Frozen peas of sweat slide down Paul's sides. With a look of distaste – pulling something nasty from a plughole – Watt produces the envelope. He looks at Paul, and someone laughs. Without putting his jacket down, Watt tears open the envelope, and unfolds the letter. When he looks up, his expression – a sort of suspicious outraged squint – seems to precipitate more widespread laughter. Paul is silent, sweating in the sunlight like a suddenly illuminated herbivore. Seemingly oblivious to the surrounding laughter, Watt feels his jacket for something. A pen – a proper ink pen. Unsteadily, using his left arm as a writing surface, he scribbles something on the letter and holds it out. Paul's mouth is very dry. Watt has written *Call me* (underlined) and a mobile number. He is already in his seat, having a sip of sour orange juice and eyeing his wet slices of scrambled egg with a shrunken appetite. Paul takes a step towards the smoking room; then – suddenly remembering who and where he is – performs a U-turn, and heads for the exit as the volume of voices swells.

For a few minutes, he hides in the locker room, pulling himself together. Then, on the lookout for Martin, he slips out into the morning. With shivering hands he lights up. He did not want to involve himself in the situation – that was the whole point of the letter. Now that Watt knows his identity, however, he is terrified that he will take it to Macfarlane – or worse, to Martin himself.

His first plan is to phone him at noon. He does not. *Tonight*, he tells himself, as he undresses, *tonight when I get up*. Heather's presence in the lounge provides all the inhibition he needs to prevent him from following through on this second plan, and he leaves for work with an unpleasant sense of omission. It is mainly to disperse this feeling that, when he finds himself with a few minutes at the bus stop, he tries the scrawled number. With his eyes on the murky point where the bus will appear, he listens to the pulses, hoping for voicemail. If it is voicemail he will not leave a message . . .

'Roy Watt.'

For a second or two Paul says nothing. 'Who is this?' Watt says.

'It's . . . Paul Rainey.'

'*Who?*'

'You know – the letter . . .'

'Oh.' Watt pauses. 'Yes. What's your name?'

'Paul Rainey.'

'Well, Mr Rainey,' Watt says. Paul sees the bus in the twilight, two stops away. 'I'd like to talk to you.'

'Okay.'

'Not in the store, of course.'

'No.'

'So . . .' There is a short silence, then Watt makes an uneasy suggestion: 'Perhaps if I could buy you a drink?'

The Stadium is a sprawling pub on the Old Shoreham Road. On Friday night the car park out front is full, and a cobwebbed yellow garden spot stares up at the swaying sign. Inside, Paul feels vague and sleepy. He has not had breakfast. The hubbub of the pub sounds muffled to him, and he experiences his own presence there as something strange. He has never been in the Stadium – an unusually large local – until today; having to pass through the foot tunnel under the railway line, and over the mini-motorway of the Old Shoreham Road, makes it seem further from Lennox Road than it is. It is only for this reason that he feels safe meeting so near the houses – his own and Martin's. He wanted somewhere within walking distance – and both he and Watt wanted somewhere where they were unknown, and unlikely to be seen. He yawns – a huge, hollow, face-twisting yawn.

Watt is standing at the bar. When he turns he is smiling like a maniac, showing the wide spaces between his teeth. He is wearing a concrete-coloured jacket with a brown corduroy collar and shape-less, high-waisted, low-seated jeans. His hands shaking, he sets the drinks – his pint of Guinness and Paul's Bloody Mary – down on the table.

'Thanks,' Paul says.

'That's okay.'

Paul is sitting on a padded bench. There are no other seats, and with a sort of desperation, Watt scans the room for a moment, and then – unleashing a strange little laugh – sits down next to him. Paul pretends to move up, but there is nowhere to move to. 'Well,' Watt says, still smiling, 'here we are.' An ex-ex-smoker, he takes a pack of ten Silk Cut from his pocket, leaning ostentatiously out to the side as he does so. While he lights his cigarette – seemingly out of practice, he puffs at it furiously, as if it might not take, singeing it halfway to the filter in the lighter flame – Paul tastes his Bloody Mary. The vodka and tomato flavours seem separate in his mouth; the vodka very unpleasant, the tomato squash only slightly less so. Watt inspects the Silk Cut now smouldering satisfactorily in his hand. He seems to have mastered the worst of his nerves, and is more like the man Paul sees in the supermarket. 'So . . .' he says, looking up, straight ahead over the small oblong of the table. 'What makes you think Martin's been using unlisted suppliers then?'

'It's what I've been told,' Paul says, with his elbows pressed into his sides.

'Who told you?'

'Who told me? Bloke who works with me.'

'What bloke?'

'Just . . . a bloke.'

'A bloke,' Watt says. 'A bloke who works on the night shift?' A frown of scepticism enters his voice. 'How does *he* know?'

'Um. I'm not sure.'

Watt, it seems, was hoping for something more than this – something more impressively sourced – and Paul says, 'To be honest . . . I want to be honest, yeah.'

'Yes?'

'To be honest, I don't *know* it's true. What I said.'

Watt sighs. 'I see.'

'I'm sorry . . .'

Watt wrinkles his nose and takes a moody gulp of Guinness.

'So you have no information? *Nothing?*'

'Only what I was told . . .'

'I mean proper information!' His voice is suddenly peevish. 'Not what your mate might have told you on the night shift.' Points of irritated sweat shine on his hair-poor pate. 'I mean, how does *he* know?'

Paul does not speak for a few moments. 'Why don't you have a look at the paperwork?' he suggests. 'There must be paperwork . . .'

'I *have* looked at it.'

'And?'

'No. There's nothing. I mean, there are . . .'

He stops, perhaps feeling unable to speak freely to someone who is a supermarket employee, and of the lowliest kind.

'There are?' Paul prompts him.

'There are things which . . .'

'Which?'

266

'Which don't quite add up,' Watt snaps. With a dozen fierce stabs he stubs out his cigarette. Unsuccessfully – it persists in smoking feebly in the ashtray for a whole minute of sulky silence. Though Watt's irritation has made him feel unimpressive, Paul is nevertheless pleased that the situation too seems to be smouldering out. His worry, of course, is that Watt will mention it to Martin, and he says, 'Are you planning to mention –' Watt interrupts him. 'On their own they're not enough.'

'What aren't?'

'The things that don't quite add up.'

'Not enough for what?'

'Not enough to take to the south-east manager.'

'No.'

And then Watt says, 'We need evidence.'

We need evidence. The implication – that he and Paul are somehow involved in something together. Paul has a slurp of Bloody Mary, wipes his mouth and says, 'What do you mean?' For the first time, Watt turns to look at him with his small eyes. 'If I'm to go to the regional manager,' he says, 'I need some real evidence.'

'Sure.'

'Otherwise it's just hearsay. It's just gossip.'

'Yes,' Paul says. And then, 'Maybe there is no evidence.'

Watt is having a second stab at putting out his cigarette. 'What do you mean "no evidence"? There must be.'

'I mean maybe it's not true, what I was told.'

'I think it is true.'

Surprised, Paul says, 'You think it's true?'

'Yes.'

'Why?'

Watt huffs and waves his hand. 'Well . . . Those questionable items, those invoices . . . You know. It's not like I didn't suspect something.'

Paul tips his glass to his mouth, but there is no Bloody Mary left and only the ice cubes slide down and strike his teeth. Seeing this, Watt immediately says, 'Another?'

'Um . . .'

He is already up, and shoving his way to the bar.

To start his day with a Bloody Mary in the Stadium with Roy Watt is making Paul feel weird. In the din of the pub he feels like he is underwater; everything muffled, the sounds shapeless submarine noise.

Setting the second Bloody Mary down on the table, Watt says, 'So. We need some proper evidence.'

Paul does not particularly want to be involved in whatever scheme Watt is envisaging – and from his unsophisticated salesman's smile, it is obvious that he *is* envisaging some sort of scheme. 'Like what?' Paul says, without enthusiasm.

'Well – what would be the best sort of evidence to have?'

Paul pouts, tastes the Bloody Mary – a double this time. 'Dunno,' he says.

'Well, the best evidence would be this, wouldn't it.' Watt is still smiling, his straight lip drawn up from his yellow, horse's teeth – and what he says is so surprising that Paul wonders whether it is a joke. He inspects Watt's eyes for a moment. Watt laughs – he has a solid, percussive, forced-sounding laugh. '*That* would be evidence,' he says. 'If I could go to the regional manager with *that* . . .'

'I don't understand,' Paul says. 'How would we –'

'Look.' Watt has turned on the padded bench so that he is facing him. 'We get someone to pretend to be an unlisted fresh-produce supplier . . .'

Paul shakes his head. 'Who?'

'Whoever. It doesn't matter. We get them to fix up a meeting with Short, offering to sell him something, some produce. We fix them up with a hidden camera, and get the whole thing on tape.'

That's insane, Paul thinks. However, he says, 'What if Martin doesn't go for it?'

'Let's see, shall we?'

For a few moments, Paul says nothing. Then, trying to sound as if he is enquiring only out of politeness, he says, 'Who are you going to get to be . . .'

'The supplier?'

'Yeah.'

'You have to do that,' Watt says. He starts to light another Silk Cut. 'You have to find someone.'

'*Me?*'

'Yes.'

Paul shakes his head. 'No, you see . . . I don't know if I want to . . .'

'You don't want to what?'

'I don't know if I want to get involved in something like this . . .'

'Then why did you send me the letter?'

Paul shrugs. Watt offers him a Silk Cut, and after a moment's pause he takes it. 'I've been wondering about that,' Watt says, as Paul lights it. 'What have you got against Martin?'

Paul pretends to be immersed in lighting the cigarette. Then he says, 'What have *you* got against him?'

'I think that's well known, isn't it? Even on the night shift.'

'Is it?'

'Do your wife, did he?' Watt says, with a smutty laugh. 'Something like that?' He is joking – isn't he? – and Paul tries to smile. 'Nothing like that.'

'What then?'

Paul takes an unhappy swig of Bloody Mary.

'The fact is,' Watt says, 'if you don't help me get some evidence, I'll just have to put the whole thing to Jock, and that means telling him who told *me*. Martin too, of course. I'm sure they'll want to talk to you about it. You can't just go around making accusations like that. Not if you can't back them up . . .'

'I don't understand,' Paul says. 'What do you want me to do?'

'I want you to find someone to pretend to be a fresh-produce supplier.'

269

'*Who?*'

'Whoever! Doesn't matter. Look,' Watt says, his tone softening, 'it's important I don't know the person. That's all. In case something goes wrong. My name can't get mixed up in this. You must be able to understand that . . .'

'What about my name?'

'It's the hardly the same. You just need to find someone.'

'Yeah, find someone, find someone. And how am I going to persuade them to do something like this?'

For a moment, Watt looks shocked. Paul's tone was insolent, mutinous – he seemed to have forgotten that he is a night-shift warehouseman speaking to a senior member of the store management. It is, however, a highly unusual situation, and Watt lets it pass. 'Tell you what,' he says, swallowing a mouthful of Guinness. 'I'll pay them . . .' He pauses, looking very earnest. 'Two hundred quid. If you can find someone,' he says, 'I'll pay them two hundred quid. All right?'

'You'll pay them two hundred quid?'

'I will. So . . . That should make it easier to find someone, shouldn't it?'

Paul sighs. 'I don't know about suppliers . . . I don't know how these things work . . .'

'You don't need to. I'll explain everything. You find someone, and I'll explain exactly what they have to do. All right?'

'I don't know . . .'

'What don't you know?'

'If I can find someone.'

'Well, you just try,' Watt says, more menacingly. 'See how you get on. I'm sure you'll be able to – two hundred quid for a few hours' work's not bad. And I'll sort out the equipment as well.'

'What equipment?'

'The hidden camera and all that. I'll sort that out. You can leave that to me . . .'

He notices that Paul is staring at something on the other side of the room, and following his eyes, sees a young woman sitting with some other people.

Paul says, 'Doesn't she . . . ?'

Work in the supermarket. A junior manager. Paul does not know her name – he sees her sometimes on the margins of his shift. She is in her late twenties, and her face, throat, arms and hands are entirely covered with fawn freckles – slightly strange-looking but not ugly, and Paul often wonders, with a tingle of excitement, whether they extend over the whole surface of her skin. 'Who is she?' he asks, in a quieter voice. Watt has turned on the bench so that he is almost facing the beige wall. 'She's . . . Her name's Hazel,' he says.

'Do you think she's seen us?'

'How should I know? Look, I've got to leave.'

'All right . . .'

'Is she looking at us?'

'No. If you're leaving, I'll come with you –'

'No! We've got to leave separately.'

'Why?'

'What if we're seen? Wait here for a few minutes. Just five minutes. Please. We mustn't be seen together.' He stands up – keeping his back to the part of the room where Hazel is sitting – and says, 'I'll call you next week.' And then, pointedly, 'I expect you'll have found someone by then.' Paul drains the last of the Bloody Mary – watery with melted ice – and stares obtusely at the tabletop.

When he looks up, Watt is no longer there.

Walking home through Amhurst Crescent, he thinks, *What the fuck have I got myself mixed up in?* He sighs, entering the smelly foot tunnel under the train tracks. And he *is* mixed up in it. Mixed up in something with someone who does not seem entirely sane. He emerges from the tunnel. Payne Avenue – not in fact an avenue, merely a quiet street – is empty and silent, except for some muffled music from the Kendal Arms. It seems extraordinary that Watt is prepared to shell out two hundred quid – more, with the equipment – on something so speculative, so shadowy, so impetuous, so wild. Of course, his whole professional life is on the line. Perhaps, Paul thinks, it is not surprising that he should be in such a state, that he should be so willing to use methods outside his normal pen-pushing modus operandi – twenty-five years of patient work and supermarket politics, store manager the prize, and just when it seems his, Martin Short sweeps past, and he is left with a modest pension, and years of senescence in which to savour the poisons of his failure.

On Saturday night Paul is still wondering who to sound out for the part of the produce supplier. His first thought was of the snooker hall. There would, however, be a possibility of Heather finding out somehow – and none of those lot would be able to persuade Martin that they were bona fide fruit wholesalers. What's more, he might have seen them in town. A stranger then? Someone from a transients' pub in Brighton? Paul imagines sidling up to a travelling salesman in the saloon of a two-star hotel and saying, 'Hello, mate. I'm looking for someone to . . .'

And then his mind fastens onto the word 'salesman'. A *salesman*. He knows a few of *them*. They would surely be well qualified for this sort of thing. They are all from out of town – from London and other parts of the south-east. And the subject of the impersonation is himself a sort of salesman. It is obviously the solution, and Paul immediately starts to think of the salesmen he knows, and wonder which of them to speak to. The first two he thinks of are Murray and the Pig, and there is no question, of course, of using them. Nor the likes of Wolé and Marlon. So who else? He looks through the numbers in his phone and finds others there. Some of them he has not seen or spoken to for years – their numbers probably obsolete – such as Mundjip from the Northwood days, and Nick and Paddy from Archway. Pax Murdoch is in prison in Thailand . . . In fact, for multifarious reasons, the options are more limited than he had hoped. In the end there is only one who properly fits what he is looking for, and that is Neil Mellor, one of his fellow managers at Park Lane Publications. Fortyish, worldly, quite well spoken, Neil would make a plausible fruit wholesaler. And he might like the look of a quick two hundred quid, too – PLP has surely folded, and who knows where he has washed up. Moreover, he did not know Eddy or Murray, and is unlikely to have stayed in touch with the Pig.

Paul phones him on Monday morning.

The first surprise – it seems utterly extraordinary – is that Park Lane Publications has *not* folded. It is still struggling on. Neil is on the sales floor there when he and Paul speak. He sounds slightly prickly – and this prickliness, obviously linked to what happened in December, is the second surprise. 'Well, well, well,' Neil says. 'Rainey, you fucker.'

'All right, mate . . .'

'You've got a nerve, phoning us up here.' It is said with a sort of smile – even so, it is not very friendly. They are still exchanging these pleasantries when Neil suddenly says, 'Look, Lawrence is about. Can I call you back later?'

'Sure.'

'I'll call you back later.'

When, the next morning, Neil has still not done so, Paul tries him again.

This time he seems to be in the smoking room, and Paul gets as far as saying that he has an 'offer' for him. Neil evidently assumes that this 'offer' will involve joining Paul at whichever outfit he is now working for, and is nonplussed when Paul starts saying that he needs someone to pretend to be a fruit wholesaler. 'Sorry?' he says, as though he must have misheard.

'I said, I need someone to come down to Brighton for a day or two –'

'Yeah, yeah. I got that. And do *what*?'

'And . . . Well, you'd have to meet this bloke and pretend you were a sort of fruit wholesaler . . .'

Neil laughs. 'What?'

'That's the job.'

'What is? I don't understand.'

'You'd have to meet this bloke, right, and pose as a fruit wholesaler.' More laughter. Paul laughs slightly himself. 'What? That's all. It's simple.'

'I'd have to sell him some fruit?'

'No . . . Well, not exactly. You'd have to pretend . . . I mean – are you interested at all?'

'I don't think so, mate. What is it? Some kind of scam?'

'No, no, nothing like that. It's two hundred quid for doing not much –'

'Two hundred quid *isn't* much. And anyway, I've got a job to do as it is –'

'We could do it at the weekend. Or you could take a day off –'

'Thanks for thinking of me, mate, but I'm not interested.'

'It'll probably be a laugh.'

'I'm sure it will . .'

'A day out by the sea . . .'

'No, mate. Seriously. I've got other priorities at the moment.'

Neil, it turns out, is now Lawrence's number two, and the myriad problems of Park Lane Publications press down heavily on his shoulders. (Since his nervous breakdown, Lawrence himself has been little more than a figurehead.)

'What you up to anyway?' Neil says.

'Oh . . . Working.'

'What – with Murray and the Pig and that lot?'

'No.'

There is a pause. Then Neil says, 'Well. Hope you find someone, mate . . .'

'You're sure you're not interested?'

'Yeah, I'm sure. Cheers. Take it easy, yeah?'

'Yeah. You too, mate.'

Slightly disconsolate, still in his blue nightshift uniform, Paul switches off his phone and pads through to the kitchen. *Fuck it*, he thinks. *Fuck Watt and the whole fucking thing.*

Exactly twenty-four hours later, however, he is speaking to Watt in person. 'Hello? Is that Paul Rainey?'

'Yeah, it's me.'

'Ah. Morning. How are you?'

'I'm okay.'

There is a short silence.

'Yes, I'm okay,' Watt says. 'Oh, by the way, did Hazel see you the other night?'

'Hazel?'

'That young woman . . . That member of staff we saw in the pub.'

'Oh.' Paul hesitates. 'No.' This is not true. When he stood up to leave, two minutes after Watt himself had left, Paul's eyes had for a moment met Hazel's. She looked slightly puzzled – as if she was unable to place him . . .

'Are you sure?'

'Yeah.'

'Well . . .' Watt laughs nervously. 'How do you *know*? How do you *know* she didn't see you?' When Paul says nothing, Watt makes a dissatisfied, sceptical noise. He has found himself the subject of some very strange looks since the weekend; some very significant smirks in the supermarket. 'So,' he says, 'any news?'

'I'm afraid not.'

There is a long pause. 'You mean you've not found anyone?'

'No.'

'Why not?'

'I just haven't been able to.'

'Have you *tried*?'

'Of course I've tried.' Somehow, Paul is aware of Heather listening to what he is saying – perhaps it is the sheer intensity of the silence – and he lowers his voice. 'I've tried a few people,' he says. 'I'm sorry. There's nothing more I can do –'

'Look, Rainey –' Watt's tone is that of someone finally taking a firm line with a plumber who has been messing him around for months – 'You're going to have to do better than that.'

'What do you mean?'

'Do you want me to get Jock involved?'

'No, I don't want you to get Jock involved. But what do you want me to *do*?'

'*Find* someone.'

'*Who*?'

'Anyone. I don't care. It doesn't matter.'

'I'm telling you, it's not that easy –'

'You've got until Friday,' Watt says. 'You've got until Friday, all right? If you've not found someone to do this by then, I'm going to Jock. I'm sorry. It's what I should have done in the first place. Do you understand?'

'Do I understand what?'

'That you have until Friday, or I'm going to Jock?'

'Yes,' Paul says, eventually, 'I understand.'

When Heather enters the kitchen, he is staring stonily at his phone. It is one of the unusual, uneasy weekday mornings when she is not at work. 'You all right, Paul?' she says.

'Yeah.'

'Who was that?' She puts the question very indifferently, with her head in the fridge, and when Paul murmurs, 'No one,' she does not press him further.

20

And he has other worries. His Friday-night date, for instance. A schoolteacher, someone Ned knows. Within minutes of Paul telling him that he and Heather were packing it in, Ned was pressing him to phone Jane. He was insistent, pestering. A balloon-bellied Pandarus wiping foam from his mouth. 'Call her,' he said, sliding the scrap of paper on which he had written her number across the bar. 'Call her. I've told her you're going to call.' And then, a week later, 'Have you called her yet? *No?* She's *expecting* you to call. She wants you to. She's waiting. If you don't call she'll be *disappointed*.' On the phone, she sounded jolly. She was surprisingly well spoken, for a friend of Ned's. Sweating, out in the garden, Paul said, 'So . . . Should we have a drink or something?'

And now he is in the Ancient Mariner, a newish pub on Coleridge Street. He was here with Heather once; their local, the Kendal Arms – a corner building of peeling green paint with several knackered pool tables on the dusty old carpet, a dartboard and live sport on TV – she refuses to go into. The Ancient Mariner, however, has leather sofas. Despite these sofas, it had been a depressing evening. Entering the loud, smoky interior of the pub more or less straight from his porridge, Paul was still half asleep, and did not feel – really did *not* feel – like drinking beer and chain-smoking cigarettes. Shy and intimidated in the fashionable milieu, Heather had struggled with his obvious malaise. On the table in front of him was a lurid vodka Red Bull, which hurt his teeth every time he tentatively sipped it. She had a vase of white wine. There was also a saucer of olives. Whenever she spoke, his lips formed themselves, for a moment, into a tight little smile. 'That's a nice picture,' she said. They had been sitting in silence for several minutes. He half turned to inspect it. 'Yeah,' he said, without seeing it. He was having trouble getting through his vodka Red Bull, and would not want another cigarette for a while. He lit one anyway.

No, it had not been an enjoyable evening. Nevertheless, when he needed somewhere to meet Jane, the Ancient Mariner seemed the place. And now he waits for her there, waits with his pint of white beer, his knees jiggling and his eyes on the door. Though it is many years since he has found himself in this situation, in his youth Paul was something of a ladies' man. A fluent talker with a winning smile; with a finely transparent line in faux knavery. Nor was he overweight then. His self-esteem, in those early salesman years, was spry, was whippet-like. On the sales floor he was one of the top men, which thrilled him for a while. The money itself – and for a year or two there was lots of it – had made him feel strong. It had made him feel self-important. He took taxis everywhere; when he left work, he would wave down a black cab and stroll unhurriedly to where it waited. Such things were tonic to his self-esteem, and he made a name for himself as a minor ladies' man. Murray was envious, for one.

Young women who joined the sales force at Burdon Macauliffe tended – if they were single, which they usually weren't; and if they mixed with the other salespeople, which they usually didn't – to fall into the hands of shambling, handsome Pax Murdoch, or of Paddy, a lean Irishman with eloquent sky-blue eyes. Paul was a sort of junior partner to these two, and enjoyed what was left over. Lucie, for instance, vivacious and pudding-faced with straw curls. With a boxer's nose. Or Valentina, sickly-looking and unable to speak in a voice louder than a mumbled whisper – she was hopeless at selling and quickly left; she and Paul went out for more than a year. Somewhat unusual was Lorna. Raven-haired Lorna was pretty – pretty enough to make Paul wonder what she was doing with him.

In her, his self-esteem found its limits, and he wondered why he merited such a woman; wondered whether she was perhaps unstable, nuts, a nymphomaniac. If he had had more money he might have understood. She was the one to initiate their short affair, practically pulling him into a taxi outside the Café de Paris, where the Burdon Macauliffe Christmas party had taken place. He presumed that he had his standing as a minor ladies' man to thank for this. From the start, though, he had been ill at ease. He was troubled by things that had not troubled him in the past. Aspects of his physique and wardrobe, for instance. In public, he felt threatened by other men. In private, he worried inordinately about his performance. When it ended, it was like a liberation. She immediately took up with Paddy. Paul did not mind – he was flattered, in fact; felt a new parity with the pale-eyed Irishman, whose friendliness towards him increased markedly from then on. And he felt too that he had had a sort of escape; that head-turning Lorna might have led him into a total failure of self-esteem – the way that being married to Brit Ekland turned poor Peter Sellers into a paranoid schizophrenic.

His standing as a ladies' man did not suffer. Nor did it suffer the following summer, when word spread through the sales force that he was seeing two ladies simultaneously. The only person who did not know seemed to be one of the ladies in question – Lisa O'Rourke, known privately to Paul as 'Weathered Statue'. Her head had a uniquely smooth, worn look. Her nose a mere nub, her lips practically not there. She had poor posture, and long thin undulating mashed-swede hair. Lashless blue eyes under low, weathered brows. She was on Murray's team – an earnest, persistent pitcher – and it was she who gave Paul the nail-biting blow job in the smoking room one evening when they stayed late to call California. Murray was still there and might have walked in on them – until the very last moments, Paul's eyes were intent on the blond wood of the institutional door. Lisa did not know, however, that he was also seeing Sharon. 'Beaky' was his secret name for Sharon – she was half-

Lebanese and had a nose like a toucan. (Between the two of them, he often thought – averaged out, as it were – they would have had a normalish profile.) He and Lisa had had no more than a fling when she went to Ireland for a funeral. In the end, she was away for two weeks, and Paul presumed that that was that. Murray's birthday fell in this fortnight, and the festivities ended in a dark, airless nightspot in King's Cross. Murray hit on Sharon there; she went home with Paul. She was a secretary in the London branch of an immense Japanese bank – these were the days when the park of the Emperor's palace in Tokyo was worth more, it was said, than the whole of California – and she took Paul to the Japanese restaurants where she went with Mr Kojima, for whom she worked.

Paul suspects that it was Murray – for whom *he* worked – who told Lisa what was happening; that when she did not pick up on the tittle-tattle he was so assiduously spreading, he just sat her down in the smoking room one morning and told her. So 'Weathered Statue' wiped her oddly lifeless blue eyes and left the sales force. (Murray tried to meet her for a drink the following week – she said yes, then stood him up.) And in September, more or less on a whim, Paul told Sharon that he did not want to see her any more.

In later years, when there was a lesser profusion of sex and money, he would wonder why he had been so nonchalant in leaving her.

He remembers how Eddy, when he heard how long it had been, marched him to the nearest phone box and told him to take his pick of the tom cards. The phone box was on Fleet Street, and standing in its packed sour odour, Paul had surveyed the festooned cards. Then, stepping out of the stuffiness, he had said, 'No, mate . . .'

'*Why not?*' Eddy shouted on the pavement.

'I just . . . I don't know. I don't want to. Do you?'

'Me? I'm a married man. But no it's true,' Eddy had said, as they walked to the Chesh, 'you want to know what you're getting into. Here.' He pulled his phone from his pocket. 'Take this number. She's in Bayswater. She's good. Really sweet . . .'

'No –'

'*Just take it!* You don't have to call her.'

So Paul took it.

'Her name's Annette,' Eddy said.

'Annette' worked out of a basement in a street of one-star hotels and youth hostels. The street was strange-looking because it was originally a mews of plain, pipe-disfigured house-backs which had been transformed into house-fronts with no more than the addition of narrow doors and a few half-hearted pilasters. The number in question seemed to be some sort of hostel, with a pine-panelled foyer where Paul made his way past a fridge and some CCTV monitors towards the stairs.

When she opened the door, he was surprised to see her wide, flat breasts. She was wearing forest-green knickers. 'Annette?' She nodded, and stood aside to let him in. She was short, solid, blondish, smiling. 'We spoke on the phone,' he said, stepping worriedly into the room. When she asked his name, she did not seem to be French, as 'Annette' was obviously intended to suggest; nor was she English. The room was quite large and smelt of cigarette smoke and air-freshener. It had a white, empty feel. He noticed a single plug-in electric hob, a sink, some bottles of household cleaning products. A small powder-pink stereo. The curtains were open and so was the window – it was summer – and passing footsteps were easily audible from the street overhead. She wanted a hundred pounds. He took out his wallet, and the five twenties that he had withdrawn on the way, and she put the money in a drawer. Then she pulled the thin curtains, stepped out of her knickers and asked him what he wanted. He just shrugged. Her doughy breasts swung forward slightly as she stooped to put her hand on his quiescent trouser front. Then, starting to unbutton the jeans, she licked her palm and went to work. Despite this slow start, once she had him out of half of his clothes, and onto the bed – and had fitted him with a condom, and lubricated herself – he finished very fast, within twenty seconds. She wiggled and slid off him, and for a few more seconds they lay there under a light sweat. Then she said, 'Do you want to go again?'

He was staring at the orange pine of the bedstead, the grey wall. 'No. Thank you.'

'I don't mean more money.'

'No,' he said. 'Thank you.'

He sat up. Once more, he was aware of footsteps and voices from the street outside. 'Do you want to clean yourself?' she said. Her eyes flicked to the little sink with its collection of plastic bottles. He stood up, naked from the waist down, and went to the sink. There he peeled off the condom and dropped it into a waste-paper basket, then tore off a square of paper towel and quickly wiped himself. He turned to look for his trousers. They were in a heap on the floor with his shorts and socks and shoes. He untangled them. Sitting on the wide bed, a sheet pulled up to her sallow face, 'Annette' smoked. 'Right,' he said, when he had his clothes on. 'Thank you.'

'M-hm.'

Walking to the tube station he felt fine. More than fine. The evening, the London streets, seemed vibrantly alive. There had – he thought – been something so kindly, so solicitous in the way she had offered to do it with him a second time for free; something so unlike the indifference of the city in which they lived, and which the thousand strangers of the mauve evening seemed to express.

Often – on tube-station escalators, for instance – he would think of her. And when, some time later, he saw Heather in the secretaries' pool of Archway Publications, and then that Friday in the Finnegans Wake, he did not fail to notice similarities of blondish solidity, of thickset shortness. The similarities were more in the figure than the face, and struck him most the first time that he saw Heather naked.

His memories of 'Annette', however, were shadowy, and the physical facts of Heather soon obliterated what was left of them, so that when he thought of her from then on it was simply Heather that he saw – though Heather herself had seemed a sort of shadow of 'Annette' when he had first seen her in the secretaries' pool.

Jane is late.

Paul is staring at the roundel of lemon in his cloudy pint – wondering whether she has stood him up – when he lifts his head and sees a woman looking lost. Ned had said that Jane was 'fortyish'; the woman in the Friday throng seems somewhat older. She is wearing an oriental padded jacket, pink on black, and her hair is tied tightly into greyish pigtails. Her face, though it shows signs of old-womanishness, a sag on the jawline and under the eyes, is somehow youthful – soft and small-toothed. She is wide-hipped, bosomless, with narrow full lips painted pink. Seeing her, Paul experiences only disappointment. What had he expected though? His expectations were silly – he sees that. The facts of life never had a fair shot. And in fact she is not so bad. He stands – she is peering worriedly into the mass of people – and tentatively holds up his hand. When she sees him she hesitates, perhaps experiencing her own moment of melancholy disappointment; then she smiles nervously.

'Jane?' he says.

'Hello.'

'Do you want a drink?'

'Okay.'

'What would you like?'

'What would I like. What are you having?'

He returns from the bar – she is joining him in a *bière blanche* – and she says, 'This is a nice place.'

'Yeah,' he says, putting the glass bucket of beer on the table. 'I think it's new.'

'Is it? Thank you.'

'I think so.'

'It's nice,' she says.

'Yeah.'

'I didn't know about it.'

'No. Well, I think it's new. Um,' he says, a moment later, 'so you're from Hove?'

'I live in Brighton.'

He smiles. 'Oh, the other place.'

'The other place. London-on-Sea.'

'Yes. Well. We're more genteel in Hove.'

'Yes.' She sips the cloudy greyish beer. 'Mm. This is nice.'

'It is, isn't it.'

She is not shy. She is wary, watchful. And she seems somehow without the tough shell of worldliness that normally forms on people in their maturity – or if she is not without it, it is translucent and ineffectual – and perhaps because of this it is easy to imagine her when she was very much younger than she is. Loose wisps of grey hair stand out at the margins of her smooth forehead. 'That's a nice picture,' she says.

'Yeah . . . I think it's for sale actually.'

'Is it?'

'You . . . interested in art?' Paul ventures.

'Mm. Yes.'

'What sort of thing?'

'Oh. I don't know really.'

'Well, it's difficult to know these days, isn't it.'

Despite this difficulty, he soon finds himself putting forward some extremely strident opinions. Suddenly he seems to have a strident opinion on everything. He is sounding off on whatever question has the temerity to show its face. To stop himself, he asks her whether she is an art teacher – 'You seem to know so much about it' – and with a sharp laugh, a shake of the head, she says, 'No, maths, I'm afraid. Sorry.'

'Well, that's more important than art.' She smiles sceptically. 'No, it is. How long have you been teaching then?'

'God, do I really have to say?' She has something of the hollowed-out, exhausted quality of some teachers; she is savagely matter-of-fact (dismissing her twenty-five-year membership of the profession with the statement 'there's not much else you can do with a maths degree') and at the same time she seems emotionally vulnerable, easily upset. 'Let's just say it's been a while.'

'All right.'

'Longer than I care to remember.'

'I know the feeling. Still, it must be . . .'

While he puts questions to her, he wonders why her face is a strange sort of reddish brown. Perhaps it is just the light in the pub. Perhaps she has slapped on too much foundation. He has plenty of time to wonder this because she is now talking non-stop. Something seems to have set her off. He wonders what it was. One minute he was asking polite, interested questions – and she was passing him polite, meticulous answers; the next she is flushed, intense, voluble, plaintive, waspish. The subject seems to be the politics of education. Initially, he listens pert with interest. He is not able to maintain this for long, however. She seems exasperated about something – PFI, top-up fees, streaming, parents, ministers . . . Something. Zoning out, he nods thoughtfully, his phatics – once lovingly wrought one-offs – now no more than mass-produced murmurs. And surely she, as a teacher – a *maths* teacher – must have noted the total lack of positive evidence that he is following what she is saying, must have picked up on the listlessness of his eyes and posture. Or perhaps not – perhaps these are precisely the things that years of maths teaching have made her unable to see. Self-preservation. Just stand there and say your words, and then . . .

'What?' he says suddenly. 'Sorry?'

'I'm sorry,' she says. 'I've been off on one again.'

'No,' he insists. 'No. Not at all.'

'I'll stop now.'

'Not on my account.'

'Me, me, me!'

'It was interesting.'

'I've got a bit of a . . . *thing* about all that.'

'Sure. And it's totally understandable.'

'What do you do?'

'Me? Um. I've been working on a night shift,' he says. He smiles. 'If I seem a bit tired, that's why.'

'You don't seem tired.'

'Well, I suppose I shouldn't. I only got up a few hours ago. No, it's a good excuse to get straight on with . . .' He hesitates. 'These.' Indicating his empty beer bucket.

Except for a slight quiver, she seems to ignore this hint of an alcohol problem, and quickly says, 'Where's that?'

'Where's . . . ?'

'Where do you work, on the night shift?'

'Oh . . . Just . . . A supermarket.'

'Which one?'

'Sainsbury's. You know the west Hove Sainsbury's?'

'Yes, of course. You're the night-shift manager there?'

He nods. 'M-hm.'

'What's it like?'

'It's all right.'

With her large, light brown eyes on him she waits for him to say more. 'You know. I just have to make sure everything's neat and tidy. It doesn't have to be perfect. It's not that demanding, to be honest.'

'And,' she says, 'if you don't mind my asking, *why* do you work nights? I mean, do all managers have to do it? For a while? Is that how it works?'

He is tempted to tell her yes and leave it there. Instead, he says, 'No. It's not like that.'

'So do you like it?' She smiles. 'Maybe you're a night owl!'

'It's all right.' His tone is sombre – unintentionally so – and she immediately makes her eyes serious. 'I s'pose I was a bit down,' he says. 'When I started. You know.' She nods. 'So. Well . . .' And to his surprise, he finds himself launching into a long spiel about himself – one which is not even true; which has to fit with his self being a supermarket manager. So he says that he used to manage the fresh produce – 'the fruit and veg, you know' – and that when his marriage – 'well, it ended' – he started to suffer from insomnia, 'and I thought I might as well work nights. It seemed appropriate somehow.'

She listens with an expression of intent sympathy, her head slightly lowered, looking up from under pencil-line eyebrows. When he pauses, she puts sympathetic questions. 'Wasn't it weird?' she says quietly. 'To work at night.'

'It was weird. At first it was very weird, yeah. You get used to it. You do get used to it.'

'You get used to everything,' she says.

'You do. That's true.'

'How long have you been doing it?'

'Not that long. Six months.'

'Are you going to carry on?'

'I don't know.'

'I know it's none of my business,' she says.

'No, go on.'

'Maybe . . . I don't know . . .' She is looking at the tabletop; then she turns to him. 'Maybe . . . Do you think you're hiding from something?'

'Like what?'

'I don't know.'

'Maybe . . .'

'I don't know. I'm probably just being silly.'

'Not at all.'

'Psychobabble . . .'

Something touches his foot, and he looks down to see one of her black trainers stepping swiftly away. 'I'm sorry. And before that?' she says, flushing. 'Before you worked nights. Did you like your work?'

'Yeah, I did. You know.' He smiles wryly. 'As much as one can. Being fresh-produce manager, it's a bit like working in a garden.'

She looks surprised. 'Is it?'

'Sometimes. You know – the fresh fruit and vegetables. Organic matter. Yeah, it is.'

'Maybe you'll go back to it one day.'

'Maybe,' he says.

'Are they good employers, Sainsbury's?'

'Dunno. Yeah. I'd say so.'

'And have you always worked for them?'

'No, not always. Since, um. Since ninety . . . ninety-five. I was on the, um, the management training scheme.' He is himself slightly shocked at what is happening. Slowly, he is spinning a whole past for this other Paul Rainey – this Paul Rainey who is a manager at Sainsbury's, and has been since ninety-five. Underlying the first part of the story, of course, the night-shift part, was a sort of metaphorical truth; an emotional or psycho-logical truth in the story of a man – 'Paul Rainey' – who slides into a sadness, and sick of this marauding insatiable world, signs on to work nights. As it spreads further into the past, though, he starts to wonder just how much material he is going to have to make up. He is telling her about the management training scheme – how it took place in White City, how it involved a mock-up of a supermarket floor. How, as part of the scheme, the trainees were sent out to work in various jobs in supermarkets all over the country. (He has heard that this happens.)

'Where were *you* sent?' she asks.

'Where was I sent? A few different places.'

'Like where?'

'Um. Darlington.' He has never been there, does not even know where it is. 'It's quite nice actually,' he says. 'Quite a nice little place, market town. Do you know it?' She shakes her head. 'All I know,' she says, 'is that it's in Yorkshire.'

'Yeah, that's right. Typical Yorkshire town. Really friendly people. People are so friendly up north, aren't they?'

'And where else were you?'

'Where else?'

'You said you were in a few different places.'

'Oh. Yeah.'

In Swansea, he says, he packed people's shopping. In Gillingham he was in the warehouse. Then he starts to tell her about his first proper posting, in London . . .

'Where was that exactly?'

'Oh, you won't know it . . .'

'I'm sure I will.' She smiles. 'Try me.'

Suddenly, though, he is unable to think of a single Sainsbury's in London. It is extraordinary. There must be two hundred of them. 'The one in Hammersmith?'

'Hammersmith?'

'Yeah.'

'No,' she says, 'I don't know Hammersmith. Is there one in Hammersmith?'

'Of course.'

'So how did you end up here?'

'Here? In Hove?'

'Yes.'

'Well. I was offered a promotion. It was too good an opportunity to turn down really.' She nods. 'And my wife was – *is* – from round here.' On the mention of his wife, her eyes droop for a moment. 'And I wanted to get out of London anyway . . .'

Finally, somewhere in the early nineties, he manages to fuse this fictitious existence with his own, saying, 'And before that, I was a salesman for a few years.'

'A *salesman*?' she says. 'Well, it's good you got out of *that* racket! Anyway.'

'Yeah.'

'What sort of salesman?'

'Well . . .'

'Not the sort who phones people up at home?'

'Well, no – it was business-to-business.'

'That must have been awful,' she says. 'Didn't you have to lie all the time?'

'Sort of . . .'

'I think that's awful. Isn't it?'

'Yeah.'

'People seem to think it's just normal now.'

'Well. I don't do it any more.'

He has needed a piss for a long time. And he is on the point of excusing himself when she starts to tell him how *she* ended up in 'London-on-Sea'. It is a long story – involving several further forays into the politics of education. It takes in a stint in India, and somewhere, some schools – the ferocious pressure in his lower abdomen is preventing him from following what she is saying – and finally 'London-on-Sea', a term she insists on using, though it sounds sour in her mouth since it was, she says, precisely to escape 'the smoke' of London-on-Thames that she fled there. (On the subject of smoke, she has spent the evening squinting in it, and swatting the fug, and staring sadly at the filling ashtray.)

When she has finished, Paul says, 'Do you want another one?'

'Um . . . A little one?' she says, indicating an inch with her thumb and forefinger.

'Okay.'

He stands up. First, urgently, he slips to the toilets. The evening, he feels – in the peace and quiet of the tiled space – has so far been a qualified success. When she listened to him, with her solid head on one side while he spoke of himself, putting her sensitive questions, he had started to quite like her. Had even started to fancy her. What troubles him is that what he told her was mostly lies. He thinks of the unfortunate Frenchman who posed as a surgeon, and sees that something similar is possible here; and he has not even opted for the kudos and sexiness of surgery. *His* lie is that he is the night-shift manager in a provincial supermarket. Which does not seem worth quadruple murder and suicide, if that is how this is to end. He turns to the sink. And the lie is wearying. Now, after only an hour or two, it seems like a load of luggage. Washing his hands, inspecting his face in the mirror – he is looking okay – he finds himself hoping – it *is* precipitous – to spend the rest of his life with this woman, this Jane, this teacher with her small teeth and weary solid face and overpowering feelings on the politics of education. (He hopes, too, that something of her youthfulness persists under her clothes.) So he should start with the truth. He waves his hands under the hand dryer. Start with the truth. The truth.

'I'm afraid I've been lying to you,' he says, once more installed in his seat, two fresh *bières blanches* on the table, hers a half. She looks startled. 'What do you mean?' He is lighting a B&H. (He thought his pouch of smuggled Drum tobacco would make a poor impression.) 'I've been lying,' he says. 'Not telling the truth.'

Smiling unsurely, wondering whether this is some sort of joke, she says, 'What do you mean?'

'About myself.'

'What about yourself?' She is starting to sound slightly distraught.

'I'm not really a manager at Sainsbury's,' he says.

This takes a second to sink in. And of course it overturns not just some small talk, but an intense section of the evening during which she listened with intent sympathy while he spoke – it seemed – in solemn, thorny earnest; and it was perhaps his willingness to do this that had persuaded *her* to do the same; to speak so openly – she had surprised herself – of her unhappy life in London, her years off work, the stalker, the flood, the insurance nightmare, the endless legal hell . . .

'Then why did you . . . ?'

'Say I was? I'm not sure.'

They sit in silence for a few moments. Her voice, when she speaks, is offended and thin. 'What are you then?'

'A warehouse operative. That's what they call it. I mean, I *do* work nights,' he says. Pink-faced, she stares at him. 'I'm sorry.'

'What do you mean "warehouse operative"?'

'You know . . .' He flicks ash into the tray, shamefaced.

'A shelf-stacker?'

'Yeah.'

'I wish you'd stop smoking,' she whispers, sweeping some from her face with a small, tense movement.

'Sorry. You should've said . . .' He stubs out his unspent cigarette.

'I don't . . . I don't feel . . . I'm sorry.' She shakes her head, looking elsewhere.

'What? What don't you feel?'

'I think I should go.'

'*Go?* Why?'

She sighs tremulously, and stands up. She seems in a hurry.

'Look, I'm sorry . . . I didn't mean . . . Are you really going?'

'Yes.'

'Why? Please . . .' he says, half standing. For a few moments he stays on his feet, prevaricating, wondering whether to follow her, whether the situation might still be saved. It seems unlikely. In haste, she is pushing her way tearfully towards the exit. He sits, and fishes his cigarette from the ashtray. On his own – feeling shaky, empty – he finishes the pint and a half of *bière blanche*. He tries her phone. It is switched off. For several seconds he hesitates, poised to leave a message. Then he hangs up, and threads his way through strangers' voices to the door.

21

Watt insists on meeting in Eastbourne. He says that Brighton is not safe, Hove even less so. So on Saturday evening, straight from his porridge, Paul sets out. He was up earlier than usual – when Marie was still in evidence, and there was still light in the sky, and shadows in the garden – and he feels muzzy and soft leaving the house. It is a mild evening. The hotel in Eastbourne that Watt has selected is part of a Victorian terrace on a side street perpendicular to the seafront. It is white stucco, several houses wide – where front doors used to be, windows with lace curtains. The bar is quiet. No one is playing the walnut baby grand; the red velvet armchairs are mostly unoccupied, the cut-glass ashtrays mostly empty. Paul advances over the maroon carpet, looking for Roy Watt. When he sees him – in one of the armchairs, his head lolling on a stained antimacassar – he is shocked how exhausted he looks. He looks utterly shot, like he has not slept in days. The weary brown shadows under his eyes spread almost to the edges of his face. 'Sorry I'm late,' Paul says, holding up an apologetic hand. 'The train took longer than I thought. It takes forty-five minutes. Did you know that? It can't be more than twenty miles . . .' Watt looks hurt. He has a sip of his G&T. Then a sip of his Silk Cut. 'Drink?' Paul says. Technically, Watt is supposed to be paying for everything. (And he is insisting on receipts.) 'I'm all right actually,' he says.

'Sure?'

He nods.

When Paul returns from the bar – which looks strangely flimsy, like something left over from some very amateur dramatics – Watt is still sulking. 'We've not got much time,' he says. From the carpet next to his seat he lifts an old-fashioned British Airways flight bag. 'The equipment. Take it.' Paul takes it. 'The instructions are all in there. I've tested it and it works. But test it again before . . . You know.'

'All right.'

Paul wants to unzip the bag and inspect the equipment. Watt is staring at him, with exhausted-looking eyes. The situation seems to be wearing him down. He has had to lie to his wife and daughters about where he is. Nor do they know that he has started smoking again – he has to hide his cigarettes and suck mints and tell them that he has been in smoky pubs with boring men. None of which is positive for his self-esteem. He peers into his glass, empty except for a few shrunken ice cubes. When he speaks, his voice is scratchy. 'So who's this "Andy" then?' he asks.

Unhurriedly, Paul puts down his pint. The tablecloth is a filthy ivory, with lumpy lace edges. He had waited until Watt phoned him on Friday – in a terrible, feverish state – to tell him that he *had* found someone. Andy. On Thursday, at his wit's end, he had tried Andy's mobile number, hoping that it would still be the same. It was. And it was not the only thing. Andy – it was almost incredible – was still at Park Lane Publications. *Everything just went on,* Paul thought. *It just went on.* He had joined Tony Peters' team. Paul said that he had a job proposal for him. He explained, loosely, what was involved – two days in Brighton, pretend to be a fruit seller, two hundred quid. Andy had not taken much persuading. The whole thing lasted only a few minutes, though it might have lasted longer had Paul been more expansive when Andy asked him what *he* was doing. 'This and that,' he said quickly.

'With Murray?' It was the only mention – oblique – of what had happened last winter.

'No. Um. In Brighton. So . . .'

So he would meet Andy at Brighton station on Monday morning. 'Oh, and bring a suit,' he said.

'No problemo.'

And that was that. Andy had not asked a single question.

'Just a bloke I used to work with,' Paul says. 'A salesman.'

'You were a salesman?'

'Yeah.'

Watt looks surprised for a second. 'Presentable, is he?'

'Very.'

'How old?'

'Mid, late twenties.'

'Hope he's not too young.'

'Don't worry about it.'

Watt *is* worried though. He looks miserable, threadbare with stress. He leans his ugly face over the low table, and says, 'Does he understand how *serious* this is?'

Paul shrugs. 'Yeah,' he says, 'I'm sure he does.'

'Tell him,' Watt says, with a cigarette in his mouth, making a mess of lighting his lighter, 'tell him he'll get no money if he doesn't get any evidence.'

Mildly outraged, Paul looks at him for a moment. 'That's not what we said.' Watt sighs, frustrated. 'I'll be able to see of course,' he says, squinting through the cigarette smoke. 'I'll be able to see if he's not trying. On the tape.'

'Yeah, you will.'

He pulls some printed sheets from his briefcase. They are neatly stapled together in two sets, and he hands one to Paul. The first page is headed 'The Strawberry Market'. Watt starts to go through the text, explaining, quickly, how the fresh-produce market works. It is a frenetic, fast-moving world. Fruit, vegetables, cut flowers. Prices hugely up and down. The strawberry price, for instance, might swing from a high of five hundred pence a kilo to a low of a fifth of that, and then up again, in a matter of weeks. Thus early season the prices are usually high, falling precipitously over the summer, then shooting up in September time. The supermarkets, with a price horizon of a month or two, try to manage their stock in line with this. Men like Martin watch the five principal wholesale markets – Liverpool, Bristol, Birmingham, and the London markets, New Covent Garden and New Spitalfields. They pore over the fine statistics of DEFRA's weekly *Agricultural Market Report*; for Martin, it is the most important document in the world. They watch the weather, subscribe to special Met Office data services. They need an encyclopedic knowledge of seasonality, of the natural processes of horticulture.

Maximising profits means fully exploiting the volatility of the market. But since the produce is highly perishable, and everyone is trying to do the same thing, margins are squeezed, sometimes to zero. To outperform the market, therefore, it is necessary to snatch hold of opportunities the moment they present themselves. 'Your mate should call the supermarket and ask to speak to the fresh-produce manager,' Watt says quietly. He has turned to the second page. Paul has done the same.

'All right.'

'He should say he's from a strawberry grower, based in Kent.'

'Strawb'rries.'

'That's right.'

'Okay.'

'Morlam Garden Fruits. It's all here.' Watt indicates the printed sheet. 'He should say he wants to meet. That's routine. It's normal.'

'Sure.'

From his pocket Watt takes a small stack of business cards – he had them made that afternoon. 'MORLAM GARDEN FRUITS' is written across the top, next to a stylised image of a tree. 'Andrew Smith' is the name; 'Sales Manager' the post. There are some telephone numbers, and an email address – asmith@mgfruits.co.uk. When he holds them out to Paul, his hand is shaking slightly. 'These look good,' Paul says, taking them. He spends a few seconds in polite inspection – Watt has evidently put some time in. 'The numbers . . . ?'

'I just made them up.'

'Well . . . All right. What if Martin phones them?'

'He'll know something's up. But he's not going to phone *during the meeting*, is he?'

'No.'

'And afterwards it'll be too late.'

'Yeah.'

Watt says that the strawberry price is very high – the early-season crop has been poor. There is especially a shortage of quality class-one fruit. On the wholesale markets the most usual price is well in excess of four hundred pence a kilo. 'A spike,' he says, summing up.

'Strawb'rry price spike,' Paul murmurs.

Watt shoots him a nervous, irritable look. 'Yes. That's why I went for strawb'rries.'

'M-hm.'

'Your mate should say he has a crop of early-season Elsantas, ripened in polytunnels, and ready for shipping. He should say an agreed sale has fallen through, leaving him in immediate need of a new purchaser – for which reason he is willing to offer the whole crop for a very low price. It's all here.' He presses on from the text: 'The fruit will be supplied in 227-gram punnets, unlabelled, with twenty punnets to a tray. A tonne of produce in total, which he should offer at two hundred pence a kilo.' Martin, Watt says, will find it impossible to withstand such an offer. Strawberries *will* sell. It is early in the season, supplies are scarce, there will be a powerful sense of post-winter novelty, of the first red berries of summer – and several thousand pounds' profit. What's more – Watt points out – Tesco's are promoting their own strawberries, imported from Spain, and pulling in the punters with summery images in their ads.

All of which, he says, is important – Andy will have to know it inside out to persuade Martin that he is not an impostor. More important, however, is what follows.

They turn to the next page.

Martin's initial response, Watt says (lighting a new cigarette with the end of his old one), will undoubtedly be to suggest that Morlam Garden Fruits join the list of approved suppliers and submit to an inspection. Andy should say, first off, that even if the inspection were in forty-eight hours, it would be too late – he needs to shift the fruit within forty-eight hours. And then he should say, 'Anyway, to tell you the truth, there might be problems with an inspection.' When Martin asks him what sort of problems, he should say, 'Oh nothing serious.' And then mention the fact that some of his pickers might not yet have secured their work visas, that the firm might not be BRC audited, or a member of the Assured Production Scheme. Having mentioned these things, he should ask, 'Would that be a problem for you?'

'And if Short says no,' Watt says, smiling toothsomely, though with fear in his eyes, 'we've got the bugger.'

'What if he says yes? What if he says it would be a problem?'

'Well. Then your mate says –' Watt puts his fingertip to the words – 'Would it be a problem for you *in principle*?'

And if Martin were to say no to *that* (which Watt seems to think very likely if he uses unlisted suppliers) then they had him too. It would not even be necessary to follow through and make the sale, though of course Andy should do so if possible. When Paul wonders aloud whether selling non-existent strawberries to someone might fall within the legal limits of fraud, Watt says that no money will move, and no papers will be signed – one-off fresh-produce transactions, he says, are always settled COD.

'Still . . .' Paul says.

Watt starts to shuffle papers, to stuff them into his briefcase. 'Well,' he says, 'I'm not entirely sure. It's another reason I wanted my name kept out of it.' Andy should be dressed in a suit, he says, and arrive with two unmarked punnets of excellent, extremely fresh Elsanta strawberries. '*Extremely* fresh. That means bought the same day.'

They leave the hotel. Watt will not stop talking. He says the same things over and over. '*Extremely* fresh,' he says. 'That means bought the same day.'

'I understand.'

'And he has to ask, Would it be a problem for you *in principle*?'

'I know.'

'And test the equipment before you use it. I've tested it myself and it works.'

'I will.'

'I've booked a room for him at the Queensbury guest house.'

'Yes, you said.'

'And I will need a receipt . . .'

They part in front of the illuminated hotel. Watt is about to hurry off when Paul says, 'The money. The two hundred quid. Plus you owe me about forty quid for expenses as well.'

Watt frowns. 'Afterwards,' he says. 'I'll give it to you afterwards.'

'No. Why? I'll need it to pay Andy.'

'Pay him. I'll give you the money.' Watt laughs. 'Look . . . I haven't got it on me.'

'Let's get it then . . .'

'Why? I'll pay you. Don't worry.'

They eye each other without much trust. Paul sighs. 'If I don't get that money,' he says, 'you won't get the tape.' Watt stares at him for a moment. Smiling slightly, he looks innocent. Perplexed. Even offended. The threat seems to have upset him. He says, 'Fine. I'll pay you. Don't worry.'

Paul *is* worried though. There is something that he did not tell Watt, something important. Two nights earlier he had once more spoken to Gerald in the frore shadows of the warehouse. When he mentioned Martin, Gerald seemed not to know what he was talking about. Then he said, 'Oh yeah that. That's all shit.'

'What?' Paul said.

'It's shit.'

Paul laughed. 'What are you talking about?'

'It's some other bloke. It's not Martin Short. Over in Soufampton. Terry told me, yeah?'

'Terry? Who's Terry?'

'Terry. The lorry driver.'

'What did he tell you?' Paul had turned pale, though in the ghostly light of the warehouse it did not show.

'He told me all that stuff. It was some manager over in Soufampton. Fresh-produce manager over there. Not Martin Short.'

'So Martin doesn't use . . .'

'No,' Gerald said.

It was a shock to hear this. In the non-foods aisle, Paul's hands had trembled as he packed the shelves with soap-filled pads. And he had intended to tell Watt. To tell him when they spoke on the phone on Friday; then he thought he would wait until they met face to face on Saturday. And he had been about to tell him – to say, 'Listen, there's something . . .' – when Watt produced the equipment. He had already paid for the equipment. If Paul *then* told him that the whole thing was a mix-up . . . Well, he would surely tell Macfarlane, and Martin, everything. This way, Paul thought, it was possible – *possible* – that he might not. It would be Andy's performance on the tape that would settle it one way or the other – a thought which did little to soothe him as he waited in Eastbourne station.

The Queensbury is one of several guest houses on Russell Square, a small rectangle of Regency terraces slowly discolouring in the shadow of the Churchill shopping centre. One end of the square is open, and there Cannon Place sends the traffic down to the seafront, past the unobtrusive patch of green and its somnolent, grubby B&Bs. The Queensbury is in the corner of the square furthest from the road. There, the decay seems worst. The house-fronts are nothing but flaking brown paint, weeds grow thickly in the corroded railings and the windows are dark grey with dirt. Even the Gothic lettering of the sign –

Tea and coffee in all rooms
Contractors welcome

– is mottled, faded, and losing pieces of itself into the damp of the sunless area below. A plastic tablet, yellow-edged like a smoker's fingers, in one of the ground-floor windows says VACANCIES. Next to it is an ancient decal promoting the tourist industry of the south-east. The door is held open by a rubber wedge. Inside – a narrow corridor with a torn carpet and a payphone on the wall.

Watt found this place. His search for low room rates led him here.

Mounting the three chequer-tiled steps (black and beige) up to the unpromising corridor, Paul looks over his shoulder. Andy is following a few metres behind with his overnight bag and suit carrier, looking up and down the quiet square with mild, bloodshot interest. He is obviously stoned. Paul is stoned himself. They were passing through the neighbouring square – Clarence, very similar – when Andy said, 'Should we have a quick doob?' The doob had a particularly pungent, skunky odour, and they smoked it quickly, under the uninterested eyes of some scaffolders. Now Paul is sliding in slow motion into the guest house, slowly immersing himself in its stale smell. 'Oi, mate!' Andy's plummy voice. Paul turns. One wall of the corridor is covered with mirror tiles, each an inch square. Pixellated, Andy stands motionless in them. The opposite wall is puffy with old wallpaper. From outside, the sad sound of gulls. 'What?' Paul says.

'Is this where I'm staying?'

'What do you think?'

Since Paul met him at the station, Andy has maintained an irritating prima donna fussiness. 'This is where you're staying,' Paul says. 'Yes.' It is a strange situation. Not having seen each other for so many months, and now here, in Brighton, neither of them wearing a suit. When the late-running ten-oh-six from Victoria finally pulled in, Paul had left his post, and was inspecting croissants under illuminated glass – most of them had lost their pep, they looked soft and greasy under the heat lamps. A voice at his shoulder said, 'All right, mate?' Startled, his speech of welcome vanishing from his mind, all he had said was, 'Oh, all right.' And then purchased a cheese and ham croissant – he was hungry, had not had supper – while Andy waited with his luggage. 'How are you?'

'Yeah. Well . . .'

'Oh – d'you want something?'

'No thanks.'

What Andy did want was to take a taxi to the hotel – his word – but when Paul said, 'All right, if you pay for it,' he spent a long time sighing and whining and looking longingly at the green-and-white taxis pulling up outside the station like motorised mints, and then finally said, 'It better not be far.'

'It's not.'

They walked down Queen's Road. In the distance, the sea glittered like static on an untuned TV screen. The pavement was strewn with rubbish, the businesses were tawdry. Paul ate his croissant from its greasy paper bag while Andy pestered him to take the suit carrier. Andy was wearing jeans and a rugby shirt with wide lateral stripes and brogues. (The only previous occasion on which they had seen each other outside of work was one Saturday in the autumn when they went to the rugby – Murray had been there too.) They passed the clock tower and pushed their way through the Churchill Square shoppers and then, in the quiet of Clarence Square, where the houses were discoloured like old newspaper, Andy stopped and said, 'Should we have a quick doob?'

Under the stairs – painted black, with a worn blue runner – there is a sort of booth, made of unfinished tongue-and-groove material.

There is someone in this booth, a fat woman. Paul does not notice her, however. He is peering into what seems to be a dingy dining room – he sees a toaster on a sideboard – when her voice makes him jump. She laughs – a tinkly, high-pitched laugh – and says, 'I am sorry.'

'That's all right,' Paul says, shock sluicing away as he turns, and smiles himself. His voice is slightly slurred. Still smiling, the woman stares at him from her plywood booth. Seconds pass. 'Do you want a room?' she asks.

'Um . . . I've got . . . A reservation.'

'All right. What's the name?'

'Well, it's under . . . Watt.'

'Sorry?'

'Watt.'

'What's the name?'

'The name's Watt. W-A-T-T.'

She laughs again. 'Oh, I see.' She turns the page of a desk diary; her hands seem small at the end of her stout, rosy arms. 'I suppose you get that a lot.'

'I'm not Mr Watt.'

'That's all right,' she says, patiently. 'Just the one night?'

'That's it.'

'Fine . . .'

'Actually it's for this gentleman.'

And Andy steps forward.

The room is on the top floor. It is small and low-ceilinged. The window, hung with a foul lace curtain, overlooks the end of the square. The floor is loud and lumpy, and when Andy sits on the single bed his buttocks sink almost to the level of the cloth-like carpet. There is a tiny sink, heavily infected with limescale, a wardrobe with a single wire hanger, and a kettle – also limescaled – on a sloping side table, the only other piece of furniture in the room. Next to the kettle are a tannin-blackened mug, two tea bags and a doily. The paper shade on the ceiling bulb is tawny with cigarette smoke and speckled with the excrement of generations of flies. 'It's not too bad,' Paul says. 'Quiet . . .'

Andy is struggling to stand up from the bed. While he does this, Paul swings the old-fashioned British Airways flight bag from his shoulder. 'This is the equipment,' he says.

'What equipment?'

'Do you want to get a pint then?'

Having somehow succeeded in standing up, Andy does want to get a pint.

There is a pub more or less next door, the Regency Tavern – a few steps down the alley which eventually opens into the wide sea-facing expanse of Regency Square. The interior is kitsch, the walls painted with wide vertical stripes – verdigris and pond green – and the light bulbs shaped like candle flames. Ormolu cherubim support mirrors and hold brass palm fronds in their babyish hands. Paul pays for the pints and they sit themselves down by a large frosted-glass window. It is only just eleven, and they are the only people in the pub. On the windowsill next to their table, an imitation stone urn overflows with white silk roses and lilies; the tabletop is painted to look like malachite. In these surroundings, Paul outlines what is to be done. When Andy laughs, he says, 'Don't fucking laugh. This is serious, mate.'

'Why? Who is this bloke?'

'Never mind. What does it matter?' He presents him with Watt's printed instructions, saying, 'Study this. Learn it. You've got till tomorrow.'

Andy is smiling in a way that does not suggest he is taking the situation entirely seriously. He snickers at something in the instructions. 'Where am I going to meet him?' he says. Paul has been wondering about that. 'Why not here? Here. You know where it is. You've got to phone him and fix it up.'

'*I've* got to phone him?'

'Of course. You. Of course. Andrew Smith, of Morlam Garden Fruits.' He looks at his watch. 'We'll try him at twelve. What are you going to say?'

Andy smiles. 'All right, mate. Wanna buy some fruit –'

'Stop fucking about! This is *serious*.'

'What do you want me to say then?'

Paul sighs, and takes a biro from his pocket. 'I don't know,' he says. 'We'll write something down.'

Over the second pint, he finds himself pressing Andy for PLP news. Who's in, who's out. Lawrence, it seems, has had a nervous breakdown, and Neil Mellor is now de facto director of sales. 'How's he doing?' Andy does not have much to say on the subject. 'He's really stressed out,' he says. 'Shouts a lot. Kind of like Lawrence used to.'

'Lawrence doesn't shout?'

'Not really.'

'What *does* he do?'

'I don't know.' Then: 'He's got an office.' And finally: 'I think he's leaving soon.'

'Is he?'

With a shy smile, Andy says, 'What happened to you?'

'What happened to me . . . ?'

'And Murray and the others.'

'Oh *that*!' Paul's eyes slide to the other side of the room, where they find some framed silhouette portraits on the striped wall. He shakes his head. 'What a fuck-up, mate.'

'Why? What happened?'

'There was some plan . . . You know. Some bloke we used to know . . . Me and Murray. Anyway it all fucked up.'

Andy does not ask what this plan was, or why he was not included in it – he must know why. Even Dave Shelley made more deals than he did. He just nods, quickly, and says, 'Yah . . .'

'Yeah,' Paul sighs.

'How's Murray?'

'Murray? I've not seen him in a while, to be honest.'

'You haven't?'

Paul finishes his pint and says, 'Let's make that call.'

22

Martin looms huge in Paul's mind. He has seen him only once since Easter Day. On Saturday night, straight from his Eastbourne meeting, he turned into Lennox Road to see him leaving his – *Paul's* – house. The tall shape was unmistakable, and it was too late to stop, too late to hide in the shadows. They met under one of the street lights, the one that shines in through the bedroom window. It was midnight. And thus ill-met by humming street light, they surveyed each other for a moment. Paul did not like to think of Martin in his house (though it would be his for only another month); he wished that he had turned into the street a minute later and been spared the knowledge of it. Especially with the flight bag on his shoulder, and the meeting with Watt still so fresh in his mind – he was worried that it would show up in his face somehow; a voice in his head was shouting out extracts from Watt's instructions. *He should say he's from Morlam Garden Fruits* . . . 'All right, Martin?' he said, shifting the flight bag on his shoulder; it was not heavy.

'Hello, Paul. Been out?'

'You know I have.'

For a moment, Martin dipped his head – hid his smile in inky shadow. 'Somewhere nice, I hope?'

'Yeah.'

His eyes moved inquisitively to the flight bag. 'Been away?'

'No.'

'Oh. Well . . . Goodnight . . .'

Stopping at the payphone in the hallway of the Queensbury guest house, Paul fumbles in his pockets for the number. Andy waits, staring at the wallpaper. 'Here it is,' Paul mutters. Despite the pints, he is nervous. Memories of Andy's hopelessness on the phone are flooding into his mind – he has already warned him that he will not be paid if he fails even to set up a meeting. He thrusts the handwritten script at him – the one he wrote in the Regency Tavern – and starts to say the number. It is the main number of the supermarket. Andy enters it into the phone, and then waits with a pound coin poised. Suddenly he presses the coin into the slot and says the first line of the script: 'Oh hello. Could I speak to the fresh-produce manager please.' Paul turns to the open door and sighs quietly. The memories sit like cold stones in his belly, memories of Andy fucking up. Memories of the sales floor. Of innumerable phone calls . . . He hears Andy say, 'Oh hello, is that Mr Short?' A tense pause. Is it? Is it Mr Short? How strange if it is – how strange that *Andy* should be talking to *Martin*. 'Oh hello, Mr Short. My name's Andrew Smith. I'm calling from Morlam Garden Fruits.' Another pause. Paul has turned to Andy and is studying him intently – he has a finger in his left ear and is leaning in to the puffy wall. 'Kent,' he says. And then, 'Strawb'rries mainly.' The smile flickering on his full lips is something of a worry. It has a loose, twitchy quality, like he might start to laugh at any moment. His self-possession on the phone, however, seems to have improved. 'Well, I was wondering if we could meet up and have a chat.' Paul wrote that line. It sounds okay. It sounds fine. 'Well, as soon as possible,' Andy says. 'Tonight?' He shoots Paul a quick, questioning look. Emphatically, Paul indicates *no*. They need more time for preparation, and he has to go home and sleep all afternoon. Standing there in the narrow corridor, he is swimmy with fatigue. 'No, unfortunately I can't do tonight . . .' Martin says something that seems to merit a laugh, and Andy says, 'I know I did. How about tomorrow?' Paul lights a cigarette and stares at the torn, balding blue carpet. 'Yes, tomorrow afternoon's fine. Five o'clock? That's fine.' Some people stop on the pavement outside. Paul turns away from them, turns to his reflection in the mirror-tiled wall. He looks like a jigsaw puzzle; where tiles have come unstuck, pieces of him are missing. Andy is saying, 'I'm afraid I don't know Brighton very well. So somewhere central, I suppose. There is one pub I know . . .' This is another of Paul's lines. 'The Regency Tavern. Do you know it?' Evidently, Martin does know it. Andy says, 'Excellent. So I'll see you there tomorrow at five. Excellent. Thank you, Mr Short.' He is about to put the phone down, when he says, 'Um. Oh. Yeah. It's . . .' And he looks at Paul with imploring eyes. Paul does not understand what he wants. *What?* Furiously, he mouths the word. Andy turns away, lowering his head. He says, 'You can get me on . . .' And then he says his own mobile number. 'Excellent. See you tomorrow. Thanks. Thanks, Mr Short. Bye.' Elated, he faces Paul. Who says, 'Yeah, well done, mate.'

'I had to give him my mobile number.'

'That's fine.'

'Was that okay?' Andy is trembling, alight, flushed with triumph. He laughs. 'Was that okay?'

'Yeah, it was okay. It was fine. Well done.' Paul hands him his lighter. 'But that was the easy bit.' Lighting a cigarette, Andy nods. 'Tomorrow's the hard bit.'

'Yeah.'

'Tomorrow's where you earn your money.'

'Another drink?' Andy says eagerly.

'I can't, mate. I've got to . . . I've got things to do.'

'Yeah, why aren't you at work?' Andy says, holding out the lighter.

'That's where I've got to go now. And you've got to learn *that*.' He points to the rolled-up A4 document in Andy's left hand.

'Yeah, yeah . . .'

'I mean it! You've got to fucking know it.'

Andy nods. 'Yup,' he says. 'Yah.'

'I'll see you later, yeah.'

'What time?'

'Tonight. I'll see you in the pub at nine, all right? Regency Tavern.'

'All right.'

Paul starts to leave. Then turning on the threshold, he says, 'And don't fuck around with the equipment. I'll show you how to use it tonight.'

'Okay.'

'Learn that stuff.'

'I will.'

'I'm going to test you on it later.'

He leaves him loafing in the musty corridor smoking a Marlboro Light, and walks through Regency Square to the bus stop. The colour of the tall terraces varies from cream to biscuit, and in the middle the windy lawn – with its few bushes and spiky palms – slopes down to the traffic of King's Road and the sea. Walking past hotels with the sun in his face, Paul squints. Gulls hop on the coarse grass. The surface of the sea is striped, like the paintwork in the Regency Tavern – white shining stripes, and dull dark ones. Out in the sea-stripes the West Pier still stands, an outline stubbornly holding its shape.

In the evening, Paul shuffles into the kitchen to prepare his porridge. His head feels heavy and throbs. His face is lumpen, inexpressive, like some naive mask fudged in grey clay. He is standing over the hob when he feels Heather's presence. He does not look at her; he watches the porridge start to quiver.

She says, 'Are you seeing someone, Paul?' It is obvious from the way she says it that she is trying to empty the question of intensity. She does not succeed. He turns to her in surprise; she seems to think, however, that his expression is one of outrage and immediately stops smiling. 'Sorry,' she says. 'I know it's none of my business.'

For a few seconds he is speechless. 'What if I am?'

'I just . . . I mean if you don't want to tell me . . .'

'No, I'm not.'

She stares at him sceptically. 'Okay.'

310

'I'm not.'

'So where do you go?'

'I don't ask where you go.'

'You know where I go.'

'No I don't.'

'I mean you know who I'm with.'

'Where *do* you go?'

'Look, Paul, I'm sorry,' she says.

'Why? I'm not "seeing someone", Heather.'

She is not persuaded. She says, 'M-hm,' in a pointedly stony tone, and pours herself a huge glass of wine. Then she withdraws to the lounge and shuts the door. Of course, he thinks, taking the raisins from the cupboard, his going out on his nights off must mess up her own plans to some extent. Having to have Martin over here, with the kids upstairs, must be less fun than the bar of the Metropole, or his extravagant extension. Or his jacuzzi. Paul had remembered a few weeks earlier that Martin has a jacuzzi; it was installed last summer – a little winch lifting it from a flat-bed truck while Martin watched from the pavement, shielding his eyes, and half the curtains in the street twitched . . . Must be fun, he muses, stirring in the raisins, to fuck in a jacuzzi. He sighs listlessly, and starts to eat. Initially, the tone of Heather's question had pissed him off; now her suspicions make him sad. Strings of light bulbs sway on the seafront. Yes, they make him sad. He is walking through Regency Square. In the twilight, the terraces look statelier – the square is lit like an expensive restaurant – with scores of softly lighted windows, and the entrances of the hotels illuminated. The scruffy lawn is lost in indistinct grey. The Regency Tavern, too, is illuminated; spotlit at the end of the mews like a national monument. The sign shows George IV in the high-collared handsomeness of his youth. Inside, the pub is lively. Andy is up on a high stool, nattering with the staff like a local. Seeing Paul, he smiles. 'Right, mate,' he says. The sloppiness of his smile, the fact that he says 'Right, mate' as if it were a single word, leave little doubt that he has been there for some time. 'Wanna drink?'

'Have you looked at that stuff?' Paul says.

Unhesitatingly, Andy says, 'No.'

'You haven't looked at it?'

'S'all under control.'

'What the fuck are you talking about?'

'S'under control.'

'No it's not under control.'

'Yeah it is . . .'

'I fucking knew this would happen.'

Andy looks puzzled. 'What?'

'What do you think?'

'Oh.' He leans unsteadily towards Paul. 'Look,' he says. 'Look. It's all worked out. All right? I'll do it tomorrow morning. D'you wanna drink?'

'No I don't. This isn't a fucking joke.'

'What's the problem? I'll do it in the morning.'

'You were supposed to do it today.'

'What difference does it make? I'll do it –'

'You're a fucking idiot, do you know that?' This seems to hit a mark somewhere. Andy stops protesting. For a moment his eyes sink to the green carpet, its woven laurel wreaths and scallop shells. When they meet Paul's a moment later they are obscurely distressed. He swallows. 'What the fuck do you think you're doing?' Paul says.

'I'll do it tomorrow –'

'What are you *doing*? You've been here all afternoon, haven't you?' Andy shakes his head. 'I'm not paying you to have a piss-up. You're not here to have a fucking laugh –'

'I know.'

'I don't think you do know. Why haven't you done what I told you?'

'I'll do it tomorrow,' he says quietly.

'This is *serious*. Do you understand? It's not a fucking joke.'

'Look, I'm sorry –'

'You will be.' Then he says, 'All right. Let's go.'

'Where?'

'You're not staying here.'

'Why not?'

'What do you mean *why not*? I'm going to be round early tomorrow morning –'

'What time?'

'*Eight*.'

'Eight?'

'*Eight*. Tough shit. And I want to have a look at your suit.'

'My suit . . . ?'

'Let's go.'

'Why d'you want to look at my suit?' Andy says, turning to search for someone as Paul hustles him out into the mews. Paul has been worrying about Andy's suit – he remembers the chalk-stripe of a metropolitan barrister or senior estate agent; not the sort of thing a shadowy provincial strawberry producer would be likely to wear.

They climb the narrow stairs of the guest house. Mrs Mulwray – the proprietress in her plywood booth – watches as they disappear into the depths of the convex mirror. They are standing outside the door of Andy's room – the paintwork is orange with age – when he says, 'Oh fuck.'

'What?'

'Forgot the key.'

'Get it then.'

He crashes down the stairs. There is then some sort of delay and it is a couple of minutes until he plods up, out of breath and smiling.

'What?' Paul says. 'What you smiling about?'

'She says . . .' Andy pants, 'she says if you stay the night, you'll have to pay.'

'What?'

'If you stay the night,' he says, sniggering, 'if we spend the night together, you'll have to pay.'

'Open the door.'

The room looks even more threadbare than it did in daylight. 'Where's the suit?' Paul says. Andy has taken the trouble to hang it in the wardrobe. He lifts it out, still in its carrier, and passes it to him. Then he sits down on the edge of the bed and starts making a spliff. Paul unzips the suit carrier, and pulls out part of the jacket. 'You can't wear this,' he says.

'Why not?'

'It's too smart.'

Andy smirks. 'Sorry, mate.'

'I'll lend you mine.'

'All right.'

'I'll bring it tomorrow morning.'

'All right.'

Paul rezips the suit carrier and slings it onto the bed.

'D'you want some of this?' Andy is holding the nose of the newly made spliff, swinging it like a sachet of sugar. Paul sighs. Yes, he does want some of that. He is knotty with tensions, furious with worries. The prospect of putting some immediate space between himself and his situation is an enticing one. His face is stony, set, expressionless. 'D'you wanna spark it?' Andy says.

'No,' Paul murmurs, 'go ahead.' Andy sparks it. 'So I'll be here at eight.'

With his mouth open, holding the smoke in his lungs, Andy nods.

'You better be up and ready to start.'

'Uh-huh.' He exhales, finally, in a long smoky wave.

'I'm not joking.'

'No, I know.'

He holds out the spliff. Paul takes it. While he smokes pensively for a minute or two, Andy flops onto the bed, and stares vacantly

314

at the ceiling. Suddenly he stands up. His face, Paul notices, is as white as a cloud. His lips look purple. He mumbles something. Then he opens the door and leaves. A few minutes later – it seems like much longer – there is still no sign of him. The silence of the small room has a piercing, singing quality; and staring intently at the swirling velvet whorls of the counterpane, Paul finds himself forgetting that Andy is even in Brighton. That he even exists. Sometimes, vaguely, it occurs to him that he is downstairs, presumably vomiting in the mouldy bathroom. Such moments, however, swiftly pass – and as soon as they have passed he has no memory of them. For minutes at a time he forgets where he is himself, and why he is there

Um.

That guest house.

The spliff has gone out, and he places it on the side table, next to the tannin-stained mug. His mouth is drier than the dry valleys of Antarctica, where it has not rained or snowed for thousands of years. These valleys must be something he saw on television – there is an associated image of a mummified seal (naturally mummified, he seems to remember, in that perpetually frozen and waterless environment) the colour of a nicotine stain, lying on a gravel slope. What was the programme? He does not know. The dry valleys, and the desiccated, weak-chinned face of the seal – which in a melancholy way resembles his own face – is all there is. Very slowly, he moves to the little sink in the corner of the room. He turns the squeaky tap and finds a trickle of water. It is not easy to drink, though. The sink is too small for him to get his face under the tap, and when he tries to use his hands the water leaks away before he is able to lift it to his mouth. Then he sees the mug. Even when he has drunk several mugs of tepid water, however, his mouth feels moistureless. Naturally mummified. If he keeps drinking, he tells himself, he will just have to piss. So he stops. Standing there, he senses that he has forgotten something ... For what seems like a very long time he stands there, with his mouth open. *Yes!* Andy. He is downstairs, sicking up in the loo. Slowly, Paul switches off the light and leaves. Humming snugly, he descends the tightly turning stairs. He seems to descend through many floors – perhaps twelve – until finally he finds himself in the narrow hall at street level.

Surrounded by the shining silence of the stairs, he had felt safe. Now, though, there are sounds. Mrs Mulwray has turned on a television. From the street, he hears quiet voices speaking a strange language. He stands on the final step, wondering what to do. He has been in this position for some time when he notices that he is visible to Mrs Mulwray. There is a convex mirror high on the wall, tilted so that from her booth she is able to see up the stairs, where he is standing. With sudden purpose, he propels himself towards the exit. The outside air seems to stroke his skin. Passing the phone, he stops. There is something else ... Something ... *He must establish the fact that he is leaving. He must, or she will make him pay.* Turning, and trying to project his voice, he says, 'Um ... Guhnight ...'

Part of Mrs Mulwray's face emerges into view. 'Good*night*,' she says.

Quarter to eight in the morning, and Regency Square looks less swanky. A street sweeper (not Malcolm, though his 'patch' is only a few metres further east) slowly plies the margin, and in the unforgiving light the terraces and hotels look their age. They look tired. They look fed up. Curtains cover their windows like flannels on mature eyes – eyes that have seen through everything, that have no youthful illusions left. The lawn is flecked with litter. Everything looks moist and streaked with dirt. A seagull squats on the head of the bronze soldier, his bronze arm outstretched, symbol of the fallen in an unfashionable war.

Entering Russell Square with a holdall in his hand, Paul Rainey looks up at the rotten brown cornices and window frames of the Queensbury guest house. The spicy odour of superskunk is noticeable on the pavement outside. On the stairs, it intensifies. Outside Andy's door it is vivid. Andy is sitting in bed in his boxer shorts smoking a spliff. Seeing his torso, Paul is surprised how fat he is. Loaves of pale flab sit on the waistband of his shorts. Downy tits, round shoulders. He looks up, pale-eyed. 'What are you doing?' Paul says, stepping into the smoke-filled room.

'Quick doob.' Andy's voice is hoarse.

'Are you out of your mind?'

'Oh, come on . . .' he says, in a whisper.

'We've got work to do.'

'Yeah, I know.'

Paul shoves aside the greasy lace curtain and opens the window. The grotty sash gives with a scraping grunt. 'You can smell that thing all up the stairs,' he says. 'Put it out.' Surprisingly, without a word, Andy does so, stubbing it out on the inner surface of the mug, which he is using as an ashtray. He yawns, showing fat teeth. 'There's the suit,' Paul says, indicating the holdall. Andy nods. 'What size are your feet?'

'Nine.'

'Fine. I've brought some shoes as well.' The big black brogues – highly polished ebony artefacts – would be as implausible as the chalk stripe. 'I'll wait for you downstairs,' Paul says. 'You've got five minutes.'

'Do you want me to wear the suit?'

'No. Why would I? You can try it on later.'

In the corridor downstairs the smell of superskunk mingles with

317

the smells of toast and tea. Quiet munching and murmuring sounds emanate from the dining room. Paul steps out into the dank morning air and stands on the discoloured chequer of the front steps.

'Where's the instructions?' he says, when Andy joins him.

'Oh.'

'Go and get them.'

Andy trudges up the stairs. 'Where we going?' he asks, when he next emerges.

'Somewhere. I don't know.'

They wander off in search of a café, ending up in the Starbucks on Market Street. There Paul studies the newspaper while Andy studies Watt's instructions. When he has looked through them a few times, Paul puts down the paper and tests him. 'What's your email address?' 'What sort of strawberries you offering?' 'How many grams in a punnet?' 'What's the most usual price this week?' 'What price are you asking for?' 'Why might an inspection be a problem?' When Andy scores poorly on these questions, he spends a further half an hour studying, while Paul purchases a lemon muffin and a second latte (wondering, in the queue, whether to expense them), and then settles down to the international news and sport. Andy also fails the second test. He is still quite stoned and only able to remember one or two facts at a time.

When Paul asks him, 'How many grams in a punnet?' he stares at him with pink eyes for a few moments and then says, 'Four hundred?'

'No.'

'Um.' Andy frowns. 'How many?'

Paul puts down the stapled sheets of A4. He has passed a long night of tedious meditations; meditations that went nowhere, like one of the kiddy-rides on the seafront. Nevertheless, he now wonders for the umpteenth time whether to tell Andy to fuck off back to London and forget the whole thing. Start looking for someone else. To proceed with him seems suicidal. Watt, though, would never wear a postponement. With a sigh, Paul picks up the pages. 'Two hundred and twenty-seven,' he says.

Andy nods. 'Oh yeah.'

Once more in the room on the top floor of the guest house – it has to be vacated by noon – they turn to the equipment. Paul spent Saturday night experimenting with it. There are two units. The first is the camera. Made of rough, unmarked plastic, it has a serious, functional, professional look. On one side there is a small hole, and on the other a socket where the wire plugs in. Were it not for the battery, it would weigh nothing. The other unit is the digital video recorder, which looks more like an ordinary item of consumer electronics, with a metal finish and some chrome buttons. Watt has prepared the bag for use himself – he has made a small hole in the side, and seems to have sewn in a pouch of the camera's exact size so that the 'lens' – it is more of a pinprick – is aligned with this hole. Ensuring that it is pointing towards Martin, Andy will simply have to open the bag and press record on the DVR. Taking out the punnets of fruit – they stopped into Tesco's for them, and have transferred them to the unmarked punnets which Paul pilfered from work – will provide an ideal pretext for doing this. On Saturday night, while Heather and the kids slept, Paul recorded some images and played them back on the TV; the picture quality was surprisingly sharp, even in low light. He shows Andy how it works, and they take some practice shots, working out how the bag has to be positioned in order to find an object in the camera's angle of view.

Then Andy tries on Paul's suit. It is more in the black economy line, very much more typical of the gangmaster sector, than his own. A bland blackish blue, with shiny patches, old creases and a missing button, it is not a perfect fit. The shoes are scuffed. The tie a dismal strip of paisley. 'You look shit,' Paul says. 'Perfect.'

'Like you then.' Andy smiles. 'Only joking, mate.'

Paul says that if he scores a hundred per cent in a final test he'll stand him a pint. 'And then that's it,' he says. 'That's it – no more booze till it's done.'

'Sure.'

He makes the test easy, and they stroll to the Regency Tavern. Sitting under the large frosted-glass window, Andy looks nervous. He is quiet – very unlike him – and smokes even more heavily than usual. Other than his smoking hand – shuttling to and from his mouth – he is very still. He has a misleadingly unpractised way of smoking, an odd manner of holding the cigarette between his plump fingers, of exhaling the smoke like a twelve-year-old girl. They sit in silence for a while. 'Look, don't worry about it,' Paul says. 'If you stay sober, everything'll be fine.'

Andy nods, and says, 'M . . .'

The hangover lends him a pallor, a slightly hollow-eyed quality, which is entirely welcome. His edginess, too, will be in keeping with the role. He should not, however, be overly nervous. And to take his mind off the performance ahead, Paul says, 'How's things going at PLP?'

'How are things going?'

'Yeah. For you, I mean. Getting the deals in?'

Andy shrugs. 'Some.'

'Yeah?'

He seems unwilling to say more.

Why are you still working there? Paul thinks. He wonders whether to put this question to him; he even wonders whether to make an impassioned speech, urging him to leave sales and start something else while he still has time, to wake up, to shake off the sedations, to stop and think, to save himself from the sort of life that he is sleepwalking into.

Instead he says, 'What's it like working for Tony?'

'It's all right.'

They leave the pub, and for a few moments loiter in the mews. 'I've got to go, mate,' Paul says. He is not happy about leaving Andy on his own in a town full of temptations, but he is exhausted. He keeps yawning. 'All right,' Andy says. Wearing Paul's suit, he has his own luggage with him as well as the flight bag. 'This Short character,' Paul says, yawning. 'He's very tall. And he doesn't drink.' Andy nods. Paul looks at his watch. 'You've got four hours. If I was you, I'd dump that stuff at the station. It's not far.'

'Yeah.'

'Get a paper or something.'

'Yeah.'

'No more drinking.' Andy smiles. 'Why are you smiling?' The smile vanishes. 'Look, mate, if you can't go four hours without a drink –'

'I was joking.'

'And no more of that.' Paul makes a smoking motion. He feels that there must be more to say. Nothing occurs to him. 'All right. Phone me when you're done.'

'Okay.'

'And good luck, yeah.'

'Yeah. Which way's the station?'

'That way.' Paul points to the far side of Russell Square. 'Turn left and just keep going. There's signs.'

'All right. Cheers, mate. See you later.'

'Yeah.'

For a few moments, with misgivings, Paul watches him totter off past the peeling guest houses. In that shapeless blue suit, it might be himself that he is watching. He has an uneasy feeling that he ought to have done more. He is too sleepy, however, for this thought to trouble him much. He will sleep. Whatever his omissions, it is too late to mend them now – a state of things which imports a sort of peace – and he will sleep through the event itself. And he turns and wanders off through Regency Square, with the sea wind in his tired face.

23

In a long series of hallucinations on the edge of sleep, he has lived through it many times. Has seen Martin and Andy meet in the green-striped interior of the Regency Tavern . . . Strawberries, flight bags . . . Light bulbs in the form of candle flames, orange and flickering . . . Each time, though, something essential seemed to be missing; whenever his puzzled head poked for a moment into the oxygen of wakefulness he wondered, in particular, whether the upshot was success or failure. Once, he threw off the sweaty duvet and left the house – was walking through streets, making for somewhere with an overwhelming sense of purpose . . . Once, more prosaically, he was in the kitchen, preparing his porridge. Often he experienced the moment when his mobile – unusually stationed upstairs – would startle him. Whenever this happened, he never managed to find it in time. It seemed to be hidden under mountains of stuff, or lost in a room at the far end of the house. He staggered down passageways pointing to infinity. And always with the panicky sense that the phone's next iteration would be its last.

When finally it does start to vibrate and twitter, his searching hand thrashes on the side table like a little bull in a china shop, and his sticky mouth struggles to form the word hello.

'Urluh,' he says. A sort of tinnitus is howling in his head. 'Ndy?'

'It's Roy Watt here.'

'Oh.' Paul sighs, and lying on his back says, 'All right?'

'What's happening?' Watt says urgently. They spoke yesterday evening, when Paul told him that the meeting with Martin had been set up.

'I don't know.'

'Did he see him?'

'He's seeing him now.' Paul shuts his eyes. The TV is muttering under the floor. 'What time is it?'

'Six.'

'I should be hearing from him soon.'

'Can't you call him?'

'Not really.'

'Why not?'

'What if he's still with Martin? He'll call me as soon as he's done.'

'And you'll call me.'

'Yeah.'

'As soon as you hear from him.'

'Yeah.'

'I'll be waiting for your call.'

'Okay.'

Paul drops the phone and turns away from the window. A wave of sweat shimmers over his whole skin. He farts. Then the phone starts again. It is Andy.

'Mate?' Andy says.

'Yeah.' Paul opens his eyes and sits up painfully. 'What happened?'

'Look, I'm sorry about this, mate.' Andy sounds nervous.

'Sorry about what? What happened?'

'Look.' There is a long silence. 'I.'

'You what? *What happened?*'

At first Andy tries to hide the fact that he is laughing – he hawks ostentatiously and holds the phone away from his face. Paul listens without emotion. 'Don't worry, mate,' Andy says when he is able to speak again. 'I was just . . . Everything's fine.'

'Everything's fine?'

'Yah.'

Surprised at his own lack of surprise, Paul leans over to the pack of Marlboro Lights on Heather's side of the bed. Extending his fingers like Adam on the Sistine ceiling, he is just able to pick it up. He lights one, holding the phone to his ear with a round shoulder while Andy talks excitedly. When he has finished, Paul tells him to wait in the Regency Tavern. Then he phones Watt and passes on the news. Then he stands up – still smudged with exhaustion – and tugs on his clothes. He is working later; his first shift since Friday.

Descending the stairs, quivering slightly, he is surprised to hear strange voices in the lounge. A young man in a suit steps into the hall. 'All right?' he says.

'All right . . .'

'Your wife let us in.'

'Did she?'

The young man offers no explanation for his presence; Paul presumes that he is an estate agent, one of Norris Jones's people. Presently, he is followed out of the lounge by some other people, a man and a woman. They nod timidly in Paul's direction, and are ushered into the kitchen. Heather is in there – Paul hears the woman say, 'Sorry about this,' and Heather says, 'That's all right.'

'Lovely garden.' The estate agent.

'Um, when's it available?' the man says, a few moments later. The agent asks Heather when she is moving out, and she says, 'A month. Just under.'

'There you go.'

In the hall, overhearing this, with the agent's sharp sandalwood scent in his nostrils, Paul puts on his jacket. Without looking at him, the viewing party leave the kitchen and start up the stairs to inspect the bedrooms. Several times, he has been woken in the middle of the afternoon by a knot of such people whispering in the doorway.

Andy seems disappointed that Paul is not up for some sort of impromptu stag weekend. He offers to fund it himself with the two hundred pounds that he has paid him. Paul, however, sticks to a single half of lager – he did not even want that, and only agreed to it because Andy looked so spaniel-like and sad. Then he tells him not to be a stranger, and leaves him in the Regency Tavern, remembering on the bus back to Hove that he is still wearing his suit and shoes. He sends him a text message saying that he will pick them up next time he is in London. Then he dumps the flight bag in Lennox Road, puts on his uniform, and hurries to work. In the morning, he is supposed to leave the flight bag in a left-luggage locker at the station. Watt says he will transfer the money when he has seen the tape; first however, exhausted though he is, Paul wants to watch it himself. So with a microwaved shepherd's pie, still in his uniform, he sits down on the sofa in front of the TV.

For a while the screen fizzes, then suddenly a picture appears. The first thing he notices is that the lens is not perfectly aligned with the spyhole – a wide band on the left of the screen is just black. The rest of the image shows the surface of the table and Martin's suited torso, his shirt front and tie; the lower part of his face – and only the lower part – makes occasional appearances. This worries Paul until he sees the moment – some way in – when Martin lowers his whole face into the picture to sniff the punnet of fruit in front of him, thus providing an undeniable positive ID.

The film opens with Andy saying, '. . . at the fruit.' He has obviously just taken it out and he hands the punnet to Martin. Martin examines it – he seems to eat one or two berries. Then he says, 'So you use polytunnels, yeah?' The voices are slightly muffled.

'Yeah,' Andy says.

Martin asks some more questions – in answer to which Andy says that the strawberries, Elsantas, will be supplied in 227-gram punnets; that he has a tonne of fruit in total; and that an arranged sale has unfortunately fallen through. It is at the end of this exchange that Martin's face makes its short appearance on-screen. There is something almost lewd about the expert way in which he sniffs the berries – perhaps it is his fluttering eyes, his slight smile. Then he says, 'Well.'

'So,' Andy says, 'would you be interested?'

Martin laughs in a way that suggests he thinks his interlocutor is something of an idiot. This is not surprising. From the start, 'Andrew Smith' has presented an image of extraordinary innocence and simple-mindedness. Which is perfect, of course – he seems *exactly* the sort of person who would find themselves forced to offload a tonne of fruit for a painfully low price. And it is only now that Paul sees quite how perfect Andy was for the job. He told him to try not to sound too posh; he does not seem to be trying, and in fact his plummy voice is only enhancing the overall effect. He sounds soft, privileged, unschooled in the painful knocks and upsets of economic self-propulsion. 'Would I be interested?' Martin muses. 'That rather depends, doesn't it?'

And a few seconds later Andy says, 'What does it depend on?'

With a forkful of shepherd's pie poised to enter his mouth, Paul smiles. 'What do you think?' Martin says.

'Money?' Andy, after a long pause.

'Got it in one.'

'All right. So . . . Um . . .'

'How much?'

'I was thinking . . .' Andy says. 'Two hundred pence a kilo?'

The price is obviously lower than Martin had expected. Suspiciously low. The situation is suddenly tense. Perhaps sensing this, Andy says, 'I really need to offload this fruit.' And for the first time he sounds not foolish but insincere.

'There's something you're not telling me, isn't there?' Martin says.

Ignoring the steaming strata of mash and mince on his knees, Paul stares transfixed at the screen. The players have left the script. Nevertheless, what Andy should do – what Paul himself would do, what any salesman would do – is obvious. For a long time Andy says nothing. Judging from the quantity of smoke pouring into the image, he is puffing furiously on a Marlboro Light. Martin makes a dry, disapproving sound.

'Like what?' Andy says finally.

Paul laughs out loud. It is not at all what he had in mind; it is impossible to imagine a more fumblingly idiotic line. And yet it is thus a masterstroke – instantly quashing Martin's suspicion that Andy might be something other than a total imbecile.

'You tell me,' Martin says.

'The thing is,' Andy says quietly, 'we're not . . . um.' He seems to be struggling. 'Oh what is it?' he wonders aloud.

'I don't know,' Martin says. 'What?'

'BNC audited?'

'Do you mean BRC audited?'

'Um. Yeah.'

'Right. Anything else?'

After a minute Andy says, 'You know the Assured Production Scheme . . .'

'You're not part of it.'

'No.'

'Why not?'

'Um.' A pause. 'We're just not.'

'What do you mean, you're just *not*?' Martin says, very suspiciously. There is a long silence.

Then Andy says, 'Some of our pickers haven't got their work visas yet.' Watching the scene on television, Paul is sure that this is an attempt to move on to a new subject, not an answer to Martin's question; Martin, however, seems willing to take it as one. He laughs. 'Well, no wonder you're not in the scheme,' he says.

'No, we're not.'

'So you're not BRC audited,' Martin says. 'You're not in the APS . . .' He is marking the points off on his long fingers. 'And you're using illegal immigrants to pick your fruit.'

'Yah,' Andy says, hesitantly. And then – 'Would that be a problem?'

'What do *you* think?'

'Um. Would it be a problem in principle?'

First, Martin simply restates the question. 'Would it be problem in principle,' he says. And he sighs. Then he inspects the fruit. This time, though, instead of lowering his face, he lifts the punnet. 'These are nice fruit,' he says eventually, having eaten several berries.

'Yeah, they are,' Andy eagerly agrees.

'How much did you say you had?'

'Um, a tonne. Yah.'

'And you want two hundred pence a kilo?'

'Two hundred pence . . .'

'So two thousand pounds the tonne.'

'Um . . .'

Twice, Martin thrums his fingers on the *trompe l'oeil* malachite of the tabletop. Though his face is out of shot, the fingers are eloquently expressive of tense vacillation. Then he says, 'Fifteen hundred.'

Andy sighs stagily. There is the sound of a lighter being lit, and waves of fine blue smoke fall into the picture. 'What about –'

Martin interrupts him. 'Take it or leave it. It's up to you.'

The pause that Andy inserts here is immense. 'Okay,' he says finally.

Suddenly, though, Martin seems wary. 'Have you got a card or something?'

'A card? Sure.' Andy hands over one of Watt's cards. Martin looks at it. Then he says, 'All right. When can you deliver?'

'Whenever,' Andy says. 'Immediately.'

'Tonight?'

'Um. Tomorrow morning?'

Martin laughs. 'If that's what you call immediately,' he says. 'All right. Deliver tomorrow morning. You know where we are.'

'Yah.'

'Fine.' He slaps his knees and stands up. 'Well. A pleasure doing business with you, Andrew.'

'And you.'

'Not too much of a pleasure, I hope! No, I'm joking. I hope I've been able to help you out.'

'You have.'

A few more pleasantries are exchanged, and then Martin leaves. Andy stands up and walks through the picture to the bar. Only when he returns with a pint does he remember to stop the DVR, and the screen is suddenly void.

Paul watches it once more while he finishes his shepherd's pie. He wonders whether Martin has since made enquiries about Morlam Garden Fruits – whether he has tried the mobile number on the card, and heard the automated female voice saying that it is not in use; whether he has tried the landline and found it to be a private home in Hastings; whether he has asked directory enquiries for Morlam Garden Fruits, and been told that they have nothing under that name – not in Kent, nor anywhere else in the UK.

He takes a bus to Brighton station and leaves the flight bag in a locker there. With sunlight filtering through the glass roof, he texts Watt to tell him which one. Then he walks down Queen's Road. He feels unexpectedly melancholy. A sort of emptiness. And it is perhaps for this reason that he spurns the shops of Western Road and walks all the way down to the sea. Success – if this is what it is – seems as sad as failure. Sadder, in a way – without the psychological detritus to moon over, there is only a sad, immaculate sense of transience. He passes the conservatoried entrances of the Grand Hotel and the Hilton Metropole; wind-tousled doormen wait on the steps, and in the still air of glassy restaurants women in white blouses set the tables for lunch. On the other side of the road, the sea and the sky are formed from the same palette of cool blues and greys. What troubles him most, as he walks, is the fact

329

that the fear is still there – fear of the future, fear of loneliness. For a week, he had lost sight of it. So much had happened – he had spoken to Andy on Thursday; on Saturday he had met Watt in Eastbourne; he had spent Saturday night experimenting with the equipment; on Monday morning – it seems a month ago – Andy had turned up. Then the events of the past forty-eight hours ... The sea thuds lazily on the tiered pebbles to his left. And now this tiredness, this sense of time passing, this strange mourning sadness, this fear.

He sees Watt on the shop floor two mornings later. Their eyes meet for a moment. They never speak again. Of course he hears from Gerald, holding forth in the night-time smoking room, his version of events. (This is a few days further on.) Gerald says that the fresh-produce manager was called to HQ in London, that he went there expecting to be told that he would be succeeding Macfarlane, and was told instead that there was evidence he was using unlisted suppliers. He was, Gerald said – and even *he* seemed slightly sceptical – shown a video of himself doing so, and sacked. Freckled Hazel Ledbetter was made fresh-produce manager in his place ...

From the night-shift, it seems like thunder over the horizon, someone else's storm. Paul inspects Heather's face for signs of it. He sees none. One morning, however, he is watching TV when the doorbell rings. He drops his spliff into the ashtray and stands wearily. *Fucking estate agents*, he thinks. He inspects himself for a moment in the hall mirror. Then he opens the door.

'Martin ...'

Martin does not look well. He looks like he has had a sleepless night – perhaps more than one. His face is bloodless – all the blood seems to have found its way into his grey-blue eyes. Smiling mildly, with mild perplexity, Paul says, 'What ... ?'

'I know it was you,' Martin says.

'What was?'

'You know what.'

Paul shakes his head innocently. 'What?'

'Andrew Smith.'

'What are you talking about? Who's Andrew Smith?'

'You're just a fucking . . .' Martin seems to search for the word. '*Worm*.'

'What are you talking about?' Paul says again.

'An envious little worm.'

'What?'

'I know it was you, worm.'

'Yeah, okay . . .' Paul starts to shut the door. 'I don't know what you're talking about.'

'Hazel Ledbetter saw you in the Stadium with Watt.'

'Who's Hazel Ledbetter?'

'I knew I'd seen that bag somewhere,' Martin says. 'That bag. You had it with you when I saw you.'

'What bag? What are you talking about?'

'How can you deny it?'

'Deny what?'

'That you and Watt were in it together!'

'In *what* together?'

'You *know* what!' He shoves the door open, forcing Paul two steps into the narrow hall. 'Don't come in . . . *Don't!*' Martin hesitates on the threshold. He is wearing his blue tracksuit. 'I don't know what you're talking about,' Paul says. He is surprised himself how wounded he sounds. He is shaking. Staring at him, Martin says, 'Why are you such a shit?'

Paul notices the cold sore on Martin's lip, the reddish stubble on his jowls. 'What?'

'I said – why *are* you such *a* shit?'

Paul sighs, and says, in a sort of whisper, 'I don't know what you're talking about,' and shuts the door. For a moment, Martin's tall blue shape lingers on the front step. Then he presses the doorbell. Presses it in. Filling the house with furious livid urgent noise.

He is looking for something in Portslade, south Hangleton or Shoreham. One morning, he looks over some properties – the sort of properties where lonely people die alone; one-bedroom flats in Victorian villas honeycombed with loneliness. Even the estate agents do not try too hard to talk up the small rooms they show him, with single electric hobs, and bathrooms housed in plasterboard boxes, over which dusty sleeping spaces wait at the top of ladders. They study the ceiling, the brown carpet, while Paul steps to the window to inspect the view – train tracks, ivy-filled ex-gardens, allotments.

'Look, Heather . . .' he says. He is hesitant, solemn. They are in the kitchen on Lennox Road. 'Is there any way . . .'

She waits for him to finish his sentence, and when he does not, she says, 'Paul . . .' Then, failing to finish her own, she sighs.

'I think,' he says, 'I think these things happen to everybody. Don't they? I know I've been selfish. I see that now.' She is staring past him, into the garden. It is May. 'I mean . . . I can forget about what happened with Martin. I understand. I let you down.'

Looking at him – sober, afraid, unshaved, pale – she worries. Worries that if she surrenders – to herself, not to him – they will soon find themselves exactly where they were. Her sadness – which once seized her with something like fear in the clamorous solitude of Martin's shower – is intensified by her sense of Paul's fragility; it pained her physically, when she stepped from the vaporous stall and pulled Martin's unfamiliar towel towards her, to think of him at that moment, on his own, preparing his porridge. Martin was waiting downstairs in a kimono, opening packs of Madagascan crevettes and a bottle of champagne. The more she thinks about Martin, the more he seems to be something unknown, a vague outline only, a worrisome shadow. He wept when she did not see him for a few days, when she punished him for phoning Paul.

Since then, she has found a peevish, wheedling, even threatening side to him, a side new to her, which has made her realise how little she knows him; his emails and voice messages – several a day – seem veined with impatience, with irritation, with self-pity. And now, in the last week, with a sort of hysteria. Something seems to have happened to him. He has started to talk of quitting his job, of taking up gardening. He has stopped shaving. And he wants her to move in with him. Whatever happens, she has made up her mind not to do *that*. Where will she live then? With her parents? Will she sleep in the single bed from which she once set out for school, through grey suburban streets, through swirling orange chestnut leaves? Will she live as she once did, a sort of asylum seeker in her parents' house? Everything the same as it was then? Thinking of the house in Hounslow, she finds herself thinking of a younger Paul – it was there that she was living when they met; there that she first spoke to him on the phone, taking it into the hall for privacy. Thinking of this younger Paul – this fusion of hope and nostalgia, memory and imagination – has often made her tearful these last few months.

He is waiting for her to speak.

She says, 'I think I'm going to take the children to London this weekend.'

He nods, very sombrely. 'Okay,' he says.

On Sunday night, she returns to Hove with her terms. There are three of them. The first is that he stop drinking. He seems to think about this for a moment. Then he says, 'All right.'

'I'm serious,' she says.

'I know. So am I. I want to.'

She stares at him with open scepticism. 'I mean *completely*.'

'I understand. I'll do my best.'

'No, that's not good enough,' she says, shaking her head.

'I'll stop drinking, Heather.' She holds him in her serious gaze. 'I'll stop drinking.'

The second is that he get 'help'.

'What do you mean "help"?'

'Help,' she says. 'Professional help.' And then, 'I don't know what exactly. There must be *something* – *some* sort of help you can get.'

He shrugs.

'And you know . . . I thought you wanted to stop taking those pills,' she says.

'I do.'

'Then you'll need help.'

'Yeah, maybe.'

'Will you get help?' she wants to know, still unnervingly serious.

'Yes,' he says after a pause, 'I will.'

'You promise?'

'I promise.'

The last of her terms is that he find a job in sales. In fact, she says 'a proper job'. There is, however, only one 'proper job' that he is able to do.

The second of these terms fares the worst. He has a short conversation with Dr Marlowe, who prescribes his Felixstat, and who advises him that, while it might be desirable in principle, in practice he should probably not stop taking it. Especially not now. He finds a few phone numbers on the Net, and sets up a single appointment with some sort of mental-health professional, which he postpones twice and then fails to turn up for. This takes a few weeks and by then – perhaps because he is making progress elsewhere – Heather seems willing to let it lie.

The first of her terms, meanwhile, is allowed to morph into something other than its original form. In its new form it stipulates, essentially, that he is not to drink *in the house*. Once he starts his new job he does drink in London, which must be obvious to Heather – though in those first few weeks he never shows up drunk – and eventually, over several months, this too, like the second of her terms, is quietly phased out.

The last, however, is fulfilled in full.

He quits the night shift, and in the morning phones Neil Mellor. 'You still looking for someone to sell fruit, Rainey?' Neil says as soon as Paul has identified himself. 'No, mate,' he says. 'I'm looking for a job.'

Neil laughs loudly. He seems to be showing off to someone. 'Went that well, did it?' he shouts.

'It went all right, actually. It was just a one-off.'

'And do you really think Lawrence is going to let you work here again?'

'Lawrence? I thought he'd left.'

'Yeah, he is leaving,' Neil admits.

'And I hear you're taking over. As sales director.'

'Do you? Who told you that?'

'I just heard it.'

'Well . . . It's not official yet.' Neil is speaking more quietly now. He pauses, and then says, 'I do have a managerial vacancy as it happens.'

'Yeah?'

'Remember Simon Beaumont?'

'Simon. Of course.'

'Had a heart attack.'

'Shit . . .'

'He's still alive. Just can't work.'

'Oh. Is he . . . ? What's he going to do?'

'Don't know. This is quite funny actually,' Neil says, 'because you know what he was going to be working on?'

'No.'

'European fucking Procurement Management.'

'What do you mean?'

'Your mate fucked it up, didn't he. I heard about that. Delmar

335

Morgan fucked it.' The name draws from Paul a delicate qualm of depression. 'They totally fucked it,' Neil is saying, 'and the federation sent it straight back to us. We started on the January edition last week.'

'I thought Simon did the in-flight magazines,' Paul says.

'He did. Till the fuckers took them away from us. World Alliance.'

'They took them away?'

'They did. So . . . Up for it? *European Procurement Management*? Only because I'm desperate, you understand.'

'Well. Yeah. I need something.'

Neil sighs. 'All right,' he says. 'I'll have to talk to Yvonne about it. I'll get back to you.'

'Yvonne?'

'Yvonne Jenkin. The MD . . .'

'Yeah, I know who she is. Why do you have to talk to her?'

'You're quite controversial, mate. She might not appreciate you being rehired.'

'All right. Well . . .'

'I'll get back to you, yeah.'

'Thanks, mate.'

Neil does not get back to him that day, or the next, and Paul starts to suspect that Yvonne has vetoed his appointment, and to wish – in view of this – that he had not phoned Neil at all. He went to PLP first, despite what had happened, for the simple reason that it seemed easier to be somewhere he knew, with people he knew, than to start again at an unknown place with strangers. There was, of course, something humiliating about it. It was the idle, the fearful, the easy option, and he almost hopes that it will not work out.

It does work out, though. He phones Neil two days later and is told that he has spoken to Yvonne and that there is a job for him there if he wants it, starting on Monday. 'Oh, and another thing,' Neil says, pleased with himself. 'You can have young Andy back on your team.'

336

'Andy?'

'Yeah. Andy. I hear he's been doing some freelance stuff for you anyway.' Neil laughs. 'See you on Monday, Rainey.'

It is a strange, quiet, somehow melancholy weekend. They spend most of Saturday in the presence of predictably smarmy estate agents. The houses they see are all more or less the same, Hove being a town of a thousand two-storey Victorian terraces. Though Norris Jones has not found new tenants and would have let them stay, they have decided to move – to escape from Martin, who has not taken things very well, and to make a new start themselves.

Emerging, with a dozen others, from the evening suntrap of Portslade station – two open platforms on a line running due west – Paul steps out into Portland Road. Waiting on the traffic island, he wonders whether to pop into the Whistlestop for a quick one. The pub sits at the junction of Portland and Boundary roads, where the former ends, outstaring its wide, low-lying, desolate length – desolate under November rain, of course, but also under the heavy stare of this July sun. At this time of day there is no shade on Portland Road. He decides against the pint. He had a few in the Penderel's Oak with the others after work, and now, seventy minutes of rammed train later, he has a lurking, indefinite headache; it is hardly perceptible, merely a shimmer of pain as he turns his head to look for further traffic, and seeing none, steps onto the tarmac. His new shoes – bright black Churches – pinch his hot feet, and as he walks he looks forward to easing them off, to peeling off his black undertaker's socks, and waggling his blind toes in the warm shade of the garden. Summer evenings, the sun is shut out of the garden, the new sun umbrella – cream canvas and solid wood – unnecessary. He knows that Heather drinks coffee under it in the morning, and on Sunday mornings when the weather is fine he reads the papers there. Occasionally he looks up from the acres of text and surveys his square of lawn – pleasingly wider than the narrow space of the Lennox Road house – with its flagstones set into the turf to form a serpentine path (true, only two stubby turns) and a displeased-looking, spiky palm at the end – the sort of palm you see outside hotels and in front gardens all over Hove. The house has a proper front garden, with some tall beige feather-dusters of grasses. The neighbours in the other half of the semi have rose bushes in theirs. The next house along has a monkey-puzzle tree.

He passes the the pink-brick cube of Martello House ('HM Customs & Excise, VAT Office') – with few windows, it looks like some sort of prison – and turns into the wide street that is Portland Villas. He wishes it were shadier – that is his only problem with the street on which he now lives. The sun glares off the expanse of tarmac, off the exposed pavements, blindingly off the parked cars. Now, even on the west side of the street there is almost no shade, what little there is falling into the gardens in front of the houses, which are mostly semi-detached, and grouped in stretches of eight or ten to the same pattern.

As he approaches his house, already feeling the jacket on his arm for his keys, he squints warily at the parked cars. After what happened in June, there is, of course, no yellow Saab; he knows, however, that Martin has been around since then – once he saw him (he is pretty sure) in a nondescript grey Ford. He stared at the car for several minutes, until its occupant started the engine and moved off. Even that was a month ago now. The phone calls, the text messages, the emails, the letters (some put through the door in the dead of night) have petered out. Yes, since the police had a word with him – it was traumatic to involve them – things have quietened down. Seeing no sign that the house is under surveillance, Paul opens the freshly painted gate and pulls the keys from the pocket of his tangled jacket. Since then, there have been only two messages. The first, an email full of foul-mouthed abuse, was followed, only a few days later, by an invitation to a barbecue – a photocopied invitation with *Hope you can make it!* added in a flourish of blue biro. Under the circumstances, this invitation was far more disturbing, seemed far more insane, than the abusive email that immediately preceded it. Yes, there had been something terrifying about that barbecue invite. On meat-red paper, there was a cartoon – so crudely drawn it seemed to have been done with a marker pen – of some meat sizzling over coals, and a knife and a long barbecue fork . . . Portland Villas throbs with the dusky peace of wood pigeons. The moon floats up pale and ethereal in the sky. Tired, Paul half turns for a last sweep of the quiet street, then unlocks the door – it has panes of glass frosted to look like silk – and enters his house.

Acknowledgements

I would like to thank the following people, for all their efforts, and for their enthusiasm most of all: Alex Bowler, Sam Edenborough, Will Francis, Dan Franklin, Jago Irwin and, last but not least, Anna Webber.

Of course many other people have also had a hand in this book, in many different ways. I want to thank them too.

www.vintage-books.co.uk